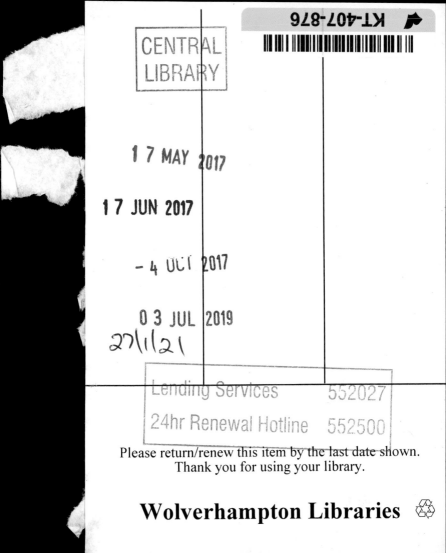

THE THIRD NERO

OR

NEVER SAY NERO AGAIN

THE
THIRD NERO

OR

NEVER SAY NERO AGAIN

Lindsey Davis

HODDER &
STOUGHTON

First published in Great Britain in 2017 by Hodder & Stoughton
A Hachette UK company

1

Copyright © Lindsey Davis 2017

Map by Rodney Paull

A CIP catalogue record for this title is
available from the British Library

Hardback ISBN 978 1 473 61342 3
Trade Paperback ISBN 978 1 473 61343 0
Ebook ISBN 978 1 473 61341 6

Typeset in Plantin Light by Palimpsest Book Production Ltd, Falkirk, Stirlingshire
Printed and bound by CPI Group (UK) Ltd, Croydon, CR0 4YY

Hodder & Stoughton policy is to use papers that are natural, renewable
and recyclable products and made from wood grown in sustainable
forests. The logging and manufacturing processes are expected to
conform to the environmental regulations of the country of origin.

Hodder & Stoughton Ltd

THE THIRD NERO

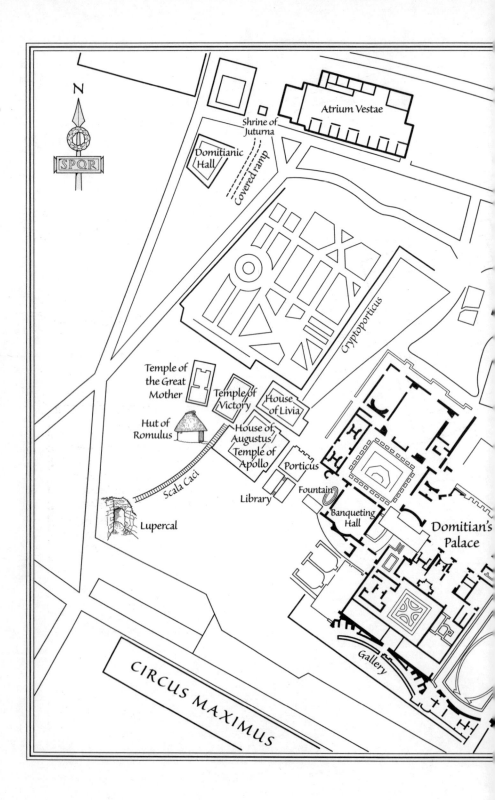

N

SPQR

Atrium Vestae

Shrine of
Juturna

Domitianic
Hall

Covered ramp

Cryptoporticus

Temple of
the Great
Mother

Temple of
Victory

House
of Livia

Hut of
Romulus

House of
Augustus

Temple of
Apollo

Porticus

Scala Caci

Library

Fountain

Banqueting
Hall

Domitian's
Palace

Lupercal

Gallery

CIRCUS MAXIMUS

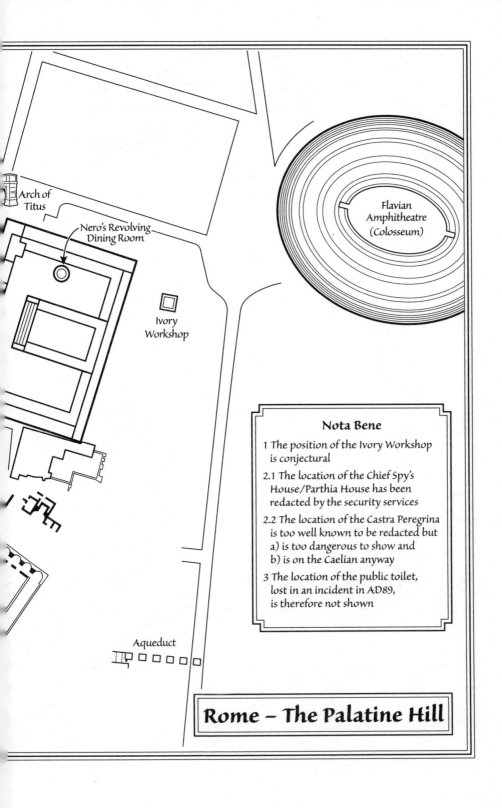

Arch of Titus

Nero's Revolving Dining Room

Ivory Workshop

Flavian Amphitheatre (Colosseum)

Nota Bene

1 The position of the Ivory Workshop is conjectural

2.1 The location of the Chief Spy's House/Parthia House has been redacted by the security services

2.2 The location of the Castra Peregrina is too well known to be redacted but a) is too dangerous to show and b) is on the Caelian anyway

3 The location of the public toilet, lost in an incident in AD89, is therefore not shown

Aqueduct

Rome – The Palatine Hill

CHARACTER LIST

Emperors

Domitian, our Master and God	a brooding presence
Nero, damned to the memory	a hero to some

The household

Flavia Albia	licensed to make enquiries
T. Manlius Faustus	her husband, not what he was
Dromo	their slave, a trial
Graecina	their housekeeper, on trial
Galene	a self-styled cook, very trying
Katutis	a secretary from an older culture
Larcius	a clerk of works, down to earth
The Fabulous Stertinius	a visiting harpist

The family

Q. Camillus Justinus	a helpful uncle, a senator
Marcia Didia	a favourite cousin, packs a punch
Marius	another cousin, packs a flute

Officialdom on the Palatine

Flavius Abascantus	a high-ranking member of Roman intelligence
Claudius Philippus	a rising (or falling) bureaucrat, Albia's handler
Trebianus	the Parthia-watcher, Albia's other handler
Rubrius	Philippus' bagman
Fuscus	a trained killer
Eutrapelus	the ultimate archivist (for the record)
Gaius Ritellius	a missing field agent
Ilia	his wronged wife

At the Castra Peregrina

'Titus'	the Princeps Peregrinorum (not his real name)

Plotios	his clerk of all trades
Alfius	a 'plumber', a nice young man
'Nero'	a prisoner (not his real name)
Paternus	an unknown quantity
Trophimus	an agent provocateur, nasty
'Simon'	a scribe (not his real name)

Under suspicion

Two highly placed widows	not colluding (that's their story)
Sallustius Lucullus	} their dead husbands, historical
C. Vettulenus Civica Cerialis	} mysteries
Lusia Paullina	who knows everybody (her real name)

From Albia's contact list

Sodalus	an archive clerk, births and marriages
Perella	a wronged 'dancer', mainly deaths
Momus	a dissolute fixer
Rutilius Gallicus	the Prefect of the City (top man)

At the Parthia House

Dolazebol	a devious envoy
Bruzenus	a duplicitous henchman
Asxen	his wife, a nice auntie
Squilla	a piece of work
Vindobona	her white cat*
Two sight hounds	who haven't read the disclaimer
'a nephew'	someone's nephew
Corellius	'counting tablecloths'
A gardener	'pruning'

Also: veiled ladies, guards, musicians, gardeners, mules (Sabine and other), kittens, cataphracts, slaves with mops, elephant

---

* *editor's disclaimer: no cats were harmed in the making of this novel*

Then shall come to the west the strife of war stirred up,
and the exiled man of Rome, lifting up a mighty sword,
crossing the Euphrates with many tens of thousands.

The text known as the
Sibylline Oracles

Rome,

September AD 89

I

Many people wanted to believe the Emperor Nero had never died. At least three pretenders passed themselves off as him. One had made a false claim within weeks, under his successor, Galba. Another was dealt with by Titus, and last year Domitian had to tackle a third. Pretending to be a resurrected Nero held a curious appeal. And it was simple: look like him, own a harp, pop up far away in Syria – then keep moving when the legions came to get you. As they certainly would.

One False Nero was caught at sea; two later ones tried fleeing to Parthia. Bad mistake. Devious foreigners in trousers and conical hats used any False Nero they got hold of as a political tool. But once Rome had negotiated the return of that particular fake, he soon ended his deluded existence, dead in a ditch. In this, at least, he matched the real Nero.

Beforehand, in establishing a claim, the harp needed to be mastered only loosely because Nero was at best a mediocre musician so any bum notes would sound authentic. Looking like him could be achieved by dyeing the hair yellow and plonking a wreath on top. Strong self-belief was a nice touch.

To be realistic, nowadays such impersonations were harder. People in Syria joined uprisings whenever they were asked, but even they were growing tired of failure and its horrible consequences. Rome has developed reprisals to its own fine art. Rome puts down a revolt so firmly that it lingers long in the memory. I should know. I come from Britain. We had all that after Boudicca.

In any case, two decades had passed since Nero died. Even in districts where he always drew a cult following, his mad appeal became more nebulous. New pretenders found it harder to tickle up rebellions, even among gullible people who convinced themselves that Nero was wonderful and had *not* cut his throat with a razor, or had had it cut for him because he was too cowardly. He went into hiding only until the moment came to reappear and conquer tyranny . . .

In Rome, Nero was seen rather differently, even though we had a real need for a protector who could see off tyrants. We had our tyrant. He spent a lot of time looking around for people who might want to dislodge him, then had them put to death. Pretenders made him especially nervous.

The third False Nero, the recent one, remained 'shadowy'. In part, this might have been because Rome's *Daily Gazette* couldn't be bothered with him. The editors wanted *new* news stories, not yet another harp-twangler, with more mischievous involvement from Parthia, leading once again to the sordid death of the hopeless hopeful. If number three was dumped in that useful ditch, who cared? Failed fakes were old news.

Besides, it was overseas. Any False Nero had to compete for public interest with the nitty-gritty of our daily life: senatorial decrees, the harvest, aristocratic births, crime, scandal, wills, portents, athletics results and the so-called military successes of our all-too-living emperor, Domitian.

The *Gazette*'s column about amazing spectacles had a cracker this week anyway.

*SHOCK NEWS MIRACLE ON AVENTINE Aedile
struck by lightning on wedding day. 'He is determined not
to miss the Roman Games,' vows weeping bride of miracle
survivor. 'Manlius Faustus will appear in his official role.'*

Juno. That was as preposterous as most *Gazette* reports. It
ranked with three-headed calves being born in a village in
Mauretania or a small earthquake, not many dead. I was
the bride so I should know. I had had no time to weep,
even though the half-killed new husband was mine. And
until I was sure he was fit again, my man was damn well
not going to be dragged out in public at the Games, even
though it was his duty to help organise them.

The mangled report did have consequences, however.
That September, the toiling bureaucrats in their vast office
complex on the Palatine were still tidying up loose ends on
the newest False Nero. They were making sure he remained
as 'shadowy' as possible. For a routine chore, they all read
the *Gazette* to ensure compliance with official policy – where
'official policy' meant 'the paranoid decisions of Domitian'.
The *Gazette*'s amazing-spectacles section was less sternly
policed than others – who cared about a rain of brilliant
green frogs in Thrace? – but the *SHOCK NEWS MIRACLE*
made the bureaucrats pause. In the way of their inquisitive
trade, they must have checked whom this unlucky magistrate
had been marrying when the lightning bolt felled him.

The report did not specify that his allegedly tearful bride
was a daughter of Marcus Didius Falco, who had once
worked as imperial informer, or that I myself carried out
personal enquiries for the general public. The *Daily Gazette*
probably left this unsaid because it does not accuse magistrates' brand-new wives of low activities – not unless they

have committed adultery with actors, and even then it has to be actors the public had heard of. But the bureaucrats existed to know who people were and what they did. They had their own resources – crude spies, torturers, death squads – or sometimes, for light surveillance, they would hire freelance investigators. They kept lists of all Rome's freelances. Whether I liked it or not, they knew what I did.

Just my luck: one of them needed a task carried out discreetly. Widows were involved, nobly born widows with élite ex-husbands. To have the usual repulsive armed men approach these matrons would be undiplomatic, even in Domitian's Rome. So when my marriage came to their attention, the officials thought of commissioning me.

My name is Albia, Flavia Albia. I carry out work for troubled people who need answers. I am efficient and discreet. I came to Rome from Britain, which makes me mysterious and exotic. But the bureaucrats knew that, as the adopted daughter of Marcus Didius Falco and Helena Justina, I could be passed off as a decent, intelligent woman whose mother was a senator's daughter and her father a man of standing in Rome. Wonderfully for the palace, I had just married a well-regarded magistrate – and, as the *Daily Gazette* said, I would soon be seen nibbling nuts with him among people of the best quality at the Roman Games.

Forget the British angle. The scroll-beetles were eager to overlook any rumours that I was a bad-tempered, straight-talking Druid. For tricky interviews with highly placed widows, I was ideal.

2

Many a bride wakes on the morning after her wedding feeling full of dread that her new husband may not be the man she had thought. In our case, if I had made a mistake, it was not his fault. The gods had struck him down and caused a great change in him; I must hope it was temporary. They were not my gods, or if they had been (if I had any gods), the whole Olympian pantheon would be answering to me.

Tiberius Manlius Faustus, a sweet and serious person, had wanted us to have the full marriage ceremony, with a big public procession from my father's house to his. He believed a show was needed. He was committing himself to an informer, a bad move socially. Even I admitted that. My father swears informing is all above board, but he is also an auctioneer, so false claims come easily to him. Besides, people knew I had come from Britannia, that peculiar province at the end of Europe. Britain fascinates everyone in Rome – none of whom would want any son of theirs to set up home with a British orphan. So, while the full marriage procedure is not a legal requirement, Faustus and I went through it as a public gesture.

During my bridal procession, a huge thunderstorm broke above the Aventine Hill. A bolt of lightning felled my new husband. Nobody had yet dared to suggest this was his punishment for marrying me, although I knew people thought it.

Three other men were killed outright. At the time I could barely take in what had happened to them, but despite the rain pouring down on us, I noticed a smell of smoke. At the second of impact, I glimpsed flashes from weapons they had been carrying. I then saw agitated helpers shake their heads, gesturing to me that I should not look at the corpses, which had been stripped by the blast, leaving their clothing in shreds and their shoes blown off.

Tiberius survived. He was thrown to the ground, briefly unconscious. Family members worked frantically to revive him; they put him on his feet again, although they had to drag him to our house for he could not walk. At first he was unable to swallow or to speak, but then he bravely managed to croak an approximate bridegroom's welcome to his new wife. I wanted to shoo everyone away but felt I must allow the formalities, because they meant so much to him.

As soon as I could, I put him to bed. It was hardly a normal wedding night. Tiberius seemed to pass it reasonably well. I did not sleep. Terrified for him, I was in anguish. We had been so full of happiness and hope. I knew how nearly I had lost him and realised from the start that he might be significantly altered.

At first, he showed few physical marks. Next morning, a huge bruise appeared on his chest. My father was to confess eventually that he must have caused it when he thumped Tiberius with a double fist because his heart had stopped. Father knew that, by horrible coincidence, I had been widowed once before in a freak street accident; Falco could not bear it to happen twice, especially right in front of me. His action saved Tiberius's life, though he would always remain rather quiet about just how hard he had whacked him.

'Try to hang on to this one, chuck. You attract disaster. I can't see any other man being brave enough to take you.'

'Oh, thanks, Pa!' No orphan could have been adopted by anybody better. He was deeply upset; I could tell by his making a joke of the chance to beat up his new son-in-law.

Examining Tiberius further, I discovered strange spreading red ferny marks, which had developed upwards from his feet to his torso. By then Mother had sent us a doctor, who told me these patterns on the skin were typical. He reckoned the lightning had made a direct hit on the other three men; it had killed them, then bounced along the ground in less-ened strength before it sprang into Tiberius. That had spared his life, although I was warned that my poor man would suffer unpredictable after-effects, probably for ever. Different people were affected in different ways, and even if he seemed unharmed, serious damage might show itself even in many years' time.

Still shocked, he was in pain and extremely withdrawn. He let me tend him, though he hurt all over and had panic attacks. Apart from his uncle, who looked in on him briefly, I barred visitors. Most of our relatives were interested only in finding out whether our marriage had been consummated (what in Hades did they think?). Fortunately, quite a few were still too drunk to leave their houses.

The event attracted strangers. People stood outside our house and stared. Other members of the medical profession scrambled to call on us, cadging fees. I picked their brains on the doorstep, then sent them packing. Mother's man prescribed mild sedation, while he advised letting time take its course. He was a doctor I approved of.

9

We had planned various parties, which I cancelled. Normally, socialising for days is compulsory for new couples, but I'd had enough at the wedding. I did consult Tiberius, who agreed we had made our point. We had announced our union in spectacular style – then when the *Daily Gazette* reported the event, our families told us people paid good money for this kind of recognition. Father's secretary was sent to the Forum to write down full details, which he brought and read to Tiberius, leaving the copy for us. I tossed it into a chest. I knew what had happened. I relived it every time I tried to rest.

I kept busy.

We had come to live in a house that Tiberius had bought to renovate for us. He was supposed to be running a building firm from a yard alongside; he intended to finance our own property out of his earnings on new contracts – but when would he be fit to work again? While he remained bedridden, I did not even discuss it with him. But I had to think about the situation.

We had a bare plastered house, empty of furniture, except for a beautiful entrance hall and our own bedroom, which Tiberius had completed as his marriage gift to me. Until the morning after our wedding I had never seen them. Now I finally managed to look properly, in daylight, at the exquisite wall frescos, the elegant floors, the fielded doors with their crisp architraves and new bronze handles, the carefully repaired ceiling coves; going around alone I was very upset. If I lost him, I could never live here. He had worked so hard, intending me to enjoy this house with him. Today, he ought to have been showing me everything himself.

His fresco painter turned up as soon as he heard what had happened, anxious about his bill. I snapped that it was thoughtless to harass a man who had so nearly died, and told him to return in a few days. If Tiberius was no better, I would arrange payment myself.

Other creditors were making enquiries of our clerk-of-works, next door. Larcius came from the building yard and mentioned this quietly, saying he, too, was putting people off. I reassured him that we did have funds; it was true, though I was reluctant to dig into my own investments in case we used up all our money too soon. In the short term, Tiberius and I both had wealthy relations. We could swallow our pride, put up with their teasing, and call on my father and his uncle to pay urgent bills. That is how things are done in Rome. We would never be destitute.

I did not at this point visit my banker, a cunning Greek woman who believed all savings must be hidden from your husband. Alternatively, you should grab any money that belonged to him – after poisoning his dinner.

I liked her, but I knew Arsinoë would see the lightning-strike as the gods' wedding gift to me: husband lost, so wife achieves wealth and independence. She had yet to learn that, if Tiberius recovered, my investments would be called in to finance our intended business. All bankers assume your money is theirs to play with. The idea that you might one day want to use it yourself is blasphemy.

Tiberius and I were planning to be a family partnership, with me fully involved in our affairs. So now I had to tackle our debts. Not for me placidly weaving at a loom in the atrium, claiming that my husband always dealt with money matters while I didn't understand that kind of thing . . . I would never possess a home loom. For heaven's sake, I was an informer, not a weaver.

I needed to organise our affairs, starting with staff in the house. So far I only had one slave belonging to Tiberius, Dromo, to assist me with nursing the patient and everything else. Dromo, a dim lad, always had a one-track mind: who looked after him? Shaken by what had happened, he became needy and anxious. If his master died, Dromo would lose his provider. There would be no more cakes, no more sleeping half the day on his mat. He might even be sold to someone who would make him work. Or they might cruelly beat him . . .

I said unless he stopped mithering, I would beat him myself. If he wanted Tiberius to survive, he must help me look after him. Grumbling, he took himself off to brew up a spiced drink for his master. I had given him a recipe, though teaching Dromo anything was hard.

I sat down to plan. We must have someone to answer the door. After years of run-ins with the foul-mouthed, eager-for-bribes incompetents who serve as door-keepers in Rome, I now reluctantly needed one myself. Tiberius was a magistrate and my own work attracted dubious types. Face-to-face with a stranger (or, worse, some idiot you already know), you lose your options. I had to obtain an intermediary. I could not use Rodan, the elderly ex-gladiator from my old apartment: he was sordid and filthy, not to be trusted in sensitive situations. Dromo was hopeless too. He could answer the door and take basic messages, but then he would forget to tell us.

Someone to run the household was urgently needed. I couldn't help Tiberius with his business, deal with my own clients, then also shop, clean, cook and make beds, let alone carry out that housewifely task of chatting to visitors politely even if they were persons I despised (most people). I might manage to sit in the courtyard handing around almond biscuits, but someone had to buy in dainties and bring them on a tray. Organising a home was not for me. I can do it. Helena Justina, my adoptive mother, had made me a knowledgeable, capable woman. But it was not what I wanted to do – any more than she did. So I had to find a good steward or housekeeper, and find them fast. Then I'd supply whatever staff they needed.

I could give instructions. I had always been good at appraising situations then expressing an opinion. Tiberius even pretended to like me for it. The housekeeper would answer to me, and would know the position. Anyone who crossed me would be kicked out.

The first addition to the steward's staff must be some biddable slave for everything Dromo refused to do.

You may think, why didn't I dump Dromo? Bad idea. Dromo belonged to Tiberius. I would tolerate the boy patiently, as he did. I did not intend Tiberius Manlius ever to blame me for dismissing his adored favourite slave.

No, of course he did not adore him. Dromo wore him down and drove him mad. But I was keeping out of that.

I did know what I was starting here. I was a wise bride, and in choosing me Tiberius Manlius had shown he was a clever man. I was not some fifteen-year-old virgin, who had never been in charge of the keys before. I was nearly thirty and had lived on my own for years. Besides, I had been married in the past.

So had he. As far as I could see, what he had learned from it was next time to choose someone different. Having met the ex-wife, I knew he had certainly done that. A crucial difference between me and Laia Gratiana was that I had my own career. A good informer can stay solvent; my earning power gave me reassurance. However long Tiberius stayed bed-ridden, I would pay our bills. I felt lonely while he was unable to share my concerns, but I stayed calm.

I was to receive my next commission sooner than I'd thought. A new visitor arrived. Dromo let him in, shouting across the courtyard that he was too busy to keep looking after people. He went back to doing nothing. The man found his own way out to me. I knew him: it was Claudius Philippus, a bureaucrat from the palace. Although he said he was bringing official good wishes for my husband, from the start I guessed there was more to it.

3

I was seated on an antique stone bench that Tiberius had bought. Philippus joined me. We were in a small, bare courtyard, facing a wall through which a doorway had recently been cut to reach the building-yard next door. Beside the door, turned up on its edge, a rough-cut stone basin leaned, a huge ugly object awaiting overdue removal. It would need a team, with sturdy ropes. There would be much cursing. I intended to watch the performance secretly from upstairs.

Something could be made of this area once we had time. At the moment the outdoor space contained only my bench and one potted oleander, a glum thing that had been brought out from where it was dying by the porch. After he entered through the redecorated hallway, Philippus must have realised the rest of our house was work in progress. Although he looked around, he made no comment. He gave a slight cough, as if reacting to the dust and expressing refined surprise that anyone could live in such chaos. I noticed him secretly making a survey of the good and the shabby. That must be to assess our financial situation.

Tiberius Claudius Philippus was lean and ascetic, with fine features. His looks seemed unexpected because his manner was that of a man with little personality or home life. (Did he eat and sleep at the palace, in case his imperial master required something?)

In his profession he followed his father, a much respected servant of the old, wise Emperor Vespasian. Claudius Laeta had been a palace freedman, so he had probably married another ex-slave of the imperial family, with their children being freeborn. Were there other children? I could not easily imagine Philippus with brothers and sisters. If so, I bet he created inventories of their toys, then wrote rules about who was entitled to play with what.

My father had worked with the older man, Laeta, whom I had met, so I knew Philippus must have gained his looks from his mother. He could have been a playboy, making a career among rich society women, yet had chosen to be a scribe. His old-fashioned attitude was all his own. None of us would have trusted his father to serve us a slice of pie – yet Laeta was always aware, a keen observer and manipulator. The son might or might not be equally acute. Tiberius and I had met Philippus recently, but had yet to learn how ambitious he was, or whether he plotted.

It seemed likely.

Claudius Laeta, the father, did plot. He had carried on a gritty feud for years with the head of the intelligence service. Laeta had come up under the Emperor Claudius, whereas Anacrites had been Nero's man. In public administration, this kind of history is critical. When the chief spy had brought their tussle to an end by dying in dark circumstances, as the best and worst of them tend to do, Claudius Laeta did not grieve for him but grabbed the role of spymaster. With him in charge, first Vespasian and then the short-lived Titus revamped Rome's security service, once merely a minor role of the Praetorian Guard. Laeta was so subtle that the public barely noticed his adaptations.

Under Domitian that altered. Spies were now openly

everywhere; they were watching not hostile frontier tribes (though they must do that as well) but all of us at home, their brooding master's frightened subjects. As I greeted Philippus, therefore, I felt wary.

'When we met, your father had just died. Are you succeeding Claudius Laeta?' I was flattering him. Philippus seemed to be in his thirties, too young to head a secretariat. He wore white palace livery, though kept it plain, with quite meagre gold trimmings, and he did not reek of fancy pomades. I could see no jewellery.

'My field of interest is similar.' This cagey reply was reminiscent of Laeta, who had cultivated his mystique. I decided to treat Philippus carefully, so I waited for him to take the initiative.

Bringing official good wishes was a normal enough reason for this visit. A magistracy made Tiberius one of the most significant men in Rome, at least during his year of office. There were four aediles; to those of senatorial rank it was a rung on the ladder to consul, though Tiberius was plebeian so could expect much less. Still, for this year he looked after a quarter of the city.

Philippus said Domitian would wish to know that an aedile had so nearly died, and in such an extraordinary way – spared by the gods. Would I describe what had happened? I did so, keeping it factual. 'Please don't make too much of this, Philippus. Don't let it sound like some divine favour, competition for our Master and God.' That was the title Domitian liked, while pretending he was too modest to allow people to say it.

Philippus pursed his lips slightly. He knew what I meant. Our emperor believed himself a protégé of Jupiter, with Minerva as his personal patron. Anybody else claiming the gods' special approval would diminish the Emperor's position. Domitian could easily take it into his head that Faustus posed a threat. 'He had a lucky escape, Philippus, but is suffering painfully. For Manlius Faustus this is no divine honour!'

Philippus wanted to see for himself. I had to allow it, so I led him upstairs. When we looked into the bedroom, Tiberius lay pale, his eyes closed. He seemed asleep, though as Philippus left he opened his eyes to exchange a look with me. I found his expression worrying. I could not stop to investigate but it left me edgy.

Philippus seemed in no hurry to leave. Back in the courtyard, he stared around nosily again; this time he commented on the lack of staff. He said I seemed to have my hands full, then pointed out that building projects were notoriously expensive.

I saw what he was doing. I let him make his play.

'You must have enough anxieties without financial pressure . . . I hope I can speak to you frankly. Would a paid task be welcome, Flavia Albia? Something so quick and easy, you could do it in your sleep?'

'My husband does not wish his wife to work,' I simpered shamelessly. Tiberius had not raised the issue or I would never have married him. He valued my work.

He could probably overhear us from the bedroom above – I had left a door open in case he needed something. However, I heard no guffaws or growls.

'I am sure we could find you an acceptable commission . . . In fact, I do have something that would be suitable – if you were interested?'

Reluctant to work for officialdom, I gave Philippus no encouragement.

He pressed on. Nothing deters a bureaucrat when he is trying to offload a task – and, as my father would say, especially when it's a stupid one. 'I feel sure your husband will approve . . . Flavia Albia, I need a respectable person I can trust, preferably female, to ask questions of two women. They are very high status, ex-consuls' wives. In fact, both their husbands were provincial governors.'

'Were?'

Philippus jumped nervously. 'Dead, sadly. Both men.'

'How?' I asked, stony-faced.

'Executed.'

I knew what this meant. 'Big men sent to help them commit suicide? Loud knocks on the door, with swords at dawn?'

'Yes, the usual.'

Philippus made it sound a matter-of-fact occurrence. To him, it was. He worked for Domitian.

Having persons of high rank removed by armed officers occurred too often nowadays. Titus had done it; even Vespasian occasionally, though he would use Titus as his frontman. They played it down. They acted as if executions troubled them. Domitian had no qualms. Under him, anyone who had the bad luck to catch the Emperor's eye might find himself doomed.

I had not agreed to accept the commission, but of course I asked who the dead men were and what they had done.

'Who they were is the easy question. Your task, my dear Albia, is to help me prove what they did.'

'What they *really* did, you mean? I assume Domitian already had thoughts on the subject when he picked them for a snap redundancy.' Any 'thoughts' from Domitian about his presumed enemies tended to be ludicrous.

19

Philippus explained. One of the men had been killed the previous year, one more recently. When I was told their names, I vaguely remembered. The deaths had been notorious because Domitian had struck when both men were in service, still out in their provinces. To execute a serving governor was unheard of. Governors had been charged with misdemeanours, usually extortion from provincials, but they had been properly brought home and put on trial.

Why did he do it? Deadpan, Philippus named the charges against them: Sallustius Lucullus, governor of Britain, supposedly 'invented a new javelin and called it after himself'. If true, it was a stupid insult to a touchy emperor. Civica Cerialis, in Asia, was simply indicted for 'conspiracy', a conveniently woolly term. It would have been difficult for either to defend himself, though defence against Domitian was never a real option.

I assumed they were killed for a connection with the Saturninus revolt; Antonius Saturninus was himself a provincial governor, in Upper Germany. Last January he made a bungled attempt to seize power; afterwards, Domitian executed senators he suspected of involvement. He could not pinpoint many.

With Saturninus, poor preparation might explain why he was so quickly defeated. To be confirmed in office would have meant winning over the extremely nervous Senate. My two uncles, who were senators, reserved judgement, never making any public comment. Most shared their caution.

Any wide-scale support for Saturninus eluded detection. However, Philippus told me that Domitian had not forgotten. Almost a year later, he still wanted revenge.

He was currently away in Pannonia, defending our borders. With autumn, the fighting season ended; Domitian would be coming home. In Rome's mighty hilltop palace all the bureaucrats were jumpy. Naturally Philippus wanted a good report with which to greet his master. He wanted me to provide it. 'Our Master would be very pleased to have his thoughts on these two men validated.'

Or much less pleased if I proved he had been wrong . . . That might be fatal for me. 'Is he definitely coming back?' I asked. 'He won't enjoy himself with banqueting and screwing fancy boys in winter quarters?'

Philippus let this pass, perhaps knowing it had some basis. 'He has made peace and is coming home. He is to be awarded a double triumph for his successes in Pannonia and Dacia.'

'Peace? I thought he bought the Dacians off!' Many people despised him for it. I might have done, but I already despised him for too many other things. 'I haven't heard anything about the Senate awarding a triumph.'

'Nor has the Senate yet.' Philippus put on a special owl-eyed dour look. His father, I thought, would never have admitted that the Senate were helpless puppets.

'What Domitian wants, the Senate must provide?'

He nodded.

It seemed incongruous to be seated in my private garden being told state secrets by a man who had seemed too junior to know them, but Domitian's administrators tended to be young. He quickly dispensed with older ones, whom he viewed as compromised. Rather than use their experience or trust their loyalty, Domitian ousted anyone who had served his father and brother – even going right back to doddery freedmen who had once had connections with Nero.

'So what's your task, Philippus? Is it suitable for me, and do I even want to try?'

The good-looking man looked down his long nose at me. 'I invite you to interview the wives of Lucullus and Cerialis. See if they will confirm that their husbands were supporters of Saturninus.'

I scoffed. The women would never admit that. 'It would be foolish to reveal pillow talk. To admit they were aware of the revolt in advance would damage themselves, any children they have, and other relatives.' Plots in Rome never went away. Executing two governors was merely the start; ripples would be flowing outwards from this incident for years. Nobody close to the men Domitian had condemned would ever emerge into the light, free from suspicion.

I know this. Something similar had once happened in my own family. We never speak of it.

'What is the fee?'

Without hesitation, Philippus named a sum. It was larger than I had expected. He seemed very sure of himself.

'Claudius Philippus, do you have clearance for that?'

'I do.'

'I am impressed. I want it in advance,' I specified.

'Oh, come, Flavia Albia! Have faith. Your father has done imperial work and been paid for it.'

'Two years later! I need income now, Philippus. That is the whole point. I have plenty to do as an aedile's wife, especially with the Roman Games fast approaching. Manlius Faustus needs me. If you want me to stop looking after him and do this as a favour to you, you will have to pay upfront.'

He sighed. 'Well. I have a special fund I can call upon.'

Special cash funds are always intriguing. They are usually secret, and meant for spending on *very* special actions. I wanted to discover more.

'I deduce this task will be more difficult than you are so blithely making out . . . Would I have assistance?'

'My staff are always helpful.'

'And do *you* think the governors were plotting?'

'It is more than probable.'

'Not a fantasy of the Emperor's?'

'The Emperor is extremely shrewd.' When you feel convinced people are out to get you, you have to stay sharp. Domitian had the knack of clinging to life.

'I still think the ladies will simply deny it.'

'I fear so.' Philippus took this calmly. He put his finger-tips together, a precise, prissy gesture. 'But we have to ask the question. So, Flavia Albia, can I assume you are willing to do this?'

I accepted the job.

The man from the palace then added smoothly: 'There is something else you can do for me, if you will. While you are questioning the women about Saturninus, please see whether their husbands were in any way connected with the Syrian fiasco. I need to know if the men had any contact with, or interest in, the third False Nero.'

'Trust a secretariat to want two jobs for the price of one!'

'You agree?'

'I agree that I can ask them.'

That was how I came to obtain special knowledge of imperial fakes. Philippus just casually tossed it in.

Of course I am not supposed to discuss that sorry business

or even hint that I know about it. My father always says, the whole Roman Empire will have to decline and fall before his sensational memoirs can be put before an astonished public. Mine will contain lively material too. For instance, the third False Nero, whom Philippus so slyly added to my commission, was not as shadowy as people think. I can say that with some confidence: I met him.

4

I should have paid more attention to the Nero request. When a bureaucrat pretends something has little importance, you can bet it is significant.

By then my thoughts were back with my stricken husband. I was wondering why, when Tiberius Manlius opened his eyes, he had seemed so troubled as he looked at me. It was as if he could not even remember who I was.

As soon as Philippus left, I went upstairs, carrying the official tablet that set out my access to the interviewees.

Dromo was there. 'I am looking after him!'

Clearly I was supposed to remove myself. 'I am here now.' The slave glared. 'I want to talk to your master in private.' I held the door open for him, pointing the way out in case he failed to get the message. I won, though I felt I could not always rely on it happening.

Tiberius had watched without comment. I gazed at him. He was washed and dressed, though Dromo had not shaved him. His skin felt too sensitive; he could not bear the razor. To see such a sturdy figure reduced to lying feebly on his bed all day was dreadful.

His grey eyes assessed me. He must see my anxiety, so at last he held out a hand, encouraging me to sit by him. His grip felt warm enough.

Perched on the edge of the bed, I waved my commission

tablet. 'Philippus wants me to conduct some interviews. I told him you refuse to let your wife work.' A smile hovered faintly. His sense of humour was lurking in there still. 'The fee will pay the fresco painter, but it carries a moral burden. I have never acted for the government; I never wanted to.'

'Your father has.' Affected by his sedative, Tiberius' words came out a little slurred.

'Yes, but never since Vespasian died. Father had respect for him. I am being hired to validate the dark suspicions of our Master and God, which is very different . . . I have to prove, or disprove, that he was right to execute two men.'

'Just because Domitian believes other people are plotting doesn't mean he has imagined it.' Tiberius was alert enough and as usual very fair.

'Oh, yes. Once a plot succeeds, his suspicions will all be justified . . . If he really is a god, then after he croaks he can look down on us all with that knowing smirk of his.' Tiberius shook his head slightly, warning me not to be outspoken. 'Well, aedile, my task seems straightforward: interviews of respectable widows. They will know who I am and why I have been sent. It is all out in the open.'

Tiberius gave me a half-shrug.

I wanted him to rant and refuse permission. I wanted a tussle. Would he care more if he was not in pain? I hated to see him too weak to criticise this new task, and perhaps, even at this stage, I wanted him to give me an excuse to turn the palace down.

I gazed at him. My husband. My husband, whom the Roman gods had snatched away into some darkness where I was no longer certain I could reach him.

'Oh, Tiberius! How are you, sweetheart?' His response was another lacklustre movement. We were honest with one

26

another. I explained how his expression earlier had alarmed me. 'You looked like a man with memory loss. I felt frightened that you were wondering who I was.'

At that, the look I had noticed seemed to clear. He reached out, pulled me down beside him on the bed and held me in his arms. Against the top of my head he murmured, with something like his normal chortle, 'Unforgettable!'

'Flavia Albia?'

'Flavia Albia. Daughter of Didius Falco and Helena Justina.' The formal reply seemed reassuring – until he went on, 'Wife of Manlius Faustus . . . But that's the problem,' admitted Tiberius, quietly. 'Who is Faustus?'

He might have been teasing. Yet his insecurity was heart-rending.

5

I decided to see the British governor's widow first. I wanted
to get Britain out of the way. I had told Philippus to fix
it up for that same afternoon.

I was to interview both women at the palace. Neutral
ground. The best place available, since I was told they had
sold their town mansions and gone to live quietly in the
country on family estates. Once Domitian had despatched
their husbands, they must have found it hard to remain in
Roman society, where most of their friends would feel
nervous about knowing them. Perhaps they managed to see
those people in the country. More likely, friendship was
another of the losses inflicted on them.

Philippus must have compelled these noble women to
journey to Rome especially to be questioned. I guessed he
was reminding them of the Emperor's power over them.

Hey-ho. Perhaps I would start with an apology . . .
Somehow I felt that was unlikely to win these ladies over.

Before I tackled the interviews, I prepared myself.

There were certain things I could deduce. The widows
must be of an older generation than me. Their men had
completed the full senatorial course of honour. That ran
through aedile, quaestor, praetor, consul and overseas legate
until, if one was cynical, it nowadays ended with offending
Domitian and premature death. For consul, the qualifying

age is forty; when their provinces were granted they would be shy of fifty, with their wives perhaps ten years younger. Aristocrats tend to marry when they are entering the Senate at twenty-five, often taking wives who are still teenagers. This is supposed to ensure no taint of scandal attaches to their brides; well, young girls are famous for concealing whatever they get up to. I had teenaged sisters. My parents were living with fear every day.

The senators might have done their wild living too, but that never counts against men. *Settle down, Albia!*

So the two ex-consuls had been mature, at the height of their powers, perhaps even wise and competent. They would have travelled out to run some foreign place, before enjoying a comfortable retirement with any money they had creamed off its locals – provided they dodged imperial disfavour.

Asia is generally seen as the highest prize available. The man there would already have served three years in a lesser province, which would have made him older though still not decrepit. For Domitian to grant him Asia was a very specific honour. How did Civica Cerialis subsequently lose the Emperor's trust so badly?

Britain, of course, is inferior. No favour there!

As I expected, nothing much was known about Sallustius Lucullus, who had been sent to Romanise the woady British natives. I knew he had been appointed in the wake of Julius Agricola, with whom Domitian had a touchy relationship; the Emperor distrusted Agricola's supposed ambition and military success. Agricola nevertheless stayed in post for a long period, conquering away; when finally recalled to Rome, it was said that he entered the city unobtrusively by night instead of proudly and publicly. After debriefing, he was granted triumphal honours, including a forum statue, but he immediately retired.

People believed Agricola had been offered the important governorship of Africa, but declined it. Perhaps he loathed Domitian – or knew Domitian loathed him. There was talk of ill health. My family, who took an interest, simply thought Julius Agricola had had enough. Civilising Britain had exhausted him. Well, it might have, they said, grinning at me.

Sallustius Lucullus, who replaced him, was ordered to avoid more military conquest. Not for him annexing Caledonian mountains. So, was he bored, twiddling his thumbs, until he began inventing new army equipment? Or was that javelin story a pretext?

Usefully, I was able to fill out my deductions. One of my uncles, a senator, came visiting to ask after Tiberius. His breezy voice calling hello announced him, in the usual absence of Dromo: Camillus Justinus, Mother's younger brother, her favourite. He strode in without ceremony, despite the purple-bordered toga, which he always wore rather raffishly.

'Uncle Quintus!'

He gave me a hug, knocking the breath out of me. 'That was some wedding, young Albia! Thundering Jupiter! How is the poor fellow?'

I sent him up to see the patient. He was gone a while. Tiberius must have been talking.

When he came down again my uncle asked sternly about my task for Philippus. So that was it! Men deciding what was suitable and safe for me.

I exploited his presence to ask about the two dead

governors. Justinus said Sallustius Lucullus was never prominent. 'My impression of him in the Senate is of a plodder.'

'He had to be thought efficient, though Domitian cannot have viewed him as dangerously ambitious. Might he have supported the Saturninus revolt?'

'Not enough gumption.'

'Was he obsessed with military toys?'

'What toys?'

I explained about inventing the new kind of javelin. My companion winced. He had served in a legion but he was no armed-forces fanatic. He liked to read, eat, and father children. He was a benign parent. His rabble of six had marauded like little barbarians at my wedding.

'So, Uncle, did you know the other man, Civica Cerialis?'

'Not me.'

'Really?'

'Never met him, honest.'

'I get it! None of you in the Senate have any idea what he did wrong?'

Justinus pulled a face. 'The general thought is that he did nothing. I mean *nothing*,' he hinted heavily.

'Didn't support the Saturninus revolt, for instance?'

'Doubt it. Too far away. He was off in the east. Anyway, I think Domitian eliminated old Cerialis before the revolt happened. More likely his crime was inertia during the Nero fiasco.'

'Ah! Enlighten me, Uncle.'

'Well, this is a guess. When the latest fake turned up in Asia, Domitian probably felt Cerialis ought to have barred him more robustly.'

'The False Nero travelled to Asia?'

'He certainly didn't stay in his Syrian village. He gathered followers and set out for Rome. When that went wrong, the idiot went to Parthia. But the whole adventure seems murky.'

'That's intentional,' I told him. 'Diminish his importance by publicly ignoring him . . . Quintus, I suppose such a situation always poses a problem for a governor. He must wonder, *What if this unlikely upstart wins?* After all, Vespasian and Titus gained the throne from the east, which seemed a crazy feat at the time.'

My uncle nodded. I knew the story only as a kind of folk tale, whereas he was old enough to remember. 'Vespasian won because the governors of various eastern provinces, in a region where he was conveniently fighting at the time, declared for him. The way he played it, it was their idea to put him up for emperor. It did demonstrate that frontier governors, who all control very active legions, could influence who holds the throne – with the possibility that they might do so again.'

'So a False Nero appearing on his doorstep could have given Cerialis ideas?' I asked.

Gazing at me with fine dark eyes, my uncle spoke as if giving a legal verdict: 'Young woman, provincial governors are supposed to have sufficient judgement to dismiss any yellow-haired shepherd lad who comes along singing and claiming to be a dead man's ghost.'

'Well, tell me something else. Cerialis was dead in Asia before Saturninus made his play in Germany. In my commission they seem oddly linked. What about Saturninus? Did you know him, Quintus?'

Once again I heard the all-innocent line: 'That misguided rebel was utterly friendless. Ask anyone!' Uncle Quintus had a particularly telling grin.

Always attractive, he had grown even more into his looks as he had matured in his middle years. His humour was drier too. He knew how the world worked, tolerated its inequalities because he had to, but among his family he deplored nonsense.

Neither he nor his elder brother would be offered consulships or provinces, although they were fully capable. Years ago, a relative had plotted against an emperor. The doors to political success closed in their faces. Instead, they became lawyers, not flamboyant ones who were famous for litigation, but the honest kind who tried to advise clients on how to avoid the courts. Politically they kept a low profile. They had managed to enter the Senate, like their father, but could advance no further.

Neither ever referred to their career disappointments; nor did they seem to bear grudges. Yet supporting Saturninus might have appealed: a grateful newcomer might have given Camillus Aelianus and Camillus Justinus opportunities they had long been denied by the Flavians. Both astute, they had judged the revolt in Germany a predetermined failure. Anyway, one plotter in the family was enough. One disgrace. Any false move now and Domitian might remember what had happened in the past. That would be typical of him. It could be fatal for them.

When Quintus was younger, before his career faltered, he had been a military tribune in Upper Germany, based at Moguntiacum. As I expected, he had views on what had happened there last year. 'Moguntiacum is a huge fort, housing two legions – both notoriously stroppy. The Fourteenth Gemina has a terrible reputation. The Twenty-first Rapax are no better.'

'You served in one of those?'

'No, the First Adiutrix. They moved over to the Danube. It was partly to empty a space where the Twenty-first Rapax could be dumped. The Fourteenth had already been drafted there for one ruckus too many. When Saturninus took up his post, the two legions had been cosying up together for too long. Then, too, there was serious money stashed at the fort, a double whack of soldiers' savings. Saturninus relied on these uppity buggers, and intended to use their cash to fund himself.' Quintus stretched his legs as if he felt uncomfortable. 'They backed him – so, Albia, I call the affair in January a mutiny, not a rebellion. The thing was never sound. It was one man who should have been cleverer, plus soldiers behaving like idiots. By no means a wide-scale political movement.'

'Why was Domitian so exercised about two legions?' I asked.

'Saturninus had four, in fact, a huge army. His other two declined to join in, though that could not be foretold in advance. Besides, his truly evil plan was to invite the Chatti to cross the frozen Rhine from Free Germany. The tribe was ready to do it but a sudden thaw made the river impassable.' I could see that, for Camillus Justinus, encouraging barbarians to attack Rome was a serious sin.

'My impression is the rebels, or mutineers, just caved in?'

Justinus shook his head. 'No, it came to battle. Saturninus' forces were defeated and he was killed. He completely underestimated Domitian's reaction. The Emperor himself was on his way to Upper Germany, with Ulpius Trajanus fast-marching a legion in from Spain, but even before they got there Lappius Maximus had rushed up troops from *Lower* Germany. He crushed the rebellion. Lappius had the

34

First Minervia. Domitian founded that legion. Your everyday soldier somehow likes Domitian and, no question, those lads would not let their founder be deposed.'

I was curious about what happened next. 'It was all kept under wraps, as I remember. Finished before the public in Rome realised anything was happening?'

Quintus' face darkened. 'Yes, it came as a shock. But Domitian must have been warned that a coup was likely to happen on New Year's Day. He was secretly ready for it.'

'He had loyal generals.'

'He had spies.'

'Hmm! And afterwards, Quintus? I know officers from the two mutinous legions were brutally hunted down in Germany.'

'They were tortured and decapitated. Domitian had the severed heads despatched to Rome, then displayed in the Forum. It was the crudest warning to the Senate – *this is what happens to those who oppose me*. We had no idea. We turned up at the Curia for normal business,' said Quintus, in a bleak tone, 'and, without warning or explanation, found a sickening row of bloody heads. Some, of course, were senators' young relatives.' Suddenly Justinus shifted in his seat. 'That's enough. Don't ask me any more.'

I was surprised he cut me off. 'Hey! Why this caution?'

'You are an informer for Domitian now.'

Too late, I grasped the implications. With our paranoid emperor, no one trusted anyone, even close family. Any indiscreet talk might be reported. Your relatives, your friends or your slaves might betray you.

Quintus pointedly changed the subject.

Like Philippus, he gazed around. He asked how I was

35

coping. I assured him I had plans for new staff to help; I knew a good steward who might be at a loose end. At once Quintus kindly whistled up his escort, extracted an address from me, and sent a man off to invite Gratus to come along later to discuss whether he was interested.

This positive action cheered me. So when, shortly afterwards, I wrapped a stole around my head for decency and set off to the Palatine, I walked with a light step as if I was making progress.

I knew my uncle's discretion was wise. Luckily for Philippus, evaluating the widows was not the first job that had made me uncomfortable. Informers have to do whatever comes along. 'Just like lawyers!' I had teased Quintus. He took it badly.

Before I began, I walked around the Capitol to the Atrium of Liberty, where some of the censors' records are kept, and asked for an old contact. Sodalus was a sludge-coloured slave in a grunge-coloured tunic, though he persuaded himself he was clean-cut. A clue to his vanity was his red-laced shoes, which must have got him noticed when he was out on the pull among his cronies.

I asked him to dig out any scrolls that contained references to the two families I was investigating. He grumbled. I said it was official. He agreed to assist but I had to come back later. 'Much later.' He scratched a boil on his cheek for emphasis.

'You're a gem, Sodalus. Tomorrow.'

'Too soon!'

'Wrong, sweetie. It is for the Emperor.' I already enjoyed this deployment of the august one to speed up results.

Well, it might work. Sodalus gave me a curl of the lip

that implied everyone tried to use 'imperial business' as a fulcrum. I stressed that time was of the essence. He scoffed, 'What's new?'

For a professional informer, gaining information is not difficult. Your problem is gaining it early enough, squeezing a story out of some layabout when you really need it. Dealing with a slouch like Sodalus was routine for me. He would have scrolls lined up tomorrow. He knew I always tipped him well.

Adequately, anyway.

'Gorgeous shoes, Sodalus, by the way.' Always leave a contact with something positive.

I strolled back through the top of the Forum and up to the Palatine.

The palace was new, though the atmosphere was very old: suspicion. In the lofty, marble-slathered corridors, everyone I passed seemed to look at me too hard. They were probably all just palace scribes, walking purposefully between offices to avoid doing any work. Some might be outsiders, maybe tourists or students of high-end design, coming to see the famous innovative architecture and the gilding, perhaps taking advantage of Domitian being away. To me, they all looked like snitches.

Of course, in the world we inhabited, clerks and visitors genuinely were potential spies.

Joking internally about this sinister environment, not to mention my own role as a hireling, I found the office where Philippus worked. This took time. Here there were rooms within halls within segmented suites. I met twists and turns and altered levels. Somewhere Domitian and his family lived inaccessibly in gorgeous boltholes, which one could regard as deserved retreats – or as hideaways for a tyrant fearful of attack. Locked doors protected them.

37

Even though Domitian was absent, he had left behind an oppressive presence.

Eventually I was directed by a slave with a mop. There were quite a few of those, no doubt observing who came and went. I found Philippus pretending to read a scroll. He and I had a short briefing session. I reminded him my fee was to be paid before I started.

There was a pause while a slave was sent for the money. I sat tight in Philippus' office until he produced it. He pursed his lips. I refused to be cowed. It took some time for the money to arrive, so he gave me some facts as a briefing.

The widow of Sallustius Lucullus was being kept on ice in an anteroom; in due course I whisked in, scarves a-flutter, full of insincere apologies for having kept her waiting.

6

Philippus did not come in with me. I preferred to introduce myself.

The widow wore dark clothes, very formal; she was
discreetly jewelled, pampered with undetectable creams and
cosmetics. Two maids chaperoned her, dressed almost as
expensively – which meant more expensively than me. Used
to sharing her husband's consular status, she did not rise
when I entered, or suggest I could sit.

I seated myself on a couch nevertheless, straight-backed,
between its tasselled cushion rolls. I let her inspect me:
unaccompanied, long gown in good pale cloth, dark hair
put up tidily though clearly by me and not some deft slave.
I, too, had a discreet necklace and ear-rings, though unremarkable. I was twenty-nine, with an accent she would not
be able to place and a restraint that failed to impress her.

'My name is Flavia Albia. I am the wife of a magistrate.
I am to interview you about your late husband.' While I
was speaking, I took out my note-tablet and stylus, though
I laid them beside me on the couch. I wanted to look
professional yet not threatening.

I began with the obvious: had she accompanied her husband
on his British posting? No. Well, that made everything easier.
She was never there. How could she know anything?

For women of rank, it was optional to accompany a

husband on tour. Wives whose marriages were cool tended to remain in Italy. Provinces with high military activity, such as Britain, could well be omitted, though a governor educating unkempt provincials might welcome the presence of a cultured wife. Wise wives, those who cared, went along anyway to deter their men from taking mistresses. 'Can I ask what influenced your decision?'

'It did not seem necessary for me to go.'

I feigned sympathy. 'The climate, the bleak amenities . . . Actually, it's not that bad. I once stayed in the governor's palace at Londinium. I found it comfortable.' To a scavenger straight off the streets it had been staggering luxury. I remembered enormous interiors, mighty halls, quiet formal gardens, heated mosaic floors, even glazed windows . . . 'I was impressed by the sense of diplomatic business. Brisk military aides. Efficient clerks. Receptions for traders and so forth. The officials I met seemed honest, people with a mission, people with vision.'

Despite my sympathetic approach, the widow made no response.

I asked whether her husband had written to her from Britain. He had, but the subject matter was mundane. Family matters. Domestic arrangements, birthdays . . . She claimed she had kept nothing. If she had any sense, she would now go home and burn everything she could find. Had she unbent at all towards me during the interview, I might have advised her to do so.

'Have you been given any documents that he left in Londinium?'

'No.'

If true, some loyal aide might have weeded the filing trays. Perhaps Domitian's executioner rootled through, looking for evidence, then carried it off. Or, so far from Rome, rather than pack up stuff to go back across Europe, it might all have been simply thrown away.

'I presume you can't say, then, whether Sallustius Lucullus communicated with other governors. You see where I am leading. First, did he contact Antonius Saturninus?'

'Not to my knowledge.' I saw the woman relax slightly. She must have known she could safely pretend ignorance. Philippus had told me there was a problem with correspondence in Upper Germany.

'Unfortunately, everything in writing is lost,' I admitted openly. 'It caused quite a controversy, as I am sure you know. When Lappius Maximus arrived at Moguntiacum, he took it upon himself to have a bonfire. Norbanus, from Rhaetia, helped him do it. They were censured later, though not punished. To be honest, I find it odd that Maximus and Norbanus got away with this.'

For once my companion showed a trace of satisfaction. 'Domitian must have been furious.'

'Well, yes,' I agreed. 'They destroyed anything that could be incriminating. Some people thought Lappius Maximus was protecting himself.'

This time she was wise enough not to react.

'If he was organised, Saturninus would have sounded out everyone,' I suggested. 'Even replies of "No, thanks" to him would have damned people for Domitian.'

'I was told,' said the widow, 'Maximus and Norbanus only wanted to defuse the situation. Staunch recriminations. Saturninus was dead, so let it all die down.'

'Quite. I suppose,' I continued, 'you cannot tell me either whether your husband corresponded with Civica Cerialis, in Asia?'

I was correct. An autocratic shrug told me she could not.

'There is a question mark over Cerialis. How did he respond to the problem with the False Nero? So you have no idea whether your husband took an interest in that?'

The widow claimed not; she said events in Britain and Asia were unconnected. Frankly, I thought she was right.

'My mistake! Anyway, uproar in Palestine would mean little in Londinium. In general, I suppose governors in provinces that are very remote from one another would only correspond if they were good friends. So, here at home, did your families mingle?'

She claimed they knew each other socially, but were never close. Uncle Quintus had prophesied this. The two families might have spent every summer picnicking together on Lake Albanus but they would deny it now.

I changed tack. 'What about the extraordinary story that your husband invented a new javelin and named it after himself? Does that sound like him to you?'

His widow only sighed and made a gesture with both hands. She might have been deploring his hobbies, blaming his lack of tact, or simply helpless before a stupid and unfounded accusation. Unable to tell, I toughened up: 'So tell me what happened about it. All I know is that your husband was not recalled to Rome. He remained in his province and was "executed" there. How exactly did he die?'

Suddenly, she lost her control. For once I witnessed emotion. Whether she loved her husband, or how much, was still unclear, but Sallustius' widow was definitely angry on his behalf and at last she showed it.

'Karus.' She was both adamant and furious. 'I was never told how, but I know who was responsible! Julius Karus

42

organised everything. And the horrible man has been foully rewarded for it.'

I picked up my stylus. Julius Karus. That I did write down.

Assessing her, I decided to stop. She was truly upset; I could see her shaking. The two maids looked daggers towards me and wanted to rush to her. She was too proud; she held up a hand to stop them. Although she quickly restrained herself and made no further outcry, I ended the interview.

7

Philippus had gone to lunch. It was the middle of the afternoon, so I took that as a euphemism.

A certain Fuscus, who was quiet with an air of menace, was in the office when I emerged. This man seemed to have no other work. He said he would attend to anything I needed, although when I asked who Karus was, he claimed not to know.

If he did know (I was thinking like one of them now), I deduced he wanted to work out why I needed the information and how it impinged on policy. People in palaces give nothing away until they believe they understand your motive in asking. He would probably check with Philippus whether I had clearance.

'There has been a change of venue for your other appointment, Flavia Albia. The woman did not wish to come here. She was offered a very private suite in the Empress's apartment as an alternative – the Empress is away, there would be no awkwardness – but she has chosen the House of Livia instead.'

'Why?'

'Palaces upset her. Since her husband died.' Fuscus then surprised me by coming out with a useful suggestion: 'Rubrius may know who Karus is.' He was probably still wary, but would pass my problem to this other person.

He led me to Rubrius, presumably an intelligence agent of some kind. On the way I asked, making conversation, 'What do you do, Fuscus? Do you tend the drop-boxes where people's slaves can leave notes betraying their masters – or are you a trained killer?'

At the second suggestion he jumped. I was surprised. Not that he *was* a trained killer, but that I had guessed right. I had only meant it as a joke.

As we walked I noticed that Fuscus paced extremely quietly and held his arms loose, with slightly bent elbows, as if he was ready to whip out a hidden weapon.

In law, even soldiers are not armed in central Rome.

In the palace, even trusted staff are not supposed to carry weapons in case they attack the Emperor.

The next man, Rubrius, also subtly gave the impression he could garrotte a sentry silently, when he had to. He had probably been on more paramilitary training courses than cyphering or shorthand lectures, though he was currently engaged in desk-work.

He introduced himself as assistant to Philippus. He was mild-mannered, though carried the air of having long experience in the field; ethnic artefacts hung on the walls of his office. I was sure there was more to him than he revealed at first meeting. If you were hiding under a hedge with him, Rubrius would know how to pee undetectably and which grubs were safe to eat.

He appeared to be sifting through intelligence reports, which he did with a slight frown of concentration as if the world depended on their proper interpretation. Perhaps I fantasised. He could merely have been auditing messengers' expenses. My father had told me that to produce a claim

45

for imperial reimbursement required skills on the same level as carving a marble nude for an arts connoisseur. According to Pa (especially if he had had a drink or two), an expense sheet that would actually be paid, without deductions, was as beauteous and timeless as the best work of Phidias.

Rubrius looked boyish, about thirty, though on close inspection was older. His manner was friendly. When I was a girl I would have thought him handsome and lust-worthy, though now I merely took note of the white portrait plaque on his writing-table of a woman who must have been his wife. He had her set to one side so he would not feel unduly monitored if he went off into a dream about someone more voluptuous.

He, too, could not help me with Karus, though when he said he would find out, I believed he might. He told me to come back to the palace after I had seen the second widow.

8

Fuscus escorted me the House of Livia. It was never open to the public. The custodian took a look at my sombre guide and let us in.

The old Emperor Augustus liked to pretend he was an 'ordinary' citizen who lived simply. Since he and his wife Livia had grand separate houses on the Palatine, this plea of an old-fashioned lifestyle was crazy. I despised it, along with the claim that his womenfolk wove all the family's clothes at home. Judging by what empresses and princesses tend to wear, they must have had a high skills level. And given his daughter Julia's notorious number of lovers, one wonders how she found the time to run up Papa's tunics too. People say he felt the cold and sometimes layered on three.

My own father hates twee gifts crafted by his children. He searches for lived-in tunics on old clothes stalls. When he finds one he can tolerate, he wears it for the next ten years.

By Falco's standards I was much too clean and neat today. I never believe women in any business have to be as scruffy as men. Anyway, I was meant to look more like a matron canvassing for temple donations than an informer condemning suspects.

When I tripped into the rich, high-ceilinged atrium in

47

my middle-class sandals (smart but serviceable), various attendants who had come with the widow were hanging about below old mythological frescos. They were fancy types who ignored us. Fuscus went to find someone in charge and say we had arrived. He made me wait and told me not to explore. According to his protocol, spies should not case a meeting-place themselves but rely on sidekicks. That explains why intelligence so often goes wrong.

Bored, I inspected the frescos. Io was having a bad day, tied up to prevent her enjoying herself. A couple of gods or heroes were posing ineffectually, with no thought of unfettering her.

Fuscus came back. 'The women are in an anteroom.' He pointed at an adjacent salon.

'Women plural?'

'She brought her sister-in-law. You go in. I'll stay here to listen to what the chaperones are saying.' They would be stupid to say anything in front of him – but if people behaved sensibly the intelligence service would collapse.

There was no slave to open the heavy double doors. I managed their big knobs for myself. I had chosen not to knock.

The grand dames waiting were relatives of men with four names: Caius Vettulenus Civica Cerialis and Sextus ditto ditto ditto. In public such women wore their nobility like a uniform. When the Empress Livia had sat with a tisane beneath these elegant painted garlands of flowers and fruits, plotting to poison her relatives, I expect she breathed with similar disdain. She, too, would have resented my low presence.

The wife of the executed governor had dressed like a bereaved matron, as carefully as the previous widow. Dark

48

gown, in fine fabric, jewellery that made pompous statements. Perhaps the two women had colluded beforehand. Girls on a spree. Sisters in misfortune. Conferring on how to deal with me.

This widow was wrapped in a heavy head veil. I asked her to lower the redundant garment. We were women together, not men at a sacrifice. Since her husband had been dead for more than a year she could not be concealing the ravages of grief. In any case, the image offered was not tear-stained.

Her back-up was a bossy madam in brighter yellow and green, shimmering with silk and twinkling with layers of gold chain. Philippus had said Civica's brother had married a certain Lusia Paullina, an equestrian's daughter. Among the senatorial class that was unusual. More than unusual. He was the only one I had ever heard of to do so.

'You are Flavia Albia? You should be ashamed of yourself, harassing innocent people for that man.' Lusia Paullina spoke her mind. At least it made a change from proud, pained silences.

'For Philippus?' I had coped with belligerent witnesses many times. Most were men with something to hide, but I could tackle women. I eased one of my ear-rings thoughtfully as I spoke. 'You know the alternative: a Praetorian inquisitor. I shall treat you with more courtesy. Be grateful.'

'I meant working for—'

'Don't!' I cut in. 'You need to be more cautious.' If I let her disparage the Emperor, the next problem could be *her* reporting *me* for treason . . .

I fetched out the standard tablet but this time kept it right on my knee, stylus ready. I sensed a tussle coming; this could be interesting.

They had stage-managed the room, I thought. They were seated in wicker armchairs, perhaps used by the Empress Livia although they were battered. I had been left an X-frame stool. They are damned uncomfortable. Faustus had one. I had rarely seen him use it, even though he was formal as an aedile. In this house, now reduced to an unlived-in heritage site, there was of course no cushion.

I smiled to myself. Someone had told them the trick of positioning a suspect between two interrogators so he cannot see both simultaneously; although the roles were reversed, they were trying to force that cliché on me. Dancing the dance ought to be my role, but I left the stool where it was. They had not twigged that I could always turn my back on one of them. I promptly did so on Lusia Paullina.

'To start, I shall ask you the same questions I put to the widow of Sallustius Lucullus.'

Lusia broke in loudly, from behind me. 'My sister-in-law is too upset. I shall speak on her behalf.'

'Very well.' Patiently, I swung back around. 'First: did she go out to Asia with her husband?'

'My sister-in-law and I,' Lusia Paullina claimed regally, 'believe a wife should always accompany her husband on a posting. She shares the experience, shouldering the same burdens. She contributes socially and in private.'

'Commendable,' I returned mildly.

'We, the Vettuleni, are from the Sabine territory. Family is *so* important!'

Lusia Paullina was talking too much. All she had had to say to my first question was 'Yes.'

I pressed on: 'Civica Cerialis will have had a province before Asia?'

'Moesia.' Lusia Paullina was primed with excess

information to throw at me. '*My* husband served there first. Sextus had a very distinguished career. After governor of Judaea he was immediately made consul, then was sent to Moesia without any waiting period, which is rare. It is a frontier province with many sensitivities, which calls for a high degree of competence. Vespasian's brother had served there previously, so he took a keen interest. Sextus governed Moesia for six years, again almost unprecedented. Caius had the honour of directly following his older brother.'

'Sextus then preceded him in Asia?' Using her husband's first name was too informal, but as the brothers shared their last three names, I had no alternative.

'No, we had Africa.' Africa was the other big prize for notable senators, equally prestigious.

I twisted back to look straight at Civica's widow again. 'I have to ask about correspondence. Did your husband communicate with Antonius Saturninus in Upper Germany? No? Was that too far away?' She assented in silence. 'I have asked the widow of Sallustius Lucullus about letters from her husband discussing the False Nero.' I tried to imply that incriminating evidence might be in imperial possession, though I guessed these two disbelieved it. 'If you were with your husband, there was no need for written correspondence.' Not unless they had had a row and she had put out a note: *Your toga is in the oven* . . . 'You could talk with him. You believed in sharing confidences, traditional marital closeness. So when you and he conversed in private, did Civica Cerialis give his opinions on these subjects?'

'Nothing material!' snapped Lusia Paullina from the sidelines.

'Did he?' I repeated for the widow. She exchanged a glance with her sister-in-law, then shook her head. She was

51

not subservient to Lusia, but Lusia was supposed to do the talking.

I may have shown my irritation. 'I find that hard to believe – especially when the False Nero came calling. That would have placed your husband in a serious dilemma. Surely he discussed his qualms with you.'

No.

Faced with a straight denial I was stuck. I had warned Philippus that this was all we could expect and now my task became impossible. I could not treat this woman as a suspect herself. Philippus had been clear: I was to find out whatever I could, yet give no cause for complaint. I realised why: Domitian had not sanctioned an inquiry. Only if I learned something significant would he be told. If I messed up, Philippus could come in for criticism, or worse. So could I.

'Did the False Nero ever visit Ephesus?' That was where the governor of Asia lived. I caught a flicker of anxiety as the widow admitted yes. She then insisted that the pretender was never admitted to the governor's presence. 'So where did he stay?' An uncertain pause. 'In the governor's palace? Was he given hospitality? Accommodation? Food and drink?'

She said no, though this was significant; she could have been covering up.

'He pitched a tent in an orchard?' Both women received this with a snort. I reproved them: 'I am not being facetious. Since the not-Nero came from a desert province, I assume he was familiar with tents. I want to know how this man was received.'

'He was never received officially.'

Presumably Domitian suspected otherwise. If he could prove it, the charge against Cerialis would have been stronger than the catch-all 'conspiracy'.

'The governor was horrified when the False Nero turned up in Asia,' Lusia hastened to emphasise. 'It put us in a terrible position.'

That was undeniable: Caius was to die for it. To shake things up, I tried the question that had so disturbed Lucullus' widow: how exactly was Civica Cerialis 'executed'?

This one's reaction was even more extreme. Her knuckles went white as she gripped the two arms of her chair. She closed her eyes and began shaking her head, making desperate choking noises. The distress looked genuine.

The sister-in-law leaped up. 'Have some charity. There is no need to remind us!'

I was shocked. 'Oh, no! You mean his wife witnessed his death?' Striding to the doors, which I flung open, I called to the maids, 'Your mistress needs you. Come at once and attend to her. One of you, ask the custodian for a beaker of water – quickly!'

While patting and mopping began in the anteroom, I jerked my head at Lusia Paullina. She joined me in the doorway, out of immediate earshot. She looked tense, standing with her arms tightly folded, a defensive posture. I asked quickly, 'Were *you* in Asia too?'

'I was,' Lusia agreed. 'My husband had passed away. She kindly invited me as her companion. I enjoy the east.'

Lusia Paullina must have been good-looking when she was younger. She had a strong face, with dark eyes. There was an Oriental air to her beauty, while she pronounced Latin with a faint accent. This is true of so many people in Rome you tend not to remark on it. Although earlier she had spoken as one of the Vettuleni, she had married into the family. Had the noble Sextus Vettulenus picked her up, this attractive, feisty equestrian's daughter, during one of his eastern postings? Was she an exotic travel memento?

'You hail from those parts?' I ventured.

'My family comes from Egypt. I belong to the eastern network. I know everyone. Apollonia, Perge, Antioch . . . It has its uses.'

The enmeshed aristocracy at the far end of the Mediterranean was both powerful and still discrete from us in the west. People out there owned extreme wealth and saw Rome as an upstart power.

'I understand. I have been to Greece and Egypt.' I saved her further elaboration. 'So tell me quickly,' I urged in a low voice, 'was Caius expecting his fate?'

'No.' Lusia also kept her voice low. Members of the eastern network are easy with concealing a discussion. 'An envoy turned up, out of the blue. He burst in with soldiers and immediately ordered them to put the governor to the sword.'

That was Domitian's way. 'The governor was given no option of suicide?'

'He had no recourse to law.' Even I shook my head. Hands should never have been laid on the man. He ought to have been recalled to Rome and allowed to defend his actions, or whatever actions Domitian ascribed to him. 'Caius had no time to compose himself. There was no point begging for mercy. He was dead on the floor before he had even finished asking what was going on.'

'With his wife watching?'

Lusia Paullina shuddered. 'She flung herself upon him.'

'Juno.'

'Fell upon his body. I think, if she could have, she would have interposed herself between him and the soldiers. They were too quick. It was all over. I struggled to pull her off the corpse. She was covered with blood. Screaming uncontrollably. I feared the soldiers might attack her, too, unless she disengaged herself . . . She still has nightmares and relives it.'

'You too?' I commiserated.

She did not want my sympathy. 'The envoy then took command of the province.' Lusia Paullina kept her control by telling a factual story in a hard voice. 'I asked to see his commission. He had instructions signed by Domitian. He showed me without quibbling – he could see I was the person to deal with if he wanted things to happen quietly.'

'What was his name?'

'Italus!' she spat. 'Only an equestrian. He should never have been placed in charge. That aspect caused an outcry later, but to no avail.' With an angry shake of her jewel-coloured skirts, she carried on: 'He worked for the governor. He was a procurator in the province. Minicius Italus. The man had no concept of loyalty!'

'Why did Domitian select him?'

'Italus was in the Hellespont. For a messenger coming from Rome, he was the nearest official.'

And Domitian trusted him. As an equestrian, Domitian had *appointed* him. Whenever the Emperor was ousting the old guard because of his suspicions, he tended to put in equestrians. They had no specific career structure; they would always be grateful.

Installing a man from the middle rank to run Asia was an insult to the Senate – also to the important local aristocracy. It might have been a temporary move, to the Emperor it might have seemed the right choice, but it showed carelessness of sensitivities in the fabled eastern network. Domitian could have appointed any of the governor's own senatorial staff – his finance officer, or a military legate. I supposed they came under suspicion along with him.

Lusia Paullina confirmed it. 'To a great degree a governor can choose his own staff. Italus immediately replaced them all.'

I took a moment to imagine this woman, fighting to stay calm in a desperate situation, coping with the distraught widow and her traumatised household, working out how they must behave to ensure their safety, taking it upon herself to check that the intruder had proper credentials . . . Yes, the procurator would have been civil to her, perhaps even grateful for her presence.

'We were allowed to hold a funeral. As soon as it ended, the ashes were scraped up and thrust at us in a wine tureen. Then we were put on a ship home. Before light, next morning.' I could see why Italus wanted the women out of his hair. And if he had known of her connections in the region, he had needed to expel Lusia fast.

'You came back to Italy?'

'Italy is my marital home, of course. My husband's home, my children's home. We all live in Reate.'

I nodded towards her sister-in-law. 'You both have children?'

'Yes.'

All disgraced. All hoping for a change of regime one day, all wishing with hindsight that the Nero pretender had pulled off his claim, with them as supporters who would be rewarded. I took a chance and asked slyly, 'So did Civica Cerialis really support the False Nero?'

Lusia swept aside the suggestion. 'No one did. The governors of Syria and Cappadocia-Galatia were his first resort. Valerius Patruinus and Candidus Marius Celsus. Two very sound men, both with eastern origins. Patruinus had been Celsus' immediate predecessor in Cappadocia. He moved across to Syria without a break in service. Of course, Celsus is related to absolutely *everyone* and Patruinus is almost as highly connected, so they form a very tight clique. I know them, know them well.' She would do. She knew everyone. She catalogued the high positions they had held almost as assiduously as a palace bureaucrat.

'Did you know the pretender?'

Lusia shot me a look. 'Even if he had been a suitable person, that would have been unwise!'

'I see.' I saw she had not exactly answered my question.

She needed to add something. 'He was nothing. Village villain. Heaven knows where somebody found him.'

'Ah! You saw him?'

'I did not say that.'

'Of course not. So. Those two governors in Syria and Cappadocia-Galatia would have been formidable backers for him. They must have had forty thousand soldiers between them, if you count auxiliaries.' I was no military buff. Philippus had given me the figures.

'Absolutely. But they both spurned him. Caius knew that, of course; there was constant correspondence. So he had decided that the problem would go away naturally. As it did. He was correct. He ignored all overtures. The pretender fled to Parthia.'

'Before Italus came?'

Lusia considered. 'Around the same time. After the murder, I believe Italus dispersed the rebels. Using his troops from the Hellespont.'

Was there, I wondered, any chance that, just before he was killed, Civica Cerialis had actually helped the pretender escape? I did not ask because Lusia was so certain Cerialis had had no idea that trouble from Rome was coming; he would not have known he needed to get rid of the False Nero fast.

'So the Nero took refuge with the Parthians, who always welcome a chance to cause embarrassment, even if they don't openly attack Rome . . . There must have been chaos in Asia!'

Lusia huffed. 'So my friends there tell me.'

Her sister-in-law's maids had finished fussing. Their mistress sat up straight again, formally clasping her hands in her lap. Clearly, she did not want to talk to me; I could see no point in forcing her.

As a matter of common sense, I absolved Civica Cerialis of support for the Saturninus revolt in Germany. He was killed well before it; there were no links between Germany and Asia, not like those between Germany and Britannia. So, I agreed with Uncle Quintus: Civica's crime was failure to respond strongly enough to the False Nero.

Even if he had encouraged the pretender, these women would never allow me to prove it. Lusia Paullina had a grip on the situation. She understood what they must say; she had schooled the widow. I bet they would never vary their story, not even under torture.

So Civica Cerialis died for indecision. It was hard luck. Historically, commanders who are guilty of weakness end up with honours, not punishment. Well, that's the cynical view.

Lusia Paullina now took it upon herself to conclude the meeting: 'We have nothing helpful for you. We shall return to Reate and live there quietly with our children, awaiting better times. My husband and my brother-in-law did not have a consular father, but nothing can diminish the reputations they both earned. Believe me, Flavia Albia, one day they will have consular sons.'

I told her quietly that I carried no brief for the current regime. If she was right in her prophecy, I hoped she and her sister-in-law would live to see their sons flourish as they deserved.

When the women left the salon, the governor's widow declined to look at me. She went ahead, sheltered by a phalanx of protective staff.

Only then did Lusia Paullina condescend to volunteer something to me. We were intelligent women with equestrian fathers, who both had colourful early backgrounds. As a consul's wife she looked down on me; even so, I liked her.

'Don't waste effort harassing true friends of Rome,' she muttered. 'Attend to the real danger. You should be looking at Parthia!'

9

With her parting comment, Lusia Paullina gave me a curt nod. I hoped she acknowledged that I possessed integrity so my report to Philippus would be fair. Despite that, she did not warm to me, for I was in no position to guarantee those who had commissioned me.

Seeing no sign of Fuscus, my dour escort, I set off alone, able to walk at my own pace, thinking over what I had heard. I crossed back over the Palatine to revisit Rubrius.

'Fuscus said you were on your way!' was my greeting. Fuscus must have seen me looking for him, yet he had nipped ahead. Perhaps he was practising manoeuvres in the field. Or had he listened to my interview at the keyhole and gone to report on me?

'Well, Rubrius, I'm glad he didn't wait around. I always like to stop at Romulus's Place of Augury and survey the birds, in case any new lovers are prophesied for me.'

Rubrius pretended to look shy. 'So how did it go?'

'As badly as I expected!' Crisply, I advised him that, as well as Julius Karus in Britain, I now wanted the facts on Minicius Italus, the man from the Hellespont.

'Yes, I thought you might. I have arranged to confer with Eutrapelus.'

'And he is?'

'You will see!'

Eutrapelus was in charge of records. These were records that I had realised must exist, though I had never expected them to be nursed with such care, or indeed kept here. Held in the palace, they could be produced at short notice not only for senior people with an interest in military personnel but on occasions – under Domitian, on many occasions – for the Emperor himself to pore over.

We went down one long corridor then around a corner. Eutrapelus was stationed close to the spies.

The room he inhabited was a complete columbarium, walls lined with pigeon holes, every hole neatly packed with scrolls. One space had been left for a large map where provinces were annotated with abbreviated numbers and names for the legions deployed there. A table served for laying out scrolls, with baskets for carrying them elsewhere if they were requested. A small, high window let in limited natural light.

Eutrapelus had the pale skin of one who laboured there by day and night, tending his records single-mindedly, as if they were a mushroom crop in a cellar or precious cheeses. Rubrius said he had refused assistants. There was only a small boy sitting on a stool, moving glass counters on a board as he played against himself. He looked up when we entered, then continued, as he was clearly allowed to. 'The little slave is here to go out for bread rolls or fetch more ink,' Rubrius told me, as he watched me take in the set-up.

He introduced the record-keeper. Eutrapelus posed like an acrobat returning to ground level. 'Fair lady, welcome to my lair!' His mannered speech, the circus gesture plus a pretend leer were slightly askew from normal behaviour. This man, now elderly, lacked human contact. He had straggly strands of unwashed hair and smelt sour. I guessed he would continue there as long as they let him, reluctant to retire.

'Thank you, Eutrapelus. I see you tend a great many scrolls!'

'I hold the complete service record of every centurion, any man who may be a potential centurion, and each ex-centurion who could be called up to the reserves.' Eutrapelus spoke with mild pride. He knew he was peculiar, but saw no reason to alter how he lived and worked. For him, living and working were the same.

'So is this for the army or one of the secretariats?'

A glance passed among my companions. Eutrapelus stated solemnly that keeping personnel records was one of the many tasks that burdened the Secretary of Petitions, Flavius Abascantus. He then added, in a hollow voice, that although Abascantus liked to boast he was the busiest man in the Empire, everyone knew that the busiest man, he who attended most closely to documentation, was the Emperor himself. Abascantus delegated.

'So, on a day-to-day basis, you work to Claudius Philippus?' I guessed drily. Eutrapelus nodded. Assessing the complex scope of his material, I asked, 'Each legion has a hundred centurions?'

'A common error. With a full complement, if they ever have one, there are actually fifty-nine. The first cohort is largest, divided into five *centuriae*, then there are nine further cohorts, each divided into six. So! Nine times six is fifty-four, plus five. Every legion should have fifty-nine centurions, and how many legions are there now?' Eutrapelus asked Rubrius, testing him.

'Twenty-eight?' Rubrius volunteered good-naturedly. He appeared to be counting mentally.

'Try again!'

'Twenty-nine?' I suggested, remembering what Justinus had said. 'Domitian added the First Minervia.'

Eutrapelus applauded. It went on too long. 'So how many centurions am I keeping track of?'

'I would need an abacus.' I can do multiplication, but not at speed and under strangers' scrutiny.

'One thousand, seven hundred and eleven!'

'Olympus!'

'Every time an emperor creates a new legion, I have to scurry through my records to find fifty-nine sound optios – men whom serving centurions in other legions have chosen as their deputies. That causes ripples when I swoop in and pinch them. Maybe not quite fifty-nine, since I must make allowance for special requests from whoever takes command.'

'Idiot nephews and sons of their favourite freedmen?' I commiserated.

'Quite! We manage. The needs of the army take prece-dence. Legates who make silly demands can always be jumped on if I go high enough for support. And, believe me, I do.'

I wondered about the executed governors. Had I been brought into this because Eutrapelus had information about silly demands made by Lucullus and Cerialis?

'Flavia Albia wishes to pick your brains.' Rubrius used a solemn tone.

'Karus and Italus?' He knew already. The men had discussed my needs, agreeing on what I could or could not be told. Well, I rode with it. 'Centurions are my pride and joy, but any man in a leading position has his record in my cache,' Eutrapelus revealed, with a wink. 'I know every post he has held, I can guess how often he scratches his fleas and, if it becomes relevant, I can predict his loyalties.'

I raised a genteel eyebrow. 'How high up do you go?'

'How high do you want?'

'Legionary command?'

'Oh, yes. Nobody wants the wrong legate in charge in some unstable location.' Any legate would probably have served as an officer before, but these men were not career soldiers; they were aristocrats on the course of honour. Hades! So Eutrapelus was even monitoring senatorials.

I could imagine the reaction of the average senator if he was told all his appointments had been settled by a scribe. People wonder how the Roman Empire can be managed so successfully. As any scribe would tell you, this is how. Emperors may come and go, bringing more or less chaos, but the bureaucrats keep the wheels turning.

Startled, I pushed further: 'Governors of provinces?'

This time Eutrapelus did not answer, merely spreading his hands as he gave me an arch smile.

'The subtle bureaucratic art of the affirmative denial!' I said.

Rubrius chuckled. He had parked his backside, a fine one, against a wall of columbaria and was listening in with enjoyment. 'Governors,' he told me, 'are chosen by the Senate or the Emperor. But Eutrapelus provides guidance.'

'*If* I am asked,' Eutrapelus corrected him, with a mock show of diffidence.

'As you are!'

'I like to be of use.'

'Be of use to me, then,' I encouraged him.

We settled down for his lecture.

First, Britain.

Domitian had decided against unforced territorial expansion. Rome's frontiers along the Rhine and Danube were volatile enough. He was always short of troops.

As governor of Britain, Julius Agricola believed in further conquest. He sent people to sail around it to prove it was an island; then he wanted to bring that whole island under Roman control. He had marched his legions right into the wild north, defeating the Caledonians, then building a string of military installations, including one huge fort to control his new territory.

Domitian contra-decided there was nothing for Rome in north Britain. He bled the British legions of troops for his own campaigns. Agricola was ordered to withdraw south and compelled to return to Rome.

Gaius Sallustius Lucullus was then made governor, with a brief to enforce new policy. Agricola was said to have had an uneasy relationship with his officers, yet many now supported expansion, which they had carried out with him for years. Soldiers enjoy victories. When Lucullus arrived, they were disgruntled that their gains had been so soon given up.

Caius Julius Karus was an equestrian, commanding an auxiliary detachment, the Second Cohort of Asturians.

'He was on your "trusted" list, Eutrapelus? So his Asturians are based in Britain?' I asked, in all innocence.

'No, they are in Germany.'

I raised my eyebrows. Then what was their commanding officer doing on his own in Britannia?

Making himself useful. Karus secretly informed Domitian that Sallustius Lucullus had not only failed to purge disaffection among his officers and officials but had let them influence him.

Whether Karus had been deliberately sent on detached duty to spy on this situation or whether he had taken it upon himself was not specified to me. But nobody needs an abacus to work out that sum.

'If the four legions in Britain had refused to obey the Emperor, while those in Upper Germany were also in mutiny . . .' I let my comment tail off. Rubrius and Eutrapelus smiled at each other again.

'What I know,' Eutrapelus enlightened me, 'is that the governor's foot guard, his personal protection squad, was suddenly shifted out of Britain on reassignment to the Danube. Julius Karus escorted them there himself.'

'All the way? To ensure they went?'

Eutrapelus gave a twist of the head in assent. 'Their new posting was dressed up as "significant", although it was inferior and they knew it.'

'Another quaintness,' Rubrius added, 'involves an auxiliary cohort in Britain, now named the First Faithful Vardullorans – *Coh I Fida Vardullorum* – where *Fida* invariably refers to extreme loyalty in a crisis. They have all been awarded Roman citizenship.'

'Every one?'

'Batch validation. While in service.'

'Unusual?'

'Unheard of.'

'So what honorific deeds had these Vardulloran boyos carried out?'

'Cannot tell you, I'm afraid.'

'But you know?'

'Cannot tell you.'

'Cobnuts,' I replied, but I decided not to argue. 'So Sallustius Lucullus was sympathetic to his officers' mutterings. Britain was at risk of rebellion. A dangerous unit was shifted out, a loyal one rewarded. Am I correct?' Neither man reacted. 'Fidgeting Furies! Rubrius and Eutrapelus, stop messing around. Domitian was right, wasn't he? He did not really execute Lucullus because of some misnamed spear. Lucullus was on the verge of defiance, in a province that has always been volatile. So he was culled.'

Rubrius winced at my term, but then produced a smile that called me a wise woman.

'This clears up another issue,' I said. 'Lucullus was killed *in situ* because he could not be brought home. The key route back to Rome from Britain is along the Rhine. You pass through Upper Germany, where Saturninus was busily plotting. The two men had to be kept apart. So Karus gave Lucullus the chop in Londinium.'

'She is quite the strategist,' said Eutrapelus to Rubrius.

'Chop is a good word,' Rubrius replied, as if adding it to his personal thesaurus.

I had no truck with flattery. 'Did Karus himself do the deed, as the widow believes?'

Eutrapelus declined to say. Rubrius frankly guffawed. 'Three gold crowns and a silver spear? You may assume he did!'

'Yes, he's become a walking jewel case. Are you envious?' I teased. People who work in intelligence are never so honoured. When they are successful, their work stays invisible. Emperors forget. I summed up: 'Lucullus *may* have backed Saturninus, but logically, he had no connection at all with the False Nero. His sin was strictly local. Some of his men were on the verge of mutiny – and he was being dragged along.'

I had been asked to ascertain whether he had confessed to his wife. I doubted it. *The lads are furious about Domitian's policy and I've decided they are right* . . . Never. Lucullus would not write this in a letter that had to be dictated to a scribe, carried by an imperial messenger and received by another slave before ever it reached his lady back in Italy. He would have known how many hands it would pass through, where the seal might be broken and the contents read and copied. The diplomatic satchel leaks like a sieve. If he had used his own courier it would have been no different.

Code would not help. The best code-breakers in the Empire were right there on the Palatine, just waiting for a test of their skills.

'The wife never knew,' I said flatly. 'He said nothing to her, so she has nothing to say to us. Perhaps Sallustius Lucullus really did mess about with javelins – but if so, he did it in a little out-house by himself. Even at home, the wife's only clue to anything he got up to in his den would be that afterwards he came indoors hungry and morose.'

Rubrius and Eutrapelus were staring.

'The way men with hobbies do,' I pointed out.

For spies, they seemed rather short on understanding of human habits. If these men had hobbies, I dread to think what they were.

IO

I became more businesslike. 'That's Karus and Britain. Now do Italus and Asia.'

Lusia Paullina had provided the back-story. Although Italus was an equestrian, he was no slouch. Eutrapelus listed a history that included postings in four different auxiliary units, then promotion to legionary tribune. That level is normally senatorial.

Minicius Italus had become a procurator. These positions are equestrian, but important. I had a relative, Flavius Hilaris, who had been procurator of the mines and procurator of finance in Britain. To us, Uncle Gaius ran Britannia.

So Italus was not simply wandering through the Hellespont picking flowers: he controlled that significant part of Asia. Asia is a large, disparate province; Italus had serious responsibility – independence too. The governor might have descended in a visitation (or not, if he was lazy), but Italus himself had smooched the traders, collected the taxes, overseen the courts and stamped on disturbances. He had had a good complement of soldiers to support him.

'Crucially,' Rubrius explained, 'when the imperial messenger was sent out, bearing Domitian's death sentence, Italus in the Hellespont was his first drop-off. Italus was briefed, and raced for Ephesus.'

'When Domitian originally appointed this Italus as a

procurator, loyalty must have been a factor,' I said. 'He was another on your special trusted list, Eutrapelus? So the messenger gave him orders, with the necessary powers. Even life and death?' This was abnormal for an equestrian.

'He was thought dependable. With his army record,' shrugged Eutrapelus.

'So now will his appointment be permanent?' I asked. My father was an equestrian. You could put him in charge of a province and it would run like silk through a finger ring. Would Falco execute people to order? If they were sufficiently degenerate.

'Oh, temporary.' Eutrapelus was definite. 'The next senatorial incumbent will go out early, hard luck for him. Italus now graces my potentials list for Egypt.'

That was a significant reward. 'Procurators of Egypt live like kings. I've seen it. If,' I said slowly, 'Domitian's reward reflects the favour Italus did for him, I presume that in the Emperor's mind Civica Cerialis needed to be snaffled urgently. Domitian was absolutely certain he had cuddled up to the False Nero?'

'No proof.' Rubrius was emphatic. He pursed his lips. Very nice lips, I noticed. 'Our Master is an instinctive emperor.'

I made no comment on that. 'According to his women-folk now, Cerialis did *not* wine and dine the man – sadly, it's their word only. But if Domitian had facts, Philippus would not be belatedly prodding hostile widows. Either way, Cerialis is dead. His family won't cause difficulties. They are going to live among the Sabine mule-breeders and be diligently rural. I'd say this incident is over. So why do you all need to carry on niggling about what Cerialis did or didn't do?'

'We want to put the False Nero problem properly to bed,' said Rubrius.

'I thought he was dead in a ditch?'

Rubrius smiled gently, while both men indulged in another of their mystic silences.

I I

There seemed nothing else the two would tell me, and there was no more I wanted to ask them. A slave fetched my fee from the main office; he was to bring it safely home for me. I parted company with the others, after leaving a message to Philippus that I would write my report shortly.

I had been at the palace for so long that day, trawling through so much material, that once I emerged I felt transported out of real time. Up aloft on it, the Palatine always seemed remote. All the city lay bathed in bright sunlight but its sounds and smells were far below. Down there, thousands had been going about their business – their lives, their loves, their work, their woes – while I was absorbed in another world. My long afternoon had left me stiff and feeling slightly soiled.

To exit the palace, I left through its shimmering public portico, which looms above the Forum. I wanted the opposite side. I knew there was a pathway down, somewhere beyond the Hut of Romulus (it's a fake, renovated with new materials many, many times). I retraced my steps to the indulgently stretched properties of simple-living Augustus and Livia, below the enormous Luna marble Temple of Apollo – their personal shrine, complete with library. The temple, I remembered grimly, had been built where a lightning bolt had struck.

For reasons of my own, I once more descended the short flight of steps that gave entrance to Livia's house. I adopted the air of a visitor who had left something behind, though having seen me before, the boot-faced custodian let me in without a quibble. I was left to my own devices. I could have taken a chisel and carried off frescos on a handcart.

All I did was steal their style. I went back into the side room, where I made sketches of the elegant floral swags, with sidebar notes of their muted grey-green coloration.

I was conscious that I had my own house, with my new husband in it. These décor details were intended as a distraction for him.

Trailed by the palace slave with my fee, I went down to the Circus Maximus on the ancient Stairway of Cacus. I trudged around the end of the stadium, then climbed up the dogleg road to the Aventine summit. I was walking automatically, consciousness switched off. I nearly found my feet taking me to my old apartment.

At home, as I must learn to call it, my knock was answered by the master himself. Tiberius, in slippers and a plain tunic, waved me in. Ah, my beloved husband. A practical householder, thank goodness.

I kissed him quickly. 'I hope I am not to be hit with a ladle and "What time do you call this to come crawling home?" Where's Dromo? You shouldn't have to open the door.'

Tiberius looked pale, but had come downstairs to take charge. It was clearly an effort, though he did not complain. I was glad to see him up and about. I handed him the fee money; cheered, he sent off the palace slave with a copper. Since we lacked an armoured chest in the atrium, Tiberius stowed the cash in an empty room for the time being, levering a plank across the doorway diagonally, as if there was work in progress. If anyone moved it, at least it would make a noise.

Gratus, the steward I was hoping to poach, had sent word that he could not leave his current post. He suggested I try a widow we knew and had sent her along. She was sitting out in our courtyard, so Tiberius and I hovered in the atrium to discuss it.

I knew Graecina was a dedicated home-maker. After her husband died, I had myself suggested she become a concierge. She needed income: she had two young children. Their present home on the Esquiline was too far away so Graecina would come as live-in staff; she would want to bring her offspring. Tiberius checked whether I objected.

We were desperate. They were quiet. I decided we could find room.

They had also owned a trying dog. Tiberius said it had passed away.

'Done!' I strode out to hire Graecina.

Her little boy and girl were politely allowing Dromo to throw a ball to them. Their mother must have told them to behave nicely. Dromo had similar orders from Tiberius. He shot us a baleful look, but they all carried on gently tossing the small ball. Things were looking up. Our home was a haven of obedience – at least temporarily.

Graecina, a free woman, was neat and conscientious. Short and stout, she had dark olive skin with darker moles and eyebrows that came almost together over her nose. Her late husband had been a house steward, adept and unobtrusive. They rented their own apartment, but she had learned from him the management of someone else's household.

Tired out by my day, I let her ask the questions. She was

practical: the tasks? The salary? When to start? Time to herself for looking after her children? Did *we* have any children?

'Give us a chance,' I muttered. I stifled the fact that my husband had lost interest, saying smoothly, 'So far, Graecina, there are just the two of us. We have one slave, Dromo.' I let her judge for herself what he was like. 'Beyond that wall is a builder's yard, which belongs to us. Workmen may come and go sometimes; their needs must be accommodated. It will be for you to suggest what other staff we need in the house, and help us vet contenders.'

I could tell she liked having choice. I hoped that didn't mean she would take over completely.

'I have had a look at your kitchen, Albia. It needs a lot done.'

'Give me a list.' I had peered in that morning, winced, and shelved the problem for later. Later was now. Well, having someone to organise was supposed to be what I wanted. Thank goodness I had forced Philippus to pay me up front. Doing a kitchen would probably wipe it out.

'Will there be a lot of visitors?' With her pre-planned questions, Graecina must be a woman who made mental lists, I thought. What was more, she could remember them.

'Friends and family will be welcome. Otherwise we shall live quietly. However, people will call here on business. A room must be kept for interviews – that gives privacy to our clients, but also steers strangers away from family areas.'

'I shall make it nice for you.'

I remembered the apartment where she lived and was suddenly nervous. Our interview room would be dressed up with stripy floor mats and fringed table doilies.

'Not too nice,' suggested Tiberius, noticing my caution.

75

'Sometimes it can be best to keep things bare, so unwelcome supplicants are less inclined to linger.'

Graecina shook her head at him. 'Well, that's why you will have me here, sir. If people hang on too long, don't worry. I can bustle in and shoo them off.'

Hmm.

You are too busy. You hire someone to help you. You are then beset with trouble, trying to make them work the way you want . . .

Oh, hell, it would be all right. It had to be.

I had brought food in, picked up at markets as I came home. Straightaway, Graecina told Dromo to serve – 'And don't pick at the food you hand around!' – enjoying herself as she decided which would be our mealtime crockery.

We possessed supper bowls. Many of them. We were newly married. Our wedding had been formal, so invited guests had presented us with horribly decorated pottery. I had to see that these things were 'accidentally' broken and tossed down the lavatory. Then I could bring out my own Arretine again.

'Oh, these new ones are lovely, Albia!'

'Yes, aren't they, Graecina? . . . We'll soon be straight,' I assured Tiberius privately.

'All normal,' he answered, as if in agreement. Yet he still sounded as if, for him, nothing could ever be normal again.

Everyone in my new household ate together that evening. I said that on occasions Tiberius and I would want to be private. I hinted that sometimes Graecina would like to be alone with her children. In general, however, we were an inclusive household. I knew that that was what Tiberius believed in.

I am not like that. Still, I had a lifetime habit of bunking off by myself if I had had enough of people, so I would escape when I wanted. Ask my family. Watch them roll their eyes and groan.

After a simple supper, Graecina took the children home to make arrangements for their move. She had instructed Dromo to wash up the dishes; when he remembered, we heard vague splashing noises.

At last I was at home, fed and at peace, with my husband. Then I established what would be the custom of our married life: telling Tiberius Manlius the story of my day.

12

He was a good listener, even quieter now he was sick. I kept it succinct, just my thoughts so far. It can be useful to let a night pass while you absorb information. Even in sleep your brain carries on churning.

Tiberius gave little more than an occasional nod. I like a man who knows not to interrupt. Relaxed by a beaker of watered wine with supper, I liked this one considerably tonight for other reasons. What is the point of a new bridegroom if you don't find him alluring?

Mine caught what I was thinking. He looked as if he was hearing from some neighbourhood thief that, even though he had pork dripping all down his tunic and was picking shreds of meat from between his teeth, he was absolutely not the person who had stolen his neighbour's pig.

I sighed but gave in. I am not a pushy lover. Anyway, he still had painful bruising and I was now too weary.

Tiberius put aside the stern expression. I knew he would make suggestions without taking over my case, so I was keen for his input.

The washing-up noises had ceased. Dromo came out to the courtyard, looking put-upon. The front of his tunic was wet through. 'Is that woman who came here supposed to be in charge of me?'

Normally when Tiberius was present I left him to grapple

with his slave, but tonight I tried to save him and intervened. 'This can be discussed tomorrow. Now don't interrupt us, please, Dromo.'

He ignored me. 'Is she?' he whimpered at Tiberius.

'Tomorrow, boy.'

'That's no answer!' The slave was about to protest further.

'No.' Tiberius raised a finger, although he had not raised his voice. Its steeliness was sufficient. If I had been about to ask for a bigger dress allowance, I would have left it until next week. Even Dromo subsided. 'Albia and I are talking. Find yourself somewhere out of the way, Dromo, and leave us alone.'

The slave stumbled off. His master did not look at me. I sat quiet.

Eventually Tiberius spoke one word on my investigation: 'Reate.'

For some time after that I simply sat, considering.

When Lusia Paullina had mentioned Reate, the name seemed familiar. I had never been there. It is a small town, about two days' journey east of Rome, though the Sabine hills are visible from much closer. I knew the inhabitants were an ancient people, that life there is rural. The region is most famous for producing mules.

It came to me. 'Vespasian! The mule drover.' One of the insulting nicknames used to demean that emperor.

He had been a new man. His family were of middle rank; his brother their first senator. Vespasian had emerged from a traditional country background, which he refused to be ashamed of; his ancestors had made their money from tax collecting and supplying mule trains. While he held the prestigious governorship of Africa, he was even accused of

79

running a salt-fish business. The Flavians got by with mortgages, trade, intermarriage for money – and sticking close together for mutual benefit.

'See what I mean?'

I thanked Tiberius for the clue. 'Yes, of course. Vespasian came from Reate.'

'He was born there,' said Tiberius. 'Or some hamlet nearby – Falacrina?'

'He always kept the family estate. He went there frequently. He and Titus both died while travelling to Reate for summer vacations. And,' I found myself growing excited, 'the Vettuleni belong to the same area. The widows have gone back to live there.'

'Mm!' Tiberius was stretching his legs, as if they ached. 'You can imagine it there, especially in summer. Big extended families, enjoying the classic country life.' He had been brought up in a rural area himself, though nearer to Rome. 'Landowners roll up their sleeves and join their workers in the fields sometimes to show they are true countrymen at heart. They hunt, they fish, they attend local markets and fairs. They teach their boys about crops, animals, the phases of the moon and what it means for sowing and reaping; they count off the stars on country nights, they listen for the owls. Dreamy days, followed by early nights.'

I nodded. 'The women organise outings and picnics, where they sit for hours at long tables under trees – along with their visiting neighbours. *The neighbours* – that's it! The Vettuleni are family friends. This brings Domitian's killing into focus. When he executed Civica Cerialis, he was not simply removing an official he distrusted. It was an incredible act of betrayal.'

Tiberius agreed: 'Vespasian, his brother Sabinus, Titus,

the two Vettulenus brothers – you can imagine they all had the stocky build, the faint country accents that Rome's better-spoken élite mocked, the same no-nonsense ways of thinking. When the men came to Rome, as they had to for power and status, they collaborated to gain advancement.'

'Neither the Flavians, Vespasian and Sabinus nor the Vettulenus brothers had consular fathers. They must have created their own niche together.'

'Out-manoeuvring the old urban smoothies who despised their background—'

'Rewarding each other, once they were in a position to do so.'

I blew out a long, slow breath. 'I thought the sister-in-law, Lusia Paullina, was being outspoken. But how restrained she really was today – and how very bitter the Vettulenus widow must be feeling.'

'They have known Domitian since he was a chubby little tot in a loincloth,' said Tiberius.

I snorted. 'I bet he was the horrid child nobody wanted to hold on their lap. Now I can see why Lusia denounced him as "that man" with such vehemence, almost the first thing she said to me. The Emperor she once saw as just an unlovable, attention-seeking brat is now a paranoid killer – even murdering family friends.'

'He lost his mother young.' My husband was a tolerant man.

'So did you.'

'Not so early . . . Domitian had to live through his loss in the shadow of a brother who was ten years older.' Tiberius might have been remembering his own bereavement. 'Anyway, Titus was off being educated at the palace with Claudius' son Britannicus, while the young one was only

81

home-schooled. Vespasian was away a great deal. So Domitian grew up feeling abandoned,' Tiberius mused. 'Desperate to be loved.'

I did not want to feel sorry for him, but I said, 'He will have heard them, all those close-knit Sabine friends and neighbours, saying how much his so-charming elder brother resembled their father, how close Vespasian and Titus were – such a shame the younger one could not be more like that.'

Everything made more sense. Tiberius said, 'When Domitian awarded Cerialis the sought-after province of Asia, he was still keeping to the old loyalty, continuing Vespasian's policy – but he's a brooder. Once he saw an excuse, his jealousy came out. His father would have been horrified.'

'Perhaps that was the point,' I mused. 'He was lashing out against Vespasian, Titus, all the old clique of friends and colleagues.'

Tiberius now grinned at me. 'You should have fun trying to write this up.'

'Thanks, love!'

'Show me your draft.' It was an offer, not an instruction.

I sighed, though I welcomed it. 'Yes, it will be tricky. *Don't blame the False Nero; the governor's death was caused by upbringing and spite.* All because somebody long ago wouldn't let grabby little Domitian hog the strawberries at picnics.'

I believed our premise. If you have better ideas on the Flavian coterie, feel free to table them. Don't try it in my house, though.

After a moment I said, in a more subdued mood, 'We should have been nicer to your nephews at our wedding. I hope they don't turn out this badly because they sense we loathed them.'

There were three. All under ten. I had not taken to them.

Tiberius shook his head. I could see him anxious over his young nephews. Their parents' marriage had stumbled. The boys had inherited bad traits from their father. It was an unhappy family. So I said, 'It probably only matters if you give unlovable children all the powers of an emperor.'

Unfortunately Rome had done that so I would have to fudge the truth. My report would end up blaming the False Nero after all. I could not point out that Domitian was guilty of personal spite.

Domitian believed people constantly lied to him. This was why. Even I, a legend for fearless plain speaking, would be forced to prevaricate. He had turned himself into a tyrant. His cruelty only encouraged the lies he feared.

I took it further. As a result of living with this cruelty, even people who really knew better might turn to a new claimant. Any ludicrous adventurer clasping a harp might succeed. People were desperate. Those who had any influence might see it as a duty to help Rome emerge from constant fear.

So, oddly enough, there could be truth in the Emperor's accusation: Vettulenus Civica Cerialis might have despaired so much, he had decided that the cruel brat spawned by his family's old Sabine friend must be removed. A change might make the Empire better and safer. So, mad as it had seemed when I began, perhaps the governor of Asia really had thrown in his lot with the False Nero.

13

We spent another chaste night. Most informers claim to have rampaging sex lives and sometimes it is even true. Otherwise we pretend that abstinence keeps your mind fresh. Gladiators may be given sumptuous eve-of-fight banquets, with fornication for their dessert course, yet how many have been killed because of disorienting hangovers and blurred vision? The celibate informer is a sad figure, but at no such risk.

So much had happened I could hardly believe it was only a day since my wedding. Tiberius had a more peaceful night. I slept enough. I listened anxiously to his breathing. In between I was aware of Rome, plagued by the rattle of delivery carts, with their antisocial drivers providing hideous thumps, crashes, loud conversations and curses. Once their noises finished, we were left with the near-lawless city in the dead of night. Up here on the Aventine it normally grew quieter in the hour before dawn; even so, there could be unexplained shouts or bursts of drunken song, often followed by neighbours throwing open shutters to yell abuse. The vigiles whistled, then dogs barked at the vigiles. If someone screamed, the protocol was, bury your head under a pillow and play deaf.

The first week I lived there, I found this terrible. Soon I was used to it. You blot it out. Next morning, bright

84

enough, I returned to see Sodalus, the archive clerk at the Atrium of Liberty. The streets were wet and washed. Stall-holders opened up, sweeping rubbish to the next stall where the owner had not yet arrived, arranging cabbages and leeks in neat rows and whorls. There were scents of fresh bread and fresh flowers, barely drowning the other smells of fresh donkey droppings and old dog dirt.

Breakfast had been bleak at our house. No one had been out to buy food. Apparently that was my job.

I left Tiberius at home thinking about what tunic to wear and what fashionable style to comb his hair into. We joked about him staying in to run our household while I, the wife, went out to work.

Our laughter had an edge. He was a Roman male: he had eight hundred years of history to overcome. Nevertheless, I said sternly it was up to him to install the new housekeeper and keep Dromo happy. I claimed I intended to work on my report undisturbed at the library.

For light relief I gave Tiberius my drawings from the House of Livia. 'Don't you bother your pretty head over anything too difficult. This should keep you out of trouble – lovely décor ideas for you to peruse when you have a free moment.'

He went along with the game. 'I suppose I am not to order anything new until you agree we can afford it?'

'Darling, we are not made of money! I'm not toiling among the spies so you can fritter my fees away on need-less luxuries . . .' I could have added quips about him not sneaking off to have affairs with charioteers behind my back, but in our present regime sex was too tricky a subject. 'I'll be home when I can. Be good!'

My husband was a man of rectitude. Olympus, I wouldn't

have trusted him alone in the house otherwise. Who wants to return and find their partner has sold all the silver and invited in pretty boys who say they are masseurs?

No chance. Dromo would never bestir himself to let them indoors.

I set off to help the intelligence service scour Rome for plots: disloyalty at home or attacks from outside. This would keep us safe so householders could sleep well in their beds and prosper: that is how spies tell it. Naturally, we believe them. We live in fear. We desperately want to feel that trained men who know what they are doing are constantly protecting our interests.

At the Atrium of Liberty, using my own skill in passing a discreet under-the-counter payment, I persuaded Sodalus to show me any documents that concerned G. Sallustius Lucullus or C. Vettulenus Civica Cerialis. As I expected, despite much complaining, he had found a few scrolls.

'This is a one-off, Flavia Albia,' he threatened. 'Don't expect any more favours.'

'No, dear.' It was what he always said. Once he had drunk himself silly in some side-street bar, he would be open to another bribe. The life of a public-archive slave is tedious otherwise.

I could be wrong. We informers pride ourselves on our keen observation and rich understanding of human nature, yet half the time we never use them. All I knew of Sodalus was his poor skin and red laces; his best quality for me was bribability. Maybe he was saving up the coins I gave him to buy his aged mother a retirement home or purchase his own freedom. I tried not to think so. If I did, I would have felt my payments were too small. He maintained they were.

But that's what everyone says about handouts and I never blame them for trying.

The material was thin. First, Sallustius Lucullus: he remained elusive. It appeared there had been no births, marriages or deaths in his family while he was in Britain. The letters his wife had said he wrote to her on domestic matters must have been short.

'This family may not live in Rome,' Sodalus pointed out, sneering at the concept. 'If he came from the provinces or worse . . .' his lip curled even more '. . . if he came from *abroad*, all his diplomas may be placed in some dump of a local temple.'

Where had this archive snob originated? A slave-trading village in the back end of Bythinia? The Lusitanian sardine shore? From out of a sandstorm in Africa, carried off by the wild-animal traders? Clearly he had forgotten – if he ever knew.

'Let us not be prejudiced.' I was tolerant, given where I came from myself. 'I've been in overseas temples that were older than Rome. The sanctuary of Zeus at Olympia is one of the Seven Wonders of the World – though when I saw that big beast, I agree you could call it a dump. It needed maintenance . . . There are senators from foreign provinces,' I conceded. 'Integration is encouraged by the wise emperors who rule us – well, they want to pretend provincials are important to Rome. But I think Lucullus was Italian.' I thought that because no one had told me otherwise. I reckoned foreign origin would have occasioned comment, as it had with Agricola (from Gaul) and Trajan (Spanish).

Sodalus shrugged and lost interest. I believed his search

had been thorough. He generally did well by me. Nothing here. Not his problem.

We moved on to the Vettuleni. Anything deposited in their home town of Reate was an unknown, though Sodalus had pulled out some birth certificates from here. 'People who want to look good register their sons in Rome. It gives them more status.'

'Or so they imagine!' I snorted.

One record was for a son of Sextus Vettulenus, also Sextus. Romans like to be confusing. Lusia Paullina had the young man keeping his head down in Reate now, with her determined he would one day be consul. The long-lived among you know she succeeded. (Thanks to Trajan, hard-bargain purchaser of my wily father's tenement.) At the time that I handled his birth certificate, Sextus Junior was approaching the age when he ought to have entered the Senate; in view of Domitian's antipathy, his chances seemed doubtful.

'You know all about his father?' Sodalus asked me. I had given him clues to my field of interest. No need to be cagey when someone can help me.

'A Sabine, thick with Vespasian?'

'Much more than that, Flavia Albia!'

Sodalus told me: Sextus Vettulenus Civica Cerialis was appointed a legionary commander when Vespasian went to quash the Judaean rebellion. Nero had had to plead for him, so in picking subordinates, Vespasian was allowed a free hand. Most famously, he took his own son, Titus. Also he selected a fellow-Sabine.

Sextus led as many significant engagements as Vespasian and Titus. He was a highly trusted member of the war council. Then, once Nero died, Vettulenus and Titus worked closely together to advance Vespasian's claim. As cronies

88

go, Sextus and the older Flavians could not have been closer.

After Vespasian was hailed as emperor and left for Rome, Titus took over finishing the Judaean campaign – though his father had left the more experienced Julius Alexander as chief of staff. This Alexander was procurator of Egypt, and among his troops he brought an equestrian officer called Lusius Gallus – brother of Lusia Paullina.

'Sodalus,' I asked, 'you keep the marriage records – wasn't it odd that Vettulenus, a senator, married an equestrian's daughter?'

'Yes, but Sabines are not prejudiced. Remember, Vespasian was living with a freedwoman, Antonia Caenis. He wasn't going to disapprove. Is Lusia a looker, Albia? Was she very rich? Or was the marriage arranged to solder friendships with the Egyptians?'

All of these, I suspected.

After Titus had followed his father back to Rome, Vettulenus was left as governor of Judaea. As Lusia had told me, this was followed without a break by Moesia. For a significant part of Vespasian's reign, Sextus Vettulenus Civica Cerialis was the Flavians' man in the east. His brother Caius then had Moesia after him, followed by Asia. For me, this clinched everything. 'So for years Sextus was as tight as ticks with Vespasian and Titus.' I presumed that Domitian had originally intended to continue this with Caius – until it went wrong.

Sodalus had more: 'Later, if there was what you could call a Titus faction, a faction opposed to Domitian, Sextus Vettulenus was significant in it.'

This caused a shiver. '*Was* there a Titus faction?'

'Not openly.' Sodalus instinctively lowered his voice as I

had done. 'But Titus' daughter Julia was seen as a potential figurehead.'

'Was Julia political?'

'Probably not. She had no children or she might have seemed more dangerous.'

Julia herself, a woman, would never have been a contender for the throne. Nevertheless, it might explain why Domitian took her to the palace after her husband died, and kept her close: he wanted to control her. He had Julia so close that gossip accused him of incest, eventually killing his niece through a forced abortion . . .

'She died this year,' I mused. 'Viewed sympathetically, Julia was the only person in his life Domitian genuinely cared for. Gods help the rest of us, now he has lost her!'

There was no way I could mention any Titus faction in the report I had to write.

Whether there was a faction or not, Sextus Vettulenus had shared with Vespasian and Titus both an exciting war and the intrigue to make Vespasian emperor. Domitian, who was never in Judaea and who was sidelined in home politics, must have resented the veteran cronies' closeness. After his accession, Sextus, as an older man who was used to taking an important role, may even have had blunt Sabine words with Domitian about the exercise of power. Sextus had died of natural causes so Domitian had retaliated against the younger brother, Caius.

When Caius Vettulenus went to Asia, his older brother's past prominence might have affected how he acted. The influential knot of people who had supported Vespasian welcomed him. They remembered his brother well, not least because of his marriage to Lusia Paullina, one of their own. Caius never had to establish himself; he was immediately among friends.

Suppose the easterners felt Domitian was destroying what Vespasian and Titus represented? They could decide that as they had once created a ruler for Rome they could do it again. In this context, to our nervous emperor, the False Nero stopped being a joke. The eastern clique, who saw themselves as powerful backers, might have been supporting him.

Perhaps when Caius arrived in Asia, the easterners welcomed him too much. Suppose they said to him, 'Let's forget the False Nero. That's a doomed plan. We respected your brother; now we have great faith in you. So how would you feel, Caius, if we put *you* up as the next emperor?'

No one had suggested this to me. I would not offer the theory to palace officials. Domitian might well have feared it privately when he had had the governor of Asia killed.

So was I now supposed to be investigating whether the impact of that death was to throw the eastern faction back into supporting a False Nero? Did Claudius Philippus really wonder whether the governor's widow and that sister-in-law with whom she lived so closely knew of some continuing conspiracy out east?

If so, Philippus was a fool not to have come clean. I had not asked the right questions. By a fluke, however, I reckoned I had the answer: Lusia Paullina had openly admitted she corresponded with friends abroad but she had also claimed to have her husband's Sabine values. Sabines were cautious. They liked the status quo. They wanted the currency stable and grain production protected. They were dignified. They had old-fashioned distaste for volatile politics.

I had never pushed Lusia into a position where she needed to divert attention from anything her eastern cronies might be up to. Of her own accord, she had warned me that the real danger lay with Parthia. To me it felt like genuine concern for Rome. That would never include support for a foreign interloper.

14

I composed my report quite easily once I had started. I had been over the ground from different perspectives. I stuck to what I had been invited to do: interviewing the two women about their menfolk.

Anyone who writes to the palace has to remember that anything they say may fall into the hands of slimy types whose objectives may not be theirs. What you say will probably even be seen by Domitian himself. Trusting no one, he famously reads everything.

In my twelve years of being an informer I had become well-practised in sensitive-report creation. Often you are simply confirming what the client feared. This is probably the easiest situation, yet you need to phrase with care. Imply that the investigation did need doing, even though the answer was obvious. Otherwise they forget to pay you.

Sometimes the information they hired you to find will be entirely factual: is that bounder who wants to wed the rich widow already married? In what hole is the delinquent father of the unborn child hiding? Spell it out. Say nothing you don't have to. Give them no excuse to fly into hysterics, making it heartless to send in your bill. You need the cash. Be heartless. If that isn't enough, send bailiffs.

It is when you have to surprise your client with

unexpected news that you need most diplomacy. You must become their comforter. That did not apply here.

Here, my formal conclusion was: our wise emperor correctly suspected Sallustius Lucullus of bending to the defiant attitude of his staff, and Civica Cerialis of being too close to rebellious elements out east. The people of Rome should be grateful for our emperor's vision in spotting these problems and containing them so swiftly.

I said neither woman was willing to condemn her husband further. They were of noble birth. No apparatus of the state could compel them. In marriage, a man should be able to trust his wife above all others and a wife should be loyal to her man. It would be improper to attempt to break that most valuable tradition, one that kept our society decent. My verdict was that the two widows truly had nothing to add to what was already known. Their connections with plots were limited, and might never have existed. Their husbands had been dealt with. The widows would not cause trouble; it was not in their interests.

I finished and went to have lunch with my mother. While we talked and ate, Father's Egyptian secretary wrote out my draft in his fine script. Mother, who had read it swiftly, suggested I rephrase the end, adding: 'They could safely be allowed to retire into obscurity.'

I told her my situation at home; she promised to give thought to that. She would lend us a slave temporarily. She had also written to a board member at the Museum at Alexandria, Aedemon, an old acquaintance who was a doctor. He treated most disease with purges; I knew Tiberius would regard that as quackery. But with use of the Great Library, Aedemon could dig out any literature that had ever existed on recovery after lightning; in the time it took to

94

make a sea journey there and back we would possess the world's knowledge. If Tiberius lasted that long, I thought we would have worked out for ourselves what to do, but writing to Aedemon made Helena feel she was helping.

She did help. She comforted me when I suddenly realised how upset I had been by nearly losing my lover. I suppose that was why I had gone to see her.

Katutis, the secretary, accompanied me as I returned to our house. Tiberius then read my draft and advised me to remove 'it was not in their interests' in case that started anyone wondering too closely what the women's interests were.

Katutis, who was entirely trustworthy, took the finalised document to the palace for me. I had hoped that would be the last of it, but he came back with an invitation. At a meeting that afternoon Philippus would present my report. He thought I should be there.

For a bureaucrat, that is code, of course. It means, *And then you can tell us what you left out.*

'Be careful!' warned Tiberius.

I suspect he wanted to come with me, but could not bring himself to leave the house. I held him close, promising to return as soon as possible.

Katutis went back with me instead. 'Look out for intrigue,' I said. 'Rome's devious palace politics almost match your fine Egyptian standard.'

'And you are venturing straight into the midst of it!' Katutis made a despairing gesture, throwing both hands wide. It appeared pharaonic, though was, I think, of his own devising. He knew how to fit in here in Rome, yet he cultivated obscure traits. I expect he was homesick. He wanted to remember who he once was. 'With your usual foolishness, Flavia Albia.'

Katutis was always frank with me. He respected my father as a venerable employer who had saved him from penury (which was the truth) and my mother as a great lady he could not entirely fathom (which was how all of us felt about Helena). As for me, I had been young and angry when he had first encountered me. He still treated me as if I was seventeen, fit only for discreet reproof by him, the wise one from an older culture.

We walked side by side. If he was with my mother, or even my sisters now they were growing, Katutis stayed a little behind. It looked like deference, though he always managed to imply he was independent. He really liked to gaze around on his own, marvelling at our reprehensible second-rate city.

He knew I saw through his Egyptian mystique. He and I shared complicity as outsiders.

Tiberius had accepted that on the streets and in the bowels of the palace I was as safe with Katutis as I would have been with him. For the Egyptian, I was Falco's daughter. He would defend me against anyone.

Would I need defending? Nobody attends Domitian's palace without apprehension. I had an official invitation, but when they know you are coming, they have time to prepare any kind of surprise. Ghastly surprises were our emperor's speciality.

The people I was about to meet now were, I was aware, those who must have provided the initial briefing for Domitian when he considered whether to execute the two provincial governors. I must avoid my outspokenness, hide my judgemental attitude. These were functionaries no one should offend.

15

The inner security council met in an apt location, given their concerns about the False Nero. Philippus, who had been waiting impatiently for my arrival, walked me there. We were followed by the silent Katutis. He had once worked in an Egyptian temple and had a way of insinuating himself that any spy would envy.

The venue surprised me. I was taken to one of the most famous features of that mad fantasy, the Golden House: its revolving dining room. My father believed he had been there, wrongly I now saw. Nero's extravagant palace, with its grandiose pleasure park and lake, had once sprawled over the entire centre of Rome. In the part beyond the Forum, amid fantastically decorated corridors and the gold-covered marble that gave the place its name, Falco had once attended a meeting with Titus in a large octagonal banqueting hall. That had a moving ceiling, so gifts, perfumes or rose petals could be released from its fretted ivory panels to the delight of guests. 'There were no free gifts for us!' Pa would grumble.

There were none for me, but at least *I* got to see the real thing. Falco would growl when I spoiled his story. Still, a house the size of a city was bound to possess more than one place to eat. It was inconceivable Nero had only ever banqueted in one room. Ostentation was his medium.

The most famous dining room stands on the south-east corner of the Palatine. As soon as we arrived I could see why: it gave diners the best view in Rome. It was dusty and echoing now, as it probably had been since Nero had fled on his final escape from the Senate. Frugal Flavian emperors might admire their predecessor's toy but would balk at paying for maintenance or technical operators. They tried to distance themselves from Nero. Domitian, who ate meagre meals, would find no joy there anyway; he took pleasure only in tormenting those who had to dine in his presence. He was a gravy-flinger, a domineering conversation-steerer, a silent starer. The host with the most horrible manners. If he invites you, send a sick note. If he insists, take to your bed and die.

Nero's fabulous creation had a ceiling decorated with all the stars and planets of the heavens. Because it was propelled by water from the nearby aqueduct, a spur off the Aqua Marcia, even now it was gently moving all the time. The complete room rotated, to provide a slowly changing view of the Forum, from the new amphitheatre and the Arch of Titus around to the glinting golden-roofed temples on Capitol Hill. Until Vespasian had replaced them with the Flavian Amphitheatre, it had looked across Nero's pleasure lake and park. It would be a delightful experience. For that, you would tolerate the fact your host was deranged.

Since we were early, I quizzed Philippus about the engineering. We had time. There was only one man present so far, though someone important, judging by the lashings of gold on his stunningly white tunic and his expensive masculine jewellery. This personage was chatting to attendants; Philippus seemed reluctant to interrupt, so we sat on the sidelines. He condescended to explain in an undertone that the room had been built around a giant brick spindle, this core operated by a waterwheel. There must be a system of gears. The floor rested on large slippery clay balls; they moved the platform gently, also using hydraulics.

Nero had attracted people with ideas, encouraged them, and eagerly paid for their elaborate devices. His best-known hobby was collecting water organs, those enormous sets of musical pipes that are used in amphitheatres. He had not stopped there. Engineers and architects had found plenty of work under the Flavians, but they would never again be as free in their flights of fancy as Nero had allowed. He had been an extraordinary character.

It was relevant. If he had been mediocre, we would not now have a climate where people wanted to believe he had never died. Nero's crazy lifetime had led to this curious afterlife, one that just possibly might destabilise the Empire. At least the phenomenon was paying me fees.

Philippus was intensely clever, yet only interested in ideas. People I knew would have wanted to nip in and inspect the works; indeed, I might have followed them, though hoping it would not involve too many ladders or ropes. I can be intrepid. I have no limits, except: will it get dirt on my dress? Philippus conceded there was a little maintenance staircase by the spindle column; he would not let me inspect it. Mechanics held no interest for him, apart from the working of his rivals' duplicitous brains.

The finger-ringed functionary ended his conversation and came quickly across to us. Effortlessly working up a warm charm, he held out his hand to me. He knew my name. 'Flavia Albia, welcome.' His grip crushed my small fingers. I hate that.

Philippus introduced him as Flavius Abascantus. 'One

of our most able talents.' He did not sound too envious or overawed, though he clearly expected me to have heard of this prominent imperial freedman.

What I knew was not good. Tiberius and I had recently been involved in an election, where we discovered that Abascantus had influenced the results. I won't say he fixed it. I can't claim we knew he took bribes. But our sources had implicated him as 'helping' one of the candidates (not the man we supported); Claudius Laeta, Philippus' now deceased father, had denounced Abascantus to us in fierce terms. Laeta took pride in being thought straight. He never was entirely – but he loathed public servants who were actively disloyal.

Abascantus had been away from Rome during the election, absent on what is called 'gardening leave'. The time-honoured euphemism for officials suspended from duty, it can be invoked for basic incompetence or laziness, but more often for corruption. Yet here he was now. I could tell he was neither inept nor lazy. That left the other thing.

He was still young enough to have thick golden hair, which he pushed back in a fetching way. I had to clear my throat at a waft of scented lotion, newly applied. He was the kind who uses a toothpick and gargles with mint before an important meeting.

Apparently he was back in favour. He was full of self-assurance, as if nothing had ever happened. How had he wangled that? Since Domitian had been abroad for a year, both Abascantus' dismissal and his recall must have been arranged by correspondence. He was in charge of correspondence. Who wrote to the Emperor about him?

Alternatively, were the suspension and its removal Domitian's own ideas? Did our Master want to keep

Abascantus on the hop? If so, it gave an insight into how insecure all the palace freedmen were.

Today Abascantus looked securely in charge. In his presence Philippus became subordinate and diffident.

Abascantus said he had seen my report. 'Beautifully put!' I felt hot pride; I could not help it.

Other people began arriving. They came in dribs and drabs because in Rome time is measured by season; with twelve hours in the day and the night, they vary in length between summer to winter as the light changes; people are only loosely aware when hours start and end. Arranging a meeting is tricky. If you live in Rome, you gain a knack of judging it – or of not minding when assignations go awry.

When a group of men gathers in a room, each arrives in a different style. Abascantus had been ahead of us, taking command of the room no doubt. Philippus was subdued. Of the others, one crashed in and paused on the threshold to make an entrance; another sidled as if trying to hide himself; one bounded; one hesitated while blinking; one stepped like a tall spider on curiously articulated legs.

Most attendees wore the white, gold-trimmed tunics that were imperial livery. No doubt it saved them wondering what to put on in the mornings. Abascantus had the richest material, the widest and heaviest braid, the finest belt. He wore not just rings but bracelets. Today was his tasteful chalcedony day, though I guessed he had a large collection.

Some of the others carried scrolls. One brought his late lunch, then chomped it. Everyone else seemed used to him: no one commented. On the whole I thought them a shambly, uninspiring, unkempt lot – types you would try to avoid sitting next to at the theatre. Nobody was introduced so I had no way to judge their importance.

We used only part of the room, because of its central column. I was intrigued that this left another area, the other side, where someone could easily have lurked and listened.

In our part, slaves stood on the perimeter with cups of water. Everyone sat on portable stools. Abascantus chaired the gathering. He alone had a throne-like armed chair, with a goat-legged tripod table to hold his documents, and had his drink poured in his own special glass cup. A slave polished it first on his tunic hem, which I happened to notice. Not too good, if you think about slaves' habits.

I noticed that Abascantus spoke perfect Latin, with a well-trained accent and in a beautiful voice. The Emperor must regard him as an ornament to the court; Abascantus knew it, too. He began, saying they would defer other agenda items and take my report first.

Abascantus had a briefing scroll that a slave must have prepared for him. *The Secretary may wish to take Flavia Albia's report at the start, so she can be released. Flavia Albia has been procured by Philippus, with the council's agreement. She is the daughter of M. Didius Falco, sometime agent for the Divine Vespasian Augustus . . .*

No copies had been circulated. Abascantus had the original written into his brief so he could read it out. (How fortunate I had kept it short.) A slip marked the place for him; as he unrolled the scroll to the position, he lifted out the marker, which he then used to stir his drink. As he slowly moved the spill around, I watched viscous honey rise up the transparent glass through a lighter liquid, mingling together.

He read well, as of course he would. He enjoyed the sound of his own elegant reading. On finishing, he let the two ends of the scroll rock back almost together, laying it on his side-table while he quickly surveyed the room; he complimented me again, then paused. He sipped his drink. It was a stagey moment.

When Abascantus put down his glass, he set it on the scroll, between the rolled ends, so it kept the place more firmly than his spill, though was at risk of marking a circle on the inky papyrus. My mother would have slapped his wrist for using a document as a drinks stand.

'Is there anything you want to add, Flavia Albia? Anything you felt unable to include in the written record?'

I chose to shake my head. However, I told them I was willing to answer questions.

Abascantus gave a grateful gleam, though he pressed on. 'Everything seems in order. Nothing we had not expected. Are we agreed, no further action shall be taken?'

Was he rushing them? Or merely a crisp chairman?

At first no one spoke. They chewed their water cups or stared at the floor. It was as if nobody wanted to offend Abascantus by contradiction. Only when he moved in his chair, smoothing back his golden hair, about to finalise the discussion, did a slumped figure pipe up.

His first remark was provocative. 'Can I say, Abascantus, welcome back? We all thought we had lost you.' *The Secretary will expect committee members to compliment him on his safe return* . . . Since presumably Abascantus had gone away because he had offended the Emperor, this was a deliberate dig.

'Reports of my retirement were, as you see, misguided!' answered the freedman, smoothly.

To me, his attitude was quite wrong. His smile was too condescending, gloating. He seemed to be taunting others who had hoped to see him in disgrace, hoped to watch his

103

fall. I found him cocky, which to me meant unreliable. He showed no sense of how narrowly he had escaped, no gratitude for survival. Anyone who thought him corrupt, and who loathed it, would be furious.

Philippus stared at the floor with mild-mannered interest, as if watching a woodlouse going for a walk on the tesserae.

This man who had tried to rile Abascantus gave the impression he was often outspoken. Every meeting harbours one of those, the routine troublemaker, harmless once he has been allowed his say. When he turned his attention to my own report, gesturing dismissively to the scroll on the side-table, his tone was one of barely restrained temper. 'There is nothing about the Parthian aspect!'

I could have sat quiet but it would have looked ineffectual. So I spoke out: 'I am sorry, I am not sure who you are. What is your interest?' He jumped. Was he never challenged?

At once, Abascantus broke in and apologised. He began to introduce people, though only some of those present. I would never remember them all but it was my only option. In Domitian's Rome it would be madness to write down the names and positions of key intelligence officers.

'On your right is Tutilius who covers Europe.' The Europe specialist seemed the most normal, even though when he had first come in he had knocked into furniture and bumped other people clumsily, sloshing over some of the wine he had brought for himself, as if what Abascantus provided wasn't to his taste. He was open in manner and almost cheery. When introduced, he waved a hand and grinned at me. I wondered what he knew about Britain.

'Our African expert is currently on leave. Amandus, over here, has the Danube frontier.' Amandus had a thin face as if he was starved, though there was flesh on him; he constantly tapped a stylus against a scroll end and was an unconscious leg-jiggler. 'And Trebianus, who just asked the question, is our Parthia-watcher. He listens to everything the Parthians are saying, not only to us but to each other. Then he tells us what they really mean.'

Trebianus looked as if he never ventured out of the palace. Endlessly tall, he had grey skin and a hump back, lolling awkwardly on his stool, with his limbs twisted up.

I explained quietly: 'The widow of Sallustius Lucullus has no detectable connection with Parthia. I learned that the Vettuleni do have links to the east. They clearly have many friends, people of influence. I saw nothing to connect them directly to Parthia, which you asked about. I can say, in confidence at this meeting, that nothing would surprise me.'

Trebianus inclined his head, in apparent shock, as if he was unused to having anyone answer his questions.

After a moment's thought, I admitted, 'There was a suggestion that I should look at Parthia, though of course this was outside my remit. Besides, you are the specialist. I have only the common rumour that the Parthians gave refuge to the False Nero. My personal opinion – if it has value – is that Civica Cerialis *ought* to have been too astute to consort with a long-time enemy of Rome. Perhaps he was. I suspect there is a lot more general interchange than people think. In the east there must be many who conduct cross-border trade, where the borders they cross take them outside the Empire. We all know how it works. The interplay of favours, hospitality, gifts. Loyalty to Rome taking second place to their own interests.'

From his initial grumpy air, I was expecting the Parthia-watcher to argue. Instead he seemed curiously receptive. Abascantus mollified the man: 'Your views exactly, Trebianus!'

Trebianus ignored him. He asked me, pleasantly enough, 'What personal experience do you have of the east?'

'Little, though I have visited Greece and Egypt.' Few women in Rome would be able to say as much. Not many more men. I suspect Trebianus knew the answer before he asked the question, because he then said, 'Your father's uncle is a *frumentarius* in Alexandria.' He made it a statement, as if *he* were telling *me*. *Frumentarii* are corn factors for the army.

I managed not to let my jaw drop. Glancing around surreptitiously, I was not the only person there wondering, *How in Hades does he know that?*

'I met Uncle Fulvius only once.' I omitted to mention that Mother regularly corresponded with Cassius, his partner, a younger man whom she liked; he ran their household, though his role in my great-uncle's work had never quite been explained. We were sure Cassius was more than a bedmate. 'Fulvius is a colourful character.'

That was putting it mildly. I decided those at this gathering had no need to know he had once run away to join the cult of Cybele, after which no one was sure whether or not he had gone through the castration rite. On our family visit to Alexandria, Father threatened to ask Fulvius to lift up his tunic, but was forbidden by Mother.

'Eccentric?' asked Abascantus, as if this was all new to him. I bet he had been briefed. *Flavia Albia's uncle is well known to the service, though colourful and awkward to handle . . .*

'Fulvius enjoys presenting himself as a mystery,' Trebianus answered.

Trebianus must have met him.

'He is elderly now, overweight and ill.' For some reason, I felt I should make out that Uncle Fulvius was in retirement – no longer of interest to them. 'We try to persuade him to come home where he can be looked after, but he enjoys life as an expatriate. I understand he used to negotiate supplies for the military, which I know often means acting for the government in other ways, but I was a young girl when I met him. What he really got up to was never explained.'

'Fulvius is well known to us,' Trebianus enlightened me. 'Corn factors see a lot.'

'They "come and go"?' I wanted to appear wise.

'Come and go,' agreed Trebianus, his tone to me now perfectly pleasant. 'Factoring grain. Venturing far and wide. Bearing news.'

News. So, foreign intelligence was what Fulvius really supplied to the armed forces. And now I was another one working for the spies. I was working for them, while unbeknown to me they had looked deep into my background first. Discussing my family made me uneasy. I was waiting to be asked about Falco, though it never happened.

There they were, the sweet heart of the intelligence service, most of them looking like oddballs. Slowly I began to see them as more competent, even though one had spilled his water all across the floor and another appeared to be sleeping. Despite appearances, they probably all had judgement and knowledge, even if narrowly focused. They slouched; they avoided eye contact; few of them were capable of relaxed social behaviour, except the urbane Abascantus and, to an extent, Philippus.

I had gained a good impression of Trebianus, so I said,

'*Somebody* must have had dealings with Parthia over the False Nero. Somehow he was extracted from their clutches, though I believe it was extremely difficult to persuade them.'

All those present stretched and shifted on their stools. Abascantus gave me an expansive smile. 'I had that task,' he said demurely, though obviously boasting of his success. 'All diplomatic correspondence comes through me.'

'Expert negotiation!' Philippus murmured. I noticed that the Parthia-watcher said nothing. The others, too, were chewing their styli and looking at their knees. Philippus might have felt he was required to say something, but interestingly the rest refused to join in with praise.

The moment passed, but I noticed.

'Well, thank you, Flavia Albia.' The Abascantus smile remained unforced and charming. I might trust the oddballs but I would never trust him. 'We are grateful for your trouble. We here can be too close to a problem sometimes. It is useful to have a wise outsider's opinion.'

Before taking the next item, the Secretary may wish to release Flavia Albia from further attendance.

He was telling me politely that I had to leave.

16

Philippus scurried after me. 'Can you find your way?'

I nodded. In any case, Katutis was waiting, sitting down on his heels with his back against the outer wall of the spindle tower. Very eastern. Most appropriate.

'What did you think?' Philippus demanded, in a low voice.

I wondered what he meant. The discussion in general or a salient aspect? It had seemed pretty bland. Would their conversation have become more incisive after I had left? Had they been disguising electric personalities? Or were they the usual troupe of weary bureaucrats, fighting for their own departments at the expense of everyone else's, wondering when the refreshments would come, finding excuses, filling their time and their brains with twaddle until they could retire to grace-and-favour villas? There they would reminisce for ever over long-gone incidents, boring to death their only audience, the slaves who wiped away their dribble . . .

I shelved it and hedged: 'I was startled to see Abascantus.'

'There was a time,' pronounced Philippus, darkly, 'when freedmen who were sent away to Neapolis understood they were going there in order to sicken fatally.'

'Convenient suicide?'

'In the old days the bastards never came back!' This was the first time I had heard him so bitter.

Narcissus, the chief minister for Claudius, was the most notorious: Nero disposed of his predecessor's richest, most powerful freedman soon after inheriting the throne. Nero came with enough emphatic advisers of his own: know-all Seneca; brutish Burrus; his shy, retiring mother, Agrippina (I jest).

'Losing favour can be a painful disease, Philippus.'

'But not always fatal, we now see.'

'Does the golden one's reinstatement change anything?'

'No, no! Business as normal . . .' He dismissed it. 'I have to hurry back inside. There are other agenda items I must hear. You and I should talk, we really should. I shall visit you this evening.'

With a whisper of the double doors, he had gone. I was left pondering what else there could be to discuss. I also noted his new emphatic approach: *must, should, shall* . . . Grammar can be telling. Listen to your schoolteachers.

Katutis unwound himself into an upright position. 'So Abascantus is recalled. Suspicions were unfounded. No action will be taken against him.' He appeared to have been squatting outside on the same spot all the time, yet he must have found people to talk to. I had brought my own spy.

'Allegedly!'

I remembered Abascantus' expression when he confirmed he had survived. Trebianus, the Parthia-watcher, had challenged him, which seemed daring. Abascantus had outfaced him, like a man who was openly getting away with it. Domitian had recalled him. Everybody else knew he was a complete crook. Domitian must need him, despite any qualms. Here he was, unassailable.

'Is this,' Katutis intoned, as if reading a sacred papyrus telling him how to dispense poison to an enemy, 'sheer madness or a clever device to make him expose himself?'

'Perhaps once he slips up,' I answered gently, 'he will disappear into oblivion finally, no reason given.'

'Oblivion!' Katutis repeated, sounding each syllable like a chant to a dog-headed god. We both glanced around us, as we walked through the elegant courts of Domitian's palace. They had been equipped with marble from imperial quarries in far-flung exotic places (polished so highly you could see an assassin creeping up behind you), extravagant gold ornamentation on every conceivable surface to impress all comers – and the most observant 'floor-mopping' slaves in the world.

'You missed a bit!' I chivvied one, before we skipped on our way.

Katutis and I went back to my house. On the journey we did not speak. The streets are full of informers.

Graecina had arrived. She had rounded up two men from where she had lived before; they had brought her furniture, which they were helping to arrange. She issued instructions in a loud, abrupt tone. They obeyed patiently.

She owned more than Tiberius and I did. After years of marriage, her accumulated goods were impressive, some items looking like cast-offs from the wealthy people her husband used to work for. He was a wheeler-dealer of renown, so had probably acquired other nice things from people who repaid favours in kind. A steward to the rich has a great deal of power with suppliers.

It struck me Graecina would run our house in that way. It would be all she knew. I would have to watch it. With

Tiberius in trade, he would inevitably engage in the to and fro of Roman patronage – but I knew he would want our carrots to be bought for their taste, not because Graecina had a private set-up with some fast-talking greengrocer.

Also making her presence felt was Galene, a slave Mother had sent. She had originally come as a nursemaid to my sisters and brother but had decided to be our cook. Typically, my parents simply let this happen. It was true she was better than previous chefs, though she had had no experience. She was still learning after thirteen years. When she had started, she could spread olive paste on bread. Now she could do that, and arrange a salad.

Fortunately my father loved playing with his brazier and its natty grill up on the roof terrace. Otherwise we would have had to live on Xero's rabbit pies; they have a bad reputation for causing epidemics. Even if you avoid stomach cramps, the bones choke you.

So far, Tiberius did not have a brazier for meat and fish kebabs. I must find out when his birthday was and see he was given one. A man needs his gadgets and I like a mixed grill.

The current problem for me was that Graecina and Galene both had the same idea of what they were there to do. I saw Galene bringing out rejected buckets and pots; they were probably things Graecina had put in the kitchen. Once *she* finished directing the placement of couches and side-tables in her private rooms (having claimed a whole suite), she would notice what her rival was doing. We were heading for conflict.

Katutis was exchanging quiet words with Galene before leaving, perhaps advising her to slow down on tossing out stuff. Graecina's children were sitting in an old dog basket on one side of the courtyard, watching the action as if they knew strife was imminent. Dromo had positioned himself on the opposite side, as far away from them as possible.

I went over to him. 'Where is your master?'

'Went upstairs.'

'Is he all right? Why aren't you looking after him?'

'He didn't want me.'

'What did he say?'

'Nothing.'

Full of apprehension, I went up to our bedroom. Tiberius had closed the shutters. He was lying down in the half-light, curled up, with his back to me. Dropping my stole on a chest I went over and sat. When I laid a hand on him, he flinched. I went to a side-table and mixed his painkiller. 'Sweetheart. All too much for you?'

He grunted. After a time he turned over, straightening out from his foetal position. Lying on his back, he forced himself to ask me how the meeting had gone. I told him, while I was encouraging him to lean up on his elbow and take the sedative. He sipped morosely. Not even mention of Abascantus gained much reaction. But with gentle persuasion I made him agree to come down in a little while and eat with the rest of us.

As I regained the courtyard, Graecina bustled up. 'What exactly is that woman here to do for you, Flavia Albia?'

'Galene?' I chickened out. 'Oh, Galene is an old family nursemaid. Very faithful. My mother, the noble Helena Justina, will have given her instructions.'

That put Graecina in a dilemma. Should she allow the intruder to care for her children, leaving her free to domineer, or should she go into a full-frontal attack over kitchen rights? She had to be cautious about 'the noble Helena', not wanting to make any error in respect of my mother, an unknown quantity, possibly a terror.

Galene had made sure she listened in, so she had to decide when to own up to calling herself a cook. Outsmarting Graecina over kitchen control would cause a furore; I could see it was tempting.

We had two people now to organise our meals. They were too busy stalking around one another. I myself fixed supper.

Katutis stayed. When he could, he muttered to me solemnly, 'I shall remain with you temporarily, Flavia Albia.' I raised an eyebrow. 'There are too many women.'

'There are two!'

'Indeed. Two.'

The Egyptian had a knack of making cryptic utterances. He could be put back into any temple and would be revered for prophecy.

Tiberius, who had just come down with his hair combed, noticed this exchange. He bent to kiss my cheek; close to, I sensed amusement. That was better. I filled him a food bowl; he picked at it slowly.

At the moment he did not look like a husband who could fire up a home barbecue. But I told myself he would like it when he saw it. Three days in, and I was a typical wife already.

We finished supper. Katutis made himself scarce indoors, Graecina was putting her children to bed, and Galene had gone to the kitchen to clear up, bullying Dromo into helping. The sky above our courtyard was still light, though draining of colour. I was enjoying a quiet sit alone with Tiberius when Philippus turned up.

Spies have no sense of timing.

17

Since we had been due to hold wedding parties, there was wine in a locked cupboard. I was the bride here; I had been ritually handed the keys. While Tiberius and Philippus exchanged polite nothings, I went for refreshments.

Galene had tidied the kitchen, studiously changing the positions of any items she thought Graecina might have arranged. At least it all looked neat and clean. Galene herself was now on her knees, furiously scrubbing out the small wood-burning oven. So long as I did not let her cook in it, this was an improvement. Dromo hung about, hoping she would dispense biscuits. I could have warned him hers were best avoided, but somehow it slipped my mind.

I took Philippus a very small saucer of hard green olives, with a small beaker of poured wine. 'Excuse us if we don't join you. We have eaten already.' Well, I tried. It seemed spies are impervious to hints not to stay long.

I sat silent, close to belligerent, as I waited to hear why Philippus had come. Tiberius had the excuse that he was an invalid, so he sank into reverie. So far, our home was none too welcoming for visitors. I quite liked it that way.

Philippus ate one olive, then put down the tiddy-bit dish. Small-talk, about the Roman Games and the part Tiberius had played in them, withered.

'Albia indicated you had something to discuss?' Tiberius made an opening. Of the two of us he was the politer host. This could be the future: him gracious, me obstructive. He could see me thinking that. If he had been feeling better, he might have grinned at me. Even so, there was a hint of a smile in his grey eyes.

'Aren't you curious?' Philippus tried on me.

'No, I came to your meeting, which seemed a waste of time. Otherwise, your fee was never intended to cover supplementary questions!'

Tiberius clucked at me gently.

'Why did you feel it was a waste of time?'

'Mainly, Philippus, because there was nothing to add. The men there, your watchers, your specialists, must have more idea than me about what goes on in Britain, Germany and the devious east. The east especially. Their agents must have told them who did, or did not, support the False Nero.'

'You felt the widows were an irrelevance?'

He was my employer; I made myself answer seriously. 'You could find out more about Sallustius Lucullus from a javelin-maker than from his wife – assuming the man really did invent a weapon. I was genuinely interested in the eastern situation. Yet even there, why harass the widow? Your expert's agents could ask around among the locals. I suspect they did.'

Philippus shook his head urgently. 'No, no! We cannot question them. They would never answer, and they would be upset that we made the request.'

'Touchy! Well, we know how they work,' I agreed. 'Tiptoeing into tents for private plotting. Business meetings that seem to be on one subject but are intended to cover something different. Too much sharing of peculiar drinks in tiny metal or glass cups.' I raised a little finger, while mimicking the act of sipping from a fancy foreign tot. 'Presents that are meant to secure favours.'

'People arriving wrapped up in carpets!' Tiberius supplied satirically, a Cleopatra joke.

'The aedile has a sense of humour!' Philippus remarked, as if joking was sedition.

'The aedile does not hold with bosh,' I answered.

The aedile closed his eyes as if the pains from his lightning strike were bothering him again.

'So what is your worry, Philippus?'

I screwed it out of him. He wanted to talk about the False Nero.

Because he was a bureaucrat, his first move was to put it in context. He had to discuss the real Nero. He ran us through what had happened when that emperor died; that is, he invited me to say what I knew about it.

'His end was up.' I was terse. I do not like powerful maniacs. I particularly hated the one who had caused the Boudiccan revolt in Britain. But for Nero, I would know my birth parents. 'He agreed to leave. He fled the palace, could not decide where he wanted to go, considered pleading for refuge in Parthia, considered requesting the Prefecture of Egypt, considered Greece where he was loved because he took part in their Olympic Games. The Greeks didn't care that he rigged the results and supposedly won a chariot race in which he fell out of the chariot.'

Tiberius continued the narrative, more soberly: 'Retirement in exile would never have been allowed. He ran out of time. He accepted an invitation to his freedman's villa.'

'Phaon.' That was Philippus. Trust an imperial official to

118

know and name his predecessors. He sounded almost envious that someone else had played a part in history.

'Nero hid in a ditch they had dug to be his grave,' I said. 'Mounted soldiers were approaching. Nero could not do it, so Phaon and one of the others –'

'Epaphroditus.'

'– helped him cut his throat with a razor. In the east, where he is so weirdly revered, some believe Nero escaped death, fled Rome, and went into hiding. He will return and, curiously, some say "overturn tyranny".'

Philippus took up the story. 'The obscure location, at a private villa outside Rome –'

'In a ditch!' I could not resist it.

'– made it easier for foolish people to deny his death. I of course believe it,' Philippus stated gravely. 'The incoming Emperor Galba had his freedman – Icelus – inspect the corpse and make a full report.'

Very bureaucratic. Lovely. Always have your mad dictators' deaths formally witnessed. Always be able to prove they are dead and gone.

Tiberius roused himself. 'I suppose the problem was exacerbated because Nero had been deposed. So he was buried not with pomp among his imperial ancestors in the Mausoleum of Augustus, but almost secretly, by his lover Acte, in the tomb of his father's people, the Ahenobarbi.'

'Immediately afterwards, we had the first imposter inflicted upon us,' Philippus glumly went on, as if he had reached the nub of some lengthy position paper. 'The first of any significance emerged in Greece. Nero's visit had flattered them and there will always be Greeks eager to oppose Rome. That first was either a slave from Pontus or a freedman from Italy, whichever obscure version you care to believe. He took advantage of the chaos in the Year of the Four Emperors. Somehow he assembled a ragged bunch of army deserters, took ship with them, perhaps heading for Rome. He was blown off course by a storm to an insignificant island among the Cyclades, Cythnus. He made that his base for piracy, arming the slaves of any merchants he captured, while trying to seduce sea captains to his side to give him a navy.'

'Galba had him captured?' asked Tiberius.

'Casperius Asprenius, on his way to take up the governorship of Pamphylia, learned the imposter's whereabouts. He diverted, stormed the ship he was on and beheaded him. The severed head was sent around the eastern provinces to prove the False Nero no longer lived.'

'It might have been helpful to do that with the real Nero! That should have been the end of fakes.' I tried to hurry him along.

'It was, for a decade. Vespasian was too strong to allow such nonsense. When Titus inherited, Terentius Maximus, an adventurer from Asia, popped up as the second pretender. He was something of a legend for his physical resemblance to Nero, and for ghastly harp-playing.'

'Oh, that should have convinced people!' joked Tiberius.

'Terentius Maximus gained surprising support,' grumbled Philippus. 'A significant armed force. He went marauding all the way to the Euphrates. Approaching the Parthians, he claimed – as Nero – they owed him a return for restoring Armenia to them. Their king, Artabanus, was an enemy to us, always looking for excuses. He received the pretender eagerly, then put plans in motion to enthrone the nonentity in Rome. But even the Parthians had to look shamefaced when we outed his true identity. After some diplomatic shuffling, we retrieved Terentius Maximus and he, too, was executed.'

'Head sent on another circuit?' Tiberius asked.

'I believe we did not bother.'

'Well, if people want a new Nero, they will find one. Now, the third?' I nudged.

'More mysterious in origin, less care taken to make him look the real thing, but for some odd reason very much harder to extract from the Parthians. They were obstinate – but we got him.' Philippus paused. 'Abascantus did good work there, no one can deny it. The third Nero was returned to us.'

'Dead in a ditch?' Tiberius prompted.

Not reacting to that, Philippus then explained, 'I am on a mission to find out who gave him support.'

'Other than the Parthians?' I asked, curious.

'We can discount the Parthians. Their motives are transparent. I mean people who should have known better.'

'People supposedly on our side?'

'If someone like that existed. The pretender might have told us, if he was kept alive.'

'If kept alive – not dead in a ditch – the pretender could have been persuaded. Inducements to talk,' Tiberius spelled out. 'Freedom. Lifelong pension. Nice house with sea views. Fast chariot. Pulchritudinous slave-girls. Boys, if he preferred.'

'If he was alive,' I repeated, as I began to suspect where Philippus was heading. Tiberius must already have been speculating.

'I have received a message,' Philippus announced portentously.

'From?'

'Best not to know.'

'If you wish.'

'Two days ago. It said, "The package you are expecting has been landed in Bruttium".'

'Code?'

'Not necessary. The security council knows what is going on. With use of the imperial post, my package should reach Rome tomorrow.'

'You may as well tell us,' I chivvied him.

Tiberius broke in and made it official: 'Your incoming "package" from Bruttium is the third False Nero.'

18

That was a stunner. More followed.

Before we continued, Tiberius held up a hand. He took the keys from me, then went for a flagon of wine and extra cups. He and I would need sustenance for this. Philippus and I waited in silence; he filled it by awkwardly drinking the rotgut I had given him earlier.

Tiberius returned. Hearing him on the move, Dromo wandered into the courtyard to see what his master was up to, but Tiberius spoke to him quietly so he lurched out of sight again.

In silence I held out my hand. Smiling, Tiberius gave me back the keys. Philippus looked unsettled.

Tiberius poured. We clinked cups. Even Philippus blinked as if, despite being preoccupied with his political troubles, he had subconsciously noticed a superior vintage. We owned fine wine. Some of our relatives were decent people; their wedding gifts had been generous.

'Thank you, Uncle Tullius!' I raised my cup again, a toast to the absent donor. In the refreshment pause, Philippus filled time by asking about the lightning bolt. Tiberius cut him off.

'My husband wants to forget.' I was terse. 'Tell us about your imposter. I would have thought it was dangerous to let him loose in Rome.'

'Oh, he will never be released.'

'So what lies in store for him?' There were various ways Rome dealt with a captured enemy: paraded in a triumph, kept in a deep pit for the next twenty years, strangled by the public executioner and his body cast onto the Gemonian Stairs . . .

'We expect to conceal that we have him.' Philippus took a deep gulp of our elegant wine. 'The man will be subjected to interrogation procedures.'

'Torture.'

'I suppose that is inevitable.' He sounded queasy. That never stops a bureaucrat. Then suddenly Philippus leaned forwards, primarily addressing me. 'I have a dilemma, Flavia Albia.'

He might have a dilemma. Now I saw where he was heading I suddenly wanted to withdraw. 'I would rather not know,' I admitted frankly, not looking at my husband.

'You object to the process?'

'It must be inevitable,' I conceded. 'Death is to be deferred. First a military torturer will make the man give up his secrets – although, Philippus, this has the same disadvantage as when slaves are used as court witnesses. Legally they must be tortured – yet evidence given under torture is always unreliable. Too crude.' I spelled it out, finding myself aggressive and angry: 'Ripped fingernails. Chains and pokers. Water. Weights. Stretching and burning. Threats, threats against his family. The victim says whatever will make the pain stop. Inevitably, it is what he believes you want to hear.'

At least Philippus was now looking shifty. 'Don't be hard on me!'

'It's your responsibility. You work for the Emperor.'

'You must be aware of how it is done.' Even Tiberius rebuked him.

'Some things are necessary.' The state servant's get-out. 'I cannot afford to dwell on the details.'

I could have forced him to hear plenty more. My father and an uncle had once had a man in our house and needed to make him talk. Mother took herself and her children away from home, unable to stop it and refusing to stay. Father acknowledged she was ready to divorce him. I was an inquisitive teenager; I saw enough, before she whisked us off.

Philippus rallied. 'I apologise. One should not be squeamish. But, as you point out, we must avoid this fellow fooling us with easy answers . . .'

Tiberius and I glanced at each other in silence.

Philippus threw back his head, like someone in the throes of a difficult confession, gazing upwards. The sky had darkened, so normally we would have asked one of our people to put out oil lamps. As it was, the evening had closed in so gradually we could still make out faces. I probably looked annoyed. Philippus looked surprisingly handsome. Tiberius looked ill.

Philippus restated that once the False Nero reached Rome, he would be secured in an official safe place. After rigorous questioning for the security council, a report with a top-secret classification would emerge; it would have restricted circulation and, once the facts had been digested and acted upon, it would be swiftly buried. After his debriefing, as they chose to call it, the False Nero would disappear from the record.

So why? Why was he not already dead in a ditch in Syria or Parthia, as everyone assumed?

I asked; Philippus told me. The reason was what he had previously mentioned: our overseas agents had said that, unlike his predecessors, this False Nero seemed to have nothing to recommend him. His success was odd. Extracting him from the Parthians had been much more difficult than on previous occasions, despite the persuasive talent of Flavius Abascantus (Philippus sounded laconic). So in Rome officials feared that the pretender was not acting for himself; he was a frontman, deliberately set up by hidden backers for their own purposes.

I remembered how Lusia Paullina had derided him as just a 'village villain'.

'The third Nero was a puppet? Whose? Domitian blamed Civica Cerialis, but I believed his womenfolk, that he was horrified when the pretender turned up in Asia.'

'Could be anyone. Parthians, eastern clique, highly placed Romans with connections east.' Philippus unconsciously shook out a few drops from his empty wine cup, then placed it on the ground beside his chair. He folded his hands and gazed between us. 'Of course, some conclusion will be prepared for the Emperor after this man is questioned. But will it be the truth?'

'Why not?' Tiberius demanded.

'I think someone will get to him,' Philippus said. 'Whoever sponsored him will stop him revealing who they are – and that is because,' he told us heavily, 'I believe, this plot comes right back to us at home.'

After a moment of reassessment, Tiberius turned to me. 'It makes sense. The objective for a pretender is to overthrow the current emperor. That is sought by plenty of people in Rome.'

'Not always for decent reasons,' Philippus agreed. 'Some disapprove of Domitian – which can disguise the fact that others have the oldest aim in the world: they seek the pure exercise of power themselves.'

'Surely the security council will expose them just the same,' I pondered. 'If not—'

'It means I suspect my colleagues.' Philippus finally said it.

Tiberius stirred. He liked to be precise. 'One of them, or all?'

'It might be more than one. I can't see how it could be all.'

'Someone I met this morning?' I asked.

'Has to be.' Was that why he had taken me to the meeting? He wanted me to see them before he told me this idea?

'Whom do you suspect?'

'I cannot say.'

'Cannot? Unwilling to speculate – or simply don't know?'

He would not answer.

I saw an obvious contender. 'Abascantus?'

Philippus writhed unhappily. 'Don't you feel he is just *too* obvious, Flavia Albia? His life is built on service to the Emperor.'

'Well, you know him,' I snapped heartlessly. 'He may have decided that service to the Emperor is not enough. He is the top freedman. If he is a traitor, that is desperately dangerous. You must not let him know you suspect him. So what would you do if he was loyal, Philippus? Wouldn't you share your fears with Abascantus?'

'I did.' Philippus could probably tell that surprised me. Did he have more backbone than he showed? 'I wanted to test his reaction. I went to him privately. He expressed horror that we might have a traitor, though on considering the facts, he agreed it seems probable. He assured me he will look into it. He said I can leave everything to him.'

'Ha! Are you satisfied with that?'

'I pretended to be.'

'Keep pretending!' I said forcefully. 'Then check what he actually does.'

'He has the best resources to investigate.' Philippus went back to looking unhappy. 'He has the ear of the Emperor.'

'He is also best placed to stop you poking your nose in!'

Philippus understood. 'Of course. Now that is why I need you, Albia. I ask you to help me investigate. It needs utter secrecy. Your role, our role, must be invisible.'

I saw that, saw it all too clearly. I wished my report had been anonymous. I wished the document was simply labelled 'from a reliable source'. 'It might have been better not to take me to the meeting today, Philippus.'

'I couldn't help that. It was his idea.'

'Abascantus?' I did not like that!

I chose not to point out to either of my companions that, if Abascantus was a traitor, he had had me invited for a reason. *He* wanted to assess *me*. There was no doubt that if Abascantus really was plotting, and if he decided that in helping Philippus I posed a danger, he would eliminate me.

Calm and steady, Tiberius asked, 'What brought you to your belief in a traitor, Philippus? Why do you feel the False Nero was being organised from Rome?'

'Recent history. There have been plots.'

'Other than Saturninus in Germany? And at home? What plots?'

'Two years ago. September. The ten-days-before-the-Kalends-of-October plot.' I groaned. I find Roman dating ridiculous. 'Domitian was quickly on top of it. Prominent men lost their lives.'

'Very quietly!' commented Tiberius.

Plots against Domitian were endemic now. It was easy to forget the ones he suppressed – or simply never to know they happened.

'Think about the way the Saturninus affair was buried,' Philippus insisted. 'Someone helped a cover-up. Someone at home, because not one senator here has ever been identified. Think, too, about the timing of the False Nero. The Empire is under serious threat from outsiders – Pannonia, Dacia, the Chatti in Germany, who were coerced by Saturninus. We know the Parthians have been making overtures to the Dacians. The Emperor has his hands full with foreign wars. There could never be a better time to depose him.'

'But he is coming home,' I pointed out.

Dimly in the dusk I saw the freedman nodding. 'They can hardly install a usurper while Domitian is outside Rome, with all the legions at his command, and many of those soldiers loving him. But that is why we need to move fast. Once he returns, he will be at his most vulnerable.'

'Can you warn him of your fears?'

'Not without proof.' Philippus was now showing how agitated he was. 'I dare not accuse someone like Abascantus wrongly – if I am right but cannot justify my claims, that will be worse. I must make the False Nero confess who in Rome supported him, Albia. I must do it discreetly before his interrogation starts. The official questioning will be compromised, I am certain.'

'So long as you doubt Abascantus, you have to do this behind his back . . . So you are alone?'

'Nominally the security council controls all counter-conspiracy efforts,' Philippus stated. 'But I can trust no one else.'

'It is dangerous, dangerous to you, Philippus. Be very sure you want to undertake it.'

He reacted earnestly: 'I realise what acting independently entails. I know that if I initiate an undercover inquiry, I am fighting for my career.'

'No,' I said. 'You work at the palace. You know the rules. Once you start any independent action, Claudius Philippus, you will be fighting for your life.'

After a time, Tiberius asked, keeping his tone neutral, 'Why must you involve Flavia Albia?'

It sounded as if Philippus had not expected the question. That was foolish of him. 'I need help. I could have asked her father, which is what *my* father would have done. But Didius Falco appears to have retired.' So he thought Falco was too old now.

'Not him,' I said. 'But never ask him to work for Domitian.' Reluctantly I added, 'If you are trying to prevent an over-throw, does this mean you approve of our Master, Philippus?'

'I am a palace official,' Philippus excused himself. 'I want stability. I approve of the proper transference of power. The Emperor must be legitimate – his candidacy open, his reign confirmed by the Senate. Once you permit individuals to manoeuvre in secret, unasked, and for their own purposes, there is chaos. The Empire is already under stress from external sources. We cannot have a civil war.'

'Agreed.' Tiberius sounded dry. Even Domitian had been suspected of murdering his brother Titus; there had been nothing 'open' about *that* transference of power.

Once more Philippus leaned towards me, his plea urgent.

'Albia, I work with documents. I understand reports. I can hold a conversation . . .' He paused a little. '*You* can make people talk. People who want to keep their secrets. I need you. You must help me.'

Tiberius Manlius stood up abruptly. Without a word, he walked away, going upstairs on his own as he must have done earlier today, taking the stairs stiffly, not looking back.

In alarm, Philippus demanded, 'Will he refuse to let you do it?'

'No.'

Tiberius would never refuse me anything. In our short time together we had survived disaster more than once. He found it unbearable to see me go into danger. But this husband of mine would allow me the choice.

He represented the best Roman values. That was *his* dilemma. He wanted to protect me but he knew my skills. If there was treachery, Tiberius, believing in a citizen's duty to Rome, had to let me pursue it.

19

Although I accepted the task, I was cautious. I had been an informer for a long time. All I agreed was that I would meet the False Nero. Then I would decide whether making him spill what he knew was a workable option.

My own plan would have been to intercept delivery of the secret 'package' from Bruttium. Not even let the prisoner reach Rome. Take him to a safe house of our own choosing, question him there. I suggested Laeta's villa, the place of retirement where Philippus' father had lived his last years; it lay conveniently just outside Rome on the Via Appia. The prisoner could subsequently come into the city as expected; nobody else in the security council need know of the journey delay.

That did not happen. Philippus lacked the resources. Since he was manoeuvring in secret, he dared not give direct orders to his usual staff. Acting like this, he had no way to contact those guarding the prisoner; in any case, he doubted the escort would accept his authority and divert.

Of course, by then I was stuck. Whatever I said, Philippus believed he had won me over. The more I felt he was an amateur, the more I was lured into setting him straight.

Then he admitted where the False Nero would be held. He finally came clean and said that, according to the movement timeline, the prisoner was due to arrive tonight. Rather than risk anyone finding out he was in Rome, they would act without delay. The torturer would begin first thing tomorrow.

I had had images of them stowing their charge deep in the bowels of the palace. It was full of buried corridors. There were reckoned to be underground playrooms that the worst emperors had used for sexual perversions; under the Julio-Claudians it was commonplace, reputedly, to starve unwanted relatives to death down there. That Nero ever survived to inherit the throne, despite the risks of exile, strangling, stifling, poisoning and genuine illness or accident, was remarkable. Growing up while his family dropped like flies around him might explain his mania.

The palace was not the venue. They had a much scarier lock-up. It came with an entire staff of sinister truth-extractors. The False Nero was being taken to the Castra Peregrina.

'Forget it,' I snapped. 'I am not going there.'

Somehow Philippus persuaded me. Curiosity is a terrible inducement.

The Castra Peregrina, or Strangers' Camp, was built by Augustus but heavily redeveloped by Domitian. The dark barracks stood on the Caelian Hill, close to Domitian's Gladiating School. Nearby streets had become a no-go area for respectable women, or even men. The bars and brothels were notorious. For soldiers getting drunk, making a noise, throwing their weight around, it was worse than the Praetorian Camp; that at least lay outside the city walls.

We went by night. Closely wrapped in cloaks, we had Dromo and Philippus' slave as bodyguards; mine was naturally useless, his a mere boy. They carried torches; these only served to illuminate our nervous faces.

As we walked, keeping our steps as silent as possible, Philippus told me how the camp was peopled. Each legion in the field had on its complement dedicated scouts. From them, the Emperor had extracted twelve or thirteen per legion. He transferred them here. They lived in their own camp. They were removed from their legions' staff list and answered directly to Rome. Their loyalty to their home legions ceased, superseded by loyalty to the Castra and direct faith to the Emperor.

Every element of their role was filthy. First, they reported on the province where they had been stationed, on suspected elements in their own legion, and even on the governor. This was likely the mechanism through which Domitian had heard of and dealt with grumblings in Britain under Sallustius Lucullus and betrayal in Asia by Civica Cerialis.

For the chosen, once they came here, their chief role was to spy on the people of Rome. They were known to go out among the public in plain clothes, inciting indiscretions. On occasion, these men would form an execution squad. After the 22 September plot two years ago, which Philippus had told us about, death sentences on prominent men would have been carried out from here. Their work was undercover – yet their existence unconcealed. That is how fear works.

Standing outside their intimidating barracks, I felt that fear.

'Philippus, this is what to say: you are a member of the security council, come to inspect the prisoner. You want to check on his well-being before the torturer begins. Be open. Better the traitor thinks you acted out of pushiness and ambition than that he learns you have been here in secret.'

'Will he find out?'

'Presumably.'

134

I would have urged him to be brave, but preferred not to remind him of his danger. Myself, I was terrified, but I knew how to pretend.

There was the usual delay at the guardhouse, though surprisingly they let us in. Entry was nothing to worry about; my real anxiety was whether they would ever let us out again.

We asked to see the camp commander. He was a big-bodied, sure-of-himself bastard, who reeked of many years of war. Battle-hardened officers can be awarded gold discs they call *phalerae* to decorate their breastplates on cere-monial occasions; up to nine are possible. This man had eight. On duty, he wore them. Every day for him was ceremonial.

He was naturally hostile, yet gave truculent respect to authority. Philippus summoned up just enough of an act. Despite hints that he would evict us, this specimen accepted that Philippus, in his palace livery, had a legitimate interest. Philippus knew the prisoner was there, after all. Luckily for us, we could say the palace was avoiding written evidence – 'So you know we can't show you a docket.'

Nearly-Nine-Gongs looked at me quizzically. He probably thought Philippus and I were lovers, or that Philippus hoped we would be, if he treated me to the cheap thrill of prison visiting. I have had lovelier treats. Being introduced as the wife of an aedile only proved I was a shameless bint, slumming. Still, so long as the commander presumed a top-class freedman was bedding me, he held off his own seduction spiel. Dear gods, I was grateful to be spared.

He told us his name. He spat it out like a challenge, saying we had better not identify him to anyone outside. Let's call him Titus. My pa says in any group you come across there will always be a big twit called Titus, the one who is messing you about.

Titus let us go to see the prisoner. He did not bother to come with us. Having a mysterious guest in the camp was routine.

The False Nero was sitting on a stool in his cell. He was eating his dinner. He was not yet formally inducted into the torture programme so he was not being starved. There are rules. A prisoner of Rome is given basic food and drink. It will be horrible, unless he can bribe his guards for better, but he will be kept alive. Well, they want him alive for punishment.

This man held on his knees a bowl of very thin barley broth. I could smell the garlic from the doorway. The watery fluid looked lukewarm and any barley in it probably had mould. Nevertheless, he was spooning it up with an appetite. He did not understand he might as well not bother. His time was up.

He had a bale of straw to lie on and a bucket so he would not soil his cell. It was a long way from what he would have known in Parthia. The beds in the east are famously soft. As a tool they could use against Rome, he presumably also rated pillows, scented sheets and helpful girls to tuck him in.

Once the torturer came on duty, bed and bowl would be removed. That is, if tomorrow's activity was to be carried out *in situ*. At the Castra Peregrina they might have a special-operations room. An end-of-life suite. Easy-clean and soundproof. Either way, as our escort told us, at dawn the prisoner would be placed in 'special measures'.

I took a good look at him. The False Nero was of

slimmish build, medium height, brown-eyed but light-skinned, with middle-Mediterranean features. That is, he could have passed in Rome without seeming exotic. Syria had been tramped through by so many armies in its long history that its people look like most of us.

This man bore one or two bruises and a great many insect-bite scratches, yet was in reasonable condition. His beard stubble and Neronian sideburns had been hacked short, but his unwashed hair had not been cut for months. The ragged tips still carried dirty traces of old blonding.

To our disappointment, we were unable to talk with him. He knew only his own language. I did not voice it in the Castra, but for me his lack of Latin and Greek was the first proof he could never have been a serious player as Nero.

An interpreter was booked, but for next day. Philippus had not thought of this. He said Rubrius spoke several languages, but he had no idea where to find him out of hours. It would be difficult to turn up any of the palace linguists, or to find them sober even if we tracked them down. Dear gods. Our visit was a waste of time.

The False Nero gazed at us, as if wondering what we would make of this impasse. He had a dull lack of curiosity over what might happen to him. It made me think that whatever was first offered to persuade him to take up his role must have been so substantial in his terms that he no longer cared. His family at home must have been given considerable wealth. He had achieved prosperity for them; his own folk would remember him for generations.

I wondered what his name was. I hoped his mother was proud of him. I hoped she never had to learn how it was all ending.

His bearing was not imperial. You could put his stinking

body in a purple toga, plonk a wreath on his sour head, let him wave at a crowd from a balcony to avoid the language issue, but nobody would mistake this grubby soul for a twig from the élite family tree of Mark Antony and Augustus.

As I had always thought, he was a typical Syrian shepherd. If he had ever possessed a harp, someone had taken it away.

The man was still eating his dinner when we left.

20

Philippus made a feeble offer to escort me home. I said Dromo would suffice. It was safer to look like a prostitute with the boy who carried her earnings and might pack a punch than to walk in the streets at night accompanied by an unworldly civil servant whose skills were all too clearly intellectual. His infant slave would never prevent us being mugged.

At a corner near the Palatine I said goodbye. Once he was out of sight, I turned Dromo by the shoulders; after a few squeaks of protest from him, we went back to the Castra Peregrina. Last time I had been preoccupied with getting past the commander for access to the prisoner; now I took in my surroundings. It was a large, square, forbidding military building, full of barrack blocks, stables, cookhouses, administrative offices and their own specialist sections: armoury, baths, shrine to the Emperor, shrine to some unpleasant soldiering god, cells. I guessed there could be women illegally inside the place, though mainly the soldiers went foraging for pleasure in the local community. The atmosphere was as heavily masculine as anywhere could be.

Indoors, there were odd smells. Belt-grease and feet. Even so late, the place was noisy, full of loud conversations, soldiers' banter, odd rattles of metal, a horn very badly played.

Nearly-Nine-Gongs, the commander, thought he knew why I had come back. Behind him he had a long fighting career in the world's most hideous places. It gave him a warm feeling. He thought girls should flock to him admiringly.

I told Dromo to squat in a corner but to stay awake. I told the commander please not to try anything because I was only married two days ago and my husband had been struck by lightning. Intrigued, as I had known he would be, he decided to be kind to me, at least temporarily.

'Let's pretend I forgot a handkerchief so I've come back for it, Titus. Then I'll tell you why I'm here again.'

'Where's your palace minder?'

'Gone home for a hot toddy, wetting himself with terror after being in your camp.'

'That's good! Not you?' asked Titus, picking his nails clean with the tip of a dagger in a centurionly manner.

I sat on the tiny stool his clerk must use, folded my arms and gazed at him. I murmured stagily, as if to myself, 'Now, Albia, can you really trust this man?'

He gave me his trust-me smile. It was hideous but, having worked with the vigiles for years, I had seen worse. At least he was either sober or could hold tanks of liquor without it affecting him. I reckoned he was abstemious. Well, fairly.

'So why am I here, Titus?'

'Let's not be formal,' said Titus. 'Call me the Princeps Peregrinorum.'

'A prince among strangers, a prince among men.' Sometimes in my work I had to use grisly flattery. He lapped it up. They always do. I did not fool myself; the man remained extremely dangerous and I was alone in his office with him. I didn't count Dromo. 'Princeps, you are a man of experience. You can surely tell that at the palace they have a situation. Listen, how do you feel if I say that what Philippus and I are doing is deeply undercover – and it is for the safety of Rome?'

He liked a crisis. He was prepared to listen. 'So what is this secret "situation"?'

'What I am telling you is in strictest confidence. The man you are looking after so tenderly in your cosy cell – you know he is the False Nero. He was transferred to Rome all the way from Parthia because there is something odd about him. It is thought that he was set up to make his false claim – engineered by a traitor at the palace. That's why I came back tonight without my minder. For all I know, even the man who hired me could be that traitor.'

The soldier looked at me askance.

I let out an exaggerated sigh. 'Princeps, that's exactly the kind of scheme such a villain would use. He might think pretending to hire me would look good and help him escape detection. But I don't believe it is Philippus. He is too mild-mannered. He hasn't a clue.'

'Too bloody ambitious,' corrected the Princeps, showing he was both observant and shrewd.

'But give him his due, he must be bright. He spotted that this prisoner, on his own, was never up to sparking a rebellion, gathering allies, leading a small army across to the Euphrates, persuading the devious Parthians to back him. So Philippus and I wanted a quiet word with your Nero, to persuade him to reveal who was really behind his attempt.'

'You got nowhere?'

'He does not speak Latin.' I bet the commander knew all along. 'So tell me,' I demanded, 'is it true your troops are drawn from every legion? That includes Syria. If your men are experienced scouts – surely the first criterion to be selected for this high-powered intelligence-gathering unit – then someone must be able to translate whatever the blond bummer in your cell does speak. I am just hoping the right men haven't all gone out to some bar.'

He looked at me. 'No,' he said.

'No?' I shrugged womanfully. 'That's a shame.'

'I have one who knows the lingo. He has gone out to a bar. Of course he has.'

'He is a soldier,' I agreed. 'This is Rome. The best bars in the world. I suppose he is now lying in a waiter's lap, stupendously pie-eyed?'

The Princeps Peregrinorum gave me a stern look. 'Don't think I paid no attention to what you and the palace prawn were up to. This is my camp. I know every spider that moves here. What – two chancers come by night to see a sensitive prisoner without a docket? Slap me in the goolies with a flounder, I can work that out.'

I managed to look admiring.

'I'd have been in there with my soldier right this minute,' claimed Nearly-Nine-Gongs. 'I'd be demanding myself that Nero coughs up his sordid secrets, but we can't find him. My soldier, that is. Nero is in his cell, sleeping like a babe. I get a report every hour. He can't sniff without me hearing he's wiped his nose on his arm.'

'That must keep you busy,' I sympathised.

He grinned. 'Only until tomorrow. Once the torturer comes, he won't have a moment to himself.'

He seemed to have taken to me. It's a knack. My work

depends upon it. Half the time, you win them round simply because their lives are boring; my enquiries are the most exciting event that week. Besides, I had been open; he was used to everyone hiding their real motives. I didn't look down upon him being a soldier; I gave proper respect to his power. Then I told him frankly what I wanted.

As a result, I wouldn't say Nearly-Nine-Gongs accepted me, but we had a workable relationship.

He signalled that our meeting was terminating. He said his soldier translator would roll up at first light. He was rostered to interpret the Nero's screams of agony; he would get back at the same time as the torturer arrived.

'Sober?'

'If he's not, you won't detect it. Or he knows I'll eat his balls in a flatbread.'

Titus then made a concession. If I was quick about it, tomorrow morning he would tell the torturer to wait while I tried my best with the False Nero.

'Thank you, sir! I shall bring fish pickle,' I said.

He looked uncertain, so I explained: to splash on the flatbread with the soldier's balls.

Sweetly, he did not know how to take it, so pretended not to have heard. 'I shall have to be present, Flavia Albia. In the event of queries, I must be able to say I witnessed everything.'

'Well, thank you again, Princeps. Actually, I would appreciate your input on whatever Nero gives up. If he does tell us who the traitor is, it may be someone rather powerful. That will require a rather delicate arrest.'

Titus looked interested, seeing an opportunity to acquire his ninth *phalera*. I noticed he did not demand names. 'So,' he said slowly, sounding as if this was where he would ask if I fancied a bunk-up. 'What made you think I would be willing to let you to talk to him?'

'I think you are loyal. Everyone is loyal to something. Gods, leaders, a woman. Do you have a woman yourself, incidentally? What would she want you to do?'

He looked as if he had slept with every barmaid from Gaul to Rhaetia, and possibly their brothers, but in what would be his final post, with his large golden handshake and retirement imminent, I bet he had lined up someone civilised to end his days with. I was right: 'I have a girl. Nice thing. Very intelligent. We never talk about politics.'

'Try it,' I suggested.

Two of his troops were assigned to take me and Dromo safely to the Aventine. Or, as the Princeps Peregrinorum confirmed, with barefaced honesty, one soldier to escort me home, another to be my witness if the first assaulted me. Thanking him nicely yet again, I said that was reassuring.

21

At home, Dromo claimed to have a latch-lifter. While I was still grinding my teeth that he should possess one but not me, we discovered he had bent his, so it no longer worked. Happily, Graecina had been nosily keeping an ear out for when the mistress returned from gadding; she opened up for us. While she inspected me for signs I had been at an orgy, I told her to call in a locksmith, and make sure a key was made for me.

Tiberius had been sitting in the dark courtyard, awaiting my return. I could tell he was unhappy. Within moments we were having the first quarrel of our married life.

I presumed this was about me going out at night, but no. All day, I had completely forgotten that this was the fourth day of September, one before the Nones. This was when the Roman Games began, an extra day added in honour of Julius Caesar, after he was murdered. There was a sacrifice to Jupiter, a procession, then chariot racing in the Circus. Had Tiberius been well, he ought to have attended. Instead, he had sat at home all day, miserably thinking about having to miss his duties.

As I pointed out, I had been here from time to time; he had never mentioned it and so far he had yet to leave the house. I was very tired or I might not have added unwisely, 'Mother's doctor said I must expect unreasonable behaviour.

Apparently when men are struck by lightning it is common for their marriages to end in divorce!'

That hardly helped. After a stand-off, we remained annoyed with each other. We had not been married long enough to have worked out whose role it was to flounce off in a huff.

Eventually Tiberius humphed and went to bed. Later, I followed and found him pretending to sleep. I crossed the room in darkness. Falling in with him, I wrapped myself around his warm body, which he at least allowed without shaking me off. I was suddenly aware of how frightened I had been at the Castra, and how good it felt to be safe again in our private bedroom with my man's steady presence.

A furtive knock announced Galene, bringing warm mulsum, one of her almond slices, a small oil lamp. Finger to lips, telling me not to disturb Tiberius, she picked up my discarded gown, which she took away for washing as if I were still a girl at home. I had been proud of surviving alone as an informer, but I could live this way.

After the door closed Tiberius relented and sat up with me. I had the drink. We shared the biscuit.

'All right?'

'All right.' We were friends. 'The False Nero was a real fake. Fresh from the sheep pen. Spoke no Latin, and no translator obtainable, needless to say. I have to go back at dawn for a quick session.'

'Want me to come?' Once he would have spoken much more eagerly.

'You don't need to.' As an aedile he would have kept Nearly-Nine-Gongs in check, but Tiberius still did not want to face the outside world. The Castra Peregrina would be a bad place for a troubled man to start.

146

He shifted against the bedhead fretfully. 'I must get over this, Albia. I need to be at the Games.'

'Stuff the Games,' I soothed him. 'You did enough to set them up. You have three colleagues who can jump on any problems. You stay in, have a nice lie-down when you need it, and let somebody else come and tell you how well it all went.'

'What about you? What if *you* need me?'

I tried to sound encouraging. 'If I do, I shall ask, I promise. At the moment I am cruising through it. The camp commander supplied a set of soldiers to see me home safe tonight; the lovely boys are coming back for me tomorrow morning. Everything will be absolutely fine.'

I was wrong there.

We spent a night plagued by crumbs in the bed. Next day I dragged on some clothes and crept downstairs at what would have been cockcrow, had any cockerels in our city survived the stewpot. I had trained my mind to wake me up when I had to work, though today it was hard.

The boys from Titus appeared promptly outside. To my surprise, these exemplary soldiers had brought me a donkey. It was a deliberate ruse: when I climbed on with my skirts runkling, they could see my bare legs. Graecina and Galene were on hand to wave me off, so they soon rearranged me decently. They vied with one another in cursing the troops, who pretended to look shamefaced. None of them gave a flying phallus, of course.

I rode down the Aventine, flogged past the Circus Maximus, around the great base of the Temple of Claudius, made it to the camp. The donkey was skittish but I managed not to fall off.

Nearly-Nine-Gongs stood, legs apart, in his office, shaving – a ceremony he carried out like a sacrifice. He used a ladies' mirror, incongruously a rather fine silver-backed one in the Etruscan style, plus a razor with which he could have killed pirates. His arm action was fussy, stroking away the stubble with infinite care. He finished by patting on a crocus lotion, using a delicate finger action and lots of it.

With him, patiently waiting on the clerk's wooden stool, was the torturer. Standing up in a corner was a clerk. He was a sleepy public slave, who looked resigned to everything. Titus had thoughtfully provided them with bread rolls, though no one offered me any.

The torturer was an unexpected treat. I had imagined a barrel-chested, boot-faced bruiser, covered with scars and grimacing. This was a nice young man. No doubt soldiers would assist him once he started, but he was a public servant, assigned to the Castra Peregrina, with a stipend, lived at home when not required, came in with his tools when summoned. He looked to be in his twenties, barely into his beard, well-mannered, nicely spoken when he greeted me. Even so, somehow I did not doubt he was skilled. There was a muted confidence about him.

He came enveloped in a large, clean, waterproofed apron, so no blood would show on him afterwards. From the neat bow in the ties behind his back, I wondered if he had been wrapped in it at home by some loving relative.

When Titus paused his razor action and introduced us, I exclaimed to the torturer, 'I bet you don't tell your mother what your job is!' She must be happy simply to know her bonny boy had an important position, with an income and work that in our city was guaranteed for life.

Alfius, as was his name, had set down a large holdall, its

148

leather stiffened and darkly creased with age. He kept it close, between his feet, as he sat on the stool. He now kicked this. I noticed he had small feet, shod in well-polished tie-up shoes. The laces were precise and even. At his kick, the bag of tools clanked, but was so heavy it hardly budged. Small gadgets for exquisitely adding pain hung from metal loops on the outside. They were all well-kept and sharp-looking. 'She thinks I am a plumber.'

She must be an idiot. A real plumber would have his tunic stuck in his bum-crack and be permanently half-tiddly.

Once Nearly-Nine-Gongs was satisfied he had a perfect shave, we all went outside. Soldiers unwound themselves from various nooks, then formed up into a camp commander's escort. This detail cannot have been for protection, for the man himself breathed physical capability. Purse-snatchers must dive into doorways when he walked down a street. However, he never moved without a group to listen to his manly words and admire his actions.

Also waiting for us was the army scout from Syria who would act as interpreter: a silent man who, as promised, smelt of wine but appeared sober. He was unremarkable physically, but sinister; I would not have liked him counting the tunics on my washing-line to see whether I was keeping a lover.

The men all looked at me curiously, though in the presence of Titus their scrutiny was subtle. I knew none of them was thinking what an elegant gown I wore and how suitably accessorised it was. They were imagining me without it.

A chill ran between my shoulder-blades. The Castra seemed no less threatening by daylight. If people jumped you in this haven of past miseries, no one would hear you

149

scream. If you stopped screaming it would be because you had gone beyond caring. Men would fling your lifeless body into the street outside. Passers-by would look away.

We moved in a subdued group through echoing corridors that I remembered from last night. There was still noise everywhere. I tried to view this as domestic clamour you might hear in any private house, even though the voices were so aggressive and loud. Somewhere a horse whinnied, then another answered. A tiny slave passed us, burdened with an enormous tray of spent oil lamps; his starveling arms could barely stretch to hold it. Cookery was going on, a military breakfast that required robust banging of immense pans, amid a scent of fresh-baked bread.

A soldier with only a loincloth hanging round his knees appeared in a doorway, saw his Princeps, grinned, gave a vestigial salute, then scuttled out of sight again. Men in the escort glanced at me. I carried on quietly, letting them know I had seen a dingle-dongle before; moreover, that this soldier's wizened specimen had failed to reach my standards.

Internally, I was preoccupied, wondering what I could say to the prisoner. Last night I had gone home far too late to think, too tired to prepare a plan. Perhaps I could first describe the treatment he would receive from Alfius, with his tools. Remind the man he was doomed to die. Pretend that if he helped me, I might intercede to obtain better for him, maybe even a reprieve . . .

Tiberius had cited possible inducements to win over such a prisoner. Given how serious the situation was, I reckoned the secretariat would agree. Whatever the pretender had already been given by his backers to take up his role as Nero, offer more. Suggest a new life, a safe new identity. Promise protection for his family.

We entered a dark, narrow, damp-smelling corridor. When we reached the cell I was furious. There was Philippus.

He had never said he was coming; I regarded this interview as mine. Yet he had arrived before me. He stood outside the room, stiff in his palace whites, gathering his toga close, uncomfortable in these surroundings. Surely a spy should be less fastidious. His attitude labelled him a mere armchair expert.

He saw my irritation. 'Nothing has happened yet, Albia. The pretender is still fast asleep. The attendant is just going in to wake him.'

Being a soldier, the 'attendant' made a crude chambermaid. His method was what he would use on a tent of dozy recruits who were trying to avoid parade duty: a stentorian yell. For added finesse, he applied a boot hard to the nearest limb of the prisoner.

At once the Princeps ordered him to stop. 'Hold it.'

The False Nero had not stirred.

The soldier stood back. He shuffled one foot, trying to hide a piece of straw from the prone man's crude sleeping bale that had stuck in his boot strap. Normally untidiness would gain him a reprimand. Sensing a crisis, he straightened and saluted his commander. The action was smart, yet diffident. A soldier's soldier to his shiny studs, I guessed Titus was much-loved.

He spoke in his usual unhurried way, but he motioned the rest of us to remain outside. Through the door we watched as he stomped in alone. He did not rush. He walked across to the prisoner, peering at him closely. With powerful hands, he lifted up the man by his tunic, further inspected his lolling head, even shook him. His shake was the hard, abrupt action you use to free the last slug of fish pickle from its container. Nothing happened. He laid the unre-sponsive figure back more gently. The False Nero returned to his straw bed like a child's cloth doll.

'Bugger me.' Not an enticing invitation. 'Why did you have to do that, son?' the Princeps asked mournfully, talking to his prisoner. 'Oh, you've upset me now, you really have. This is my camp and I did not give permission for you to disturb its nice routine.' He turned to address the rest of us. 'This is awkward, awkward for somebody. Your False Nero has gone and died on us.'

22

'Are you sure?' Philippus was beginning to annoy Titus. The prisoner was dead. Anyone could see it.

The camp commander would have preferred to decide his next move away from official scrutiny. Get your story straight. Fix it. Then tell the bastards. When you do, tell them as little as possible.

I went in for a look. Now in full Princeps mode, Titus was affronted by my disobeying his order to stay out. I didn't let that stop me. I reckoned this would be my only chance.

There were no marks on the corpse that I could see. The old bruises remained, but no new ones showed. Nobody had thumped him after we had left last night. Stooping close, I saw no frothing on his lips. No ligament cuts. He had not been stabbed: there was no blood. If he was hit on the head, nothing showed on his scalp among that pathetic, dirtily dyed hair.

Grudgingly, Titus let me conduct this inspection. He watched how I did it. It was beneath him to approve of a woman's actions, but he made no move to interrupt.

Still standing outside the cell, Philippus found his voice again; on his dignity, he announced that there would have to be a full inquiry. 'Too right,' agreed Titus, his voice laconic. It was lost on no one that the death was a failure on his part. He had not kept the False Nero safe. Important information had been lost. He, the officer in charge, had let it happen.

'Perhaps he died of fright,' suggested Alfius, the torturer, showing his youth. Perhaps being tortured by him was such a prospect that people collapsed before he had even arrived . . .

'Or perhaps he had a really bad cold!' snorted Titus. Then he uttered, in a disgusted voice, what we were all thinking: 'Somebody got to him.'

'Foul play?' quavered Philippus from the doorway, still hoping not.

'Poison.' Titus kicked the bowl from which I had seen the prisoner eating broth. *He was eating his dinner . . .* The Nero was being killed before our eyes though we never knew it. Could we have saved him?

The commander became even more morose. 'This man was in special measures. Who the fuck gave him food?'

All the soldiers present managed to look blank. Every man became certain *he* was not on watch yesterday evening. Titus peered at each of them, but he knew the rosters. These were not to blame. Others would be. Gods help them.

Alfius shuffled into the cell with us, taking care of his shoes. He picked up the bowl, sniffed, threw it down again angrily. 'I gave instructions. No food, not even water from the moment he arrived. I wanted him hungry. I wanted him starved. It's best if my subject is light-headed when I start!'

'It's best if he is still alive,' I said. He stared at me blankly. No torturer understands irony. If you are ever a prisoner of the state, absolutely do not try it. I called out to Philippus, 'Do you want me to investigate?'

154

'Not allowed,' interrupted Nearly-Nine-Gongs. 'My juris-diction, my inquiry.' Seeing me unrepentant, he insisted, 'There have to be protocols!'

Pretending I had not heard him, I told Philippus quickly, 'You will need a list of everyone who had access to the man. The Princeps must supply a statement to confirm whatever orders were given for his custody. But the contacts list is most important. Anybody on it,' I instructed Titus, 'must be confined to quarters until he has been interviewed.'

'My jurisdiction!' growled Titus again.

I told him quietly, 'You might prefer that somebody neutral exonerates you, Titus.'

'I do not think so!' answered the Princeps Peregrinorum, shepherding me from the cell.

Since it was indeed his jurisdiction, that was where we left it.

So long as Philippus and I were still there, Nearly-Nine-Gongs appeared to take his responsibility seriously. He had the cell locked after us all.

'What can we do with the body?' Philippus fussily demanded, keeping his voice low.

'I'll have his head shaved,' Titus answered at once. 'Make him anonymous, get him chucked in the river.' It seemed a practised routine.

'No!' Philippus sounded strangely decisive, as if he, too, had been in this situation before. 'Strip him and burn all he came with. Wait until tonight when the roads are full of vehicles. Take him some distance outside Rome in a covered cart. Dump him. Make sure no one sees you. Then delete any record that you ever had him.'

That suited the Princeps.

155

And so, just like his illustrious predecessor, the third False Nero would end up ignominiously lying in a ditch. Unlike the real one, he would never be lifted out of it and placed in a marble mausoleum.

23

What now?

The commander had Philippus and me removed promptly from the Castra. No escort was provided for our onward journey; we were put out and stranded in the daunting porch, with deadweight gates slammed behind us, like unwanted door-to-door salesmen. This was nothing new for me, though I could see Philippus felt his position as a palace official was compromised. He seemed astonished. Astonished that the Princeps had done it, astonished at himself for letting him.

Since Alfius, the torturer, had been hustled out at the same time, I grabbed him and took him with us to a nearby bar – not choosing the first we came to or one within sight of the Castra.

We settled in a quiet corner, while I sent Philippus to order. The palace could pay. This was their mess. Since the bar was used to soldiers who needed to be sobered up for duty, its breakfast victuals looked promisingly substantial. Without disrespect to the late False Nero, I was now ravenous.

While we were on our own, I double-checked with Alfius his instruction that the prisoner should not be fed. 'This is not your fault, then. Now, Alfius, you can help us. You don't want to be tainted by what happened. It's in your interest to discover who did provide the bowl of broth. Maybe you are going back to the Castra for other work.' He agreed; in that dark place, they tortured people all the time. 'Keep your ears open. If you hear anything useful, please tell me. Tell me urgently.'

I gave him directions to find me, remembering that I now lived not at the fabled Eagle Building, Fountain Court, but the aedile's house in Lesser Laurel Street. When I spelled out that this was on the Aventine, Alfius looked frightened. 'Bear up, lad! Fear of the unknown is what you impose on other people. You're immunised. The Aventine is fine if you keep your wits about you. Trust me.'

His work had left Alfius doubtful of the trust concept.

Philippus rejoined us so I sent him a warning glance not to start talking business yet. Alfius had little appetite. He was upset by seeing a dead man. Although the subjects he worked on often died, he never had to witness it. So now he picked at his food moodily.

Philippus had a healthy put-away. Death did not faze him. I had been right: he seemed like an innocent scroll-winder, but he had seen murdered men before. I wondered if he had ever killed any.

I tucked in. I knew how to compartmentalise. The False Nero stayed in a pigeon-hole that I could revisit, but for now I had closed the columbarium door behind me.

We were all silent. Unfortunately, this gave an opportunity for another customer to come over and sidle into the free space beside Alfius, uttering a cheery greeting.

We were all too demoralised, some of us too busy munching, to say how unwelcome it was to have our table invaded by this garrulous idiot. It had still barely passed dawn. At that time of the morning all normal people are glum, but this pest, who called himself Trophimus, kept asking impertinent questions about who we were and what we were doing in Rome. Philippus tried to be polite; Alfius was inclined to gossip, though I noticed he never revealed his day job. I refused to speak.

'A lot of people have come in for the Roman Games,' burbled the inane one, trying to find out if that applied to us. Alfius said he never went; Philippus only smiled, which was no deterrent for this man.

I started privately inspecting him. I picked at a nut bowl to cover it. He was plainly dressed, giving nothing away about his profession or position in society. Clean enough, shaved not too many days ago, no status ring. He was muscular, in a way that comes from daily work rather than the gymnasium. His accent was plebeian; his cheeky-chatter attitude came straight from the streets. He could have run a market stall, selling stolen cloaks from bath houses. If he had belonged to a better class, he could have been a bent book-keeper. There are plenty of those in Rome.

He seemed innocuous. He seemed artless. He was a friendly fellow who hated to sit quiet on his own, so he liked palling up with other people when he was out in public . . .

No, he was not. He was the loyalty police.

Alfius had eaten all he wanted; he went home to his mother. His bag still clanked like a plumber's toolkit. The barman called out to him: could he fix a fountain for them? Alfius said sorry, but he had too much work already.

The chattering man limpeted himself to us.

I sat quiet until, as I expected, the intruder blathered his way to discussing whether the Emperor would come home from Pannonia to preside over the Roman Games. The mole seemed to be still digging away at his theory that our party was in town for the festival, but once I spotted what he was up to, his intended move was obvious. Chewing a bread roll, he asked innocuously, 'So, do you think the Emperor is doing a good job – between friends?'

Time to act. I half turned to the scroll-beetle, who was seated alongside me. 'Philippus, if there's one thing this deviant is not, it's a friend. I thought our problem was that he would palm our purses. But, trust me, he wants something worse.'

Philippus breathed wry amusement. 'Ah, you have noticed too!' He had these moments when he emerged from his vague persona and became openly astute.

I gazed at the chatterer, waiting for the idiot to realise we were absolutely on to him. I went on staring until most people would have wilted but he was too deeply committed to his act; he feigned surprise at my challenge, determined to keep going. He had chosen us. We were today's marks.

When I had stared long enough, I tackled him. 'We cannot be the first people to see through you. But you never let a simple thing like exposure end it, I see! Cough up. You lie in wait in bars, luring the public into slandering our Master. You want us to say something that lets you whop us into court. What do you have – a daily prosecutions quota?'

Philippus drew himself up, with a pained expression. 'I am a Palatine official. This lady is an aedile's wife.'

That was stupid. I was so miffed that under the bench I kicked him viciously. 'Sorry, my foot slipped . . . Silly move, man. Now this slimy chancer thinks you and I are here for an illicit tryst. Adultery will serve his purpose, though – if it's true.' The agent looked as if he had not

160

thought of that; he was too narrow; he could handle only one set script.

Trained by relatives who were informers or lawyers, I complained bitterly, 'We go straight into court, and the Treasury pockets our assets for Domitian . . . Of course it's not true, is it, Philippus? You are running a spy ring and I am an agent you're handling for state security. This crass bastard is ruining our secret meet.'

The crass bastard wanted to say something. I cut across him ruthlessly.

'Push off, vermin. Assuming you're based in the Castra, Claudius Philippus controls the man who controls your promotion record.' Doggedly he attempted another interruption. Full marks for trying! It got him nowhere. 'The first thing my colleague will do, back on the Palatine, is call up your personnel scroll. Then he'll scratch a poison-stylus note to your commanding officer. Are you enjoying Rome? Make the most of it, because you're heading back to whatever bog or desert your home unit is stationed in.'

'He may not have a unit,' suggested the handsome Philippus, mildly, in his cultured voice. 'But if not, I can have him deleted from the freelance list.'

'Well, there you are, Trophimus.' I smirked at him. Trophimus looked surprised that I had remembered the name he had used. As an informer he was an amateur. 'That's Rome,' I stated. 'Even men who use fear as their weapon can themselves be threatened. We all have something we don't want to lose. Now it's your turn.'

Trophimus finally took our hints and pushed off.

The bar-keeper, who must have seen Trophimus in operation before, brought us new beakers of mulsum with a sympathetic grin. It seemed he was none too keen on having a provocateur in his bar. 'On the house.'

We thanked him for this rare treat, drank up slowly, but then left without saying any more. The bar-keeper would have listened in on any conversation, which he, too, would have reported somewhere.

This was Rome, the city of informers. I should know. Trust nobody.

24

We held the conversation we needed outside, by a street fountain. A woman who had been washing clothes had just left with her sodden bundle, so we parked in her puddles, hoping to finish before the next thirsty donkey came along.

'Here's what you do, Philippus – well, my advice if you want to take it.' He nodded, buckling before a strong woman. 'Go back to the Palatine. Tell Abascantus you came to oversee the torture session to ensure it was done right.'

'And to hear for myself what was said? To report it accurately?' Against my expectations, he had a prepared excuse.

'Good. Admit it seems the Nero has been poisoned to thwart the intelligence service. Say the Princeps Peregrinorum is conducting an investigation, then look satisfied to leave him to it. When Nearly-Nine-Gongs gives his results you can judge for yourself whether he is scrupulous, or whether he didn't look too hard.' For all we knew, the Princeps himself had been in on the murder.

Philippus meekly nodded again. I grimly considered how this biddable man held the safety of Rome in his hands.

We stood, arms folded, looking into the water. A pigeon joined us.

The new development left Philippus stuck with his traitor,

assuming he was right that one existed. 'It's over,' I urged. 'The third pretender's gone. The timing is inconvenient, but if people were using that poor creature to challenge Domitian, they can't continue. Any plot is foiled.'

'No, they will try again,' he concluded despondently.

I was used to supporting unhappy clients. 'If they want to subvert the Emperor's reign, they are bound to. But until they start, what can you do? Next time you will be waiting to catch them at it.' He still looked like a badly stuffed dormouse. 'Won't you?' I insisted firmly, feeling like his mother.

Even I did not see what else he could do. A traitor who was clever enough, skilled enough, trusted enough to work in a high position would avoid leaving traces.

'Philippus, you can only watch for clues. Past mistakes, future activity. You know what is wanted.' Sighing internally, I elaborated: 'Anyone who slips out to meet people they shouldn't be seeing. Letters that go unrecorded in the proper system. Someone who vanishes on leave unexpectedly, then comes back and never says anything about the weather, the villa they stayed at, or how the wife catastrophically ate a bad oyster . . . Any clue to who was behind this, or what they are planning next.' Philippus looked more confident, though he remained downcast. 'I can't help, Philippus. I cannot come in and audit your colleagues.' Even if I wanted to – which I did not.

'The Princeps may find out who did the poisoning,' he mumbled hopefully.

He was fooling himself; he knew it. I did not even bother to challenge his statement.

I said I was going home. I had a new house, with dis-orderly staff and a sick husband. We had a neglected business. I was needed on the Aventine.

Actually, since no one at home would expect me back so early, privately I had other plans. I was heading for Prisca's bath house, looking forward to a long soak in whatever remained of last night's hot water. I hate the feeling of unfinished business. I wanted to consider all this alone.

25

A quiet day at home. That would have been welcome. Dromo let me in. He looked shifty – the usual.

I could hear women's voices. It sounded as if two people were working amicably together. I felt doubtful, but enjoyed the novelty.

Graecina's children were sitting on miniature stools in a shady part of the courtyard, while a young man I had never seen before taught them alphabet letters. When Dromo noticed me looking, he whined that Graecina had said he, too, must learn to write, sharing their lessons. 'She's wrong. Tell her she's wrong. I don't have to do that.'

'Dromo, it sounds very sensible. This will be a big benefit to you.' If he could read and write, he would be so much more useful to us . . . 'Learning will last you all your life. Do as she says. Go straight over now and join in.'

'My master doesn't want me to!'

'Yes, he does. That's ridiculous. Where is your master now?'

'Those children are cleverer than me.'

'They are only about four and five. Don't be silly. Pay attention to the teacher and he will help you catch up.'

'I don't want to!'

'Dromo, life is not about what you want, but what we, who have your interests at heart, want for you.' That sounded pompous but, inevitably, sweet replies had failed. I was losing patience.

'That man will beat me if I can't do it.'

'I see no stick. He uses a kinder method. Get going or you'll have no cake for a week.' That worked. 'And where, I asked you, is Manlius Faustus?'

Dromo jerked his head towards a room by the atrium. Dragging his feet, the bullied boy slouched over to attend the lesson. The teacher gave him a letter board and began to explain perfectly gently. I could see Graecina's shy little children liked the young man. He looked friendly, wide-eyed, hopeful that he could achieve miracles through the wonder and joy of education. Life had yet to sour him.

He had not worked with Dromo until now.

Graecina had transformed a previously empty anteroom. Assigned as our interview salon, it was already housing my husband and a visitor. They were holding a strained conversation while they waited for me. Since I had not hurried home, they might have been waiting for some time.

Tiberius had had a simple ochre wash painted on until we fixed up fancier décor. Hello! The furnishings were mine. The contents of my old apartment, mainly bedroom stuff, had already come from the Eagle Building in time for my wedding. Now someone had toiled up six flights of crumbly stone stairs to lug down the contents of my office. They would have risked the staircase giving way. My father had used that eagle's nest before me, but I had chucked out his battered possessions, which even the Aventine homeless then rejected. My own replacements were comfortable, to encourage my clients to relax.

Everything I used for work had been brought on a cart

and installed here. Though it felt good to see familiar things, I hated the way this new room was arranged. My basket armchair had been pushed against a side wall, but I quickly pulled it out to a more dominant position, then plonked myself down in it. Once I could reclaim my couch from the visitor, its throw and cushions needed to be rearranged in the way I liked them. Graecina had given Faustus his own curule seat. I must find him something more comfortable. On new display shelves stood Greek vases I had borrowed from Father's auction house to show I was a cultured informer who charged high fees. My housekeeper had worked fast to find a carpenter to put those shelves up – though I guessed she had gone into the builder's yard and snaffled someone. It would stop the workmen thinking that while Faustus was sick they could spend all day eating pies.

As I had feared, in my absence today Graecina had prettied up the plainly painted room with vivid floor mats, a set of twinky-winky drinks coasters and a truly hideous Cupid candelabrum. That had to go – it had to go right now. I picked it up by one horrid winged child, taking it from the room and dumping it in the corridor outside.

'The putti from Hades! I am not looking at those plump little bottoms every time I come in here.'

Tiberius gave me a wan smile. 'I told her! She had tried phallic fauns first.'

'What's wrong with a simple hanging bowl?' I grinned at the visitor, including him in the conversation. I knew him, and he must have introduced himself to Tiberius: thin, lanky, extremely tall, faintly musty. Trebianus, the Parthia specialist. The odd man with sallow skin and washed-out colouring had ventured out from the Palatine to our house. Whatever could he want? Could I bear to know?

He was bursting to tell me, but at that moment doors were flung open to admit Graecina and Galene, vying to cause a commotion as they brought food. 'I happened to mention I had not eaten,' Trebianus said, almost apologetically though not quite humble enough.

That was Rome. Full of people on the cadge, desperate for free meals. Our first week here, yet Tiberius and I had already acquired a client; no doubt he was hoping we would toss him a present, some dear little purse of coins to take home. We were lucky he did not have a wife and several children hanging around in a carriage outside, also avid for free food and drink. 'I hope you don't mind, Flavia Albia?'

I said it was a pleasure. My first chance to play the gracious housewife! I would not bungle that.

Anyway, since I had left home so early, it was still only mid-morning. If we shoved a few olives and cheese bites down Trebianus now, he might have safely gone by the time Tiberius and I wanted our lunch in peace. Mind you, I thought giving a palace official sliced egg, gherkins, nuts, fresh rolls and cold Lucanian sausage was an unnecessary extravagance for a first visit.

We could iron out that problem later, when I played the domineering matron, hectoring my feckless staff. As Graecina and Galene served him, they glanced at me furtively, as if they anticipated my reaction.

That was good. Keep them fearful.

Trebianus ate while he talked. The mad-looking members of the security service were clearly used to speaking with their mouths full. Imperial staff are given a thorough education, which I believe includes social etiquette, but good manners in public must have been edged out of the spies' cram-packed syllabus by vital tricks like leaving messages with twigs or invisible ink.

'So what is this about?' I wondered if my husband had already been told, though he stayed out of it, picking at the olive bowl.

'As soon as I knew what happened at the Castra, I rushed straight here!'

I raised my eyebrows, now tidied and reshaped at Prisca's baths (so I was slightly sore), while I asked what, in the official view, had happened and why Trebianus had galloped around to us.

In the short time, short as I saw it, that I had allowed myself at Prisca's this morning being bathed, manicured, hairdo-ed, oiled, and pampered with delectable gossip, Philippus had gone back to the Palatine. He had reported the Castra murder. The inner security circle had met, digested, reacted. The Princeps Peregrinorum had turned up in person and reported on his inquiry.

'Fast work!'

The Princeps had taken no time to concoct a good story: an agent deployed to the Castra was implicated in the poisoning. He had since gone missing. The Princeps had men out looking for him. He thought it unlikely the killer would be found.

I sighed. 'What's his name?'

'Paternus.'

'Does Paternus have a wife who is to be seen these days showing off a valuable necklace? Has he recently purchased a pointlessly fast chariot?'

'They tend not to be married,' replied Trebianus, gloomily. Having met one that morning, Trophimus, I felt no surprise. Even if he praised her food and was kind to her mother, a wife with any self-respect would find him unbearable. 'The Princeps Peregrinorum believes he will turn up floating in the Tiber, Flavia Albia.'

'Well, when he does, you had better assume the Princeps had him dropped there.'

'Oh?' Trebianus paused, with a roll half bitten through. His next words were muffled. Crumbs flew in every direction. I would need to sweep the couch. 'We generally consider the Princeps Peregrinorum one of our own.' Relieved of this aphorism, he chomped energetically.

I felt free to be cruel: 'You are taking a risk! There's a man who despises palace freedmen for sure, so not naturally on your side. But losing the False Nero while in his custody leaves the Princeps in a lonely position. He must reckon blame will be landed on him.'

Trebianus still looked unconvinced. He reached for another gherkin, only to find he had eaten them all. He had had his lot. I would not send for refills.

'The Princeps let this man be murdered in the Castra,' Tiberius intervened, 'The harsh view must be that he was either coerced – or he is hopelessly incompetent.'

'Thank you, aedile. Is there a gentle view?'

'No.' Tiberius had on his most dour expression. 'So what is the palace intending to do?'

'Call the incident unfortunate and drop it. Abascantus declared the matter closed. His position is that the pretender was always meant to be executed, after all. Somebody spared us the trouble, an optimist might say.'

'I find myself a pessimist. What about information the False Nero might have given?'

'Irretrievably lost, sir. We shrug. We move on with normal business.'

'You approve?'

'No.' Trebianus neatly echoed the aedile's own terse response. Maybe this man had hidden finesse. He must be bright, surely. Watching the Parthians was important to Rome.

'So "normal business" is the Abascantus approach,' I said. 'What about Philippus? And what are you doing here, Trebianus? So agitated about it all?'

'Philippus is a past master of shelving difficult problems.'

'Really?' The Philippus I had seen in the past couple of days seemed to blossom occasionally. Today his orders about disposal of the body had been crisp. He had shot shrewd orders at the Princeps, despite that man's overbearing style.

Trebianus seemed to adjust his line: 'Oh, he has a fine mind. Excellent heritage from his father. One day, if he manages to survive, Claudius Philippus will be a man to tackle anything.'

I glanced at Tiberius, then we both looked at Trebianus.

'Philippus will just let the issue die quietly,' he insisted. 'He is an old woman, wants no fuss.'

Of course that was not my experience. So Philippus was doing a good job of concealing his aim to uncover the traitor.

'Why have you come here, then?' I demanded bluntly, not giving Philippus away.

The Parthia-watcher slumped further on our couch. He had folded up his long length like a resting stick insect. To fill in time, he moved egg pieces round and round in his bowl with bony fingers, staring at the food. Eventually he admitted the truth: he knew Philippus had suspicions, suspicions he shared.

'We are not close colleagues. Nevertheless, colleagues we

are. We devote ourselves to a common interest, which is the good of Rome. So Philippus and I, individually, have come to suspect that someone, someone with the power to influence events, has chosen to follow the wrong path into the mountains.'

'Philippus has hinted this to you?'

Trebianus jerked. 'People in our world rarely voice such anxieties. Premature action alerts the opposition.'

'So have you done anything about your own suspicions?' Tiberius asked, sparing me the need to be so blunt.

Trebianus looked shocked. 'Done? Done, aedile? This is not a situation anyone should disturb without evidence and certainty.'

Tiberius fell silent. Since it was my inquiry, he made a slight gesture, handing the initiative back to me. It was not abdication: I knew from working with him that avoidance was not his style. Tiberius Manlius addressed issues. He assumed it was his duty, because otherwise the world is packed with fearful fools who will never take the right action.

I shifted in my chair. Tiberius made a smaller movement, uncomfortable on his curule seat. I was aware that Trebianus unconsciously mimicked our actions, also disturbed by the point we had reached in the conversation.

'So, Trebianus,' I kept my tone neutral, 'what has brought *you* rushing to see *us*?'

'Parthia,' he said.

26

My husband was a background man. He called for a résumé on Parthia.

I cursed. Much as I loved Tiberius, his obsession with detail could be gruelling. I had swallowed enough foreign background: Britannia, Germania, Asia. Filthy frontier provinces with restless tribes and haughty locals, all crammed with Roman agents observing loyalties until their eyes watered.

At least Parthia was not our province, or likely to become one. Parthia was an empire in its own right. Parthia was huge. According to Trebianus, Parthia made Dacia, the wealthy and warlike society that so exercised our emperor, look like a moth-hole in the map.

'I don't suppose you *have* a map?'

'We are setting up house. We do not even possess a calendar of markets and festivals!' snapped Tiberius, who needed one for his work. He could consult a list at the aediles' office, but had not felt up to going there since the lightning strike.

The Parthian Empire stretched between Rome and China. Its vast distances were crossed by the Silk Road, which gave it all the power and prestige of exotic trade, and by the Persian Royal Road, which provided excellent communications. That could be a disadvantage: Alexander the Great used the Royal Road to invade. Even so, from here in the west its capital at Ctesiphon was only to be considered for the most ambitious commercial enterprise. Rome and Ctesiphon did not easily communicate.

Though heavily influenced by Greek culture in the past, the people spoke many languages. Politically, it was a conglomeration of nations led by a variety of satraps who had never truly settled to allegiance to the Parthian King of Kings. For us, this was useful: it kept the King of Kings tied up at home, lest the kings of whom he was nominally king tried to usurp him. Often attempts to overthrow him involved his close relatives.

Rome had a long history of wars with Parthia, which included the ghastly battle of Carrhae, perhaps its greatest military disaster. Crassus, one of the First Triumvirate, was, naturally, attempting to invade. A spy had exhausted his army by leading them to and fro all night on the promise of finding a safe route. Crassus had seen his weary troops terrified and disoriented by deafening war drums, then mown down by long-range archers. After one blunder succeeded another, it was said twenty thousand Roman troops were massacred and ten thousand more captured. It was rumoured that because of his reputation for financial greed, the Parthians had poured molten gold down the dying Crassus' throat.

Major Roman figures attempted action in the east there-after, Mark Antony among them. Most successful was Nero's legendary general, Domitius Corbulo, after Parthia invaded Armenia; in the teeth of defeat, Corbulo overcame distance, harsh climatic conditions and the enemy's tenacity to forge a compromise. It took him years. The envious Nero gave him no thanks; he forced Corbulo to commit suicide.

The compromise Corbulo negotiated was: Rome would be said to rule Armenia but would install Tiridates, a charismatic brother of the Parthian ruler, as king. Tiridates travelled to Rome, and in what Nero called a triumph – a weird piece of international pageantry – Tiridates and Nero had bonded like brothers.

'Nero loved the theatricality – he was entranced,' growled Trebianus. 'Tiridates taught him magic. Nero supposedly became a Zoroastrian priest – all the more ludicrous since the principle of the magi is that you take responsibility for your actions. With the maxim of "good thoughts, good deeds, good words", only Nero the supreme, blind egoist could believe himself equal to it. But Tiridates knelt at his feet like a slave – this handsome, popular figure who had travelled to Rome in the midst of a small army, cheered at every town along the way. Nero, who never even saw an army, wore a triumphal purple robe and behaved like a conqueror. Tiridates went along with it. I can tell you Tiridates despised Nero. But since then Parthia, while loathing Rome, has claimed admiration for Nero.'

'A convenience?'

'Their choice. Being Parthians, they have their reasons.' Trebianus was revelling in the mystique of his subject. 'When the second False Nero, Terentius Maximus, jumped up ten years ago, Artabanus of Parthia was preparing war. Terentius would have been installed in Rome as his cat's paw. Officially we claim that Artabanus abandoned his war plans because Terentius was exposed as a fraud. Not so. We were lucky: the king was beset at home by the usual relatives out to knife him. He was glued to Ctesiphon.'

That said, Parthia was the great enemy. Rome lived with a dark fear that unstoppable hordes would come galloping from the Euphrates to swamp our borders and obliterate our way of life. Barbarians would pillage our national treasures, slaughter noble Romans, rape their virtuous wives, enslave their children, soak the Forum with blood, impose harsh alien gods, destroy our ancient liberty – all the while gabbling in their impenetrable languages, most of which no one in Rome spoke.

Well, we knew Greek. Rome's nervousness of Greek-speakers is intense.

'Only two things prevent the Parthian threat,' Trebianus said sombrely. 'The ceaseless in-fighting for their throne and the fact they never have a standing army. When they go to war, they rely on retainers from the nobility, which is disparate, self-serving and completely unreliable. If Parthia ever sets up a professional army to match Rome's, we are done for.'

This scenario called for a dedicated Parthia-watcher. According to Trebianus, the foreign empire in which he was so expert posed unique problems. Specialists always say that. They claim their realm of interest has singular qualities, which demand individual treatment and permit breaking rules. Anyone who is an expert in a 'unique situation' counts as extraordinary in his own eyes.

A cynic would say this is a good excuse for that expert to claim extraordinary expenses. Treasury auditors tend to disagree.

'So is it your contention,' Tiberius asked Trebianus, 'that whoever is trying to manipulate events here is in collusion with Parthia?'

'Must be.' Trebianus made an expansive gesture. With the extreme length of his skinny arms, this was impressive. 'The third False Nero clinched it. We could tell from the defiance with which the Parthians clung to him. They thought they had us.'

'It was claimed we "nearly came to war",' I said. 'If Parthia was being intransigent, what stopped it? More troubles at home for the King of Kings?'

Trebianus replied, in an arch tone, 'The talented Abascantus claims credit for extracting the pretender while keeping the peace.' Once again his contempt for the leading freedman was obvious. I wondered if Trebianus felt that, in liaising with Parthia, Abascantus had encroached on him. But surely the role of a 'watcher' is to lie low, never to engage directly?

Trebianus leaned forward to me, avidly intent. 'Someone invested a great deal in this pretender. You actually saw the latest Nero? What was he like? Was he a genuine prospect?'

'Fresh from a byre. Dung between his toes. But people believe what they want to believe.'

'You have to remember,' Trebianus brooded gloomily, 'Nero has a huge pyramid tomb on the Pincian, with a Carrara marble sarcophagus, where flowers are still left to honour him. For some he never died. Or death leaves him undiminished. Nero somehow conquers death.'

'An excuse for the Parthians, a tool for a would-be Roman king-maker? Trebianus, I still don't see,' I challenged him, 'why you have come to us.'

Trebianus squirmed. He was not a man who should wriggle like that, wrapping up his interminable limbs. If he locked himself in too tight, we might have to extract him from his own Gordian knot.

'I believe you find people, Flavia Albia,' he said.

'It has been known.'

'I want you to find someone for me.'

So there he was on my client couch, struggling to bring out his request. He was embarrassed, uncertain, anxious. How many times had a prospective client sat below my shelves of elegant vases while squirming so miserably?

I asked a crisp professional question: 'Who is lost, Trebianus? And where did they vanish? If it was in Parthia, don't even ask me.'

'One of my agents. He did go missing in Parthia – he disappeared from Ctesiphon.' I groaned. Trebianus continued excitedly: 'But he has been seen recently in Rome.'

27

My husband turned to me, smiling. 'Albia, this is for you!'

Tiberius then stood up abruptly, as he did these days. Although he said nothing to excuse himself, he left the room with the air of a man who would not return. I assumed he was in pain again. I saw him catch at the doorframe as if in one of his dizzy fits. Then he carried on and I had to set aside my anxiety.

Before I clarified the task, I set out in plain terms that Trebianus would have to pay me. I was not an informer because I hoped one day someone would award me a small temple, with my name on a plaque as a benefactress. I listed my charges, a daily rate plus a finder's fee. Trebianus assured me there was a 'Parthian fund' to cover this, but as I had with Philippus, I asked for cash up front. Interestingly, he agreed. That must be how he paid his agents.

I piled up bowls, taking them out of the room on a tray for tidiness. I told Trebianus I was fetching writing tools, so left him to mull.

Taking advantage, I used the facilities. Graecina must have cleaned the cubicle. It now looked much less like a builders' closet, which was how it had been left before our wedding. She had supplied a jug and new sponges on sticks. I could let my fussiest teenaged sister use it – though perhaps not Tiberius' octogenarian aunt. One sniff and Valeria would tremble with distaste.

I inspected the rest of my domain, making sure all the staff saw me doing it.

At the front door, Katutis was supervising a locksmith, with his snootiest Egyptian attitude. I flashed the workman a smile, for balance. He had just cut his hand with a chisel so it failed to cheer him.

The kindly teacher had gone. The two children had Dromo on a tiny stool and were testing him on Greek letters; they gleefully mixed him up over *pi*, *phi* and *psi*. Any moment now he would run away crying.

Satisfied, I returned to the anteroom.

'Right. You want to go ahead? Give me details, Trebianus.' As Tiberius had said, this was familiar work for me. Better than slogging through Philippus' task with the widows. 'First, have you in person met this missing agent?'

He nodded. 'Know him well. I prefer to assess them myself, before sending them out.'

'Name?' As he supplied answers I took notes in short-hand.

'Ritellius.'

'Age?'

'Fifty plus.'

'Raddled! I thought spies had to be athletic young men who can get out of tight corners.'

'He has some skills – well, he did have originally.'

I sensed that things might have deteriorated. 'Nationality? Rank?'

'Roman, more or less. His father was equestrian, held minor positions, had funds. Ritellius dropped down the scale. But his paternity made him educated, personable, able to trough with anyone, free to engage in trade. He was right for us.'

'What is his cover?'

'A negotiator.'

Most people assume power abroad is imposed by the Roman army. Territorial power, perhaps. The Empire's true wealth comes from the movement and sale of commodities, both luxury goods and staple foods; this is often handled by negotiators who bring together buyers and sellers, in many cases fixing prices and organising transport. These unsung men have at least as much influence as the military.

'What did he negotiate?'

'High-end furniture.'

'Io! I'd like to see his portfolio . . . Was he knowledgeable?'

'Adequate. We didn't want him spending too much time on it. An agent doesn't need to be too good at his cover. A hopeless demeanour gives him more colour. Colour is needed. I want people to think of him when they have exciting gossip. In our trade, mediocrity is death.'

'So it doesn't matter if the locals think him a drunken bum? . . . Tell me about him.'

'Past his prime, if he ever had one. Seedy. Raffish. As a man he is a disaster, given to excess, prone to trouble. He drinks, womanises, moves from one unreliable situation to another, lets people down all along his path, yet always charms his way out of it. That was what I needed from him – everybody knows him, they like him, he can go anywhere. A good agent can strike up a conversation with anyone – even if they are suspicious of him, they go along with it. Ritellius was just right. Nothing ever happened in the bazaars without him hearing.'

I distrust that kind of person. 'Someone like that sounds a little risky?'

'He was oddly efficient. He did take trouble. That was why I assigned him to Parthia. Whenever he turned in a report, it would be high quality – and even in fine hand-writing. It was the contents I liked. He prided himself on the high value I placed on his material.'

I thought of the idiot Trophimus, that morning. He under-estimated his powers of striking up conversations; I bet he could not evaluate material. When I mentioned the encounter to Trebianus, first he looked stunned, then he laughed himself silly at the thought of an attempt to subvert the clever Philippus.

'Have you heard of this fellow?'

'We receive weekly figures for arrests,' Trebianus replied. 'Trophimus frequently features. He rakes them in. Well, normally! He will be a bit light this week.'

'I spotted him as soon as he sat down . . .' I pulled the subject back: 'Talking about the people you watch, you said "even if they are suspicious" – so when you send an agent to a country like Parthia, do people understand why he is there?'

'Unless they are stupid. Any foreigner will come under scrutiny. But a good agent can bluff his way, even though everyone knows what he is doing.'

I was surprised. 'I had assumed spies worked deeply under cover.'

Trebianus nodded. 'Sometimes. Positioned in a local community, they may observe for us for years, in complete secret. If I do have anyone like that in Parthia, I won't disclose it to you, or anybody. Even Ritellius, who was on the spot, will never have known.'

'If there is a traitor on the Palatine, will *he* know about your hidden spies?'

'I bloody well hope not!'

Trebianus became aggressive in defending his undercover cells, explaining he always had to protect their identities. Otherwise, they could be tortured and killed. I calmed the conversation. 'So you have hidden sleepers but Ritellius was working for you in plain sight . . . How would you communicate?'

'Infrequently.' I waited. 'Letters through intermediaries, mostly, with the proviso that we know such messages are intercepted and read. The wording has to be oblique. Otherwise we have a system. Signals. Watchwords. Codes. Codes for me to summon my people into action, codes for them to indicate when they have vital information. Codes, very urgent codes, when they need to be brought home in a hurry – assuming Italy is home for them. Which it may not be.'

I thought again of Uncle Fulvius in Alexandria. He had travelled there like a man of exotic tastes, too scandalous for Rome; he had ensconced himself in a tall, expensive townhouse with a roof terrace, where he had stayed for years, mingling with officials, traders, senior staff at the Museum and Great Library . . . Fulvius and his partner Cassius gave the impression they were on nobody's payroll, but that was a useful front. They looked like nonconformists, with free loyalties. Private men. It made good camouflage.

'Going back to your Ritellius: you considered him a valuable agent?'

Trebianus did not hesitate. 'One of my best. Intuitive, a

184

natural. He was my protégé. I allowed him more freedom than anyone, perhaps too much for his own good.'

I could see the disadvantages. 'I guess he cost you! Pinched too much of the budget?'

His handler grunted quietly.

This Trebianus was an easy client to question. The intelligence services work as I do, so he understood the value of gathering as much information as possible, then plucking out crucial details. He listened patiently to my questions, answering each in turn without growing restless.

'How long had Ritellius been in Parthia?'

'Some years.'

'Run to seed?'

'Not especially. Disreputable enough to do his work. He looks as if he would drink the war-chest dry, then run off with the legate's wife. Worse, run off without her, leaving her pregnant and broken-hearted. She has to appeal to our officials for aid, he is permanently gone. Turns up in some other armpit of the world, starts again with a new, equally shady life.'

'His bags have been repacked quite a few times?' I smiled, because Ritellius struck me as a dirty Adonis, like half the shiftless swine my female clients hire me to track down. 'If I am to trace him, I need a description.'

Trebianus looked blank. I explained patiently I must have pictorial details to use when questioning people; then if I finally ran down Ritellius, I would want to be certain it was him.

Trebianus responded. Ritellius was tall, a figure people noticed. He was heavy-boned, usually carrying too much weight, often unshaven and dishevelled, though he could tidy up for a diplomatic reception, or to seduce a woman, even though women often took to him because they thought he needed mothering.

He had no remarkable features. That would have made my task too easy. Not a birthmark on him, no quirks, no tics, no startling habits.

'Well, a spy needs to blend in,' I grumbled. 'Even so, a limp might have been helpful. Red hair and a limp would have been perfect.'

'Ah!' Trebianus jumped. 'I forgot to mention he is gingery.'

'You are joking!'

'No. Must have originally looked like a Celt. Perhaps that was his origin. Ritellius was a redhead last time I saw him, though it was some years ago and he was losing it. He must be bald by now.'

'A lot of fair skin then! Freckles?'

Trebianus havered. He could not remember, probably never noticed in the first place. I did not bother asking again whether Ritellius had a gammy leg.

'Right. So – as to his vanishing. Exactly what happened?'

Nothing had happened. That was how Trebianus had been alerted. Normally, Ritellius posted regular reports, hoping that juicy details would lead to a financial bonus. He was always in need of money. Not long ago, Parthia had replaced their ambassador to Rome. Since Nero's extravagant bonding with Tiridates, King of Armenia, it had been customary to pretend we had a diplomatic friendship. Hospitality gave us some control. Or so we thought.

Naturally Trebianus expected his agent to respond to this personnel change by providing advance information on the incoming Parthian. Rome (Trebianus) demanded a full brief. Ritellius sent nothing. Reports completely dried up. He failed to respond to reminders. There was silence from Ctesiphon.

He might be dead, though if he had drunk himself into Hades, it should have been possible to find out. If he was hiding from creditors or angry business colleagues, there would be rumours locally. Trebianus possessed other contacts, none of whom had seen Ritellius in his customary stamping grounds; nor had they heard anything about him. If the Parthians themselves had taken against him, they would either tell Rome he had been arrested (in the hope Rome would buy him back, like a hostage) or they would kill him openly, as a cruel message. None of that had happened.

He could have fled from one of his broken-hearted women, though in that situation he normally told Trebianus where to find him next; any sudden flight for domestic reasons always left him desperate for extra cash. Silence. Too much time had passed with no plea for funds. This was no moonlit flit to avoid a private crisis.

'So, Trebianus, let's move on. You say he has been seen in Rome?'

'We are pretty certain it was him.'

'Recently?'

'Two weeks ago.'

'How come?'

'I watch Parthians wherever they are, including Rome. *Especially* here. We do not want an incident. I monitor anyone they send for diplomatic reasons – where "diplomatic" always means suspicious. Their envoy is lodged in a house we provide for him at public expense.'

'That gives Rome some access?'

'Exactly. It is made plain that travelling elsewhere in Italy

187

would be unwelcome, but the envoy is free to live here and receive diplomatic courtesies.'

'Parthians in Rome?' I queried sceptically.

'Often been done. Sometimes we deliberately took hostages, sometimes high-ranking Parthians sought refuge from strife at home. Rome has long encouraged foreign princes to live here and absorb our customs.'

I had heard as much. Then they were sent back to rule their own countries as established friends of Rome. Imperial Roman women had households full of such fosterlings. Trebianus' Parthian royalty had lived in Rome for long periods, bringing up children who had never seen their homeland.

'We have been extending hospitality ever since we covered costs for Tiridates – *that* was horrific,' Trebianus grumbled. 'Nero allowed him eight hundred thousand sesterces a day for his enormous retinue, which took nine months travelling here! Thank goodness what we cough up now is less. The current envoy also came overland – they say it is because a magus cannot cross the ocean; a Zoroastrian priest should not pollute the waters with any bodily excrescence. This one made a disgusting parade of it, camels, war elephant, the lot. Even those ghastly armoured men they call cataphracts. He now stays in a substantial property. I have a man in the house.'

'Of course you do! So your man saw Ritellius? Is he actually living with the Parthian diplomats? Did he come to Rome with them?'

'We do not believe so. They had to provide a list of retainers and associates. He was never on it.'

'Coming with the diplomats would lend new meaning to "going native"!' I commented.

Trebianus, po-faced, gave me a lesson in what 'going native' traditionally meant – adopting foreign food, ethnic customs, living with a non-Roman wife, growing a beard, liking obscure footwear . . . The point was that the dissolute man lived that way in his adopted country, not that he came home in peculiar clothes with barbarian habits.

I thanked Trebianus patiently for this helpful lecture. He looked as if he suspected satire.

'So Ritellius was spotted – once only? What did your witness think he was doing?'

'No idea. Morning visit. Difficult to eavesdrop.'

'Was Ritellius under duress?'

'No. He came of his own accord and left when he wanted to.'

'Could it have been some operation? Observing the Parthians in Rome on your behalf?'

'No, it damn well could not!' Trebianus must be tiring. He answered me grouchily. 'I can watch them in Rome myself. I have a reliable man in the house to do just that. I need Ritellius in Ctesiphon! He had no remit to come home. He is off track, gone maverick, breaking orders, risking my planned programme. I have stopped paying the bastard.'

I soothed his raving. 'By the sound of it, if you cut his cash, he'll soon reappear! All right. So when he was in Rome originally, before you sent him out as your agent, where were his haunts?'

Trebianus shook his head. 'Not something I would ever have known.'

I sighed. 'This will be tricky for me. People usually go back to places they know, visit previous contacts. If you can't say where or who, then I'm stuck. Can you at least steer me to his old friends? Surviving family? Are any of the sad women he has abandoned living in Rome?'

To my surprise, Trebianus at once said Ritellius had a wife. She was one of several he had picked up along his life's complicated path, but this was his first, his wife in Rome, who seemed to be the one who mattered – in so far as Ritellius ever displayed any nostalgia or loyalty to women. Until he disappeared, his payments from the palace were all made through that woman, who apparently viewed herself as having an unbreakable claim. She and Ritellius had remained on decent terms.

'Did they have children?'

'Not as far as I know.'

'Children might have explained them keeping in contact . . . but no. Yet he uses this wife as a conduit for funds?'

'She holds back some of the money, with his agreement. It is something we do for our agents. They are not like soldiers who are barred from marrying. We often recruit them as mature men, bound to have acquired personal baggage. If we take her man abroad for very long periods, we give a wife security in return. With Ritellius, her involvement was his choice. There seems to be a romantic attachment, even though he cannot have seen her for decades.'

'So he kept other women, had affairs, yet this one always retained her hold? She even received pin money out of what you were paying him.'

Once Ritellius vanished, his payments stopped. So she lost hers too. That cannot have pleased her. Trebianus had already sent a man to ask what she knew. Because of the terminated pay, she had seen off his messenger with a heavy cauldron.

'Straight off the cooking fire.'

I said I liked the sound of her. The cauldron did not worry me. So I made Trebianus tell me her name and where I could find her.

He then suggested that if the wife said nothing, I ought to try the new Parthian embassy, where Ritellius had been spotted. I told him to forget it. The Parthian official would think I was being sent as a sexual favour. Even before I was a new bride, seeking information in that way had held no appeal. For one thing, it never works.

'Last question, Trebianus. This is the most important. I see that, for all his faults as a man, Ritellius is a superior agent. You do not want to lose a contact of that calibre. You seem heavily exercised by his abrupt disappearance. Is he your secret love child – or what's the urgency to find him?'

Trebianus considered more of his writhing act, but under my stern gaze he controlled himself. Sitting stiff, though with his head at an awkward angle, he said, 'I had asked Ritellius to scrutinise the Parthians' support for the False Nero. I wanted him to identify our collaborator. His last message hinted he might have something to tell me.'

So there I was: looking for a man who knew the identity of the most dangerous traitor in Rome. Thank you, Trebianus!

28

The tolerant wife's name was Ilia. She was called after a famous female painter, Ilia of Cyzicus – an ancestor? Ilia the wife of Ritellius was connected to a decorative trade. She worked at a big ivory saleroom below the Palatine.

As I walked there, I mused on how Cyzicus was capital of the Hellespont in northern Asia. It was there that Minicius Italus had been holding office when he was summoned to deal with his provincial governor, Cerialis, though presumably that had no relevance to Ilia.

These Romans were a curious people. Gripped by reverence for the past, emperors would nevertheless sweep away anything that stood in their own way. Nero had remodelled the whole eastern side of the Palatine. He had buried layers of historic works, even a shrine where cult worship went back to Romulus. After hundreds of years of veneration, it was destroyed for his self-aggrandisement.

The Great Fire had obliterated most of the city centre, allowing Nero to build his Golden House. Vespasian, the modest Sabine, had given back that extravagant personal home when he filled in the lake to gift the Flavian Amphitheatre to the public. The opposite statement.

On the Palatine flank, Nero had created a marble-sheathed revetment. He cut into the hillside to allow a sweep of colossal halls and colonnades. Stuck with this, the Flavians improved it with buttressing and repairs. The rest of the Golden House remained an embarrassment. Domitian would rebuild elaborately on the heights, but Vespasian and Titus had tried to reuse space for useful purposes. So, among the grand Neronian planning at the foot of the Palatine there were a few commercial premises. One was an ivory establishment. Positioned behind a row of shops, it had the air of somewhere that might survive, centuries later, when all the imperial flummery above was fading and barbarians were taking over. Hordes from the east, say; Parthians maybe.

I had never really noticed the place. That, too, was typical of Rome. The workshop was a stone's throw from the Amphitheatre and new Arch of Titus. The proprietors did not bother to advertise. If you wanted what they sold, you would know this was the place to come. If you had never heard of them, they did not want to know you.

The business carried on its high-class trade among very superior neighbours: the Amphitheatre, the Vestals' House, the mighty Temple of Claudius, the palace looming over-head. If you looked up, you could see the revolving dining room; as it worked, you might catch the *grunch-grunch* as it slowly turned on its clay balls. There was much compe-tition: workshop noises and a constant footfall by day, before groaning carts every night, lumbering in with gigantic tusks, then carrying out awkward, delicate loads, accompanied by annoying shouts from porters and drivers. Craftsmen make poor neighbours. I saw cattle carcasses being dismembered for bone. The reek of fish glue was dreadful. Glue manu-facture was restricted to less reputable areas of the city but strong odours rose here as it was used to attach veneers.

Their products were wondrous. Primarily they built fine furniture, mainly biers to carry important corpses at rich funerals, but also domestic reading-couches and beds, beautifully decorated with ivory, sometimes also inlaid with glass enamels or amber bosses. There were many, many tripod tables with carved ivory legs. Anyone who thought himself rich and powerful would clutter up his numerous houses with scores of such tripods, whereas normal people might think themselves lucky if they owned a snail spoon.

You could buy ceiling panels or shelf ends. They offered vases in all sizes. Most expensive were chryselephantine statues of mixed materials, ivory to represent the subject's skin, with gold for hair, jewels, clothes or armour; some shone with precious or semi-precious stones. Offcuts were turned into smaller items: hairpins, needles, fan handles, combs, styli, cosmetics spoons and sweet little dolls.

At the other end of the scale, they did a large trade in much-cheaper bone. It was worked just as beautifully; when a salesman saw me browsing, he told me openly that most people could tell no difference in looks. In price, the difference was huge. Elephant ivory cost almost as much as its weight in silver but butchers' bones could be had almost for nothing.

I began by pretending to be a customer. This gave me time to acclimatise. Besides, it was tempting. Their stock made me wish I had brought a shopping list for home – though we would have to wait before we could afford most things here. However, since Trebianus was paying me now, I could not resist a box of alphabet pieces; I allowed myself to buy the smallest, cheapest bone ones. I knew Dromo would prefer dice and gaming counters, of which I saw plenty, but the letters would help me educate him. The salesman tried to sell me a waxed tablet and stylus set too, then produced a three-hole bodkin; he failed, but was not too pushy.

We settled up, then I confessed I was looking for someone. Business in Rome often involves an additional discreet enquiry. Might your uncle give me another loan? Has any of you seen my brother? He went on a bender three days ago . . . Please tell your foreman to stop dropping in on my wife when I'm not there, or so help me I'll kill him . . . Want to acquire some knocked-off fine red wine, almost qualifies as Falernian? . . .

After hearing of her hefting a cauldron at an unwanted visitor, I expected the salesman to snigger, but Ilia's reputation seemed normal. Her father ran the place, had done for many years. They were both viewed with respect. I was led to a room where craftsmen were carving ivory tablets. Among them sat a dark, middle-aged woman who must be Ilia. She was carefully engraving patterns with a fine cutter.

Shamelessly, I said she had a lovely name: was she a descendant of the famous Ilia of Cyzicus whose paintings commanded higher prices than men's? Looking up from her work, she replied no, though she had been named after her. Ilia of Rome had been allowed to learn painting and engraving, even though the men thought it unsuitable work for a woman.

Ilia claimed she was only working there at the moment because she had had an unexpected financial let-down. I admitted I knew Ritellius had vanished and the palace had cut off her funds.

As she turned more hostile, I told her who I was, who had hired me and what I wanted. She could have thrown the tablet she was engraving, then stabbed me in the eye with her carving gadget. Perhaps because I was a woman, she showed less fight than I expected. Perhaps since the first messenger upset her she had calmed down.

Her expression said it all, however. That tight pursing of

the lips and suddenly faster breathing. She was a typical Roman of the working classes. Her bone structure was good, beneath relics of a hard life that had left her skin taut, her eyes pouchy. She stared out, unafraid of anyone.

'Ritellius is not the best of husbands?' I decided I may as well be frank.

'Never was. Now he's proved he's a beast.'

'A beast! What's he done?' I asked, genuinely sympathising.

'You may well ask – and *who* has the pig done it with this time?'

'He is something of a womaniser?'

'I am his wife,' snarled Ilia. She had an impressive snarl. I tried to deconstruct how she achieved it, for future use myself. 'I was his first. I was the one he left in Rome but never let go of. I looked after his money for him. Year after year I did that. One day, he was coming home to me.'

I doubted that, but made no comment. Working with my female clients had taught me only to go so far. Instead I asked how she had met him.

'He happened to have money at the time. He had inherited from his father. A small legacy, but enough to set him up in life if he handled it well – which he was incapable of doing. He came to buy something – anything. He had never possessed cash before; he just wanted to spend for spending's sake. I was the foreman's daughter. Sweet fifteen and sassy with it. I sold him a few things, caught his eye, liked him in return, soon we were living together. He was very attractive,' boasted Ilia, needing to explain away her folly. 'Tall, strong, unmissable.'

'But he never settled down?'

'Not him. He left. By then I knew him. Only surprise was how long it took him to flit.'

'Did you ever think of travelling abroad with him?'

Ilia laughed. 'That's not for women, is it?'

Actually I disagreed. I thought of my parents – Father always homesick if he was dragged elsewhere, yet he went and generally coped with it, Mother ever keen to see new places.

'Anyway,' Ilia went on, suddenly conventional and complaisant, 'I had to bring up my daughter.'

The daughter was news. 'You and Ritellius have a child?' Trebianus had seemed to know nothing of offspring. For some, paternal responsibility might be grounding, though clearly not Ritellius. In fact, I thought all spies might do better without families, while the families would do better without them.

Ilia became angry again: '*I* had her. *He* fathered her. That was the end of his role in her life, poor darling.'

'But money came to you from the palace, didn't it? That must have helped you to live, helped you to look after your child. He arranged that. Then if you were passing funds to him,' I suggested, 'he must have always told you where he was?'

She gave a curt nod. Like all her reactions to questions on Ritellius, it was fuelled by old grievance and new bitterness. 'I gave his portion to a banker. The banker sent a letter to another, in whatever country he was living. Then he could draw on funds. Until he used up his credit – which happened pretty fast, most times.'

'He travelled extensively?'

'I guess you can't go further than Parthia. He went to other countries first, but he was one for daft projects. I thought Parthia was because I had taught him about ivory.'

That puzzled me. 'What's the connection?'

197

She liked questions where she could show her expertise. Ilia and I had a short conversation about elephants. People automatically associate them with Hannibal and Carthage, but she said the huge war elephants, those that could carry a tower full of archers on their backs, had always come from India, not Africa where the beasts are smaller. Their habitat once extended all the way through Persia, now part of Parthia.

'So, using the ivory trade as his introduction, Ritellius could get by there?'

'They have workshops like this – we don't export, nor do they send stuff this way. But the College of Ivory Dealers in the Transtiberina maintains contact. So he could vaguely call himself a trader, and do what passed for negotiating. Madness,' Ilia spat. 'You wouldn't buy a used stylus from him, despite his laughing eyes and banter. And I, more fool me, had given him the know-how. What's happened now, I did it to myself.'

'Did what to yourself, Ilia?' I asked quietly.

'I helped to put him where he met that Squilla.'

Her naming of a woman hardly came as a surprise.

If Trebianus knew of this other female involvement, he had withheld the information. That would not surprise me either. He could be testing me to see whether I dug deep enough and found her – or he, a man working among bureaucrats who all looked as though they never engaged with anything feminine, might not see the significance.

But the woman was crucial. I knew that straight away.

Squilla was blonde. 'She would be!' I commented under my breath. Ilia and I shared a snatch of disapproval.

'Have you seen her?'

'I wouldn't damage my eyes looking.'

Ilia had done her homework. It cannot have been the first time she had sized up a rival at long distance, but who knows how she had found this out? It sounded as if Ritellius was stupid enough to have told her himself. That, I thought eagerly, meant she had seen him. I bided my time, letting Ilia commit herself further.

Squilla was younger than Ilia, more carefree, less responsible, and to Ritellius much more alluring. She probably carried out vigorous acts in bed. To an ageing, foolish, rapidly decaying man, Squilla was exciting and dangerous. She had a grip on Ritellius that none of his other women after Ilia had ever achieved. Squilla was his last chance. He had met her in Ctesiphon. There, she had put up with him as long as it suited her; then one day she had taken off, like a gorgeous migrating bird. Ritellius had decided she was the love of his life. Wherever she flapped to, he must follow.

'Anyone could have told him it was stupid, but the howling fool left his work among the traders, dropped all his tasks for the government. She isn't even Parthian – but he reckons she is living with some of them here. So back he's come, slavering, whimpering after her.'

So that was why Ritellius had called on the Parthian diplomats. He had thought his girlfriend was there, living it up on silk cushions, conducting her sexual athletics for Rome's great eternal foe.

'Ilia, I take it he has visited you since he returned to Rome? He told you all this?'

'Seen him? He wouldn't dare come squirming back! Oh, no. Word just gets around in our business.'

Though she protested, from what I had heard about Ritellius a visit to his betrayed wife was horribly likely. Up until this point, she had told me the truth, but now Ilia was lying.

'So what is so wonderful about Squilla?' Her winning talents as a lover were probably what mattered, though I did not say that to the disgusted wife.

If this really had been just word getting around in the business, there were plenty of details. Squilla was a carpet merchant's widow. She had acquired money when her husband died; anyone with funding was always attractive to Ritellius. It was unclear what she really saw in him; perhaps she had mistaken him for a refuge or perhaps she liked risk.

They had run through her cash, living wildly. That was the end of joy for Ritellius. Squilla had begun cosying up to a Parthian, who gave her what she liked in life. This Parthian was an important man, who had then come to Rome.

Trying to get Ilia on my side, I assured her I had no desire to go in among the Parthians to ask about Ritellius. So I needed Ilia to give him up. Pointedly, I looked around.

'You won't find him here!'

'No.' I commented that although the place was filled with implements – lathes, drills, chisels, knives, saws, carving and smoothing styli – one item was lacking. 'So where is your famous cauldron, Ilia?' She glared. Intelligent and quick, she knew what I meant. 'I see no cooking facilities in this workshop. Yet when Trebianus sent someone to ask you what was up with your husband, you hurled a heavy pan at him so he left in a hurry.'

'Soup in his hair!' Ilia agreed. 'Lovely! I shan't have *him* crawling round again.'

'Crawling around where?' I demanded sternly.

'Where I live,' she answered, sounding feeble.

'And where is that?'

'I live with my father.'

'Oh, stop it! I'm not stupid, Ilia. Never mind your father, who else was hiding in the house? Why were you so keen to get rid of the palace's man that you wasted good soup on him?'

She shook her head mutely. She knew I had guessed.

'You didn't want the palace man to spot him. Ritellius is with you,' I said.

'Not any more!' She flashed a fast denial. 'My father kicked the bastard out. He confessed all about Squilla, so it's over. Everything's over for ever.'

'What about his daughter?' I shot in.

'She died. She died last year, having a baby. I had written and told him. The bastard hadn't even remembered we had lost her.'

Ilia squared up defiantly. Male engravers had been ignoring us, though no doubt listening in. Now they stopped work, looked up, let me know they were ready to gather around Ilia and make me leave her alone.

I had no wish to cause the woman more grief. I said I was sorry I had had to ask so many questions. I left my address, in case Ritellius reappeared. She might be prepared to pass word to me, although I felt it more likely she would continue protecting him. She was his wife, his first, his wife at home. That was how it had always been. Why would anything change now?

29

Since I was by the Palatine, I went to tell Trebianus what Ilia had said, then see what he wanted me to do.

I reached the palace via a new covered ramp that Domitian had built. This sliproad up the Palatine enabled the imperial family to come and go unseen, but was also available for visitors, at least when the Emperor was absent. You entered through a massive arch. Rising against the side of the hill, tall covered corridors turned around tight hairpin bends as they climbed in seven steep sections. The passageway was wide enough and high enough to ride on horseback, or even to drive, though the ramp was primarily designed for ceremonial entry in a carried litter.

Inside, it was cool and dark, muffling out the noisy bustle of the Forum as I climbed towards the palace above. The interior flights were sometimes dimly lit with flares, though there were high-up openings to admit natural light. Towards the top, small steps were beside the roadway, which was easier on the legs.

If Domitian had been at home, I would have run the gauntlet of guards, but he had taken the best Praetorians abroad with him. Those who remained were either past their best or too new to ask proper questions. I even persuaded these second-raters to let me use their welfare facilities, halfway up. It was only a bucket in a cubbyhole, but better than leaving them to make their own arrangements. Anyone could guess what that would mean.

One of my new friends agreed to help me find the Parthia-watcher's office. I could have asked Philippus, but I was unsure whether Trebianus wanted Philippus to know of our new work arrangement.

Yes, I had plunged myself into the dung-heap of palace politics. Among the maggoty secretariats, it was all intrigue, jealousy and backstabbing. My position was increasingly awkward. I could never be sure I trusted either Philippus or Trebianus. I was sure they did not fully trust one another. At its simplest, I was not included in their networks so they would hold back information from me.

I still knew that the traitor in government could be either of them. If so, purporting to seek a defector must be a ruse. For all I knew, Philippus had had the False Nero killed, with the poisoner, Paternus, working for him. Or maybe the collaborator was Trebianus; did his field agent, Ritellius, disappear because he had learned his own handler was in bed with Parthia?

The Praetorian and I emerged from the last ramp onto a high terrace with breath-taking views. I was escorted inside the palace via a private entrance. Pleased with himself, the inexperienced guard asked an usher the way and found the right office for me. I slipped him a thank-you coin, which he took with far too obvious gushing. He needed the Princeps Peregrinorum to lick him into shape. Titus would know how to palm bribes unnoticed.

I found Trebianus with four slaves serving him a full-table banquet. It appeared to be his normal early-afternoon activity. I wondered how someone so thin could guzzle so much yet remain flab-free. Perhaps gorging was his idea of getting into the Parthian mind, spoiling himself with excess.

He put aside his linen napkin. While the servers padded out with the salvers, he led me to a reading-couch for our discussion. I managed to snatch a small beaker of water from a passing tray. One of the slaves then took it upon himself to bring me a bowl of gingered prawns.

They still had their shells on. For me, there would be no silver fingerbowl afterwards. For the rest of the day I would be ginger-breathed and fish-smelling. But ending up sticky does not faze an informer.

The first thing Trebianus told me was that the Princeps, of whom I had been thinking just moments before, had now found the corpse of Paternus, the Castra poisoner.

'That was quick! Perhaps he knew where to look . . . Where was the body?'

'In the Tiber.'

'Surprise! We'll get nothing out of Paternus, then.'

'No, he has been silenced. Somebody is one jump ahead of us,' complained Trebianus. I pulled legs off my prawns while he settled down. 'You're right, Albia. It was inevitable. Paternus will have been bribed, but we shall never know who paid him.'

I disagreed. 'We might. Somebody set up the killing, someone handed over the bribe . . . Still, he is conveniently disposed of. We can only concentrate on things we are able to deal with.'

I tackled him about Ilia: why had Trebianus sent me to the ivory workshop without mentioning that his first messenger actually visited her at home?

Trebianus looked surprised. 'Never thought twice about it. It is true she lives with her father, has done for years, since Ritellius first left her – maybe even when they were living together as a couple. The father's house is where we always sent the money. My man must have known that – he was the one who generally took cash along. He is asking for compensation, by the way – not just for the dent in his head. The cauldron she heaved at him was full of boiling liquor. He was badly scalded.'

'Soup, I believe.' I said I was sure Trebianus would deal with that in a sympathetic manner.

I reckoned the soup-throwing had been to divert attention: Ritellius had been with Ilia. She now swore she had cast him off when he confessed his passion for the alluring Squilla, yet Trebianus should have her house searched, then watched in case Ritellius sidled back.

'Surely not, Albia!'

'More than probable,' I growled.

'But he has treated Ilia abominably.'

'So?' I had finished the prawns, and drunk the lukewarm water. For me this finished the interview. 'Use your resources to double-check what I was told by Ilia. Then, unless you can identify anyone else Ritellius still knows in Rome, I'll have to do as you said: I must get into the Parthia house to speak to Squilla.'

Trebianus began to say something but I held up a fishy hand to stop him. 'Ask your man in the house whether she is really there and anything he knows about her. I don't want to go without the best preparation possible.'

'Of course. And I shall give you a brief on the new envoy.'

'I intend to avoid him.' He nodded. 'You knew nothing of Squilla?' I demanded.

'I assumed Ritellius had a new mistress; that was his normal pattern. I never supposed this one was particularly significant . . . I did hear a murmur from a different source that he had taken up with someone sophisticated and very beautiful.'

Hmm. Squilla was one of those!

'So,' I asked coolly, 'where is the official residence?'

When Trebianus told me I nearly refused to continue. Twelve years ago I had known that house. It held bad memories for me and all my family.

'Oh, brilliant! You do know who used to live there?'

Trebianus looked evasive.

'That,' I explained calmly, 'used to be the private residence of the Emperor's chief spy.'

Trebianus said it was nowadays kept as a grace-and-favour residence to offer to visiting dignitaries. After a scandal and cover-up involving the last incumbent, the post of chief spy remained vacant. The work was covered by the Praetorian Guard and, behind the scenes, little-known agencies at the palace. I managed not to snigger. 'At least I know where to find the place.' I also knew of a back exit. With a Parthian envoy, the need to make a fast escape seemed likely. Never trust a man in silken trousers. 'It seems I have to do this for you. Though to be honest, Trebianus, I had hoped never to enter those miserable doors again.'

I said I would tackle Squilla tomorrow. It allowed more preparation time. For that house I would need back-up, though I told Trebianus I would supply my own. I knew just the person.

I left the palace.

30

I was starting to see Lesser Laurel Street as home. I entered, using my new key and hoping to slip in unobserved. As I crossed the small atrium, sweet sounds were coming from upstairs.

I was beset by Graecina, full of righteous complaint. 'As you can hear, Flavia Albia, a *musician* has imposed himself.' She spoke as if he was an uninvited drain-cleaner, some operative from local administration who claimed we were polluting the street.

'That must be the celebrity citharode, the Fabulous Stertinius. I recognise his art. He played for us and our guests at our wedding. My mother managed to secure him. Most people will be wild with jealousy that we now have him in our house, jamming for free in the master's bedroom.'

Graecina would rather have had a leg amputated. 'How long do you think this person will be staying tonight?'

It was still only late afternoon.

'As long as we can keep him,' I replied cruelly.

Graecina said Stertinius had heard about the lightning. Touched that it had happened to a man he had played for on a happy occasion, he had generously brought some fellow musicians to see whether wonderful music would help the patient. 'I was asked to keep the children quiet and Dromo occupied. Your *husband*,' said Graecina, as if mentioning my filthy gladiator lover, 'had me give those people refreshments!'

'Is it a whole theatre band? Any request from my husband should be obeyed.' I really was not helping.

I could see Galene listening in from the kitchen corridor, with a smirk. Katutis lay stretched on the dolphin bench, letting the fine Roman music sweep him into a rhapsodic trance so he could ignore all surrounding tension.

I went upstairs. On my appearance in the doorway, Stertinius and two other players burst into triumphal chords, an improvised paean of greeting. Tiberius looked happy and rested. Harp music must be consoling. I kissed my fingertips and waved them over the musicians, like a predatory social hostess congratulating herself on the grand success of her stylish salon.

They rattled off a few more numbers. I listened alongside Tiberius, holding his hand. Stertinius had brought a flautist and drummer, though the drummer pattered discreetly.

They had to go on to an evening concert, so I took them politely to the front door. I gave Stertinius profuse thanks, telling him honestly that we could never afford his normal huge fees, but any time he wanted to practise at a friendly house, it would console my husband if he came to us; we would be happy to share our humble meals with him and the others. I made sure Graecina heard me.

'You are a delightful couple.' Stertinius bowed over my hands. 'It is an honour.'

His companions never said anything, but smiled and also bowed to me. They had long hair with curious moustaches, more or less clean and combed, and wore colourful robes with dramatic sashes. Either they were foreign, or they chose to look so to give them validity as artists. They didn't need to. They all played expertly.

'No, Stertinius, the honour is ours.'

Rome is full of music and somehow we had collared the best of it. I grew up on the streets. I had lived alone for years. I felt bemused now to have such a household.

I found Dromo, who went into a long moan because Tiberius had snapped at him earlier. 'All I wanted was some money for a cake. He could have just said he hadn't got any. He yelled at me. He was horrible.'

'You have to bear with him. You know it's because of the lightning.'

Dromo kept grumbling. I sent him with a note for my cousin Marcia. She was to come with me tomorrow.

I had worked with Marcia Didia for years, whenever I needed a female aide. She made a good chaperone, watchful and fun to giggle with afterwards. She was witty, extremely bright, and at twenty-two had managed to avoid encumbering herself with a husband. This was despite stand-out good looks even among the Didius family, who all boasted of how handsome they were (often not quite as true as they thought). Her mother had been strikingly beautiful, though she had grown fat and slothful. In their home, Marcia now took the place of the parent. She was the only child of Father's dead older brother, or so her mother claimed when touching Falco for support money.

The real reason I worked with Marcia was that she could judge a situation before trouble started. If it did, she could run fast. Also, once when a drunk had tried to assault her, I had seen her punch his lights out. Knowing she was too attractive for her own safety, she had learned boxing at the gym on the Vicus Tuscus where my father did weight training.

We would be posing as respectable matrons. Even so, I did not want a wimp with me. Marcia would be ideal.

Tiberius seemed unwilling to come downstairs, so we ate supper in our room. Though soothed by the musicians, he remained very quiet. At one point, I caught him with a walnut in one hand and a nutcracker in the other, staring at the tool as if he had no idea what to do with it. It was a two-part hinged gadget I had owned for years and had come from the auction house. It was made of bronze, with crouching lions along both sides. You put your nut between the two arms, then crushed its shell between serrated teeth. The way it worked was obvious. In any case, at my old apartment, Tiberius had used it.

I gently took the nutcracker from his hand and started preparing nuts for him. I thought he might flare up at me, as earlier with Dromo. However, he accepted my intervention, seeming relieved. Frowning, he ate each walnut as I handed it to him. After a while he fed one or two to me.

Once he settled, I decided I must tackle this. For the first time, I persuaded him to talk about the lightning strike. It troubled him that he could not even remember it happening. He thought there had been a flash of blue light around him, a terrible noise in his head, an odd metallic taste. He had no recollection of falling down unconscious, or even of being brought home. The agony of the moment had been superseded by mysterious physical and psychological symptoms. Nothing was normal any more.

'I keep feeling I no longer know who I am.'

'You said yesterday *who is Faustus?*'

'Exactly. Everything seems to have changed. Whatever things were like before is all gone. It's so incomprehensible that I am lost.'

Heartbroken for him, I held him. I hid my own feelings, once more feeling isolated. I missed the man I loved. I wanted him back.

He was in pain again. I knew he was trying to wean himself off the poppy-juice. Strong-willed, he refused to be taken over by the drug. I respected that.

'I told Stertinius they could come again. Was that all right? The music seemed to help you.'

'Yes. Yes, I liked it. I seemed to be taken out of my confusion for a time.'

I had been intending to spare Tiberius anxiety over what I was doing in my work. But when he asked, I told him about today and what I had to do tomorrow. I even explained why I felt so uneasy about the house I had to visit.

'I have been there before. When Vespasian was emperor, it belonged to his chief spy, Anacrites. My family knew him. He had worked with my father. He invited us all to a Trojan Hog dinner once.'

'Not as much fun as it sounds?' Tiberius had gone on the alert. At least this was taking his mind off his pain.

'He was a bad man, hostile and dangerous. My father and Uncle Lucius were caught up in proving his involvement in terrible crimes. Cruel multiple murders, committed by his relatives, whom he sheltered – in that house – and even encouraged in their killing.'

'I never heard about this.'

'All hushed up. The security services wanted it settled without scandal.' I had never talked of these events to anyone before, but in the circle of Tiberius' arm I felt safe to discuss anything.

He spoke in a low voice, as if spies might be outside listening. 'Something happened to you at his house?' he asked.

'I talked to the man. I was a young girl, completely oblivious to danger. I even went back there, to his house all on my own, believing I could persuade him to give up secrets. Then I did get scared and ran away. Looking back, it terrifies me more, because I understand what very great danger I was risking.'

'Your parents must have been appalled.'

'They thought he seduced me.'

'Did he? Did he try?'

'It was worse than that. Much cleverer. More horrible. His aim was to make *me* want to seduce *him*.'

Tiberius kept his voice neutral. 'Did you?'

'No. But the effect was insidious. I still feel soiled from having been put in that position with him. That is what he was like. Utterly corrupting.'

'What happened to him?' asked Tiberius.

'He was executed.'

Like so many. Yet not like them, because my father and my uncle had done it.

After a time, Tiberius rasped, 'I should come with you tomorrow.'

'No, love. I cannot let you. I am taking someone else, don't worry. This is women's business.'

31

Old age must have doomed the watchdog, an incandescent brute who used to bark himself hoarse, letting you know he wanted to kill you. Behind the fierce metal gates his kennel stood empty now, though a gnarled rope remained.

The property was guarded instead by a matched pair of moustachioed guards in narrow-ankle trousers, with crossed baldrics over their shoulders. The baldrics were for show. I looked, but they seemed legal; I could see no arrows.

The guards seemed like mean cheats whose knives would fly into their hands if they were offended – but they behaved politely. Why do you think I brought Marcia? Though she was not quite so lovely as her fabulous mother, men melted when she batted her dark eyes. I was in charge of our party, but their concentration was on her. That left me free to gaze around discreetly.

Marcia and I had planned in advance to appear like girls any guards would treat well because we reminded them of their little sisters – a good plan so long as they liked their sisters. We prepared carefully. My mother had travelled almost to Parthia, to Palmyra, which is a long way east. So Marcia asked Helena, who gave us a steer that the grand dames of Palmyra wore far too many necklaces, with ranks of bangles and heavy ear-rings, topped off by neat turbans under flowing head veils.

'Party time!' Marcia gleefully relayed this news.

Spoilsport me, I said we would be decently Roman, though we could wear our best dresses. In my clothes chest I found an azure number that had barely had its hem tripped over, while Marcia came in the gown she had worn to my wedding. Graecina obligingly scrubbed the wine stains off her front while Galene sewed up my skirt.

We did keep light stoles over our heads, holding up one hand by our cheek, as Helena had instructed, as if ready to hide our faces. We had no real intention of that; this was our city where the women went bare-faced. Hiding Marcia would be a real waste, though I, of course, was a married woman. In Parthia only my husband would be allowed to look at me. As a Roman wife I would count myself lucky if he bothered.

The guards accepted us as bringing good wishes to the ladies of the house. They believed we were respectable – even though when Marcia and I were together, the tone tended to lower rapidly. We were asked to wait in an ante-room. Soon my chaperone was fizzing with pent-up mischief.

'Calm down, Marcellina. We must behave, or this will cause a big diplomatic row.'

'So who are we supposed to be?' asked Marcia. It was rather late in the escapade for clarification. 'Are you asking me to play a hired woman of the night?'

'No! We have come at mid-morning to show we have no sexual motive.'

'Where have you been, Albia? Sex in the morning is wonderful – or so people tell me!' Marcia was incorrigible. I loved her.

'We could say we are canvassing for donations to good causes, but they'll hide from beggars the same as we would. Keep it vague. Trebianus says the women here are never let out socially. The poor ducks must be screaming bored.'

'Up to us to entertain them?'

'Yes, but go easy! We'll just say it's a courtesy call.'

'Diplomacy – yuk!'

Marcia pouted. She had a round face below mad dark curls. Her neat figure was well honed by boxing practice – or whatever else she did at Glaucus' gym, where she was a big favourite. Young Glaucus, who now ran the place, was an ex-Olympic athlete, a serious, dedicated man, but that wouldn't stop Marcia being a handful.

When an attendant came for us, my cousin followed meekly while I led the way like a dour matron. We were taken to a large, over-sumptuous room. Colourful carpets on the walls, silk hangings, enough fringing and tassels for a haberdashery shop. The seating comprised long divans, their cushions plump and slithery. We dropped and lolled in the eastern fashion, rattling our jewellery.

Four big-bodied veiled women covered up with little curtain face-veils. Over the tops, they stared at us. Swathed in silks, they looked as plump and slithery as the cushions. They had been playing with a basket of grey and white kittens, which is no proper diversion for mature adults. I shot Marcia a look that said she would have to deal with the animal life. She liked cats. It was her one bad trait. Even for work, I draw the line at being spiked with claws. If one of the little demons jumped in my lap, I would fling it out of a window.

I asked the Parthian dames to unveil again since we were all female. Obligingly, they pulled aside their face screens, though long swoops of diaphanous stuff still hung from the tops of their headdresses. Now framed by those, they had handsome faces, with long straight noses. Curses. Their colouring was only slightly darker than our own. Not one was blonde. No Squilla.

Older than us on average, they must all have been striking in youth. If anything, they had layered on even more gold chains than Mother said. And beneath the so-called modesty veils they were painted up like Egyptian gods in wall frescos. I had never seen so much kohl in one room, not even in Alexandria.

We spoke Greek. They seemed as rusty as we were, but we all got by; laughing over language issues broke the ice. I talked. At that point Marcia listened. I gave them the courtesy-call excuse; they looked flattered. Saying I was an aedile's wife worked as validation. For the next few months it would be true; I might as well milk it.

They told us their names, which were all unpronounceable so we had fun with that. We said ours. They played more games, pretending these were difficult too. As I thought, they were desperate for new conversation, so when Marcia chipped in with how I came from Britain, where names were even crazier and the blue-painted people matched, that warmed up the ladies even more.

She chucked in that my new husband had been struck by lightning. That went down a hoot. 'Imagine waking up a bride, thinking your husband crackled last night but is now a permanent invalid!'

The women chuckled raucously with Marcia. I was quieter, as I tried not to believe 'permanent' was true. One, called Asxen or something that sounded like that, must have spotted my troubled mood, for she leaned over and patted my hand gently. Could it be Rome's enemy's womenfolk had kindly hearts?

As Marcia established herself as a good gossip (who would also pick up the damned kitties), I set aside my worry for Tiberius, forcing myself to join in with our plan to be entertaining. I mentioned that I had been in this house before, whispering that murderers once lived here. For bored women this must have been the best morning they had had in Rome. Pastries were rapidly sent for, as we settled in for a bout of squeals, giggles and lurid story-telling.

This was going well. I hoped a hum of excited voices, amid gales of laughter, would entice Squilla out from wherever she was hiding. It worked – though not as I wanted. She did come to see what was going on – though the idiot brought her paramour.

Perhaps she had no choice about it. He looked that kind of man.

As soon as she floated in, I knew we had found her: a piece of work with hair so pale it was barley white and apparently natural. At first glance she oozed sophistication. On closer scrutiny I defined her as what our waspish aunt Maia called 'a slut-heeled goddess'.

She wore the hair loose. It was caught on the top of her head with a couple of skilful jewelled pins, but then cascaded over her shoulders. I wanted to put it away in a tight plait. Better still, lay my hands on a pair of shears and cut it all off. I mimed harmlessness; Marcia gave me a sharp glance.

The gorgeous Squilla had a calm, regular, self-assured face that had to be accepted as true beauty. Her wide mouth naturally set in a mysterious half-smile. Squilla was tall and slender; she gleamed with near-transparent silk, beneath which were more than hints of breasts and loins. The clothes were fine, the jewels exquisite, her slut's heels in fact were cork and stacked fairly high, so she overtopped the man on whose arm she dangled.

Being a carpet merchant's widow had set her up for a lifetime of relying on the male sex. No doubt she believed she used them. She had the clothes, had learned the attitude, and passed herself off as extremely high class. She probably drank money with her breakfast. His money, of course – whoever 'he' was at the time. I knew she and Ritellius had run through all hers.

She was unveiled and I noticed the other women did not cover up. I suppose they were at home, among their own menfolk. Only strangers called for formality.

Squilla's current provider walked through the door in a gust of powerful importance. It was like a cloud of desert dust blowing in. He was no longer young; he must have been a big force in Parthia for some time. He had long dark hair peppered with grey and a full beard, all stranded in fine rows, beneath a straight-sided flat-topped headdress. His trousers had large roundels down the front from waist to ankle, from which the fine material swung in miniature swags. He had a hard body and an attitude to match. Fawning on him, Squilla either never noticed or ignored his untrustworthy eyes.

For the ambassador, she was blonde, western, entrancing. Back home in Ctesiphon she must have made an exotic trophy. When she sought him out, he cannot have believed his luck. The fact this party was abandoning a Roman spy for him must have seemed exquisite.

She had her work cut out now, however. The beauteous one had just run into competition. The couple came in with the air of having just left a well-used daybed, but as soon as he entered, the man's eyes fixed upon my cousin Marcia. It tended to happen. The good-looking, straight-backed, single-minded women of the Didius family can grab attention just by being there. All Marcia had done to catch his lecherous gaze was flick a flea off a kitten's fur.

She was less perfect than his elegant doozy, but the envoy immediately spotted that the characterful newcomer was humming with promise. He could probably guess that she might have dipped a toe in the water, more than once, but she had never found a man to interest her. I knew how that would work with him. The challenge was irresistible.

32

The Parthian envoy, a man of rank and standing, was called Dolazebol. He was the type who, on meeting a woman, lifted her hand to his wet mouth, then kissed it while gazing up in a suggestive manner. He did this to us, even though the room contained his harem, including Squilla. I kept my disgust in check. Marcia wiped the back of her hand on her skirt quite openly.

Although he must have noticed – as he was meant to – Dolazebol kept smiling. He had us trapped indoors. He had not even started with Marcia. She would learn.

I hoped we could get through what we had come for before she kicked him in the groin. How many Parthian guards could my boxing cousin send reeling before she lost the advantage of surprise? I had never liked the idea of coming here; now I was more than apprehensive. I could not have come without a chaperone, but maybe I should have picked a mousy one, for her safety.

Another man had been drawn there by the noise. He was a mighty round bundle, his huge bulk perhaps caused by disease. It had made him a wobbly pyramid of blubber on huge legs, beneath a big turban that bulged like the swollen body of an octopus. As he waddled in, he had to swing to shift from leg to leg. He might have seemed comic, but any henchman who thinks himself the equal of his superior is dangerous. He glittered with obsessive suspicion of us, and I took him very seriously beneath his rolling bluster.

As he entered, he somehow balanced on one grossed-up leg, then arced a vicious kick with the other. Behind him a big white cat had been trying to slide into the room. Had the foot made contact he would have sent the creature flying down the corridor outside. But the cat must have known him: it shot off, with a loud protest.

Though they froze, none of the Parthian ladies raised a complaint, which was telling. The man was clearly import-ant. His name was Bruzenus. He wore a torque. Coming from Britain, I saw it as a gauge of masculine inadequacy.

'Are they spies?' he demanded, in crude Greek. Sure of it, he spat, 'They are Roman spies!'

Dolazebol must have disagreed with his attitude. The two Parthian men had a short fiery exchange in a language of their own, evidently quarrelling, though it soon ended; the one in the torque made an appeasing gesture, generous enough. The other clapped him round the shoulders like an elder brother, though they looked like noblemen from different tribes. I sensed that Bruzenus chafing with rivalry was pretty routine.

I gave both men an innocent stare. 'Aren't spies meant to be narrow-eyed, hairy-chested men who single-handedly save democracy?'

'With the biggest knives and the fastest chariots. When the men are men,' Marcia chimed in, irrepressible as ever, 'and the women watch admiringly.'

'My parents knew a female spy once.' Working hard to relieve the tension, I kept my tone gossipy. I was amusing the Parthian women. 'Her name was Perella, her disguise a rather ripe Spanish dancer. She travelled the world slitting throats for the Emperor Vespasian.'

'No!' Marcia rolled her lovely eyes.

'She is still alive, I understand. She has a little grandma apartment somewhere on the Esquiline, where she dreams of her days of glory while she drinks nettle tea . . . How can you call us spies?' I shot accusingly to Dolazebol, feigning amazement that our bona-fide status could be doubted. 'We are decorous females bringing overtures of friendship to your wives. What is supposed to happen? That we shall croon of love, you will submit on the spot, then we shall prise out your secrets? Please tell your friend that's a mad idea.'

My appeal for support allowed Dolazebol to overrule his belligerent aide once more, this time in Greek for our benefit. 'These charming, intelligent ladies visiting our womenfolk cannot be engaged in espionage, my Bruzenus. What do we have here for spies, anyway? Our mission to Rome is not hidden. We are welcome visitors, guests of the state, keeping lines of communication open.' This was hypocritical from a nation that had sustained a trio of False Neros, one only last year.

'Not hidden indeed! You arrived on a camel train.' I had this from Trebianus, who said the homesick beasts of burden were now quarantined in the imperial menagerie; several keepers had already been bitten.

'I arrived on a war elephant,' Dolazebol corrected me, slightly put out that I had belittled his style. I said I heard it was very popular with the public now that we were keeping it in our zoo.

Dolazebol took it upon himself to tell me Trebianus' story that a magus might not cross the ocean. Liking the sound of his own voice, he trotted out more details of

Tiridates and his jaunt to see Nero, especially the niceties Parthia had insisted on: their prince was to suffer no signs of subjection and would refuse to surrender his sword; Tiridates had cleverly made that possible by carrying it, but nailed inside his shield. En route he was not to be denied the embrace of provincial governors, or kept waiting at their doors . . .

Letting Dolazebol drone on, I recalled my conversation with Lusia Paullina about the False Nero appealing to the governors of eastern provinces. Denying their embrace and keeping him waiting at their doors would have been a well-known signal, it appeared.

Dolazebol had also travelled to Rome in magnificent style, presumably being embraced diplomatically by governors with their teeth gritted. I returned my attention as, once again, he emphasised that his coming had been from the best of motives. *He* was not here to spy on *us*.

I responded to that, now thoroughly grave: 'Do not under-estimate the Roman psyche. I, too, have observed them as an outsider. They are very straight, an open people. Collecting intelligence by undercover means is, for them, an unRoman activity.'

Unacceptable behaviour had never stopped Rome – but, faced with lying men in silken trews, I felt free to dramatise.

Dolazebol pompously agreed. 'Indeed. Julius Caesar had ample intelligence of the plot to assassinate him – but he brushed it aside.'

He was pontificating on our own history, yet I smiled. 'Very foolish!' Things were different now. If an Artemidorus today handed Domitian a list of plotters' names, those names would be on memorial plaques by evening.

The sidekick, Bruzenus, said something short, in a harsh

Parthian language. Dolazebol answered, a couple of words telling him to shut up. There is a theory that it's a good start to set your opponents arguing with each other, but I never favoured it. The air was thick with aggression; I wanted calmness and acceptance. But I made a note of them bickering.

The Parthian women, by now our allies, joined in with open protest. Bruzenus snapped back, aiming his anger at one in particular, Asxen. She must have been his wife. That was her misfortune, but she bore it with spirit, firing off abuse. You wouldn't have wanted her telling you to take off your outdoor shoes in the house.

As the white cat scratched at the door, Squilla fetched it in. It seemed to be hers. Marcia made room, gesturing for Squilla to come on the cushions beside her, with the big cat in her arms. This at least meant Dolazebol could not snuggle next to Marcia. Heads together, the two women made much of the indignant cat, which was called Vindobona for some reason. Its white fur was thick, with a lion-like mane cascading over its front. Squilla told Marcia it was a gift from Dolazebol, the white cats of Ancyra in Galatia being more highly prized than the similar greys found in Parthia.

She stretched and flexed her arm, where several bangles jostled, one of them exquisitely carved ivory. I wondered whose gifts they had been. The carved one could have been from Ritellius, whose wife was an artist in ivory. To a man, giving Ilia's work to another woman would not seem a betrayal. Many lack sentimentality – at least when they are three thousand miles from home, and home is where the wife resides.

Squilla relayed various tales of Vindobona's cuteness: how

he was once put in front of a cornered mouse but fled; how he liked to sit on the top of doors to survey what he considered his realm, then jump off on people; how he was sick in a tribune's toga; the precious vases he had knocked over and destroyed . . . I concealed my boredom. We had to make friends with Squilla. Her light, sweet voice rose and fell while I sank my teeth into a date pastry.

The white cat Vindobona stared at me as if he knew I was a dog-lover.

'Ladies!' cried the envoy eagerly. 'What entertainment can we give you? Food? Drink? Acrobats? Poetry? *Music?* In Parthia we are extremely devoted to music.' Was that why they liked Nero-pretenders?

Music it was. Distractions would give him his best chance of assailing Marcia. As we waited for instruments to be brought and melodies chosen, Dolazebol eyed up Marcia while I, too, was considering manoeuvres: somehow I had to corral Squilla outside this room, to talk to her privately. That cascade of hair, pallid as oats in goat's milk, made her very visible. Wherever she went people knew she was there. If she left, everyone would notice.

She and the paramour were knotted too tightly for me. He had slid in beside her, the other side from Marcia, slowly stroking Squilla, as if she was his own pet white cat. It made me queasy.

Having taken it upon ourselves to visit, we could hardly decline hospitality. The food and drink were tasty, the music easy on the ear. Drinks came in pure gold rhytons, horn-shaped cups that must have been fabulously expensive; I sipped very cautiously but the contents tasted mainly of honey. I noticed that, even in this intimate gathering,

Dolazebol's titbits were routinely sampled by a food-taster. I tipped my cup, showing I had seen it. 'How sensible, sir. You wouldn't want to go to bed after a hot garlicky broth, and be found in the morning poisoned!'

He smiled vaguely as if my true meaning was lost on him. I wondered. Was he aware the third False Nero had died only yesterday, after eating broth? I felt he knew all about it; my Roman side came to the fore, full of indignation on behalf of the not-Nero.

Musicians had been brought from Parthia; they gave us pleasant, rhythmic tunes on a variety of stringed instruments, long flutes and small pattering drums. Their presence made me assess how many retainers of various types the envoy possessed. The chief spy's house was an old republican-era mansion, built atrium-style with a peristyle garden, but it had plenty of rooms in side wings where a large retinue could be housed.

I watched how things worked domestically. The servers, guards and food-taster, the maids who slipped in to fan or titivate the women, were all the Parthians' own. But I knew Trebianus had his man here. Where was he? What did he do? I guessed Rome provided the house with a skeleton staff who had to be accepted by the incomers. This was a glorified five-star mansion for overseas dignitaries, but Rome's planted cache of slaves would closely observe its occupants. Their true purpose must have been obvious.

Vindobona had tangled his claws in Squilla's hair cascade. As he struggled in panic Marcia hastened to the rescue of both, the whites of their hair almost indistinguishable as she painfully freed Vindobona and Squilla from each other. The Parthian envoy leaned in to put Squilla's locks into place again, with more disquieting stroking movements.

Squilla tipped back her head like an animal that enjoyed petting.

Dolazebol had seen my indifference to the white cat. Across Squilla and Marcia, he winked conspiratorially. We exchanged chit-chat. Learning my love of dogs, he clapped his hands. Not long afterwards a servant brought in a matched pair of tall-shouldered, extremely elegant hounds. The two had long silky fur that must have been a nightmare to groom (more retainers the Parthians had brought here: dog-handlers). Creamy gold, with black faces and dark tips to their fringed ear fur, the lovely hounds had incongruously thin tails that curled into rings at the tip.

The Parthian women squealed and slapped a lid on their kittens' basket, while Squilla clasped Vindobona to her shoulder. The two dogs were hunters.

'My sighthounds!' Dolazebol confirmed. Yes, this excellent pair were showing interest in the cat; I could imagine them taking off after it . . . 'They are friendly, Flavia Albia. You may stroke them if they are interested, although they choose for themselves whether they wish it. Come, Tazi!'

One dog stepped fastidiously up to him. The other came to me of its own accord, putting the top of its soft head against my hand and nudging. I stroked between its ears.

'Ah!' their master exclaimed, as the dog and I bonded. 'I wish we had puppies. I would present you with one, Flavia Albia.'

Beware Parthians bearing gifts . . .

I shook my head. I had no time to exercise such fast-moving creatures, no wish to be beset by neighbours whose little pets they murdered. If ever I was to own a dog, it would need to be much less obtrusive than these. I could hardly conduct discreet surveillance in some Roman street

227

with a long-coated mountain-leopard-hunter drawing all eyes. 'Dolazebol, you are kind, but these are not for me. I am more of a scruffy-mongrel girl.'

He pretended amazement. 'Yet you are married to an aedile!' Did he know that because he had eavesdropped the conversation when Marcia and I had first arrived – or had someone else told him about me?

I laughed. 'My man is somewhat unusual.' Since we had been on the subject of gifts, I added, 'Manlius Faustus is an organiser for the Roman Games. If you like, I can ask whether he can obtain good tickets for you.' Special seats are made available for important foreigners; I felt safe taking it upon myself to suggest it.

The idea went down well. It was unusual for me to have such a tempting bribe to offer. How strangely my life had changed.

The musicians had been playing and singing, but now they took a break. To stop the dogs making the white cat and kittens restless, the aristocratic pair of hounds were fed titbits ceremonially then led out. Vindobona preened. Triumph is so unattractive.

A hiatus was useful. 'You and your dear ladies have been very gracious, Dolazebol, but I must go home to check on my poor husband. As you may have heard, he had a too-close encounter with a thunderbolt.'

Amid cries of alarm on the invalid's behalf, the roomful of strangers went into fervent well-wishing, as if they were all our cousins. But after fake pleas for us to stay longer, the Parthians agreed to let us go. They were tiring of us as much as we were tired of them.

We had achieved too little. I fell back on the usual ploy:

I asked to use the facilities. This enabled me to say that I already knew how to find them. Since I had been a guest in the house before, I wondered if on our way out they would allow me to show my cousin the interesting public rooms . . .

33

Marcia jumped up and, like any girlfriend, said she would join me on the toilet expedition. She urged her new crony Squilla to come on the room tour, saying she had heard there was once a rather naughty art collection here.

True. Anacrites had shown me part of it, until the erotic content had hardened me against him. It made an excuse to lure Squilla, so I did not say that after the chief spy's death his pornography was sent for sale; I knew, because it was disposed of through our family auction house.

With many goodbyes and pledges of eternal friendship, we extracted ourselves from the silken salon.

'I wonder who has the rude statues?' Marcia burbled, pulling Squilla along with us, as we headed for the lavatory. I led us across the interior courtyard garden; this was virtually unchanged since I was last there, though perhaps a jasmine on a trellis was more neatly trimmed.

I was heading for a corridor near the kitchen. As if he had heard unusual Roman voices, a polite man in a brown tunic appeared. With a napkin over one elbow and a serving tray under his other arm, he asked if we needed directions. There was braid around the tunic neck. He spoke in Latin, not quite meekly enough.

I brushed him off, saying we could find our way and

needed no one's help to pee, so he retreated. I left Marcia in the colonnade with Squilla while I went first. I wanted to get comfortable. I could trust my cousin to whisper to the lush-haired *femme fatale* that I needed to speak to her.

But when I came out, Squilla had gone. Marcia shook her head. 'As soon as I broached your missing man Ritellius, Blondie blanked me and backed off.'

Squilla had done more. She had gone straight to Bruzenus to reveal our true motive in visiting. He was shouting orders. I know an arrest command when I hear it.

'Scram, coz! This way!'

Grabbing Marcia's hand, I hauled her down a narrow corridor in the service section that led to a back door. I had once escaped that way in Anacrites' time. Whether the exit would be open was an unknown. If locked, we would be stuck in a dead end. Behind us a commotion confirmed we were being hunted.

We rushed down, noises coming closer. From the colonnade behind, the guards would see us. Would Parthians risk chasing Roman women out into the Forum? I preferred not to test it.

A door opened. The man in brown blocked our path. 'In!'

We had no choice. We jumped into the room he indicated, falling over each other. He stayed in the corridor. When the door closed behind us, the swine locked it.

Since we were now prisoners in what seemed to be his bedroom, Marcia went over to his neat bed, where she sat down and began tidying her hair. Few things perturbed that girl.

'Getting ready for when he comes back?'

'He seemed nice,' she answered, smirking.

Interesting, anyway. When I applied my ear to the locked door, I could hear the man telling Bruzenus and the guards that no one had come that way. Given his Latin, his support for us was not entirely a surprise. 'I think we are safe. Temporarily. He has popped us out of harm's way.'

'I can always spot potential,' Marcia retorted.

'No, I think what you spotted was the official Roman spy.'

'Ooh, thrills!'

'Shush.'

The man in brown volunteered to help the Parthians look for us, though did not reveal our hiding place. I heard muffled sounds of searching through the other rooms nearby; at one point someone tried our door, rattling the handle briefly. I looked around for a weapon. Even Marcia paused in her hair-combing. But Brown Tunic's voice said something; the room was not broken into.

After a while all noises died away. We were left on our own, waiting.

34

'Is this how you always work, Albia? Find out nothing at all for your case, then end up stuck in trouble?'

It had been known.

I asked Marcia what she had said to alarm Squilla. She claimed that all she had done was ask if it was true Ritellius had come visiting. 'I just told her we needed to know his whereabouts.'

That was how I would have broached it myself. It was the only way to tackle it, so I had no complaint. 'Fine. Judging by what we saw of her relationship with Dolazebol, an ex-lover barging in demanding to see her will have been hideous. It must have nearly wrecked her position as his love-conquest. I don't imagine the other women would support her – she is the loathed intruder.'

'That one knows ways to smooth things over,' sneered Marcia.

I shook my head. 'They're a bad fit. She drools over her awful cat; he is a dog-lover.'

'He *gave* her the cat, Albia. And did you *see* her silver ear-rings? Outsize!'

'She'll develop holey lobes . . . He is a monster. Manipulative. He wanted to give me a valuable puppy. How was I supposed to explain that to my darling new husband? He showers presents around to buy people. I bet most are tempted.'

'He's a fool, then.' Marcia remained good-humoured. 'He wouldn't need to bribe you with a pricey hunting hound. All he had to do was pick up the mangiest, ugliest stray from the next street corner.'

'Turnips. I cannot be bought.'

'One sad-faced mutt . . . Pushover!'

I was silent, wondering if Dolazebol had ever loaded gifts on the third False Nero. And what riches had he, or his master the King of Kings, promised to our home-grown Palatine treasonist?

Marcia and I gazed around Brown Tunic's small, rather plain room. It was painted all over in fresco red, done years before. Previous occupants had knocked hell out of the surface.

He had left us there; what we did in his room was his lookout: with one accord, we wedged a chair against the door, then started to inspect his private possessions.

Trebianus' man was not a slave. He kept his room too clean and sweet.

He travelled light. If this was the only place he lived, he owned very little. I had been married to an ex-soldier; I recognised the way things were organised. Foldables folded. Packables packed away.

The furniture looked as if it came with the house; there were no homely touches. The best piece was a marble-topped wine-table he was using as a nightstand. I bet he had pinched it from one of the good rooms. On it he kept a redware beaker, a folding knife with an antler-horn handle, a strigil. All typical, though good quality.

The bed was basic. I said nothing to Marcia, but I feared it had been used years before by Anacrites' henchmen. I could never have slept in that bed. But Brown Tunic would not know its sordid history.

There were no under-the-pillow letters to him from lovers, male or female, and no half-finished duty letters from him home to Mother.

His boots were excellent, the leather oiled and the feet kept in shape with stuffing. A spare tunic, in a different brown from the one we had seen him wearing, was hung up with a pole through the armholes so it kept its shape. But in a nearly-empty chest we found another. Tucked out of sight, this was good woollen material, in white with gold edging.

'Palace livery! That absolutely clinches it. Your lover is the man Trebianus planted.'

'He is not my lover, yet,' Marcia answered demurely.

'How were you so sure he had "potential"? He was gone in a flash. I barely saw enough to recognise him.'

Marcia gave me a sickly smile. I raised one eyebrow.

Marcia listed: 'Medium height. Good build. Nice legs but such a shame about that limp.' What limp? I never noticed – and I had once lived with a man with a damaged leg. 'Brown hair, curly. Straight teeth, clean nails, strong hands, nice eyes. I liked his voice.'

'You rascal. You took a full inventory!'

'Certain items remain untested. You wanted me to take notes.'

'I wasn't thinking of male assets. Not Parthian?'

We agreed that. 'Never. Home-bred.'

'Well, that's good,' I commended Marcia coolly. 'I'm not telling Falco his most treasured niece is sleeping with the enemy. Even one with a romantic limp.'

There was another small table, from which we had taken

the chair to wedge the door. On it were note tablets. We opened the tablets and read them all. In firm, readable handwriting the man had started memos to himself. Recipes, shopping lists, to-do items of maintenance – Trebianus had him here as a steward.

He wrote fluently. He could even spell.

When Brown Tunic returned, he unlocked his door so quietly he might have intended we would not know he was coming. If he hoped to overhear anything indiscreet, he failed. Instinct, that great tool, had warned us when to call a halt to our merry banter and remove the chair. Marcia and I were sitting side by side upon his bed, as if we had been there quietly the whole time. We were as close as two podded peas – caused by the sagging mattress. Our expressions were as innocent as if we had never looked under that mattress for anything hidden.

Even so, he glanced around, quickly checking. He saw no disturbance to any of his property. We were too good for that.

Closing the door gently behind him, he laid a finger to his lips, warning us to speak quietly.

'You took your time,' I whispered.

'Lulling their suspicions.'

In answer to his querying look, I murmured introductions: 'Flavia Albia, Marcia Didia. And you?'

'Corellius.'

'Don't let's muck about, Corellius. You are under cover for the Palatine?'

He assented with a nod. 'And you?' he threw back at me neatly.

'The same. Trebianus sent us.'

He tutted. 'How come he sanctioned this? The man must be flipping. You could jeopardise everything we have set up. Now I want you out.' Irritably he acted as if we were invaders on his turf – and he thought we were idiots. No doubt because we were women, he viewed us as amateurs.

'Bruzenus suspects you are still in the building. He has men on watch. With luck, by now they are growing bored . . .' He took a cloak from a hook on the back of the door. 'Come along, I really need to move you. At the end of this corridor there is a street door. When I tell you, follow me quickly and silently. I am going to take you down to the door, which I shall open for us. Once outside, immediately turn left and start walking with me. If we are pursued, I'll tell you what to do. We need to put a safe distance between us and here. Obey my orders. Please,' he added, although we understood the danger and neither of us showed any sign of arguing.

35

Corellius seemed sure of what he was about, but he had frightened us. Our hearts pounded; we were too jumpy for safety. Still, we followed his orders and did not give ourselves away.

While he was re-locking his bedroom, Marcia and I scuttled down the passage. As soon as he unbarred the street door, we slipped out. No time for relief: we were still too close for comfort. The three of us made off quickly. I noticed Corellius had the limp Marcia had mentioned, though it seemed not to hamper him.

He steered us around the side of the house, then away. There was no pursuit.

I let him choose a place to talk. Most people would have gone into a bar. He whipped along the Forum to the Shrine of Juturna. This sacred spring, where in legend Castor and Pollux had once been seen letting their horses drink after a battle, is famed for its wholesome water. Coming from a family in which everyone believes the best cure for anything is wine, or at my wedding over-drinking it, I could see Marcia having second thoughts. Now Corellius was a drag.

Ignoring the newer basin, we moved around to the more sheltered area behind. There we stood beneath the very tall entrance to Juturna's ancient shrine, with its two slender columns and elegant pediment. This was a quiet, private nook, mainly out of sight from the Forum.

'You locked us in!' Marcia accused the steward in a cold voice. She treated them rough. Those who responded well stood a chance with her; wimps were discarded.

'I saved you, I'd say.' Corellius defended himself calmly. 'Excuse me, but I never leave my room unlocked. I am there to watch them; I do not let them check up on me.'

'You are acting as their housekeeper?' I was determined to appear professional. Who knew what my mad cousin was after? I hoped he never twigged that we had searched his things. 'Is this only to watch Dolazebol, or have you been there longer?'

'Five years. Stewarding is my speciality. I organise refurbishments to match foreign tastes, change locks, mend shutters and supervise the other staff – general man-of-all-work.'

'Folding tablecloths? You could make someone a wonderful husband!' Marcia had warmed to him again.

'I am unmarried.' Corellius confirmed he was available.

She smiled, knowing she had a nice smile. Corellius unbent enough to smile back.

'What caused your limp?' the brazen girl demanded.

'Fell off a horse, rolled on me. Put an end to my career, scouting for the army. Unfair – but in a while I learned: adapt or die. In a strange way, the routine of folding tablecloths saved my sanity. So!' Corellius took the initiative. I was annoyed, but hid it. 'What exactly were you two doing today?'

Pulling together the shreds of my dignity, I said we went to the house for Trebianus, though I myself had felt doubtful all along. We wanted to ask Squilla about Ritellius, since Squilla was the only person who might pinpoint his whereabouts.

'What is so urgent about him?' asked Corellius.

I decided to be open: 'Trebianus believes he knows the identity of a palace mole.'

Intriguingly, Corellius received this as if potential betrayal was not unheard of. 'Is this a new mole, or the ones we have had digging tunnels under the security fence for decades?'

'It's thought this one colludes with Parthia. Ritellius was asked to sniff him out at the Ctesiphon end—'

'That went pear-shaped?'

'Ritellius did a disappearing act. Now the palace moguls have learned he returned to Rome, potentially bearing information, though he seems to have turned renegade. He ceased all contact. His wife here refused to co-operate; she claims to have kicked him out – though we don't buy the story. Have you ever come across Ritellius?'

'He is something of a legend.' Corellius balanced respect for a good agent against what I thought was more dubious admiration. 'He was a generation ahead of me. We never met. Well, not until he caused such trouble at the Parthia house that it became my task to eject him.'

Folding his arms, he described what had happened that day. Ritellius had knocked at the door, asking to see Squilla. Normally no male, a stranger and a foreigner, would ever be admitted uninvited. I myself had got in with Marcia only because we looked like respectable women, bringing good-will.

'But Squilla is not Parthian?' I suggested. 'Do eastern restrictions apply to her?'

Corellius looked disapproving. 'She makes her own rules. Her having a maverick caller will not have seemed too odd. The guards assumed Rome is her home town. They let

Ritellius convince them he was some old friend from way back, maybe even a relative, and that he had visitation rights.'

He was allowed inside, but Squilla had refused to see him.

'If she wants to keep Dolazebol,' Corellius said, 'she had no choice. At least it was clear she had not invited Ritellius to come. A visit from a father or brother might just have been acceptable, but if Dolazebol ever thought she was engaging with a lover, even an ex-lover, the Parthian would kill her.'

'So what happened?'

Drunk or sober (it was impossible to tell which), Ritellius grew agitated. He was a big man, throwing his weight about, as he shouted for Squilla to appear and talk to him. This was unacceptable behaviour in any private house, let alone an eastern residence that contained close-confined women.

'I bet the women were thrilled,' said Marcia.

I thought Corellius was taken with her, but he fixed his attention firmly on the Pool of Juturna. The well-head was a fine round marble structure installed by one Marcus Barbatius Pollio, who, I noticed with peculiar pleasure, had been a curule aedile.

'Ritellius,' said Corellius, 'began fighting the Parthian guards. I heard the racket so I weighed in, thinking I could speak Latin to calm him. He was too crazy or too wine-soaked to be a real problem. I pinned his arms behind his back, then frogmarched him through the gates. For some time he continued raving out in the street; the guards threw stones and chucked buckets of water, so in the end he wandered off. Wet through. Still shouting.'

I could see Marcia sizing up how strong Corellius must

be to have tackled a raving intruder. Any moment now they would be exchanging gymnasium details.

'What happened afterwards?' I asked. 'Between Squilla and Dolazebol? How has she managed to keep in with him?'

Corellius looked serious. 'There was a bad quarrel but he kept it private. He locked her away in a room with him; when she emerged, she was bruised all over.'

'It doesn't show,' Marcia commented.

'Two weeks ago,' I said. Trebianus had told me.

Corellius looked dour. 'She manages to disguise a beating.'

'Risk of her trade,' I told him. 'I imagine it wasn't her first experience.'

Corellius looked surprised. 'Trade? You see her as a professional?'

'Don't you?'

'If so, I do not envy her life. When the room was cleared next morning, my staff found hanks of that gorgeous hair pulled out. Even so, the Parthian must have taken her to bed again that same night; I imagine it was rough. But next day they were billing and cooing just as usual.'

'How do the other women react to her?' I asked.

'Loathe her, but never intervene. I assume they feel whenever he is with the foreign whore he will not bother them. Bruzenus has a go at him about her, but Bruzenus is jealous of Dolazebol's position generally.'

'Where does Squilla come from?' Marcia asked. 'Her cat is called Vindobona — is it significant?'

Our informant nodded. 'Home town. She came out of Pannonia. Vindobona is one of the big legionary forts on the Danube frontier; Domitian is in the area at the moment. I served there, so I asked her. She was cagey about her

242

past, but I gathered enough. There are civilian settlements, but it is restless country under constant threat of war, so a girl with hope for a better life might slip away with a passing trader. Then, being passed from hand to hand, she could easily end up far from home – and Squilla pitched up in Parthia.'

Marcia whistled. 'Pannonia! Can it be that the white-blonde hair is actually genuine?' she asked me snidely.

I smiled it away, refusing to be jealous of a Celt, however fair-haired and willowy. 'So, Corellius, you sometimes get to talk to her? Can you ask our question? Does she know where Ritellius is in Rome? In fact,' I said, 'I am surprised Trebianus never put this request to you.'

'That could be,' replied Corellius drily, 'because Trebianus is the Parthia-watcher. I am attached to Philippus. Any instructions for me would have to come from him.'

Oh, spit. Palace politics again. Corellius did not elaborate but I could see his rule was to choose one master and stick to him. It was the only way to negotiate secretariat touchi-ness. Ultimately, apart from the traitor, all the upper-echelon freedmen wanted the security of Rome, but only to preserve their own positions. It never helped them collaborate. Their staff had to negotiate their tireless ambition and jealousy. Now so did I.

Marcia suggested that, since the answer was needed for state safety, maybe Corellius could ask the question for *us*? We were neutral. Corellius, who had a po-faced stubborn-ness, said that would depend on whether he could see Squilla alone. But if a chance arose, he would.

I then asked whether he had noticed any questionable communication between the Parthians and palace freedmen. 'Anything clandestine? Anything out of the usual?'

'Yes. Philippus whispered there may be a problem.'

'Seen anything?'

'Only normal courtesies. Philippus came down to formally welcome Dolazebol as an attaché. He is their official contact. The Parthians must know who Trebianus is, but he keeps away.'

'Abascantus?' I asked.

'Flavius Abascantus, no.' Well, I had had to ask. 'If the envoys are holding hands with someone outside the accepted conventions,' Corellius responded dourly, 'they are never going to do it where they will be seen. They know they are watched. It is my job to notice any connections they make in Rome, any at all. Mind, the Parthians are skilled at stopping me.'

I put it to him politely that at this stage he need not clear with Philippus any actions he might take for Trebianus. I spoke the language: if anything came out of his intervention with Squilla, we could ensure retrospectively that lines of communication were not compromised between the rival palace specialisms.

'Very elegant gobbledegook!' exclaimed Corellius, finally redeemed by humour. 'You don't want to snaggle any lines!'

I did not give a merman's conch for palace sensitivities – I simply required somebody to turn up an address for Ritellius, so I could claim my fee.

We made an arrangement. I was to send a messenger that afternoon. Corellius unbent and now seemed confident he could obtain a private word with Squilla, and soon. Marcia volunteered herself as go-between but I refused to let her near the house again. I would send a different cousin, a male one.

'You know a boy in our family you can trust?' scoffed Marcia. 'Who is this – Postumus?' Postumus was my eleven-year-old brother. I wouldn't trust him even if he was asleep.

'Marius. He's a philosopher and a flautist so on both counts he is sensible, yet he's terminally short of cash.' I gave him bits of extra work; he was reliable. He could certainly be trusted not to bat his eyes at Corellius.

Marius would ask for the steward in person, saying he had come about the night-soil cart. The aesthetic Marius would love this disguise; he had a dry sense of humour. Lavatory matters were guaranteed to make anybody else who opened the door opt out and run for their supervisor.

'Will you send notes in invisible ink?' teased Marcia. Only to her, smooched Corellius – a spy's chat-up line. At least he did not sink to 'How was Mount Olympus when you left it, Venus?'

Yes, I have had that one tried on me.

Of course, a man whose notion of a good meeting-place was the Pool of Juturna would never make cheesy advances. Luckily for him, he could rely on Marcia Didia to do it.

Marcia was probably still hoping for 'Dreamboat, if I follow you home, will you keep me as your pet?' but he left us with a prim salute and walked back with his near-unnoticeable limp towards the chief spy's house. My cousin and I bought flatbreads from a Forum hawker, then we, too, went our separate ways.

The streets throbbed with midday heat. People washed to and fro along the Sacred Way and Via Nova, like a contaminated tide. In the foaming crud of the Roman crowd, someone could well have been watching us. I gazed at their tense, self-obsessed faces, but saw only the usual Forum occupants: businessmen, slaves, idlers, temple acolytes, women who were past their prime hoping to encounter their lovers 'by accident', pickpockets sidling up behind bemused tourists, the occasional morose poet looking as if a sharp stone in his sandal was giving him gyp, lawyers.

High above, on the Palatine, the secretariats awaited the return of their emperor with fear, based on old knowledge of his whims. Domitian would be back among us any day. In the lofty marble corridors suspicion – of him, of the public, of their colleagues – would redouble. Normal bureaucratic rivalry would become more vicious, inter-secretariat intrigue much more intense. If there really was a traitor among them, the Emperor's return would bring new urgency to any plots that man was hatching. The return could be the moment his plotting fully flared into life.

Out of respect for decent public service, I had tossed a copper into the well-head of Marcus Barbatius Pollio. Then I walked home to my own aedile.

36

Marius was a couple of years younger than me. I felt a special bond with him because he was among the few people I had known back in Londinium, before Falco and Helena had brought me to Rome. His mother, Aunt Maia, had been travelling with my parents; Petronius Longus, then about to become his stepfather, had been there too. It was a moment of transition for both Marius and me. We spoke of it sometimes, when no one else was listening. We treated that family upheaval as a shared trauma.

On the long journey from Britain to Italy, Marius, at the time aged about what my brother Postumus was now, had taken it upon himself to teach me Roman history. I bore him no grudge. He had flogged through from the Seven Kings as far as the Battle of Trasimene before good nature got the better of him. He had let it rest, but we still sometimes croaked '*Numa Pompilius!*' then went off into giggles while other people stared at us.

Numa had what Marius and I still regarded as a quaint relationship with a very pale water nymph. Egeria 'communicated Law to him'; that was their story. Even for myth, it was shaky.

Marius was now twenty-five. His build must have come from his birth father, a vet who had looked after the horses for one of the chariot factions; Marius was short and stocky.

He had also inherited implements that could be used for horrible purposes. Every time I had a female client whose husband needed castrating, I wondered whether to borrow them.

He was blessed with his mother's attractive features, which worked better on him than on his brother or his two sisters. He always had a dog at his heels, which was another way we bonded.

When this intellectual boy, an oddity among the Didii, announced he wanted to be a philosopher, Maia and Petro went through the usual dramatic stages of trying to dissuade him. Philosophy was equated with political subversion; there were imperial purges. After everything failed, even threats to sell him into slavery, they wisely caved in; however, they insisted he took up a paying trade as well, something suitable to help him survive if he was expelled from Rome.

So Marius, who was an unusually practical philosopher, had learned the flute. He reasoned it was light to carry if he went on the run. I knew he harboured a romantic vision of playing his music around a campfire for a raggledy group of passionate fellow activists. So far, political exile had not happened.

I had no idea which branch of philosophy he followed because he said it was too dangerous to talk about. It is possible that Marius did not know either.

Marius lived in a one-room eyrie, much like my office at Fountain Court, though higher and smaller and even more ghastly. This was a deliberate choice. He wanted to suffer, to elevate his mind above the physical. His mother worried, his stepfather made bad jokes about the dangers of the neighbourhood, but Marius managed. He had skills. He could make friends with beggars, stay cheerful even if it rained, darn holes in his tunic.

Despite the tunic-maintenance, he looked unusual. It was part of his image as a thinker, an image he cultivated to the point of not cutting his hair (though on his mother's orders he had to wash it, so long as he wanted to come home for family dinners). Sometimes our Marius spent more time and effort on how he appeared to the world than on actually thinking about what the earth and a man's place thereupon should be. He wore battered sandals (it had taken hours of work to make them sufficiently distressed), an ankle-length robe that he tripped over, and what passed for a long Greek beard. When he remembered, he carried a full-length knobby staff. It was better if he forgot, because leaning on it made him walk lopsidedly. His beard was the big problem. All beards risk being dire, but his was the Aventine's worst.

You may think me wrong to entrust an intelligence mission to someone so unusual. Surely a spy's messenger needs to be invisible. My thinking was: people would assume no one who stood out like Marius could possibly be spying.

Besides, he was always a joy to work with and he needed my small payment. My other male cousins were either working or idiots. As an informer, I had to take what I could get.

Summoned by Marcia, who was good-natured about him replacing her, Cousin Marius duly arrived at my house. For a short while he played to Tiberius, though with less good effect than the Fabulous Stertinius. Marius was a competent musician, who had played for our wedding procession, but as a competent philosopher, too, his mind

constantly wandered off into fundamental problems of existence. Then the flute wavered.

Before I gave him instructions, I quizzed him. Was civic
loyalty a concept he could follow? Checking on Marius was
especially important since Falco, as head of our family, had
decreed that Domitian was a paranoid despot, so any of
us who helped dethrone him could claim a safe passage to
the province of their choosing plus a paid refuge for life.
'Marius, I can't have you deciding all rulers are monarchs,
all monarchs are tyrants, so you will side with the unknown
man who is betraying Rome with Parthia.'

'They have rulers too. A King of Kings or, if there is a
dispute, two simultaneously. Are they then each called King
of Half the Kings, I wonder? Currently Pacorus the Second
and Artabanus the Third, I believe . . . So what's my position?
All Parthians are warlike; all warlords are anti-democratic; I
am a man of peace and democracy,' Marius solemnetised.
He could talk his way out of anything. For a passionate intellectual, he could even look like an honest man while talking.

However, as one of the Didii, he often did not bother to
look honest.

The Greek robe was no use for a night-soil operative. I
put him into one of Dromo's tunics, which made both
of them complain. 'Shut up, Marius, you need to stink
for this.' The tunic was too short but his sturdy knees
looked workmanlike. Marius insisted on taking his flute;
I agreed waste-management contractors could have an
artistic side.

I went to wave him off, only to see outside an enormous
palanquin, swathed in red and gold, variously pronged and
tasselled, with moustached bearers fore and aft, giving away

whom it must contain. It had stopped by our front doors. One of the bearers was making enquiries of our building foreman. Larcius gave him a sarcastic run-around on principle, because he looked foreign.

I whisked Marius quickly out of sight, sending him out through the side door and the builders' yard. He thought that a highly exciting start. I watched him go, dog at his heels, like Orion. Despite having two ethereal jobs, he walked off on his errand like a true heir of Romulus: pacey, athletic, aware of what was happening in each corner of his vision. Nobody jumped the Didii unless the Didii were drunk. Often, not even then.

I ordered Graecina to tell the new callers that I had not yet returned home. This left an interesting confrontation between my husband, who had been placed under an invalid's lap rug, and Dolazebol: the wan-faced aedile versus the devious Parthian envoy. Since Tiberius had been dealing with my family over arrangements for our wedding, he handled this well. After discussing costs with Falco, Tiberius Manlius could duck and dive.

Apparently, Dolazebol wanted to assure himself that Marcia and I had not skipped off from his house in such a hurry because we had been accidentally offended. To my husband's clear amusement (I was listening from outside), the Parthian managed to beg confirmation that he could have tickets for the Roman Games. Then he slyly asked if Tiberius knew the delightful Marcia Didia's home address – just so he could personally check whether she was offended.

Tiberius truly did not know that Marcia and her mother Marina lived in the ludicrously named Street of Honour and Virtue. He could say only that he would pass on the

visitor's concerns. He sounded like a protective male relative – as if he had just checked in the Twelve Tables of
Roman Law what penalties might be exacted for looking
too hard at an unmarried woman.

Tiberius carried on the hypocrisy, claiming both his wife
and her cousin were reasonable women, Roman women
who would never notice any unintentional lapses in etiquette
– 'Of which I am sure there were none, sir.'

Implied: there had better not have been.

Dolazebol retreated into politics. He gave the honourable
Faustus a more detailed lecture on Parthian intentions than
he had deigned to give me, a woman. Parthia, he said, had
never been the aggressor with Rome, but always sought
peaceful coexistence. Rome, however, had for generations
followed the lust for gold and the wish to make Parthia
submit its sovereignty, invading or interfering ceaselessly.
Rome insulted the Parthians and tried to bully them.

He cited examples. After the great defeat at Carrhae,
then later Mark Antony's ignominious retreat, the Emperor
Augustus had persuaded Parthia to return captured standards. To do this, Augustus had carried off the king's son,
a shameful piece of hostage-taking and blackmail. More
bad behaviour included Rome sending a slave-girl, Musa,
who lured King Phraates into marrying her, learning to
love her, raising her to be his queen – after which this low-
grade female agent poisoned the king who had valued her
so highly so her son could inherit ahead of older heirs. A
dire example, Dolazebol asserted, of Rome constantly trying
to control Parthia and its client kingdom Armenia.

Tiberius listened courteously. When he did interject, he
agreed that Rome found it difficult to tolerate another empire
as large and powerful as its own, right on its borders. History

had shown that invading Parthia was so difficult logistically that any Parthian fears were groundless. Parthian client kingdoms, and even disgruntled relatives of Parthian rulers, constantly appealed to Rome for support and Rome would always offer a safe refuge to those in distress. But, Tiberius asked wryly, did that excuse Parthia's very recent liaisons with Decebalus, the aggressive King of Dacia, while he was making war on us? Not to mention Parthia harbouring False Neros?

Dolazebol ignored these accusations, maintaining that he had come to Rome solely to further diplomatic ties.

I was startled by how firmly Tiberius crushed him: 'You mean, now that Domitian has subdued Pannonia and negotiated peace with Dacia, he no longer has targets on our other borders – so you are afraid Parthia will be next?'

Parthia, restated Dolazebol, wanted peaceful co-existence.

Rome, agreed Tiberius Manlius, only wanted the same.

Circular arguments were tiring for him. I arranged a rescue. Graecina went in with a dose of medicine, taking it upon herself to shoo away the Parthian. For once we were grateful for her interference.

When Tiberius was alone with me, he gave his verdict.

'Very colourful! But all steel. Under the exotic dress, the moral platitudes and the whimsical pleas there lurks a shrewd, hard man. I wasn't fooled by his artless requests for seats at the Games. He understands our conventions. He knows what you were up to at his house. He came here to assess what you have taken from the incident.'

'He believed he was playing you?' I wondered.

'I think he knew I saw through him. Clearly he has realised you, too, are someone with whom he needs to be extremely careful.'

'I don't want him in our house again, Tiberius.'

'Well, you invaded his! But no. I was glad to have inspected the man for myself, but if he turns up again let us both be unavailable.' Tiberius then asked, cautiously since he knew how I regarded instructions concerning my work, 'Will you accept a request from me not to visit that house again, Albia?'

For once I nodded easily.

Much more welcome that day was another visit from Stertinius. The citharode turned up with his fellow musicians almost as the Parthian left. We were slightly surprised that his first remark was to ask whether he had spotted Dolazebol going off in his sensational palanquin. Apparently Stertinius knew him, from playing a home concert for the envoy and his household.

His fees for private recitals were stupendous, I knew. Still, the Parthians lived in the height of luxury: silken carpets, golden cups, expensive animals, a high-class mistress . . . They would want the best, also want Rome to see and hear them having it.

Besides, Parthians were dedicated music-lovers.

37

When Marius returned he was still walking proud, though looked as if he knew his message would depress me: Corellius had spoken to Squilla. He had found a chance while Dolazebol was out of the house annoying Tiberius.

Squilla told Corellius that until her old lover Ritellius had turned up causing trouble, she had been unaware he had travelled back to Rome. She had not spoken to him that day. She could not risk jeopardising Dolazebol's trust. So she knew nothing of where Ritellius might now be living. She wanted us to stop asking, and leave her alone.

'Is that all, Marius?'

'Afraid it is.' His dark brown eyes looked soulful. He was teasing. 'Oh, I nearly forgot something!'

'I thought so!'

'I wonder if it's important.'

'Don't mess about.'

Marius grinned. Like all my father's family, he had a corking grin. It had come at birth, with the knowledge of precisely how to use it, especially when talking to women.

'Spill, Marius.'

'We had a chat. Seeing my flute, Corellius said if I was any good, which I assured him I am, and if I own a presentable tunic, which thank Jupiter I do, he will wiggle me in to play for the Parthians. They are always needing diversions. If I look cute and innocent, they are bound to relax their guard. People do so with hirelings. I may over-hear something. Besides, I could do with the money.'

'Well, please don't let on you are related to Marcia and me. I don't want the Parthians to feel bombarded with my whole family . . . Did the house steward ask for your gorgeous cousin's address?'

'No.' Another grin. 'But he did suggest that after I play, he and I should go for a drink . . . To make a party of it, I may like to bring our Marcia.'

'He wants to show her how to fold dinner napkins . . . Code!' I explained, allowing for a philosopher being slow on the uptake.

Marius winced. He was too poor to have much of a love life. He had not progressed much further with girls than 'Am I dead? Because I seem to be in Elysium.' He would then go on to tell them that for a philosopher this raised knotty issues about whether there was an afterlife. As a girl's eyes started to glaze, he would sweetly add that he hoped there was (an afterlife), so she could permanently be in his . . .

He claimed this technique worked. I fear it sometimes did. Girls will fall for anything.

After he had dressed again in his own clothes, I made sure Galene fed him. Then, while she grumbled about the number of lost souls I was encouraging, he twiddled on his flute to flatter her cooking, practised his Didius smile on her, then took his leave.

Graecina, jealous that I was sitting in the kitchen with Galene, then came to mention a letter. As it was addressed to me, she had given it to Tiberius. 'You'd better hope it's not from one of my lovers!' I snorted.

I saw Katutis, the exemplary secretary, watching with a derisive smile. I wagged a finger to call him over, because if someone had written to me formally it might require a formal answer.

The note was from the palace – from Philippus, not Trebianus. Even before I knew the contents, I wondered if after Dolazebol had left our house he had taken himself over to the Palatine to complain of harassment.

Tiberius handed the letter to me unopened, though I knew he expected me to read it in his company, then tell him what it was about. We had no secrets. Well, none he knew of. In any case, I could see he was bored to tears and longing for something he could apply brains to.

It was short. Polite but clear. It thanked me for my services, stating baldly that nothing more was required. I read it aloud. We all pulled faces. 'Oh, glory! It's the big hands-off.'

I asked Katutis for his professional opinion. He composed correspondence as well as taking down dictation. When we had found him in Alexandria – where he had latched onto us – he was in the faded long tunic worn by most of the population there, demanding attention like the kind of street beggar you desperately try to shake off. He had kept popping up, clinging like a crazy barnacle, until he had done a good turn, which compelled my father to employ him. Only then did it transpire he was educated, a trained scribe.

Katutis bowed, acknowledging my courtesy in asking, though not too grateful. Now he lived in Rome he affected hauteur. He had come to this madhouse from a more ancient, more sophisticated society and must endure our upstart ways nobly. He managed. He knew that with Falco and Helena he had landed himself in the softest of swansdown options.

'Flavia Albia, we can assume they have written, rather

257

than speaking, in order to avoid awkward confrontation.'

'They think I shall argue.'

'I think so too! Interpreting the words, these compliments to your skill really mean *even though you have caused us a severe headache by your intervention this morning,* while the elegant thank-you intimates *so now cease meddling before you get us into any more trouble.*'

I looked at Tiberius. 'Darling? Warning me off almost suggests it is Philippus who is hand in hand with the Parthians.'

He shook his head. 'Too crude. No, if Dolazebol has complained, they must respond. Telling him they have terminated your contract is a way to keep him quiet. I imagine Philippus is merely assigned as an official minder. Abascantus is far too lofty, so he has passed day-to-day liaison – fielding complaints – to someone he sees as more junior.'

'Philippus may still be unaware Trebianus commissioned me . . . Should I contact him for different instructions?' I wondered.

'If you ask, then he will feel obliged to hand you the official line,' Tiberius answered. 'If you don't ask, well . . .' Nothing coloured his voice; he left decisions to me.

'He can say he assumed I obeyed Philippus. But if I am willing to go on, he can leave me to run . . .'

'So will you ignore the letter-writers, Flavia Albia?' Katutis asked, clearly relishing this.

I pulled a face.

Tiberius Manlius, my dear husband, allowed himself to smile. For me, he had as much subtlety, not to mention as much delight in strong women, as anyone from Alexandria – or even the Didii with their wicked charm. Personally, I thought him a match even for a bunch of Parthian envoys.

I had been married only for five days. I was still in love.

I took his hand gently. This confirmed what I was going to do. He must trust me and not worry.

Having an inquiry aborted was common in our business. My father even liked this stage. It usually proved we had strayed too near important evidence. Someone was agitated. Someone needed to prevent us going further before we tipped the embarrassing truth out into the open.

If I made no move to contact Trebianus, I gained some leeway, though there was a snag. Trebianus might have to stop paying me. Philippus and Abascantus might find out and force him to. Unfunded, that would be the end of us paying the fresco painter, not to mention the baker, fish-monger, greengrocer, cheese and cold meat suppliers, doctor, housekeeper and – assuming there was one for this house – night-soil collector. I made a note to have Graecina check whether we were drained by a working sewer, a crucial point.

I could give the task one more day, I decided. (That old delusion.) It was, after all, a question of right and wrong. The safety and good of our empire, our city, our people, even possibly our emperor – though on the whole I discounted him.

I reassessed my position. I could no longer rely on the bureaucrats for support. Assistance was officially withdrawn. I needed to call on my own resources.

In my years as an informer I had gathered contacts. I was already using my family. If you are wise, you also assemble a collection of possibles, people you know, or people you have heard of, who occupy some special pos-ition or have specialist knowledge. These are people you may never contact – but who exist in your subconscious for future consideration.

The aim of my task, both for Philippus and Trebianus, had been to pinpoint a traitor. I wanted to discover more about the current freedmen who worked on the Palatine. I would ask someone who had no vested interest now, but who had worked for the palace in the past. I had mentioned her to Marcia. She worked under disguise as a dancer but was a professional assassin, once secretly used by both the old chief spy Anacrites and by Claudius Laeta, father to Philippus.

She might tell me to get lost but she might help, if I asked her the right way. So I would go to see Perella.

38

Perella had been stupendous with her tambourine and foot-stamping. She had good facial lines, which she emphasised by drawing back her hair severely, as Spanish dancers do until they suddenly let it out and swirl their shining locks around as part of their act. When she let me into her tiny apartment on the Esquiline Hill, she still stood erect and moved gracefully, yet she was slow. Her dancing career must have wreaked havoc physically.

I would have liked Perella's opinion on Squilla's long-legged floaty walk. I could guess what she might say of Squilla generally. No woman who builds a career on hard work and talent will ever compliment a much younger one who uses the shallow gift of her looks.

Perella sat me down and moved around, gathering the paraphernalia of hospitality. I guessed this was to give her time, a chance to assess me. Assessment could work both ways. I watched her putting together a tray and cups, patiently waiting until she was ready to talk.

We had met once before, when I was just a girl. She had come to pick Falco's brains as to why Anacrites had disappeared. It was so top secret that Falco never told her. So between Perella and my family any habit of sharing information had limits. That would guide me now.

My parents and various uncles had last seen Perella at

work in southern Britain, dancing and acting as an imperial agent. It was the year they had found me in Londinium. They all still spoke with awe of how she performed: a woman who looked like a grandmother, using her body with enough art to surpass any pretty youngster. Her beautiful movements, her spiritual intensity, her experience had quite silenced a barful of hard-drinking tribal trash and gnarly traders who had travelled the world and thought themselves too canny to be impressed by anything.

My relatives also spoke of brutal deaths. Perella often used a slim knife to cut throats. It was a bloody way to die, but she was quick and silent. She would stake out her victim; move in for the assassination; disappear. In the panic after a horrible corpse was discovered, few people ever realised who had done the deed. If, rarely, a manhunt occurred, she outwitted pursuit. An escape route was always set up in advance.

In her apartment now, she kept a singing bird in a cage as her companion. She fed it with the delicate movements of a practised performer, finger and thumb tips together, wrist angled gracefully. She called the bird Fido, for Faithful.

'It can't avoid being faithful when it's behind bars!' I commented.

'Always a good system.' Perella cackled. She handed me a cup of something sweet, not wine. I tasted herbs and hoped they were not poisonous. 'You have a man? Keep him shackled, girl.'

The weather gods had done that for me, but I smiled, then plunged into business. 'Perella, I'd call you a clever woman – yet you worked for Anacrites?' I made it a question, exploring her old motives.

'That bastard. I worked *against* him too. I gave your father clues, that time when the spy was under investigation. Soon after, Anacrites was mysteriously no longer with us. Was it true, Flavia Albia, he took a short drop into Hades via a manhole?'

'I never knew.' I was lying. Possibly Perella saw it but she did not press me. 'So who became your employer afterwards, Perella?'

She moved, easing her aches. She flexed her hands, almost unconsciously. She stretched out one hand at a time, transferring her juice tot between them. 'I always answered to myself.'

'But freedmen on the Palatine commissioned you. They paid your expenses.' My parents had met her in Spain as well as Britain; I guessed she had travelled to other places. None of it would have been cheap.

She sniffed. 'I was the best. They could trust me to do whatever was needed – with no follow-on. If they wanted information, I found it. Could be, no one ever knew their secrets had been passed on. And when I fixed up a disposal, there was no scandal.'

'Given your lurid methods, that was remarkable!'

'Nothing ever pinned on me. Never pinned on my so-called employers either, therefore. The lofty freedmen liked that.'

I was starting to warm to her. 'So what did *you* think of *them*, your lofty employers?'

'The same as you would!' I was Falco's daughter. Perella decided she knew my opinions. She chortled, but was bitterly disparaging. 'Incompetent, idiotic, backbiting male bunch of noodles.'

'Yes, I recognise the description! The mighty freedmen of the Emperor's cabinet . . . Falco and Helena thought you wanted Anacrites' job.'

Perella tossed back her tot of liquor. 'I certainly did. I should have had it. I was better than him, better than any of them.'

'That's Rome, Perella.'

'It's madness.'

'It makes sense to them. You are a woman. They will never give a woman an imperial post, never have a woman in liaison with the Praetorians.' In theory the head of security gave the Praetorian Guards orders, though that stroppy unit perhaps saw it another way.

'More fool them.' She still sounded bitter. Perella's old eyes, watery but still shrewd, gazed at me. I was probably a blur, but she knew how to pretend. 'Since they never tried it, they will never know how wrong they were.'

'After working for Vespasian, who could stand working for Domitian?'

'I could! It's the job that counts. And if Domitian wants to be safe, he can rely on me.'

Not brave enough to tell her she was now too old, I tried to ingratiate myself, saying that I understood. 'For a skilled operator like you to be despatched on stupid missions by an inefficient clown like Anacrites must have hurt.' I was quoting my father. Falco viewed Perella as utterly efficient and so dangerous he would never turn his back on her. As an agent, he admired her. He thought her skills were wasted on Anacrites.

I knew there were times when Anacrites had tried to eliminate Father, his long-standing rival. Whether he used Perella in those schemes was unclear; I suspect not. Pa would be dead. As assassins go, Perella was as good as she claimed.

I wanted to explore her use of 'backbiting'. 'What did you mean by it?'

'At each other's throats.' She knew about throats. She had slit enough of them. 'Always yearning to be top man. Intrigue and betrayal all through the marble corridors.'

'Falco speaks of Laeta and Anacrites as bitter rivals. Is the new generation feuding in the same way?'

'I don't know the new ones.' That was the problem with young high-fliers, like Philippus and the suspect Abascantus: old stagers like Perella simply had not met them, had no experience of them or their methods. There was nothing for me to prise out. Nevertheless, Perella said frankly, 'I don't need to meet the bastards. They are all the same. Jostling and back-stabbing. Don't trust any of them. Every man of them is out for himself, Albia. Every one will treat you badly to get what *he* wants.'

'I hear you.' I decided to be frank. 'Have you heard of Abascantus?'

'The name is familiar.'

'Young, said to be talented, inordinately wealthy, supremely confident.'

'Sounds a true bastard!' There was a moment of silence, then Perella told me, 'Pushy wife. Older woman, brought him money. Making a position for herself by setting him up as petitions king . . .' So she did know him. It was no surprise. Despite her disclaimers, I reckoned she monitored the current complement, as she continued to brood over the supposed injustice done to her. Suddenly she leaned forwards. 'So what do *you* want, Albia? What have you come for?'

'Just a visit, in honour of old times.'

'Don't insult me!'

What did I want? To pick her brains about anyone who could be the traitor. I thought the fact she had retired might make this easier; she might be more neutral, more trust-worthy, than back when she was nursing ambitions of her own. Now she had no paymasters, I hoped she might open up, glad she could still make a contribution.

I told her the truth. 'Someone has gone bad. Possibly Abascantus. There is a security council—'

'Oh, that's new. The Emperor had his advisers, old pals of his own, but we never had a formal committee looking at intelligence. Still, life was easy. Nobody wanted to put daggers into the Emperor, not when it was Vespasian. In any case, he was a tough old bird. He simply didn't care.'

'I need background. I can't interview them.'

'Well, you could ask!' Perella scoffed. '*Are you betraying Rome? Oh, yes, that's me* . . . You sure it's some turncoat up on the Hill?'

'Knowledge and opportunity. No one else would carry the clout to mix it with Parthia.'

'*Parthia!*'

'Did you ever go there, Perella?'

'Too far. Too many questions asked if I did, too few ways of escaping. And if this is a Parthian tangle, I assume you don't want to take a camel-train yourself to look from that end?'

'I do not!' I agreed. 'No, the best I can do is ask the Parthia-watchers here. One of the freedmen specialises – I think he is straight. There is a rogue agent, back from Ctesiphon, but he ducked underground.'

'Who's that?' Perella demanded sharply.

I told her Ritellius, though if she knew him she made no comment. 'Another man was implicated in a death at the Castra Peregrina – but he turned up drowned in the Tiber.'

'Surprise! I never liked death by water. Sometimes the

cold shock revives them and they swim away . . . Who was drowned?'

'Man called Paternus. I never met him.'

'Me neither. Why was he bumped off?'

'Get him quietly out of the way. He had killed someone at the Castra. Poison. His paymaster must then have wiped him out to ensure his silence.'

'Who was killed?'

'A prisoner.'

'What's new? . . . Oh, I see – you cannot tell me.' She was sharp. She knew how they worked. 'Now, I wonder which naughty little captive that might have been? You knew?'

'I knew.'

'Will it ever get out?'

'Never.'

'Juicy! So this Paternus was employed by your traitor?'

'Apparently.'

I decided to ask what she thought about the Castra Peregrina. It had existed in Perella's time, though under Vespasian it had never impinged on her work. However, mentioning the commander, Nearly-Nine-Gongs, drew a raucous reaction. 'The Princeps Peregrinorum? Oh, Momus knows *him*!'

Momus was another of the old spying fraternity. My father sometimes spoke of him and winced. 'I know the name, Perella. Need I talk to Momus?'

'Only if you are extremely brave!' Perella roared. 'I'd tell you his mind has gone – but that sad lump decayed years ago. He always was a brainless blotch; the palace only used him because he was a vicious brute who could handle anything foul. If it smelt or leaked, or it involved rot, grot and slime, Momus was their man.'

I shuddered. 'So what did he do?'

Even Perella pulled a face. 'If you didn't just want someone dead, you wanted them to die after endless pain and suffering, then Momus had a concession for supplying slaves to the mines. Prisoners disappeared without the cost and trouble of a trial. They were safely gone, and would be enduring misery for years. The rest of us just counted ourselves lucky that mildewed old Momus was there to fix that, so we didn't have to do it.'

'You disapprove?' I asked, smiling.

'I was more subtle.'

Really? I could have quibbled: was it 'subtle' to take victims by surprise, without a legal hearing, then garrotte them and leave them where their loved ones would come across the corpse?

'Finesse. Ask your father.'

'Falco would not want anyone to suffer prolonged agony.'

Perella laughed harshly. 'You think?'

I tried not to feel disconcerted. 'So,' I persisted, 'where shall I find this Momus?'

She looked me up and down. Kindness, barely faked, crept over her features. 'Better not. Falco would have something to say if I let you; Helena would kill me. I'll go. Momus still lurks on the Palatine. I can ask if he has heard whispers.'

I told her how to contact me and thanked her for listening. Perella replied that she was glad to hear news, even if it was news that nothing had changed among those insanitary, scheming turds of freedmen, the men who had taken the lovely job that should have been hers.

39

Twilight.

All over the Empire the long pools in elegant gardens were attracting midges, bats, swallows and swifts. In the narrow streets of cities, adulterers and burglars sneaked along beneath unlit overhangs or dawdled in doorways awaiting their moment. Tired children mithered – including the two who belonged to Graecina; I left her to deal with them. I had already calmed Dromo, who had muddled up his box of alphabet letters, and Galene, who had become upset when my mother had visited Tiberius and reminded her cook she was only there on loan. Helena needed her back. At home, my siblings were fretting because they were tired of Father's sardine barbecues, while he was restless at having to come home every evening, constantly remembering to bring fresh sardines, even if he had found something really interesting to keep him out . . . Katutis went home with Mother. He left a message that my house was too noisy.

Twilight. Not so noisy now. With supper done, it ought to be a time for lovers, even if he was reading and she was pondering her recent long days with their complicated conversations, and no obvious way forward. But along with the midges, twilight brought out the spies.

★   ★   ★

The arrival of Trebianus was, to some extent, welcome. Tiberius and I had been sitting together, although we were sitting in silence. Everyone else had found other things to do somewhere else in the house. Tiberius had ventured to say he thought I was working too hard. Staying out too long. Coming home exhausted.

I had other views on that, so a deep silence had occurred. He was now reading Pliny's *Natural History*, which I had given to him. The volume he had was only the Table of Contents, a dry list. Ostentatious reading was merely to make a point. Reading my gift showed he was decent, tolerant, and unfairly hard done by at the hands of his wife.

If he chose to be unhappy, I would not stop him.

It was all because of the lightning, I knew that, really. He wanted me present, to cling to when he felt confused, yet he had himself agreed to me doing my work. Behaving illogically was part of his illness.

Eventually he could not help softening enough to read something out loud. Since I was still being snooty I let him rattle on: 'You may be interested in this.' I might, though I did not encourage him. 'When I get Book Six, apparently it will contain "sites, races, seas, towns, harbours, mountains, rivers, dimensions, present and past populations of Pontus, Paphlagonia, Cappadocia, region of Themiscyra and its races, Heniochi, Colic region and races, Achaean races, other races in the same area, Cimmerian Bosphorus, Maeotis and adjacent races" – I am coming to the good bit . . .' I managed not to let my face express *about time!* 'Listen, "Lesser Armenia, Greater Armenia, River Cyrus, River Araxes, Albania, Iberia and adjoining Gates of Caucasia, Black Sea Islands, races towards the Scythian Ocean, Caspian and Hyrcanian Sea, Adiabene, Media, Caspian

Gates, races round Hyrcanian Sea, Scythian races, regions towards the Eastern Sea, China, India (Ganges, Indus), Taprobane, Arians and adjoining races, voyages to India, Carmania, Persian Gulf, *Parthian kingdoms.*'

'That is interesting,' I said.

To receive Book Six, he would have to stay married to me for six years; if this was what he liked to read aloud after dinner, we might never get there. Astute as he was, he kept pretending not to notice what I was thinking.

'"Mesopotamia, Tigris, Arabia, Gulf of Red Sea, Troglodyte country, Ethiopia, Islands of Ethiopian Sea. The Fortunate Islands. Totals: 1195 towns; 576 races, 115 famous rivers, 38 famous mountains, 108 islands, 95 extinct towns and races; 2214 facts and investigations and observations." That will be useful to you, Albiola. Eventually.'

Since he had used the diminutive, I softened myself. 'Thank you, darling.'

It was not complete cessation of war. I hoped to finish working for the freedmen long before I gave him the right volume and he reached this useful information. So, just possibly, Tiberius Manlius was being sarcastic about Book Six. Me too, in saying thank you.

After a moment he added, 'His authorities are Marcus Agrippa, Marcus Varro, Varro of Atax, Alfius Nepos, Hyginus, Lucius Vetus, Pomponius Mela, Domitius Corbulo, Licinius Mucianus, Claudius Caesar, Arruntius, Sebosus, Fabricius Tuscus, Titus Livy Junior, Seneca, Nigidius and about twice as many foreigners, all of whom I've never heard of. Presumably your spies have a copy of Book Six, permanently unrolled on a desk.'

'Sounds better than relying on a maverick merchant to sniff around the bazaars.' However, the long-winded recital had shown the awkwardness of discovering information.

'At least,' Tiberius suggested, now more conciliatory, 'the agent Ritellius did physically go outside the Empire. What can someone like Seneca have genuinely known of the 576 foreign races?'

'The encyclopaedist may have consulted other people,' I said. 'He's just too snobbish to say so. My father carried out an undercover survey of Nabataea for Vespasian, but I bet Falco isn't credited as a source.'

'At least this suggests things about Parthia,' Tiberius said. 'Not only are its territories immense, the Parthians deal with peoples we have never even heard of. Settled or nomad, it is another world. We see them as slippery merely because our rules and social systems are not theirs. Rome cannot tolerate such a large power butting up against its borders, yet in fairness Parthia must feel the same. Even if we conquered them one day, we shall never have the resources to control what we might gain. I doubt whether we *can* gain anything except on a temporary basis. The losses involved in war have always been untenable.'

Going back to what he had suggested to Dolazebol that afternoon, I asked Tiberius if he believed that Parthia really would be Domitian's next military goal. Until he came home, who could know? But perhaps that made his return to Rome a significant moment in Parthian eyes.

We were still discussing this when we heard knocking. We broke off our conversation. A distraction would be welcome. For once, Dromo rolled off his mattress to let in our visitors, who turned out to be the lanky Trebianus, bringing Rubrius.

Since Rubrius was supposed to work with Philippus, I frankly asked why. Trebianus said Philippus was fully aware of what I had been doing, and that the two were here together tonight. Philippus could not actively sanction it, or join in, because Abascantus had vetoed further contact. Rubrius had come instead.

'So it is Abascantus who wants me to stop my work?'

'It was Abascantus Dolazebol went to with a complaint.'

'Then Abascantus made Philippus write to me?'

'Philippus is your handler, as far as Abascantus knows.'

Nobody 'handled' me. But if Trebianus would still cough up fees, I would not haggle over definitions.

Dromo brought lamps. I had heard Graecina telling him he should know he had to do this, then he answered back. Nevertheless, lamps appeared. He even set them a short distance away, to stop dive-bombing insects landing on us.

Our guests might have expected refreshments. Then they should not have disturbed a husband and wife who were having an argument. Neither Tiberius nor I would summon any; Dromo was determined not to have the idea; Galene and Graecina were pointedly holding back, each hoping the other would land in trouble for not doing it.

Sensing an atmosphere, Trebianus weighed in quickly. From someone who appeared unworldly, was he really a clever spy, able to pick up clues? I wondered. He said Rubrius had been watching the home of Ilia, wife of Ritellius, in case the missing agent returned there.

Rubrius took up the story. 'There was a bar within spitting distance, but too obvious, so I positioned myself in a barber's chair. It's my preference for surveillance. Along came Ritellius – I have met him, so I knew. He acted as a trained man ought. Walked casually past, taking a surreptitious look at the house. I saw him discreetly inspect the bar for planted observers. Under my warm towel I was less conspicuous so I'm sure he never saw me.'

'Did he not know Ilia would be at work?'

'He might have meant to go in and wait. Her aged father was at home. We believe there is no love lost between the two men, though who knows? It never arose, though. Something must have spooked Ritellius, because he should have come back on the other side of the street and knocked – but he never showed.'

'So he did see you?' asked Tiberius, in a mood to fling reproof.

'I doubt it.'

'He saw someone else?' I asked, equally scathing.

Rubrius and Trebianus raised their eyebrows.

'Juno, boys!' I did not hold back. 'There are so many intriguers at the palace, it's no surprise if other people were looking for Ritellius. Your traitor, for one. It could even be the Parthians – Dolazebol may want to beat him up for mooning after Squilla. He won't hold back because of diplomatic niceties.' They were looking crushed, but I sailed on: 'I wish I'd been in that street. I bet it was as packed with observers as fleas on a rat's bum. You could have all sat down in the bar together and bought each other drinks – while you were waiting for nothing to happen.'

Trebianus answered mildly. All agents used by the palace knew each other. If ever their missions overlapped, any spares would back off.

Knew each other? I said I bet the famous collaborator kept one or two unknown specials hidden up his fancy tunic sleeve. Trebianus and Rubrius exchanged nervous glances.

Tussling with Tiberius earlier had fired me up but, just

274

in time, someone else arrived. After Dromo grumbled about having to let in yet another person, we were joined by Fuscus, the quiet man with a menacing air who also worked on the Palatine.

Tiberius shot me a wry glance at the way our house was being used as a clandestine meeting place. Suddenly he and I were back on good terms. I smiled at him ruefully.

Fuscus brought an emergency message. 'Philippus was night watchman, so he received the tablet and had it decoded. It's genuine, the cypher Ritellius uses for you, Trebianus.'

'What does he want?'

'He wants to come in – or at least he wants a meeting to discuss it. But he will only talk to you.'

'Of course,' said Trebianus. 'That's what I would expect.' Trebianus then had a decisive moment. His tall figure straightened up. 'When and where?'

'Tonight,' stated Fuscus. He had an impassive way of passing on intelligence. 'The Greek Library at the Temple of Apollo. Both of you will arrive alone. He did not specify unarmed, because he knows that won't happen. Any minders must stay at a distance, preferably visible.'

'All ready?'

'Yes, I have set it up as a safe incident space, with a sanitary cordon.'

I asked what that meant; Fuscus said, without a flicker, that he had sent a team of men with buckets who were pretending to clean pillars. They had fenced off the area with trestles to stop the public wandering in.

'Will you arrest him?' Rubrius asked Trebianus, as if excited by the thought.

Trebianus replied brusquely, 'Certainly not. I want him to talk, not clam up and demand the right to appeal to the

Emperor. Good gods, I do not want him ever to be allowed within hearing of our Master . . . He knows me; I know him. I shall take precautions, but everything ought to pass off quietly. Settle down and stop nannying.' Rubrius made a small gesture of apology.

They all stood up. Trebianus made excuses, as if he was abandoning a party early. We accepted this politely. They left.

Tiberius and I sat on alone.

'Forget it, Albia,' he urged me quietly. I had bent down to fiddle with my sandal straps. He had read my thoughts. 'Stay here. I won't interfere with your work, but I can stop you being an idiot. Leave Trebianus to handle his agent. You are too weary to go trailing those men to the Temple of Apollo, however much you want to listen in.'

I drew breath, considering defiance, then let it out again. He was right. Weariness crushed me like a dead weight.

Perhaps there was a reason to be married. Once I would have been in a dark cloak and outdoor shoes by now. Somehow I had obtained for myself a sensible, affectionate man. He gave good advice. I was even prepared to follow it.

40

I contained my impatience through another night. Straight after breakfast, I went to the Palatine to ask Trebianus what had happened with his agent. Philippus had asked me to stand down, but I was taking no notice of that. When Trebianus saw me, he jumped up and whistled me out of his office, begging me to follow him at a distance, so it looked as if our passing through corridors together was a coincidence.

I sighed. Never work in espionage.

Even when he was outside, Trebianus seemed happier if I sauntered a few paces back from him. If he had been my husband I would have clipped his ear, but I went along with the deception.

He headed for the site of his adventure last night. He led me to the northern corner of the hill so I feared we were to have our clandestine talk inside the Hut of Romulus. Nothing rural has happened there for centuries, but it still smells of very ancient sheep droppings and probably ancient shepherds. Drunks have been known to throw up in it.

Avoiding this experience, Trebianus made a beeline for the House of Livia, but still carried on. He finally climbed the huge podium of the Temple of Apollo above Augustus' house. Glaring across the great vale of the Circus Maximus to the Aventine Temple of Diana, this glittering pure white monument was the earliest and finest of Augustus' public buildings, a hundred years old but recently reconstructed by Domitian. It had been elegantly Ionic but was now overbearingly Corinthian Composite. I like Ionic; Composite is horrible.

Trebianus took me briefly to the Greek library, recounting how he had turned up there last night. Large enough to have hosted Senate meetings, the grand apsidal room had the usual two storeys of shelves around a ground-floor reading area, medallions of bearded authors from the remote past, very few readers, even fewer attendants. Nevertheless, last night a library slave had been on duty; he had brought the waiting Trebianus a note to say he should move to the main temple. The slave had not properly seen the messenger. He had hidden his face.

'A ruse?' I guessed.

'Standard practice. The first was a decoy instruction.' Trebianus seemed proud of his agent's tradecraft. 'Helps avoid an ambush. Ritellius will have been secretly watching, to check that I arrived alone, not bringing an arrest posse.'

This library seemed large enough to converse unheard, though eavesdroppers could have hidden by book-cupboards or on upstairs balconies. That might have worried Ritellius. More likely he just enjoyed subterfuge.

My guide whisked us out of the library, then hurriedly zigzagged through the vast temple colonnade. Its elegant yellowish columns were *giallo antico*, which I must report on to Tiberius, who had inherited a family speciality in marble. Between them stood fifty black marble statues of the daughters of Danaus, who were ordered by their father to kill their fifty bridegrooms on their wedding night, together with equestrian statues of their unfortunate short-lived husbands, his brother's sons. A nice Greek family saga. Myths are so cheery.

Beside a cult statue of the temple god, there was the usual outdoor altar, a huge one. This grand specimen was flanked by four extremely lifelike stone oxen, poised as if ready for sacrifice. They were famous statues by Myron, looted from Greece by Augustus.

Ahead of us towered the temple, its tall pediment crowned by the chariot of the sun, the whole thing newly cleaned and 'improved' with those over-complicated Corinthian columns. Trebianus climbed the long flight of steps to the high interior and slipped through the ivory doors. He quickly pulled me after him and closed up, before I had time to admire the famous door panels. For spies, art is something about which you must pretend to have intimate knowledge when bluffing international statue dealers, who may be agents of a foreign power. You don't stop to have a look.

Glimmering with torches, the cella contained another, larger, statue of Apollo, plus his sister Diana and mother Latona. No sign of Jupiter, the archetypal philandering absentee father.

Inside was crammed. In my view, this was a worse place to meet than the library. Many other statues stood around, providing useful hiding-places. Augustus had deposited golden gifts he didn't need, and plunder that showed what a good conqueror he was, while one of his nephews had made it a convenient repository for his collection of seal-rings and other jewels. It was like an extremely expensive version of the cowshed where boys are told to store the treasures they never play with any more, after their mothers have despaired of dusting their clutter and made them clear out their rooms.

'He sneaked into the cella through a back entrance.'

'Ritellius? Come on, hurry up with the story.' I felt nervous of being in this dark interior, in case indignant attendants banned us; they left us alone, however. Trebianus took it as his right to be there. I had been taught that temples were private places, but he reckoned this was an imperial shrine and he was an imperial freedman.

'I saw him at once, waiting by the cult statue.'

It was a handsome piece, though in long Greek robes and with hair flowing down over his shoulders, Apollo looked oddly feminine. The traditionally beardless and youthful god of music, truth and prophecy (not to mention healing, the sun, light, plague and poetry) was holding a very solid box lyre; he must be golden, beardless and strong. We gazed up at his serene features until Trebianus at last revealed what Ritellius had told him, starting with how he had packed up his life in Ctesiphon. The freedman's voice was low and urgent. I did not interrupt with questions, even when the story struck me as ludicrous.

Ritellius had seen his abrupt return to Rome as a momentous decision; he set about it as if it was the last adventure of his life. When he packed up in Ctesiphon, he left behind everything he did not need. Travelled light. Travelled simply. Before he went, he gave away his possessions, bestowing one or two items he valued on the few people he had genuinely liked. He said nothing to anyone else. He told nobody his plans.

He stopped being a slob, started getting into shape. He had done it before; he could be active again. He attended gymnasia, both in Ctesiphon before he left and along his journey whenever a large inn provided exercise facilities. He gave up drink – well, nearly. There are limits. He was paring down his life until he was burdened only with whatever he would strictly need.

Ritellius believed that, whether he failed or succeeded, at the end of the day he would most likely be dead. He felt it would be worth it. 'He was sober, but like a man in drink,' complained his handler. What Ritellius was doing now gave him integrity. This great adventure would validate an otherwise rather pointless life. 'I sensed,' Trebianus told me, 'in some wild way, he is enjoying himself.'

'Extraordinary,' I answered, commenting for the first time. 'But explain. What made him suddenly take flight, without orders from you?'

It was simple enough. Ritellius had wanted to rescue his girlfriend. Trebianus looked as scornful as I felt.

We tried to accept the situation as Ritellius saw it: in the clutches of Dolazebol, Squilla could neither bear her role nor make the Parthian let her go free. For me, this was her hard luck: she had chosen to live with him. It must have been clear before she started that he liked exercising power.

But the runaway agent explained everything another way. Ritellius claimed he and Squilla had always been inseparable: she had never dumped him for a richer man; it only looked that way. Squilla had seduced the Parthian in order to watch him; Ritellius had sent her in to learn who the Roman conspiring with Parthia was. Her personal sacrifice was all to help Ritellius.

Well, that was what he thought. I had seen her. I had seen her with Dolazebol. Was Ritellius fooling himself about Squilla's motives? Somewhere in this mess there had to be a double agent; I could quite believe it was Squilla. She had found herself a better life, being the Parthian's white kitten, so she had simply bamboozled Ritellius, pretending to go along with him but forming a real bond with her powerful new lover.

Trebianus said Ritellius was convinced she was honest. When she suddenly had to accompany Dolazebol to Rome, Squilla had barely had time to let Ritellius know she was leaving. A cryptic message said she thought she had learned something important that was unsafe to trust in writing. By the time her note reached him, she had gone.

Ritellius had followed. He had had to. He wanted to hear what she had found out – then he was desperate to free her. She was the love of his life. 'At least,' I muttered, 'the latest one!'

'He hardly dares think of the future,' Trebianus continued, with sorrow. This agent, now reduced to romantic frenzy, had been his special protégé. 'But he imagines that if they two expose the collaborator, Rome's gratitude will enable them to have whatever life they choose.'

'Will it happen?'

'If he can bring it off. The Emperor will be appropriately grateful.'

That seemed likely. I thought of Julius Karus gathering in his three gold crowns and silver spear for saving Domitian from a supposedly subversive British governor. 'Rather hard on Ilia!'

'Ilia?'

'*His wife!* Trebianus, the wife your swine Ritellius actually stayed with when he popped back here to rescue his sinuous girlfriend.'

'Oh! His wife.' As Parthia-watcher, Trebianus was too obsessed to care about Ilia.

A snag struck me. 'If this is all true, why did Squilla refuse to see him? Why did he make a great fuss at the house – and leave her there? If she was in danger before, it must be far worse now. Ritellius has revealed his interest; the Parthians will see Squilla is a plant. They'll soon guess exactly what she is trying to find out. This is all madness!'

Trebianus said Ritellius knew that. Hence his urgent request to be received back by his handlers. He wanted Trebianus to help him extract Squilla.

'She is done for as soon as anyone shows they want her out!' I commented. 'Never mind her spying, Dolazebol has only to think himself losing his trophy to a rival and he'll finish her.'

'So Ritellius fears. He was in a great state,' Trebianus said. 'He is keyed up for some messy stunt. He believes this is the exploit he has always been waiting for. It is why Gaius Ritellius has existed on the earth.'

Jupiter!

I saw parallels here with the prisoner at the Castra Peregrina, the man with dung between his toes who was set up to play Nero. He, too, cannot have expected it to end well. He, too, was risking everything including life – *especially* life – to gain something. A future for his family, personal renown. Something thrilling that made death worthwhile.

For me, such men are mad. Of course, for them there is glory. Their desperate caper beats the mediocrity of normal life. But it is their kind of glory and for me it stinks.

'So what are you intending, Trebianus? Can you somehow pull the girlfriend out – yet without jeopardising the friendly relations we are pretending to have with Parthia?'

Trebianus pulled a face. 'A rescue could be achieved, I dare say. Relations are bound to suffer.'

'So? Do it! Why wait?'

'Ritellius is convinced that, after Ctesiphon, Squilla stayed on with Dolazebol because of some other secret. That was why she wouldn't see him when he went to the house. She wasn't ready.'

I blinked. 'If she knows the traitor, what more can there be?'

It did fit what she told Corellius: that she wanted people to stop messing with her and Dolazebol, and leave her alone. She had more to do.

'Ah!' replied the lanky man. 'You have met Corellius.'

'I know he works for the palace. He helped my cousin and me to escape when the Parthians turned nasty. Afterwards he spoke to Squilla at our urging. If she's really finding out things for Rome, I don't know why she didn't just tell Corellius while she had the chance.'

Trebianus seemed cagey. 'He told you what she said to him? He told you everything?'

I was scathing. 'He is a spy. I don't expect he did that! Why do you ask? Trebianus, has he said something else to you?'

'Not to me. Philippus is his handler.'

'So what has Corellius said to Philippus? Has Philippus informed you, or are you both intriguing too much against each other?'

Trebianus ignored my reproof. 'He has told Philippus that Squilla is extremely secretive. She wouldn't say anything important to him. He thinks she is keeping back whatever she knows until she sees Ritellius, so he can gain full credit. However, as insurance she has sent out an oblique message.'

'Why didn't Corellius tell me?' I was annoyed.

Trebianus brushed it aside. 'Protocol. Corellius will only pass material information to his handler. Philippus told me, and I'm telling you now. She said, *It is the man who has been consulting the Sibylline Books.*'

I could not help myself; I groaned.

Thanks to Marius teaching me the history of Rome, I did know what these antique treasures were.

The Sibyl of Cumae, a fabled prophetess, once offered to Tarquinius, one of the ancient kings of Rome, nine books of prophetic verse. The king declined to purchase them, due to their exorbitant price. She burned three, then offered the remaining six at the same stiff figure. Tarquinius again refused. She burned three more. Tarquinius decided he must be missing something really good so he purchased the last three books at the original price. My father, a true auctioneer, called this classic bargaining.

The expensive verses were originally stored in a vault beneath the Temple of Jupiter on the Capitol, with high-powered custodians. If an emergency threatened, they consulted the Sibylline Books, not to discover exact predictions of future events because seers never work in that way, but to see what religious observances might avert calamity. As with all oracles, the prophetic words were open to misinterpretation. If an oracle doesn't work, that makes it your fault.

The original prophecies had supposedly been collected in the neighbourhood of Troy. They were written in Greek hexameter verse, so the curators had to employ interpreters. When the Temple of Jupiter burned down, as it regularly does, those first books were completely lost. That did not deter the stalwart Romans, who sent envoys east to acquire replacement sayings. Versions in private hands were also gathered in and evaluated by the custodians, who retained only those that appeared true to them (surely subjective).

They made it illegal for anyone to possess a private copy.

Augustus, as Pontifex Maximus, transferred the books from the Capitol to his personal Temple of Apollo on the Palatine: right here.

Trebianus pointed to the base of the statue of Apollo Citharoidus. 'There they are!' His voice was hollow, his tone almost awed.

The books were in gold containers on shelves in the statue base, behind a grille, under lock and key. 'So who gets to consult them?'

'The custodians. The Emperor, if he believes occasion demands. It would be conducted very formally, a religious observance, with the custodians present.'

'Could you or Philippus look at them?'

'No.' Nor me, then.

'Abascantus?'

'Not even him.'

'So is Squilla's message a cheat?'

Trebianus writhed. Apollo Citharoidus gazed down at him, as if perplexed at the way he was tangling his extraordinary limbs.

'I have, Flavia Albia, discussed this question with one of the custodians. No one officially consulted the books recently and he will not let me see them. However, when I explained my reason for wanting to examine the books, its importance for Rome, I was told that at the start of the year, Domitian was extremely exercised by the Saturninus revolt, following upon the episode of the False Nero. He had a secret copy made so he could consult the books in private since to do so openly would cause public alarm.'

I huffed. 'So much for *owning a private copy of the Sibylline Books is illegal.*'

Trebianus shook his head. 'You tell that to the Emperor!'

I was terse. 'Did he take his set to Pannonia with his military kit – or has he left it behind under his pillow?'

When Trebianus would not answer, I was even more brutal. 'Trebianus, whatever the traitor has read there, we need to know. I won't incite you to bring a crowbar and break into the real book cache, but if the duplicate oracles are in Rome, we have to look at them.'

41

What? Oracular prophecies?

I had never involved myself with this kind of Roman toshery before but, oh joy, a revered collection of Greek verse was relevant to my inquiry, so among obscure old utterances I now had to poke. If I ever told my father, he would go nuts.

My husband was a pious Roman – and a reader. *He* would want me to get a sneaky squint at the Sibyl's hoary hexameters. For him, this would be even more interesting than his home encyclopaedia.

I am forbidden to provide detail. Officially only one set of Sibylline Books exists, secure in its specially constructed vault beneath the sandalled feet of Apollo Citharoidus. *If* another set temporarily existed, *if* it could be accessed by someone with privileged connections, and *if* a large enough sweetener was therefore provided to the stately chamberlain Parthenius, keeper of Domitian's secrets, plumper of his pillows and (unbeknown to us at the time) a future assassin, don't expect me ever to confess I was there.

The Books were dire. I would have preferred to sit listening for hours to my dear husband reading aloud the Table of Contents from his Pliny.

Trebianus took me to Parthenius, a wise, steady, understanding man, as he had to be if he dealt intimately with

Domitian. Trebianus explained that he was investigating a possible breach of security at the highest level. That is the best way to make high officials jump. The sweetener, which I witnessed being handed over, clinched it.

'Oh, more dirty rumours about Abascantus!' commented Parthenius, with a light laugh. He had a cultured accent, yet common vowels were surreptitiously lurking. When I was brought to Rome I had had to learn to speak nicely myself, so I notice this. Parthenius had been a slave. They had tidied up his delivery but, suave as he was, his ear was not quite good enough to fool me.

It was unclear whether he sided with those who held the suspicions or with their bumptious object. He neither accused the narrow-eyed of envy nor saw Abascantus as a much-wronged man of talent. He took no view. Parthenius was an even better civil servant than those in the secretariats. Besides, he had seen it all before. He would observe events with a neutral eye. He certainly did not appear to be shocked. It struck me that possibly Parthenius himself had warned Domitian to send Abascantus on gardening leave; he was one person who would have the facility to send letters covertly, even when his master was abroad. But if Claudius Philippus had discussed his fears about a collaborator, the chamberlain showed nothing in front of me and the Parthia-watcher.

With us, he gave every appearance of taking a hands-off attitude. Even then, I felt it was deceptive. Parthenius involved himself all right. This was the man who would one day stage-manage a successful murder. He was such a good actor, he made the real spies look crude.

Parthenius chose to give us a tour of the imperial quarters, saying, 'Let's go into the inner sanctum for privacy.' He unlocked handsome doors, several in succession. He led us down beautiful corridors until we reached the Emperor's own bedroom. It smelt like a room that had been uninhabited for months. Dead flies lay on the floor.

None of this grand suite was homely. The large marble-heavy gilded room seemed to be Domitian's own, not a marital space; there was no sense of his wife. If he wanted intercourse, he must summon Domitia Longina – or some other selected unfortunate – to him. My impression was that marital relations tended to happen infrequently these days. They had lost a child in infancy and there was no sign of another coming.

Domitia's opinion of their situation was not on record. In that sense, she was a good wife to him. Knowing about abstinence, I told myself to learn from our wonderful empress. While Manlius Faustus was not himself, I, too, must stay loyally button-lipped.

The room contained a niche with a lararium, the shrine currently bare of offerings. The candelabra were monsters, standing taller than I was. Domitian had statues, none of which I would want in my bedroom though they were all fine art; my father would have happily accepted them for auction and made a killing. I assumed the absence of clothes-chests meant that huge closets of robes, togas and uniforms were kept elsewhere; a choice of outfits would be carried in as required. Other things were in the care of accessory- and jewel-keepers – plus, if rumours were true, a trusted wig-master. Fresh wreaths must arrive from florists on a daily basis. Domitian had been offered a supply of Egyptian roses even in winter, but had declined, saying we grew more here than all the gardens of Memphis and Alexandria.

'Well, this is a privilege!' Trebianus was clearly impressed by the monstrous bed with its bronze fittings and finials, ivory-clad legs, big fat cabochons of precious stones in rare colorations. As we wandered about like tourists, I was more interested in a fancy corona of luscious drapes. Poets begged Parthenius to slip their latest collection beneath Domitian's pillow as suggested bedtime reading, so I wondered if the Sibylline Books were kept there. I hopped on a big footstool and naughtily lifted up one tightly stuffed bolster, so I saw the famous dagger that was kept under it, in case our Master was ever jumped by a violent intruder. I glanced at Parthenius, quickly dropping the bolster. Parthenius simply gave me a knowing smile.

Some years afterwards I remembered this. When Domitian was eventually killed, Parthenius had removed his dagger's blade . . .

Now, Domitian was away and, as I had been told when I interviewed the two widows, so was the Empress. Nobody was about, not even servants. In the hush of this deep palace interior, Parthenius felt safe to speak. At the end of last December, with rebellion threatening, the Sibylline Books had been brought here discreetly for Domitian to examine. He used his bedroom as a daytime office, away from other eyes.

'Apart from being in Greek and their ghastly versification, the prophecy was extremely long and obscure.' The chamberlain managed to imply that obscurity went down poorly. Some of this was snobbery about anything intellectual, though I gathered his real beef was the terrible text. I liked Parthenius; I liked his attitude. 'Our Master has a well-known love of poetry. But he reads with immense concentration.' I wondered if Domitian was a backward reader. I bet those old family friends, the Vettuleni, could say. Back in Falacrina, had little Domitian needed extra coaching? Was our Master and God a slow learner?

'The Sibylline Books could not be skimmed in a hurry; the custodians wanted them back, of course,' Trebianus prompted.

'Indeed. So we were to have them copied for studying at leisure. Then the Emperor had to dash away to the Saturninus revolt. We had begun, and might have continued, but we discovered the scribe had a private agenda. As Domitian wasn't here, I put the work on hold.'

Trebianus jumped. 'Who was the scribe?'

'Your colleague Philippus assigned him. I don't remember his name. I could find out for you . . .' Parthenius slowed down suggestively.

'Need-to-know basis?' Trebianus understood the code. 'I can ask Philippus, if it turns out to be important.'

Parthenius made a graceful gesture. Again, the style revealed his origins in Oriental slavery. 'Thank you. He came to us routinely from the pool of scribes. He had been vetted, must have been, after being picked out for the quality of his handwriting. He cannot have expected this particular assignment; he probably thought I wanted him for inventories.'

'So what went wrong?' I interposed.

'It turned out he was a Jew from Alexandria, with hidden religious motives. As soon as he was given the task, he saw it as an opportunity to create his own biased version of the prophecies. It would be for subversive purposes – though not necessarily a plot against the Emperor. He was a religious fanatic. He wanted to threaten his own people with plague, war and pestilence, then exhort them to good living.'

'Unspeakable!' I murmured satirically.

Parthenius hid a smile. 'Fortunately a supervisor noticed what he was up to. I called an immediate halt to the copying, then packed the original books straight back to the Temple of Apollo. The scribe was dealt with.'

'Who did that?' asked Trebianus, a professional question. I let him do the asking.

'The Princeps Peregrinorum had his team investigate. The bodge was all sorted quietly. Thankfully, once the Saturninus revolt was crushed, our Master never felt he needed to consult further, so he has not had to know. He does worry so.'

'A lot of your time goes on sparing him anxiety?' Trebianus seemed fascinated by the workings of the inner imperial circle. Perhaps he used Domitian's foibles to compare with whatever he knew of the King of Kings in Parthia. Certainly an ongoing wish to assassinate our ruler was a thread we had in common.

'I try to ease his mind.' Whenever Domitian was anxious, he became paranoid and violent. Rome owed Parthenius more than people knew. 'Now, if you have no further questions . . .' Parthenius felt he had given us enough privileged interaction. He subtly steered us out. Then each door was carefully locked behind us. The imperial suite stayed out of bounds to most people, even when its noble occupant was a thousand miles away.

Trebianus was gibbering over our glimpse of Domitian's private life. I could not stand that kind of adulation, so I made excuses. He went for one of his three-hour office lunches. He thought I was going home.

Not so, easily fooled handler! I walked down to the Forum,

293

skirted the Amphitheatre, washed my hands in the Sweating Fountain on the way; I felt sticky with élite dust. Then I nipped along to the Castra to quiz its Princeps. Trebianus would probably do this in due course, but I put myself ahead of him. Intrigue was not confined to palace secretaries.

Titus was polishing his desk. Maybe a suspect or a chastised subordinate had leaked blood on it. 'You again! People are talking. My ladyfriend is getting jealous.'

'Assure her, my friend, I am trustworthy. I plan to wait at least a month after my wedding before I start looking around again . . . Now, tell me quick – what was the story on a scribe you took care of, after the perverting-of-Sibylline-oracles fiasco?'

Nearly-Nine-Gongs screwed up his eyes with suspicion. 'Are you allowed to hear about that?'

'Absolutely. Special clearance. I have come to you straight from the exalted Parthenius. What an impressive operator. Such efficiency. I bet he personally wipes up the vomit when the Emperor has had too much to drink.' In truth, the joyless Domitian was virtually teetotal. 'I hope he's not called Parthenius because he originates in Parthia . . .' It seemed unlikely. Wars in the far east had never been successful enough; more often they captured us. 'Still, he's a Roman smoothie now. Top class. He told me you know what the anarchist scribe was up to.'

'Parthenius said?' It must be rare for a rough commander to admire a cushion-plumping chamberlain, but Parthenius had achieved this feat. Presumably it was because he had decided the Princeps Peregrinorum was the right man to summon in an emergency. Titus was a simple enough centurion; he approved of men who approved of him.

I sat on his little slave's stool, smoothing my skirts down neatly. 'Parthenius told me it was an Egyptian from the general copy pool. The man had ideas of his own?'

'Religious nut.' Titus did not need to spit: his tone was dismissive enough. 'The private staff did their best, according to what they know of security. Your friend Philippus had devised a routine. They kept the scribbler locked in a room on his own, only let him out to sleep. Food on a tray, bucket for piss. Gave him clean papyrus daily, confiscated his pens and ink jars every night. Counted the sheets when he finished. Locked up his notes.'

That sounded efficient. 'His work was supervised? That was how they exposed him?'

Titus nodded. 'He was taking his own papyrus in. One day they searched him when he left, found he had wrapped some notes around his body under his tunic. The supervisor took one look at the writings, went all heebie-jeebie, then the scribe copped it. Parthenius was shitting marble blocks when I got there. I pretty well had to throw a bucket of water on the supervisor. What a party. Amateur!'

I gazed at the derisive Princeps, pretending to admire his expertise. 'So what happened next, great one? You and your lively boys held the scribe here? Did you torture him? Was it horrible? I don't suppose you still have him dangling from chains somewhere?'

'You don't suppose right.' Titus enjoyed disappointing me. Me, a woman who intended to wait a whole month before cheating on her bridegroom.

He stretched, easing his brawny shoulders. Our relationship had reached a point where he felt secure confiding in me. The way he saw it, no other commander would relax with me like this, but they were hidebound fools, whereas he, subtle and flexible, had seen how to exploit my potential.

'Cough up, Princeps!' I cajoled good-humouredly. 'What did Alfius wrench out of the penman?'

'I didn't bother with that. Stuff the Alfius paraphernalia. That quivering scribe would have foamed at the mouth and died of terror. I had a little chat myself. The fellow was harmless. He didn't start out as a secret intriguer. If that copying job hadn't fallen into his lap, he would still be making laundry lists, no nuisance to anyone.'

I was surprised. 'You are taking a liberal attitude!'

'He was a Jew. My lady comes from Judaea. Lovely woman. Fantastic cook. Wonderful sense of family. She said it sounded as if he just liked religious raving; sitting all day on his own in the Emperor's anteroom must have gone to his head. Solitary confinement isn't for everyone. Well, I know that: we use it here when it's the right way forward. So she said, "Just take his dangerous literature away and put him on a boat back to Alexandria. Let him go home to be a scholar."'

'That was back in January?'

'February.'

'But he is long gone. Well, in case this mess goes as far as sending someone after him, can you remember his name?'

Titus laughed. 'We don't do names. Anyone we get in my camp is too secret to identify. Our code for him was Simon. That's Jewish.'

'True.' I changed my tone. I made it significant: 'So did you, Princeps, gain any idea that "Simon" was in the pay of the palace traitor?'

Titus pulled up short. I watched him considering this dangerous new suggestion. I hoped it would not occasion any loss of trust for the woman who had taught him to be more liberal. She who had said, 'Send Simon home, he's harmless.'

'Nobody asked me to look into that.'

'No one knew. Assuming it was true,' I said.

'I thought he was a loner.'

'Perhaps he was,' I reassured him. Somewhere along the line I had taken his welfare into my keeping. Now I hated to see old Titus looking nervous.

'Anything he did, it seemed to me, was only because he was a complete crackpot, Albia.'

'He was. Don't worry about it. Well, not about Simon. The traitor is something else. Word is, he took an unseemly interest in the Sibylline Books. Although there seems to be no prior link from him to Simon, I think Simon was gathering information for him.'

If the books were locked up in Domitian's private quarters, and the scribe worked alone, how else would the collaborator manage to consult them? Philippus had been in charge of security and we could feel sure the collaborator did not want him to notice his interest. That is, assuming Philippus himself was not the traitor.

I sighed gently. 'Is this all you have for me?'

'That's all,' agreed Titus, pleasantly. He left it long enough for me to travel past any expectation of suspense. He liked to play with people. He waited until I was about to go home. 'Unless,' he said, with a betraying gleam, 'you want me to ask my filing lad if he still has the documents we confiscated?'

42

The public slave who acted as runabout was summoned, a hairy mite with an old oversized tunic of his master's tied in folds around him. His normal sleepy look disappeared as soon as he learned he was needed as an archive clerk. He was a lad of a hundred jobs; archiving seemed an activity he was fond of. I suppose no one else took any interest. He could get on with it on his own, with time to think and no fear of a beating.

'This is my boy, Plotios. He has his uses. Plotios is going to tell us what he did with the documents written by that crazy Jew from Alexandria. I'm talking about Simon. You remember. Give it up, Plotios!'

Plotios remembered. 'The palace people took all the copying off him, Princeps, then our team brought the scrolls in for expert scrutiny. The papyrus was very nice quality, but the writings stank. So you had one of your chats with him – not too bad, he didn't cry for long. Simon wanted to compose a set of prophecies for his people, to inspire them. *"Ho, ho, Simon! If that means inspiring them to rebel against Rome, you can think again, you piece of slime!"* you shouted at him. He whimpered that he was sorry but his God had made him do it. You sent him off to Ostia to be took home to Egypt.'

'Why did I do that, I wonder?'

The Princeps seemed to use the slave as a human aide-memoire. Plotios happily expounded: 'He said he was just a historian, Princeps. His parents had needed him to work on their farm. He loved being a scholar so he sold himself into slavery. Then they used the money to employ a farm manager. Because he had education, Simon was brought to Rome to get a better price for him, so he ended up in the palace. You said that was very touching, so Simon could be sent back and sold as a history teacher in a school. That was, if anyone wanted to buy him; if not, he was going to the Egyptian stone quarries. First, you had the palace documents all burned in the yard, for security reasons. You made him watch, as a bit of fun. Even the ashes were buried after.'

'I remember. We gave the Sibylline copies an exceedingly good funeral,' Titus said to me. 'So that's our gen on Simon, Albia.'

I had been promised something to look at; I waited. Plotios was dying to say more. His commander let him jump up and down for a time, then slowly turned his gaze upon the slave. 'So what's bugging *you*, my excitable little ant?'

'You did send the lads to search his sleeping cubicle, Princeps. They came back with a bunch of notes you didn't like the look of. Another set.'

'A search?' Titus pretended to be surprised. 'That was extremely efficient of me!'

Plotios told me the Princeps had decreed that these other notes were rubbish. 'They were only written on one side, so I kept the papyrus in case it came in handy for writing something on the back one day.'

'That's very economical. Was it good-quality papyrus as well?' I asked.

'Yes, but not the same. For copying the Sibylline Books for the Emperor, the secretariat issued top-grade Augustan, the new Claudian type with stronger cross threads so that ink won't blob through. This is standard for Domitian's correspondence. Simon's notes were on Livian papyrus; it's still very nice, but a grade lower.'

'You know your stationery, Plotios!'

He blushed. 'It came to us a bit discoloured because Simon slept with it tied under his tunic.'

Titus acted out horror and disgust. 'Not in front of this delicate young lady, boy! Albia doesn't want to think about a nasty Egyptian scribe's sweaty chest.'

'Sorry, sir.'

I applied my woman-of-mystery face, as if I had inspected a few nasty male chests in my time. To a degree, it was true. I turned back to Titus. 'I am thinking that this renegade could never acquire quality papyrus for himself. He was a slave, he had no money.'

'Agreed. Unless he had previously pinched material from another high-end job, somebody gave him extra sheets – specifically to write up secret notes of the Sibylline Books,' pronounced Nearly-Nine-Gongs sonorously. 'Right! See if we still possess this seditious crud, my Plotios.'

Plotios led us to a tall cupboard, housed in a small, smelly anteroom. It was crammed with whatever he had saved up in case it came in handy. The moment he opened the cupboard door, out fell stacks of confiscated documents. He squatted among the jumble of papyrus sheets, note tablets, maps and scrolls, a huge haul from people who had been dragged to the Castra as dangerous social elements. I preferred not to think what had happened to them all. It was unlikely they were released back onto the streets. Some would have been philosophers; I tried not to worry about Marius.

Finding his way through the piles, Plotios produced our evidence. In triumph, he held up a few individual sheets of papyrus. 'Simon's cubicle notes!'

The Princeps told his slave he need not concern himself with this frippery but could stay behind to tidy up his cupboard. Plotios looked resigned to being left out of any excitement.

Titus and I huddled in his office to inspect the notes. A long-in-the-tooth soldier can read, though this one held back, mainly letting me point out the damning parts. He was at ease with rosters, passwords and letters to the commissariat. Religious exhortation threw him. Apocalyptic mysticism was not to my taste either, but I plunged in.

I speed-read, trying to summarise. 'Talk about indigestible – it gives you worse wind than onions. The first part is a lurid vision of world history. Wild stuff. He's got Chronos, Titans and Lapiths, and the children of Gaia and Uranus. He moves from myth to reality, insulting nations merrily: "*But then shall come the Greeks, proud and profane people*", followed by Alexander's lot: "*confusion and disorder, filling the world with evils, through base-living love of gain, and that in many lands, but in Macedonia most of all*". Excellent: the blondes get it. "*The terrible Phrygians shall all perish, and evil shall come upon Troy. Evil shall come to the Persians and Assyrians and all Egypt and Libya, upon the Ethiopians, on the Carians and Pamphylians a ruin of exile, and to all men alike.*"'

'Bugger me.' The Princeps must have been reading over my shoulder more than I had thought because he had picked up on Simon's joy at destroyed cities and rivers surging with blood. 'He does like his ruin and evil. He seemed pretty meek when he was talking to me.'

I could imagine a reason for that.

'What's going on here, girl? He been weeping over his pen?'

There was a smudged ring on the papyrus. 'My mother would smack somebody's hand, Titus . . . Either the scribe or someone he had with him has stood a wet-bottomed beaker there.'

So who could have been looking over his shoulder in the way Titus was with me? Whom had I once seen placing his fancy cup on a scroll as a place-marker? . . .

I was considering the scribe's own motive. 'Simon seems very driven: "*When my soul ceased from the hymn inspired, then I besought the great father that I might rest from my labour; but again the voice of the great God rose up in my breast, and bade me prophesy over every land, and to kings, and to instruct them of things which should come to pass.*"'

The Princeps snorted. 'That was why I let him go. If he survives in Alexandria, just let him try instructing kings about what will come to pass. He can sing of that until he chokes. No big prick in a diadem will listen.'

It could be so, though scared rulers like Domitian tend to pay attention to prophecies. I moved on through the lines until I reached Simon's doom-laden view of modern times: *From Asia a king shall come, lifting up a mighty sword, in countless ships, walking on the wet ways of the sea, and cutting through a high-peaked mountain; trembling, Asia shall receive him back, as he flees for refuge from the war.*

To the men of Jerusalem also shall come an evil storm-blast of war from Italy, and shall lay waste the great temple of God,

302

when putting their trust in folly they shall cast away godliness and do hateful deeds of blood before the temple.

'So Nero at last. He is trying to cut the Isthmus at Corinth – an unfinished project that I have seen, Princeps, by the way. Then we get the destruction of the Temple in Jerusalem. Which I have *not* seen.' Father's brother was killed in Judaea; Falco would not go there.

'Arse-about-tip,' sneered the Princeps. 'The temple was Titus Caesar. Nero was well dead by then. This is it, girl – "*And then shall a great king from Italy flee away like a deserter, unseen, unheard of, beyond the ford of Euphrates, after he has polluted his hands with the hateful murder of his mother, doing the deed with wicked hand. And many around his throne shall drench the soil of Rome with their blood.*" That's Agrippina paying the price for hosting Nero in her womb, thanks for that, Madam, so the bastard murdered her. And it's all the other victims Nero killed.'

'Then Simon dodges back to the east: "*To Syria shall come a Roman chieftain, who shall burn with fire the temple of Jerusalem, slay many of the Jews, and lay in ruin that great land of broad fields.*" Anyone can see old Simon is a Jew himself. And now look, Titus, Caesar's punishment for it – the eruption of Mount Vesuvius: "*But when from a cleft in the earth, in the land of Italy, a flame of fire shoots out its light to the broad heaven, to burn up many cities and slay their men, and a great cloud of fiery ashes shall fill the air, and sparks fiery red shall fall from Heaven, then should men know the wrath of the God of Heaven, because they destroyed the blameless people of the godly. Then shall come to the west the strife of war stirred up, and the exiled man of Rome, lifting up a mighty sword, crossing the Euphrates with many tens of thousands.*" So at last this "exiled man of Rome" is Nero, brought back to life or never died. And, Titus, he is heading this way!'

The Princeps, who would make a good audience for reading out an adventure story, shuddered. He was so eager to hear the rest he did not bother to waste time saying, 'Bugger me!'

The tenor changed. Ancient lore and fiery prophetics became a practical list of qualities to look for during an employment interview – assuming you were head-hunting to fill the throne of Rome. 'Princeps, now we have the recipe for False Neroism.'

'Catch me a centaur and strap a dildo on him! Albia, hand me that piece of shit!'

The Princeps Peregrinorum took up the papyrus sheet in question between a finger and thumb, as if it was something even he found unhygienic. I now listened with my hands clasped around my knees while he sonorously declared the phrases:

- Great one flees Italy like a runaway slave
- Maternal murder and other crimes, sins against spouses
- Cutting the Isthmus
- Much bloodshed for the Roman throne, wise and clever ruler returns to overthrow successor
- Brandishing a huge spear
- Crossing the Euphrates
- Playing theatricals, honey-sweet song in melodious voice
- Lurking with the Medes and Persians
- War in the west
- Champion of the east
- Whole creation shaken and kings perish
- Destroy every land and conquer all
- War to end all war, eternal peace for the godly

Titus was innocently appalled. 'Disgusting. This is really supposed to be the False Nero, him we had in our cell?'

I sat up straighter, breathing slowly. 'Someone chose that man and prepared him for the role . . .'

'They didn't choose very well, then.' Titus jerked with anger, throwing the papyrus onto a table. 'They prepared him very badly indeed! He was piss-poor. Anyway, this twaddle is no good for Rome. I'm a soldier. What will I do if another Nero rises up and they have a war to end all wars?'

'Enjoy a peaceful retirement with your lovely lady,' I suggested gently. He blinked as if he could not take that in.

These notes of Simon's had started off for what he called the blameless people of the godly. As far as I knew, it had never been suggested that any of the three False Neros had appealed for support from the Jews. Not even back during the Jewish Rebellion.

'Princeps, I don't know how much comes direct from the Sibylline Books, or how much is Simon's own version to inspire Jewish readers, but this particular list has been prepared for Rome.'

'It stinks,' Titus agreed. 'The palace traitor was creating a new emperor to foist on us.'

'He still is. The Nero who died in your cell may never have known much about any prophecies he was meant to fulfil. For the traitor, validating his new Nero is essential. With this list he can always prepare a better candidate.'

I could see the commander growing more nervous as I spoke. He certainly followed my argument. 'The turncoat wants to put his puppet in power, then he can open up the Sibylline Books, crying, "Look, my Nero fulfils the sacred prophecies!"'

'I don't like it,' decided Titus. 'It was hilarious at the time but one Nero was enough.'

A thought struck me. 'Copying the books all went wrong. Someone exposed it. Princeps sweetie, who was the palace supervisor who caught out Simon?'

He looked embarrassed. 'I hoped you would never ask me that, Flavia Albia.' He confessed awkwardly, 'I really got him wrong, I'm afraid . . . It was that Paternus.'

'*Really?*'

'Bit of a complicated history there. When I did my old inquiry into Simon, at that time Paternus worked for the fellow you know, Philippus. Philippus was in charge of keeping the Sibylline Books safe while Domitian had them out on loan.'

'Paternus was his man?' I was astounded. 'Are we talking about the same person? Paternus who, you thought, poisoned the False Nero?'

'That Paternus. And he did do the poisoning.' Titus spelled things out. I should never forget that his position as Princeps meant he was thought to be bright and a shrewd judge of men. 'Two alternatives, Flavia Albia: *either* your Philippus is the collaborator and has been all along.'

'Hard to believe! In that case why did he let Paternus haul up the scribe for moonlighting?'

'Exactly. *Or* Claudius Philippus is straight enough, but afterwards Paternus began working for someone else. By the time he was assigned to my Castra, he had somehow been turned. Presumably with money. I always thought Paternus was a nasty piece of work; he must have been available to anyone who paid him.'

'So when the False Nero was brought here, Paternus was already on the spot, working for the traitor? It confirms what I have always thought: the traitor has to be someone who knows what the inner council is planning. How long had Paternus been deployed here?'

'Oh,' Titus grumbled, accepting my theory, 'just about as long as it must have taken to bring that prisoner to Rome from the east.'

Fairly sympathetically, I said, 'Not your fault, Princeps. But it's a shame this Paternus ended up drowned in the Tiber. Otherwise we could have asked him!'

'I am sorry we lost him,' admitted the Princeps. 'When he was first assigned here, I thought it was a reward for his honesty over Simon.' He could not help seeing his Castra as a plum posting. 'I didn't like him, but I don't care for half the shoddy characters I am sent. I have to hone them up to my standards. When the False Nero died, knowing Paternus had been a palace man, I wondered. Half of them are bent. I pulled him straight in here for a scouring. He had all the right answers – but he did a bunk straight after. It would have been better if I had kept hold of him, but he had denied being the poisoner and I was still looking for evidence.' Titus picked his teeth. 'I know what you are thinking, girl. The river, drowning him, that must have been his paymaster's solution. It was not me who put him in there.'

When we had first met, he would never have dreamed of being so open. Nor would I have so readily believed him.

I hid a smile as I realised this is what spies try to achieve, of course. They charm their way in. People stop noticing their presence. They come and go, invisibly part of whatever is happening . . .

I had engineered that here. Titus was now my crony. Even so, I still did not take him at face value. He was a soldier. I never would.

'What are we going to do, Titus?'

'Sit tight. Don't tell anyone we worked it out. Watch what happens.'

We were such good pals that as I left Titus asked if I wanted to go out for a drink with him. 'Nothing heavy, don't worry, we both have commitments . . .' It sounded harmless, though with wine, temptation becomes inevitable for some people (not me). I declined politely, reminding my new friend that indeed I was committed: my new husband, the aedile, had been struck by lightning so I ought to go home and spend time with him.

The Princeps went along with this, though he did insist on walking with me. He came so far I felt apprehensive he would take me right the way home and want to have lunch with us. Somehow this loomed as worse than venturing to a bar on my own with him.

However, he said he was going for a haircut at the popular Ad Tonsores, near the top end of the Circus Maximus. He had heaved off his breastplate so as to pass more or less incognito through the streets, though his bearing was so military he might as well not have bothered.

We had gone as far as the starting gates, when a race must have ended. The noise inside the Circus was still tumultuous. The exterior gates flew open, then a couple of chariots rattled out at high speed. Their factions were the reds and the whites, and neither had the winner's palms; still inside, the greens, blues, golds and purples were either shipwrecked in splinters, or one must be a winner parading in triumph. I had no family reason to support the emerging teams; nor did the Princeps seem interested.

These were sore losers, tearing off in different directions.

It must have been a quadriga race. Four strong horses effortlessly pulled each flimsy wooden chariot, where the driver had almost nowhere firm to place his feet and the backless box he stood up in rested almost on the axle. Those drivers needed balance, as well as skill and courage. In their helmets, very short tunics and wide stomach bands, equipped with whips and curved knives in case they fell and had to cut their reins, I could see they were still fired up after seven laps of dodging and danger. Their horses swept by, ears pricked up, awash with sweat, each team of four beautifully matched. Bouncing behind, the weightless chariots almost took off flying. One careered so close, I jumped back across the pavement to avoid injury.

If the Circus was full, and if they had reached the lunch break, a hundred thousand racegoers or more could spew out. I needed to hurry to the Aventine side before the crowds became impassable. Saying goodbye to the Princeps, I pushed on towards the Trigeminal Gate.

At one point I glanced back. I saw that the camp commander had not gone towards the popular barbers' quarter, as he had said he would. Instead he had turned back at the Forum Boarium, the meat market. His unmistakably solid figure was now heading towards the Palatine.

Who was he going to see there?

43

Nobody home.

My head was so full of godless nations being laid waste by war and the blameless godly being exhorted that it took me a while to understand this unexpected hush. Had pestilence carried off all my people?

I laid down the packages of lunch ingredients that I had bought on the way home. Because of the daily races, there had been plenty of snack-sellers milling around outside as I came by the Circus. I wondered whether Tiberius had been summoned to the Games, and had taken everyone, but discounted that. As the aedile's wife, I would have been obliged to tag along.

I opened the door from the courtyard to the builders' yard, but no one was there either, only the kennelled watchdog. He woke up, eyed me suspiciously, experimented with a growl, remembered he knew me, changed the menace to half-hearted tail wags, then put his nose between his paws and went to sleep again.

I returned to the courtyard, where I sat on the dolphin bench. Fortunately, a key rasped; after two attempts to turn it, voices announced the return of Tiberius and Dromo. Tiberius waved but went straight upstairs. Dromo came and told me his master was changing into a fresh tunic.

'I got him to go to the baths!' announced the slave, proudly.

'I took him, but I was so busy encouraging him that I forgot to take the clothes basket. He didn't have to talk to anyone there – I strigilled him down in a corner as quick as we could. Then he did me, even though I said he needn't bother.'

I hid my surprise, not to mention relief, that Tiberius had finally been persuaded to leave the house. 'Good boy! What made you think of that? He was clean. You were sponging him.'

'I wanted a cake,' admitted Dromo, darkly. This was his established reward for bathing, a concept he otherwise ignored.

I asked where everyone else was. My mother had been here to reclaim Galene; though she had left a message that I could have her back if I was desperate, it was a subtle maternal hint that I should organise my own staff now. Hinting seems to be something they gain with pregnancy or, in my case, it had come along with the adoption diploma.

Although this had left Graecina in sole charge, Graecina had left too. *That* was unexpected.

'What a shock! However did you wangle that, Dromo?'

Dromo, a guileless lad, let his delight show. The official explanation was that the children's teacher had refused to come so far, while the tots were badly missing their friends. Graecina knew an elderly gentleman on the Esquiline, a very respectable Egyptian widower (or so he said, I thought cynically), who wanted a housekeeper. So she had done a flit while I was out, unable to face telling me.

Since she had taken all her belongings, the departure could not have been arranged on a whim. I admit I never saw this coming. I admit I was not entirely downhearted.

'She left her horrible vase mats for you, as a present. I'm

glad those little children have gone, but have I got to do all the work now?'

'No, Dromo. You will have to help out for a while, though no need to set place-mats everywhere. Your master doesn't like them.' Always blame your husband. 'I shall find someone else. Don't worry. Here's some lunch. Go and fetch bowls and beakers, please. And perhaps that portable serving-table?'

'I'm full of cake. I don't need lunch.'

'I do! So will your master. Fetch the things we need, please.'

'Do I have to?'

'Yes, I think so, Dromo!'

He went. He must have been able to see that his master was coming.

Tiberius leaned down and kissed me, smelling of bath oil. He had combed his hair flat while it was wet, though when I touched it, it was dry. He dropped onto the bench beside me. Ruffling his hair back to normal, so he looked less severe, I checked his mood: uplift. That was cheering.

'Marius called when you were out,' he said. 'He is going to the Parthia house this evening with his flute. I told him to be careful.'

'Thanks, love.'

Tiberius had not only made it to the baths without panic but afterwards had felt able to go over to a warehouse he owned. 'I have the workmen cleaning up; they will carry out repairs. Sparsus knows a fellow who will lend us a dog – a good ratter, to see off the vermin – then Larcius is devising an advertisement so I can lease the space.'

'That's good. But I didn't want you to worry over anything like that.'

'I need to pull my weight,' answered Tiberius, broodingly. After a moment he said, with more enthusiasm, 'Nepos has taken one of the shops to sell his cheese. I've done a *quid pro quo* on the rent, to reduce the last instalment we owe for this house.' Metellus Nepos was the man who had sold us our new home. He had been anxious to shed the building firm because he was a dedicated cheese-maker. We liked cheese, so we had encouraged him. 'I shall let the other shops now as well.' The warehouse had small commercial outlets along its street boundaries. Everything had stood empty for years so it was high time Tiberius exploited his asset. 'Your father's man, Katutis, wrote out tenancy agreements for me. I have not been completely idle, Albia.'

I reassured him that I had never thought so. I only wanted to look after him, spare him exertion before he was ready for it.

'I am ready,' he snapped tetchily.

'That's wonderful! And you have mastered telling your wife not to fuss.'

Tiberius opened his mouth, about to answer back. He paused. He saw I was teasing. He grinned. 'Nearly fell for that.'

'I love you.'

'Thank you. Love you too.'

I took his hand and we sat in silence together in the sunshine until Dromo reluctantly brought bowls and serving platters. He made no move to unpack my parcels of bread and stuffed vine leaves, or some smoked cheese that Tiberius had bought from Nepos, so I did it. I was saving my strength for more important arguments.

Despite his cake, Dromo put away more than us. I made no comment. I was too pleased with him for persuading

Tiberius out of doors. For the time being, I was prepared to feel the boy was not all bad.

That would never last.

We had just finished eating. Of his own accord, Dromo was carrying things back into the kitchen. He would polish off any leftovers then complain he felt sick. I was about to urge Tiberius to go upstairs for an afternoon siesta, while wondering what were the chances of romance if I joined him . . .

Somebody knocked. Thwarted again.

Dromo kept clattering pottery loudly, to show he was busy, so Tiberius, napkin in hand, went to the door. To our surprise, in came Philippus.

On this occasion, the stylus-pusher wasted no time. Barely seeming to notice that the master in person had had to let in visitors again, he gave us unsettling news. Trebianus had been suspended from duty. Rather than accept house arrest anywhere close to Rome, he had agreed to have an open-ended vacation on the Bay of Naples. This was a traditional destination for freedmen who came under a cloud. The traditional outcome was either suicide, or soldiers with swords were sent to make suicide unnecessary.

The Parthia-watcher was in deep trouble. Suspension was ominous enough; his enemies must be scheming to impose a much deadlier punishment.

44

I groaned briefly. 'Well, that should please Dolazebol. Trebianus given the push? No one watching Parthia? Juno, the great eternal enemy could put in place all kinds of contrivance.'

'*I* am watching Dolazebol,' Philippus corrected me, sounding peevish. 'I have a man in the house.'

'Of course you do, the po-faced Corellius! And Trebianus had someone else there, though he never told me who.'

'One of his half-drunk reprobates. Acting as a gardener, I believe,' Philippus conceded sniffily. I thought of the over-trimmed jasmine. Hacking back produces more flowers next season, but that climber could end up very bald if there were a large number of peristyle conversations to monitor. Nerves clouded his handsome face as Philippus made a conscious effort to set aside inter-service jealousy. 'I have taken over. I volunteered for the extra workload to prevent our traitor inserting a saboteur.'

'Lot to learn?' suggested Tiberius, with sympathy.

'I am bedding in . . . For the time being, I cannot do much about Ctesiphon. I have to discover what Trebianus had in place there. His record-keeping is deplorable – he's so secretive, anyone would think he was afraid of surveillance. Rubrius is to sit in his office temporarily; he can open any despatches, then we shall have to see.'

'Messages may be in code,' I warned, remembering what the Parthia-watcher had told me about how he communicated with his far-flung agents.

'Rubrius is a fine decoder. If we find ourselves absolutely stuck, I'll just have to send a courier down to Neapolis on the sly for Trebianus to translate. Apart from the time that will take, we don't want Abascantus to know we are still communicating.'

I asked what had happened with Trebianus. 'You said he was suspended? Is he actually under arrest?'

Philippus looked between Tiberius and me, as if satisfying himself he could trust us. Apparently so, for he shared the story. It was Abascantus, from his senior position, who had imposed Trebianus' suspension; he implied it was a painful measure taken on orders from elsewhere. Philippus did not believe him. For one thing, in the civil service 'measures' are always 'painful'. For another, why was it necessary?

Even in the Emperor's absence, Abascantus lacked further authority over colleagues, though he might yet try worse sanctions. If Trebianus survived long enough, Domitian would be the final judge.

'Presumably Domitian knows nothing about this yet . . . What crime is Trebianus supposed to have committed?' asked Tiberius, ever a stickler for form.

'With gardening leave, we never name the reason. The guilty party always knows.'

'What if he is innocent?' I demanded. I paused. 'As Trebianus presumably is. Or do you genuinely know something against him?'

'Oh, I know what he has done!' rapped back Philippus, in an acid tone. 'He has gone against Abascantus. Abascantus, lord of all, wants to flatter the Parthians by loading favours

316

on his creature, Dolazebol. Dolazebol has complained to Abascantus that Trebianus is pressing too hard upon him. So Abascantus ordered *me* – which we can assume was a test of *my* loyalty – to fix the immediate suspension of my colleague. Trebianus had to drop everything and go. He understood I was under duress – in fact, my acquiescence was our only way to keep someone with the right motives in his place. The whole burden falls on me now.' He was human; he sounded worn, although I detected the warm burn of discreet excitement.

'Was Trebianus expecting to be banished?'

'He probably had his bags packed from the moment he began to pique Abascantus.'

Tiberius asked thoughtfully, 'What will happen when Domitian comes home?'

Philippus tensed. 'Crisis point. As soon as Domitian returns – that is, before Abascantus can get to him – I must be able to show the Emperor everything the traitor has been doing, with full proof. The logistics won't be easy. I shall have to know when our Master is close, then slip away from the palace and ride out in secret to meet him. Otherwise Abascantus will get to him first and poison his mind. If that happens, Trebianus is finished – so, no doubt, am I. Without us, the collaborator – whoever he is . . .' Philippus paused. 'He will set in action whatever coup he is planning.'

A moment of reflection passed over all of us. I then announced quietly that I could say what the traitor was planning. He would present Rome with a new Nero, validated by the Sibylline Books.

Raising a hand to stop me, Tiberius stood up. He sent Dromo out on an errand, telling him for once that he could take his time. Usually the slave took no notice of our conversations, but it would be typical that this was an exception. What the boy did not know could never be tricked out of him by others.

After checking that the workmen had not yet returned to their yard, Tiberius put a bar across the communicating door, then rejoined us.

I had used this pause to assemble my thoughts. I was succinct. 'This is what I know: the collaborator has used the Sibylline Books. After constructing a prototype, using the ancient prophecies, he must have invited the Parthians to join him in overthrowing Domitian. In the first instance they set up the man from Syria, the one murdered in the Castra. He was so bad they are producing a more realistic contender. I presume they have found one who looks like the real thing and possibly is a true musician.'

A *fourth* False Nero? One who could play? Tiberius and Philippus were startled.

'That poor inadequate prisoner got by initially. He was what Romans expected after what had occurred in the past – a blond harpist in Syria with a swelling train of followers. Abascantus supposedly negotiated his release to us, Philippus, though if he was colluding with Parthia it can't have been as hard as he pretended.'

Tiberius joined in: 'Once he was in Roman hands, I imagine it was soon realised the third Nero was hopeless.'

'Perhaps it even happened earlier,' I suggested. 'When he tried approaching provincial governors, they may have been so disparaging in their despatches to Rome, the plotters recoiled. Abascantus would have received those letters, of course.'

Tiberius agreed. 'Someone of Abascantus' calibre would

never risk a coup with a dud figurehead. Knowing this man was unacceptable, he must have scrambled to organise a better substitute. I imagine he now has him right here in Rome, under his control, being given a stiff course in public speaking, together with a portfolio of Nero's old musical creations.'

Philippus groaned. 'I blame myself. I wanted the pretender brought here for questioning, but that fits their plans! Nero is back, rumour will say. For many it will have credibility.'

'A pretender who turns up in Rome will be lethal,' I agreed. 'People are mad enough to accept him, just as they tolerated the real Nero for so long. Listen – the plotter has gone to extraordinary lengths to find out what the Sibylline Books say. He definitely wants his creature to fit the oracles.'

'And how does that help?' Tiberius asked cautiously.

'Those books prophesy a messianic figure who will arise in the east and come west to destroy tyranny. Tyranny, everyone knows, can only refer to Domitian. Even Domitian knows it.'

'But everyone sensible knows Nero is dead,' Tiberius pointed out, still testing my theory.

'And a lot want to be rid of Domitian – maybe at any price. This Nero will be fully groomed to fit. He won't be what remote crazy Syrians think a Roman leader is, but what a cynical Roman, here on the spot, *knows* he must be. It doesn't matter that the third pretender was cavorting in the east, where new Neros traditionally appear. The game has changed. A star performer will take over. This time, the resurrected heroic figure finally will reach the west.'

Philippus looked more and more anxious. 'They will

announce that the third False Nero was brought to Rome?'

'Sounds natural enough – after all, it's what you really did!' Tiberius reminded him.

Philippus again looked sick at how he had been unintentionally drawn in. 'Yet the Princeps can say he was murdered at the Castra.'

'Really? Can you produce a corpse?' I asked, reminding him of how the body's secret disposal had been conducted on his orders.

'So then here is Nero, breaking free from his chains, such a good image,' Tiberius followed up. 'We know he will be a puppet emperor. We know a clever Roman will control him.'

'With the willing connivance of Parthia.' Philippus spoke with as much high-minded Roman disgust as if he were the thwarted Octavian watching Cleopatra's asp in the fig basket.

'So it seems,' I said. 'Dolazebol and his sidekick Bruzenus have come here to see things through at this end. Meanwhile the King of Kings is sitting on his lion throne in Ctesiphon, just waiting to hear that their plot against Rome has been successful.'

Tiberius stirred. 'You will have to shift to stop them,' he told the stylus-pusher. 'But the plotters need Domitian to be here.'

I agreed. 'That's right. They cannot try to overthrow him when he is running free, in command of twenty-nine legions.'

Tiberius continued pressing: 'If Domitian's return to the city is the critical moment, that's any day now.'

Ever since I had read the scribe's notes with the Princeps, I had been thinking. Now I put into words my curious conclusion: 'Philippus, if the substitute Nero is being coached here in Rome, at least we have a chance of finding him.'

Philippus leaned forwards, becoming more earnest. It was no surprise that he asked me if I would help. I had come so far, it was no surprise that I agreed.

45

We discussed how we could find the pretender. Plotters could have their new Nero hidden anywhere in Rome while he practised wearing a wreath. He might even be somewhere outside, within a short radius of the city, though we discounted that for practical purposes. They wanted to keep tight control of him. They wanted him easy to present to the people at the best moment. I thought his hiding-place would be central.

A search for him must be carried out in utmost secrecy. We knew it would draw dangerous attention to us. However discreetly it was done, anything so wide-scale would be noticed. The traitor must be waiting to see what we did next. Any manpower we used could be compromised, despite any checks we carried out. Then as soon as we started looking, we had to assume the plotters would secure their man even more secretly. Once we began, we must move extremely fast. Once we began, there could be no going back.

I had two questions for Philippus before anything else happened. First, I challenged him to explain how he had been using Paternus to supervise the scribe who had copied the Sibylline Books, the very agent who had ended up killing the third False Nero.

Philippus admitted it was a disaster. 'I checked my files. Paternus came to me with a recommendation; Eutrapelus held records that confirmed a good history. I never had any complaints about the man's work; his exposure of the cheating scribe showed loyalty. However, I now see he was tainted. You may guess the source: he was originally suggested to me by Abascantus.'

Paternus probably exposed the scribe after he had completed making notes for the traitor. From that point, Simon was doomed. The traitor probably hoped he would be executed in the Castra, and so silenced completely. They could have had no idea Simon had taken extra notes for his own religious purposes and that the Princeps Peregrinorum still possessed them. They certainly could not have realised that the Princeps had sent the man back to Alexandria, alive.

Abascantus had presumably continued using Paternus for his own purposes, even after he was nominally assigned to Philippus. In the palace there were reporting lines, but all staff ultimately worked for the Emperor so they could be given instructions by anyone with the right seniority. Philippus now had to accept that Abascantus had adroitly placed a mole in his team. I left him to struggle with his discomfiture.

'The other question is Squilla,' I said. 'As well as identifying your traitor, potentially she has learned of the groomed Nero. So, does Squilla know where this Nero is? Exposing that plot will make Ritellius a hero through her. I think she is holding out for more information to enhance his glory. It's brave – but her timing is dangerous. She needs to leave. Philippus, before Trebianus was exiled to Neapolis, Ritellius had been pleading with him to rescue Squilla. It is urgent – she may hold real answers. We have to get her out now. So where are you on that?'

'I have inherited the problem. Trebianus feared his

volatile agent might do something ill-advised regarding Squilla. I need to find him, and keep him out of the way.' Philippus sounded as if this was the kind of nonsense *his* section never held with. 'From the meagre briefing material I was left, I gather that you, Flavia Albia, suggested Ritellius still visits his wife at her father's house. My men Rubrius and Fuscus have been tasked to track him down. They will tell the wife that if she sees him she should pass on that Trebianus is away on assignment, so I am his new case officer. Then we have to hope she will give Ritellius up. If and when Rubrius and Fuscus make direct contact, they will take him into custody. I do not want a loose malcontent getting in our way.'

I hoped Ritellius did not guess this intention. If so, he would be a loose malcontent who plunged down a secret bolthole.

'And Squilla?'

Philippus nodded. 'She will be removed from the Parthia house. Corellius is keeping me informed about what happens there. I have entrusted the logistics to Rubrius; he is my bagman but also a good strategist.'

'Soon,' I urged. 'If Dolazebol thinks she endangers the Nero plan, he won't hesitate. Corellius believes he would kill her.'

Philippus pursed his lips and put the tips of his fingers together as he did. This made him a good-looking, intelligent man who was considering a grim situation. 'We have seen what measures these people will adopt. They murdered the False Nero; they eliminated Paternus. Control of Rome is such an extreme goal. Nothing will stand in their way.'

★   ★   ★

The three of us talked through a clandestine search for the groomed Nero. I said that if I were the traitor I would keep him incognito at my own house. But no search could be conducted there. Assuming we meant Abascantus, his home was out of bounds.

Philippus smiled. It would have been smug, though he was never that kind of man. 'I can give orders that every room in the home of Abascantus and his wife Priscilla must be checked for suspicious occupants. Abascantus need never know.'

'You have someone there!' Managing not to gulp, I asked sweetly, 'And do you ever suspect Abascantus has a spy of his own in *your* house?'

'I live too simply,' claimed Philippus, though he acknowledged the possibility. 'I have one slave, who has been with me from birth. I find this easiest.'

'No wife?'

He never answered that.

Tiberius muttered, with mock-gloom, 'Living "simply" rules out marriage.'

I did not bother to kick him. He took my hand and kissed it.

We moved on. Since the chief plotter must be an imperial freedman (for the reasons we had once talked about: he had to have knowledge, influence and access to the Parthians), we must search his area of work, the imperial palace. Obscure corners in which to secrete people existed, and he would have access to them.

Again, Philippus produced a suggestion. Trusted staff would wander everywhere with note-tablets, as if they had instructions from the Superintendent of Works to spruce up the palace in advance of the Emperor returning. They would check Domitian's new building, the old palaces that had been superseded, and remaining portions of Nero's Golden House. Particular attention would be paid to underground rooms and hidden passages.

'In the aedilate we have public slaves; they should be untouched by your traitor,' Tiberius offered. 'They are due to have time off to attend the Games. I can disappoint them and make them available to you.' That was hard, but they were slaves. Tiberius then said, 'If you can trust the acting commander of the Praetorians, he should have his men on high alert at the palace to report suspicious activity. Anyone carrying a harp should certainly be arrested!'

Unmoved by the joke, Philippus replied sadly that he was not sure he could trust the Guards' high command. The men most devoted to Domitian had gone with him to Pannonia. Those left here might be inexperienced, or doubtful, or any of them could have been suborned; anyone plotting to take over the Empire would need to woo the Praetorians heavily. But he would see.

The last point we discussed was how to reach Domitian with our story before anyone else could intervene. Tiberius recommended Philippus to approach the Prefect of the City. This man, Rutilius Gallicus, was of consular rank and wide experience, a tough old adherent of Vespasian. As prefect, it would be his task to open the gates of the city to admit Domitian formally as he returned for his double triumph. So he had to know exactly when the Emperor was coming.

My father had worked with Rutilius; Falco thought him a fusspot traditionalist who wrote terrible epic poetry. But he was straight; he was utterly loyal to the Flavians. The idea of a Nero imposter would fill him with horror. We could guess his distaste for the Parthians. As controller of Rome, Rutilius Gallicus was the highest-placed official we could call upon, the highest there was. He had access to significant resources. If Philippus could make a clandestine visit and persuade him of our theory, the prefect would help us.

We agreed to reconvene as soon as searches had been carried out and a plan devised for Squilla. Philippus left me a runner to help us keep in contact.

The first errand I gave the runner was to go to Perella's house. I sent her a message, with a hint to look out for invisible ink, telling her there might be a new danger. A king with a long spear was coming from the east. The men who had stolen the job that should be hers were helpless. Had she any news for me?

When the runner returned to our house, a hired chair containing Perella herself came with him.

46

Perella never even stepped into the house. I was summoned out to her. We spoke through the chair's window curtains. Perhaps it was a precaution, so neighbours in our street would not see her. Perhaps she was just an old lady who could not walk far.

'I saw that Momus for you. Still ghastly. Flavia Albia, you owe me a free holiday at Baiae for it!' I blinked. Baiae is a notorious pleasure spa on the Bay of Neapolis. I believed its glorious baths and casinos accommodated long-haired professional gigolos who tended women of any age with their skilful scented hands, but Perella should only go there if she had no moral qualms and was feeling athletic. Waste of money otherwise.

'Sorry, Perella, I have to consider your welfare. If your information is good, I might run to a nice little health hydro with doctors dispensing sleep therapy.'

'Get lost!' barked the creaky one. 'I don't need my dreams interpreted. I try not to have any.'

With her murdering past, that seemed wise.

'My mother knows a man in Alexandria who does serious purging.'

'Respect to your wonderful mother, but she can keep him. Do you want my news or not?'

'Enough gossip – I do.'

'First,' commanded Perella, peering out of the chair. I noticed her hair was scraped back extra severely. Even seated, she had sensible leather bags slung on her, their straps crossing over her bosom. They looked like the trappings of her old work, probably full of weaponry. 'What was that mad message of yours I needed to hold by an oil lamp? Nobody does that these days, girl. It's too old-fashioned and the letter-searchers know the dodge. I burned all the hairs off my arm.'

'Sorry.'

'The modern way,' Perella instructed, 'is to carve your message on a giant mushroom – a man must have thought up that idiocy – or stick it up a mule's bum. Still not secure: you'll see most guards at checkpoints lifting up animals' tails and poking. It isn't to give them or the mules a thrill.'

Obediently I apologised again. 'I thought you had to write it on a slave's shaved head, but I didn't have time to wait for the hair to grow back and hide the message . . . Thank you for teaching me.'

'My pleasure. Come to me for lore. I can see you have potential. What's the emergency?'

Now we were past the small-talk, I saw no reason to hold back. 'It's this: a spare False Nero is being groomed to take over Rome.'

Perella chortled. 'Oh, simple as that, is it? Bombast and harp lessons? Operated by the cunning one you mentioned?'

'Apparently. With Parthian collusion.'

'Well, of course. What are those useless freedmen doing?' Perella exploded with exasperation. 'Venus and her golden girdle! I can't leave them alone for a moment without the idle barmpots getting in a twist.'

'I know,' I murmured.

'Bloody men!'

'I know, I know . . . So what did Momus contribute?' I ventured.

'Speaking, as we were, of numskulls? That one is more of a steaming turd. Fresh laid. I shall need two hours in a tepidarium to dispel the stink of being in the same room. Not that I ever was: I value my health. I stayed outside the door.'

I smiled as patiently as I could. Sometimes you have to accept being spun a long thread.

'Being back in the palace gave me the creeps, I am not joking, Albia. The first thing that may be of interest,' Perella finally deigned to say, 'is that when I got there, Momus was with the fellow you mentioned, the Princeps of the Castra.'

'Nearly-Nine-Gongs?'

'Let's call him Titus. There's always a twerp called Titus.' Yes, Perella really did know Falco and his sayings.

I remembered how I had seen Titus heading up to the Palatine after he had claimed he wanted a haircut. So he had been off to confer with the smelly grub, Momus?

All became clear when Perella said, 'The Princeps was asking about a man that Momus had disposed of for him earlier this year. Sent to hard labour in Egypt, the mines or marble quarries.' So much for his lovely lady persuading Titus to let the scribe Simon go home to be a scholar! 'Titus, pure lunacy on legs that man, wanted to know the chances of getting back his prisoner. Momus replied, in his charming way, about as much as getting a Vestal Virgin pregnant with twins.'

'I always think the one called Cornelia looks up for it,' I riposted.

'No, she's too bright to be found out . . . Titus went all

serious and threatened Momus, who didn't care, but he admitted there was news of the scribe. On the quiet, once the prisoner came to Alexandria, he gave his guards the slip and made off into the silage like a dung beetle. Alexandria's a big city, I hear.'

'It is.' I had been there. 'Even supposing he stays there. His parents own a farm. Who knows where that may be? But sending out orders and returning him to Rome would take too long, Perella. He might never confess who his paymaster was, in any case.' His paymaster tended to have prisoners killed before they could betray him. I thought sadly of the expendable third False Nero, whose death now seemed even more pointless and vindictive. 'We can't wait. We could have a hideous new Nero prancing on a tribunal in a huge purple cloak by the end of the week.'

'Is he collecting up his city-burning arson kit?'

'Nice big flames, just to prove it's him,' I agreed dourly. 'Expect harping.'

Perella winced. 'I'm old enough to remember Nero's compositions. Perhaps you have to be trained to appreciate talent . . . About returning the scribe – they gave up on that stupid idea. Momus, in his disgusting way, reminded Titus there wasn't time to fuck a goat. We know that. They are men, they have to work it out slowly.' She sounded like an aged auntie agreeing that a young niece's parents were horrid to stop her seeing the over-sexed stable boy. 'They only think with their willies. To see a problem coming would put too much strain on their jewel casket, wouldn't it?'

I nodded meekly, the expected answer. 'So how did you hear this conversation?'

'I stayed outside the door. Keyholes are not just made for turning keys in. The simplest methods are the best.'

The thought that she merely bent over and eavesdropped genuinely amused me. 'So what, then?'

'Old Titus grunted his disappointment, with legionary phrases. He stormed out, so I laid into him sweetly with *"Ooh, Princeps dear, you nearly knocked me flying!"'*

'Does he know you, Perella?' If so, I was only half surprised.

'He had no idea. That's because I am a high-performance agent who should by rights be in control. He's just a bloody great soldier.'

'Nice physique!' I mentioned.

'Needs help with brain work, though. Off he went, all fired up with nothing. I tapped on the doorframe, then tackled Momus. And, in the gunked-up filthy sewers that Momus inhabits, your answer is yes. Some high-placed office-holder close to the Emperor has gone rotten.'

'Sewer-rats ever say his name?'

'They're not stupid. But if they ever whisper a clue, it tends to be *"Abascantus"*. They all hate the golden boy. They would all like to see Abascantus toppled. I would, and come to that, I'd like to topple that rich-widow old wife who pushes him so shamelessly.'

'Goodness, what has his wife done?'

'You never heard? When the godlike Abascantus was promoted to Petitions, Priscilla flung herself flat on the ground in front of Domitian, drooling thanks.'

I mimed throwing up, while I agreed this was seriously over the top.

'Now listen to me, young woman.' Perella leaned right out of the window. Clutching at the top of my tunic so my necklaces jangled, she drew me close. Amid the old-lady whiffs that hovered around her, I imagined I caught the lingering Momus miasma. 'The word is: something big in the offing. They are all twitchy. They don't know what it is, but Momus said to tell you that you had better bring in your father.'

I broke free. I actually stamped my foot with fury. 'Why, Perella, do people always keep asking for Falco? I do a good job. This is my mission!'

'That's right, my dear,' replied the elderly dancer, with her knowing expression. She released her grip on me. 'And you will do it right, we know. This rotter may think he is clever, he may seem untouchable, but you and I will spade up that nasty lump of compost and use him on our rose trees. We can ignore the other fools. Let them scamper around feeling busy. A man needs to be caught here. It's woman's work.'

47

After Perella had left I returned indoors, where Tiberius was talking to his clerk-of-works. Larcius must have been let in through the door in the wall. They nodded to each other as Larcius left again, then Tiberius came across to me.

'Some fellow has been here pestering the men. Asking for work is usually an excuse to get into the yard to case it for theft-worthy materials and tools. After he had sent him off, Larcius went outside and noticed two other men lurking in a doorway.'

Tiberius strode to our front doors, opened up a crack and exclaimed, 'Yes, I see them! Love, our house is being watched. *We* are.'

They must have seen Perella's chair; I wondered if she had spotted them and that was why she stayed hidden. She could have told me!

They would not have known who I was talking to and had not followed her.

I stopped Tiberius going out to accost the men. 'You can arrest them. But professionals won't confess whom they work for. My father always says if you are under observation, leave them alone. At least that way you know who it is and where they are squatting. If you have to go out, just run them ragged.'

Tiberius was torn. But after a moment he closed the doors tight and slowly came back across the atrium. 'You're right. If we scare them off, we may not spot any replacements.'

'What's your plan, aedile?'

He looked like a man who had made a decision, possibly before this had happened. Checking that nothing from Perella required my immediate attention, he made a proposal. For the past few afternoons he had retired to bed, where he either dozed and had bad dreams or lay miserably fretting. Now he said he was ready to make an appearance at the Games. He wanted me to go with him.

He sounded so apprehensive I disputed that he was ready. But this was marriage. He wants to go out. You don't. You end up going.

While we adorned ourselves in the necessary finery, Dromo was sent to borrow the big litter owned by Uncle Tullius. By the time it came, Tiberius was in his whitest tunic, over which I had helped arrange the enormous folds of his purple-bordered toga. I myself had jumped into the fine dress I had worn to go to the Parthia house, plus enough layers of necklaces and bangles to distract attention from my hair, which had a basic up-do, precariously pinned. For an aedile's wife it was too hasty and ham-fisted. Still, I was with the magistrate who had been struck by lightning. No one would be looking at me.

Uncle Tullius had been to the races that morning but was now home for lunch, which in his case meant unspeakable sexual practices followed by two hours dead asleep. He let us have his conveyance. It was huge, carried by six hefty Numidians; those bare-chested heroes were all oiled

335

like polished ebony, but the palanquin was plain, much less flamboyant than that flaunted by the Parthians. As a businessman, Tullius Icilius liked to strike a balance between showing the world he had money and moving unostentatiously from one meet to another as he ran his warehouse empire. He spent a lot of time sipping mint tea at tavern tables, while ruthlessly doing the dirty on other men of commerce. He was good. He had made a small fortune.

Some of the fortune belonged by rights to my husband. Uncle Tullius followed the Roman tradition that family funds belonged in the tight fists of the older generation. We would see. Tiberius was making cautious moves on his personal inheritance. As his wife, by tradition I should push him. So far, I was biding my time.

We clambered aboard the uncle's deluxe transport. I sized up the two observers, unsmiling loiterers in dark tunics; I did not comment to Tiberius, but to me they were so obvious they could only have been put there as a threat. We were intended to notice them. Well, where we were going we were safe: our seats would be too public and they would be unable to come close.

However you attempt it, descending from the Aventine cliffs to the flat valley that contains the Circus Maximus is never easy. Even in a rich man's giant litter, you slide gently forwards frequently as the bearers go down the steep slope. At least bracing and repositioning took our minds off the coming ordeal. There were even giggles. Out on a spree, we were remembering we were newly-weds.

During the long drag down outside the stadium, I tried to keep his mind occupied but I watched Tiberius regretting his decision. Around the Circus on festival days a throng mills, of spectators, food-sellers, prostitutes, gamblers and hustlers of all kinds. The little shops and specially imported stalls that huddle there were doing a good trade. There were scents of smoke, sweat, food and dung. Noises of music, chatter, fights, creaks, crashes. All this hubbub was beginning to bother my man.

Our bearers eventually reached the huge new triple arch that the Senate had created in honour of the Emperor Titus; to gain entrance they had to tell the gate-keepers whom they were delivering. Too late, we discovered that announcing the aedile who had been struck by lightning was a spec-tacular event. Worse than we feared, it happened during a break between races. Accompanied by loud trumpets, our litter – with its big curtains opened – was sent through the main arch, then around the track inside. The special area for magistrates was halfway along on the Palatine side; we were lucky the event-managers wanted to keep to the programme so did not inflict a complete walking circuit on us.

Nerve-racking uproar assailed us as we moved along between the seats and the spina with its water-feature, markers, temples, refuges for track-workers and emergency assistance. We had to travel down towards the high grey granite obelisk that Augustus had transported from Heliopolis. There was an official box; this was contained within a monumental temple, raised high, about opposite where the Temple of Sol sits beside the track. With the best view of the finishing line, this shrine was called the pulvinar, after the long cushioned couch that represents a seat of honour for gods. Augustus built it as a seat of honour for himself. Now it was waiting for us.

All the while cheers increased as word passed along of

337

who we were. Clapping and stamping started. When Tiberius emerged, the whole arena erupted.

He went white. I slid out to my feet, and took his arm firmly. We climbed up to the viewing platform. On this utterly formal occasion, I had expected to be the more nervous of us. Again, this was marriage; I had to help Tiberius. Thank goodness I had come with him, because I was certainly needed.

We reached the top. When a Roman arrives at a venue there is always a useful moment to stabilise: he has to readjust his toga. I assisted like a good wife. Fortunately, when my father had to go togate, it required all his female relatives to stand him still while we made the folds hang right as he cursed us, so I knew how. This task invariably made me reflect on what a mad nation I now belonged to.

'Listen to the people. Congratulations, aedile!'

Tiberius quavered a grin. A wreath appeared for him. A garland for me. We progressed to cool seating under the celebrities' awning, while consuls and other notables stood up to clap us politely. Tiberius diffidently acknowledged the clamour with a raised hand, thanking everyone for their good wishes. We sat. There were cushions. Even footstools. Slaves produced cold drinks. More slaves brought us nut saucers and fruit. Everything began to settle down.

He had made it. To my own surprise, tears were trickling.

We were here. Once he had finished having his hand gripped by his fellow aediles, once their wives, previously strangers to me, had stopped hugging and kissing me in sympathy, Tiberius turned to me while the others were paying attention to the chariots. He was overwhelmed. I smiled. Despite his anxiety, he winked one grey eye back at me.

At last. Now we had achieved the aim of our formal wedding five days ago. Here we were, as one in public – and about as public as it ever could be: Tiberius Manlius Faustus and his wife, Flavia Albia.

48

A really grand imperial box had been created at the top of the new palace. It gave Domitian the best possible view of the Circus, while allowing him to remain virtually invisible to the massed public. When he was in Rome, he might invite officials to join him up there. When he was away, the imperial box remained empty. The pulvinar was prepared for VIPs; they had front-row seats. Wives were allowed to peer over their togaed shoulders from behind them. Exceptionally, I was positioned beside Tiberius. A bride's privilege.

The consuls were together at the other end of the line. Titus Aurelius Fulvus (his father had been consul twice, so Domitian must really be having trouble finding excuses to pick on that family) and Marcus Asinius Atratinus, best known for being unknown. I only remembered their names because the year was officially named after them. Every time you wrote the date, you had to work out how to spell them. These noble ones did not come and speak to us, though they nodded benignly in our direction.

Another man of power must be the praetor, Rome's chief attorney. His wife had acquired extra twinkly jewels in honour of his year in office. I assessed them like an auctioneer's daughter (unlikely to make a profit).

Also present was the man I knew to be Quintus Julius

Cordinus Gaius Rutilius Gallicus, Prefect of the City. A north Italian somewhere over sixty, my family had first met the stomping old buffer when he was a legate for Vespasian in Tripolitania. Later he and my father, who never ducked disaster, held a joint poetry recital in the auditorium of Maecenas; it was still talked about, though not for cultural reasons. After a decent career that had begun under the great general Corbulo – so Rutilius would have an interest in Parthia, I remembered – he had passed through a consulship, governing Galatia and Pamphylia, then Asia *twice* – again, curiously topical – until Domitian had given him his current post, overall charge of Rome itself. As he acted as deputy to a man who called himself a god, the strain was beginning to show.

I suddenly wondered if the chance to meet Rutilius and seek his aid was what had made the dutiful Tiberius brace himself to come today. I would have found an excuse to go along the row and introduce myself – Falco's daughter, wife to the aedile: my accreditations were growing longer. Rutilius had recognised me, or heard about my marriage more likely, so he came to say hello. Perhaps my pa should not disparage him so much.

A race began, so Rutilius actually squatted on the row behind, leaning through to talk to us. For the Prefect of the City, extra cushions were hastily brought. More titbit dishes were handed. Wine was offered.

So, once the slaves had receded, and under cover of the race, I half turned around and spoke to him. With a hundred and fifty thousand people present, I asked for permission to raise an issue in confidence, then warned the trusty Prefect of the dangers aimed at Rome. In the turmoil of a horse race nobody could overhear us. If a hundred and fifty thousand lip-readers were in that audience, we were done for. Luckily the laps on the track were far more important than the distant conversation of two people in the special seats.

Head tipped forward to hear me, Rutilius listened. I was the young wife of a junior magistrate, so he had no need to do that, but he was the type who never turned away work. It would give him a mental breakdown soon, but in this period he was still managing to stay active. Domitian's absence had relieved the strain, temporarily.

I kept things short, little more than signposting, though I named our chief suspect, mentioned Parthia, the Nero substitute, listed our plans to go forward. When I finished, I thought Rutilius sighed to himself, like a man who already had enough burdens. He showed no surprise. He said absolutely nothing, merely handed me a bowl of walnut savouries with the gallant gesture of an older man being courteous. But in taking the bowl, I felt him squeeze my hand. He was not the type to grope a woman; that squeeze was a 'leave it to me' message.

As the City Prefect went back to his own seat, a newcomer entered the pulvinar: Flavius Abascantus, positively glittering. Rutilius Gallicus shook his hand in greeting, then kissed the cheek of the mature, handsome wife who stood respectfully behind, plastered with large Indian pearls. Neither man was effusive. They must work together all the time, so had both mastered the bureaucratic art of acting like friendly colleagues with people they despised. (And, yes, I do suspect distaste went both ways.) No warning was passed to the freedman. No warmth passed from him to the prefect.

Rutilius Gallicus took his own position. He offered another

nut bowl to his wife, Minicia Paetina. She had managed to avoid even a nod for Abascantus and Priscilla. Watching closely, I noticed that Rutilius leaned towards a slave, spoke quietly, then not long afterwards, without people noticing, the Prefect of the City slipped away.

Since I was not required to talk much, I spent time looking at the crowd. Eventually I spotted the seats reserved for foreign dignitaries and other favoured guests of Rome. Among the riot of colour all around the Circus, Parthian envoys stood out in slightly different hues and hats, with much less white than characterised holidaying Romans; they were all under parasols, which would not please those sitting behind. Squinting against the sun, I took a careful register. There were Dolazebol and Bruzenus, plus the veil-wearing ladies Marcia and I had met, and they must have brought all their retainers.

No Squilla.

I motioned to Tiberius, showing him where the Parthians were seated. 'Did you send them tickets?'

'Someone else must have done.'

'Abascantus,' I growled under my breath, then murmured, 'The lovely Squilla must be home alone.'

I had a wonderful husband. He gave me a long look – though not the most reproving in his repertoire. Without my even asking, he whispered to another aedile that the Circus Maximus commotion was a little too much for him today, so he was making his excuses. He intended to go to the theatre tonight instead, where a play called *The Spook Who Spoke* was being performed. He had to go to that. His father-in-law had written it.

We left by a back route this time, the way the Prefect of

the City must have gone before us. Rutilius was probably collected in a comfortable litter; ours had gone home to Uncle Tullius. But since most people were staying at the races until the programme ended, a line of empty carrying chairs with bored bearers stood waiting.

It took us a while because Tiberius Manlius believed it was the role of a husband always to ask what a journey would cost before he let his wife climb aboard (however much her sandal-straps were hurting as she stood in full sun going nowhere). I looked around nervously, in case I saw the two men who had lurked outside our house. Tiberius had to argue. As an aedile, whose job was to monitor such things, he claimed there were official fixed fares with penalties for not sticking to them; the bearers assured him it had been agreed by long tradition that on Games days all prices were doubled.

This was true. It was agreed by annoyed customers who grumpily paid up because otherwise they had to walk home.

While he was still hotly negotiating, we heard our names called. Claudius Philippus came scurrying up. He said he had seen us in the pulvinar, then noticed us leaving. So we all walked off to find somewhere to confer urgently, followed by the bearers' curses.

49

We walked briskly along the side of the Circus in the shadow of the Palatine. Despite promising Tiberius I would not do it again, I had been intending to go around the hill to the Parthia house. I explained to Philippus how I thought Squilla must be there on her own, and that I would try to see her. Perhaps Corellius would let me in. If everyone else was out at the Games, maybe I could even spring her. In fact, why didn't Corellius just do it?

Philippus explained and dashed my hopes. The situation at the house had changed. Earlier, Corellius had sent word that Dolazebol had turned on Squilla and made her his prisoner. Today she had been taken away under guard. It had not been possible to follow because Corellius had been despatched on an errand while it happened. By the time one of his trusties told him, she was gone.

I sighed. 'I suppose it has always been obvious to the Parthians that Corellius was watching them.' Presumably they followed my father's rule: when you know who the observers are, leave them alone. 'What about the gardener, Trebianus' man?'

'Unfortunately he was gardening. If he had suddenly downed tools, it would have blown his cover.'

That was the trouble with planting a spy who had a specific job. If he stopped, it drew attention. There must always be a risk, too, that he would like his work, becoming so absorbed in it that he missed crucial events. The jasmine on the trellis, tended so assiduously, had a lot to answer for.

There was no point in causing a disturbance at the Parthia house if Squilla had been transferred elsewhere. We all agreed we hoped she was still alive, wherever they were keeping her. Then we walked along to where the Steps of Cacus come steeply down from the Palatine, at which point Tiberius and I would go home and Philippus would leave us. He was going back to see if anything had come out of the searches for the new Nero. He complained that it seemed unlikely because the Palatine was such a rabbit warren. There were old and new corridors, endless collections of storage rooms, abandoned imperial quarters, areas that had been infilled with rubble so more buildings could be developed on top, and other parts damaged by subsidence.

I wondered if Squilla and the new False Nero were being kept out of sight in a single location. It seemed unwise. I wouldn't do it myself.

I wondered who was looking after Squilla's cat.

50

We spent a quiet afternoon. This is a luxury during an investigation. To enjoy it properly, you just have to stop believing your task is hopeless. But relaxing can make you miserable. We stood little chance of finding the groomed Nero and I had few hopes of retrieving Squilla. This meant proving the existence of a palace traitor was also unlikely. We had all put ourselves in danger to no purpose, I thought bitterly.

That evening, we went out again, to the theatre. Tiberius had told his colleague how one of the plays had been written by his new father-in-law, Falco. With typical reticence he omitted to say he wanted to check up on the festival dramas. Aediles organised these Roman Games; Tiberius had selected the plays and their performers, then fitted them to venues. He couldn't just leave it at that; being him, he had to make sure everything worked out well.

The Spook Who Spoke was hilarious. Its first and previously only performance had been in the desert at Palmyra. That had literally caused a riot. My mother always became misty-eyed with laughter when she remembered, though my father, the sensitive author, tended to be huffy. We all knew he saw the ingénu hero as patterned on his younger self. This time, he had tried to grab himself the part of the ghost, but the producer had persuaded him to stand down 'so a novice can be given a try-out'.

The play was to be performed in a small temporary theatre in the Forum Boarium, the cattle market. Tiberius had told my father he thought it would be 'more intimate'. He really meant he did not expect a large audience to put their backsides on the wavering wooden seats. I suspected he purposely set *Spooky* at the same time as a rude mime at the Theatre of Pompey, which would be popular because it was rumoured there were nudes, and a choral event in the Theatre of Marcellus that featured a particularly fine tenor. Nobody cared about his singing; people would crowd in to hear him because he was having a scandalous affair with a senator's young daughter. Everyone hoped the senator would turn up incandescent. Tenors know how to advertise.

The original actors were performing *The Spook Who Spoke*, undeterred by notoriety. Their company was owned by Thalia, my young brother's birth mother. This gave us an added reason to go, for my family is hot on loyalty – when it's loyalty that you hope will give you much to talk about next Saturnalia. Besides, we wanted Postumus to experience the heritage he had luckily escaped when Falco and Helena so generously adopted him.

Before the prologue, Tiberius had to accept the applause of this crowd. Better prepared now, he managed bravely, even though the audience was bigger than he had expected. People are attracted by the hope of disaster.

In fact, everything turned out quite well. That was disappointing. We took Dromo. He loved it.

Afterwards everyone else trundled off to my parents'

house for celebrations, which were to include one of Father's grills and much wine provided by Uncle Lucius. Tiberius and I went quietly home. He looked exhausted, though was in good spirits.

At Lesser Laurel Street, two spies remained on duty, still standing in their doorway, motionless as caryatids. Their menace was lessened by the fact we now expected them.

Tiberius went to the yard where he spoke to Larcius. The clerk-of-works told him the watchers had been no trouble. They had bought themselves fried squid for supper, drunk from a flask, tossed leftovers into the gutter, kept the flask because they could claim a discount next time if they took it back. They spoke to no one. If they peed in the doorway they did it discreetly and it was not our doorway. Larcius had taken the watchdog out for a walk, encouraging him to bark at them. Larcius himself pointedly called out, 'Evening!' just to let them know they had been spotted.

While we were out, the Fabulous Stertinius had called on the off-chance, hoping for supper. Larcius said he had been in a mood; Stertinius had gone to give someone a lesson that evening, only to find his student had climbed out of his bedroom window and bunked off to a bar.

'We offered a share of our pies, but he said no thanks if they came from Xero's. He has a concert tomorrow and can't risk being laid low with the runs. I told him the trick is to avoid the rabbit version, because Xero uses rats in those, but he mooched off. Shame, really. The dog was all keyed up; a lullaby might have calmed him.'

The watchdog was quiet now. Larcius said that was

because he had been fed. He liked a pie. Even Xero's, though they gave him flatulence.

Not long afterwards, my cousin Marcia came. Her evening had begun with a drink with Marius. Like Stertinius, he had been let down: the Parthians must all have gone on somewhere after the races so he had had nobody to play his flute for.

That had not stopped him meeting Marcia. They were later joined by Corellius, though he could not stay long because he wanted to be home to check on the Parthians' return.

'So did you leave Marius all on his own?' Solitary drinking could be bad for a philosopher. Marius might upset himself, commentating mentally on society's ills.

Marcia shook her head. 'He was all right. He had some mate with him. I could tell they were intending to make a night of it.' Because of the Games there would be a good atmosphere out on the streets, for lads who liked to party.

I teased Marcia about losing her chance with Corellius. 'Oh no, it's all on. He has asked me back to his place later.'

'Not the Parthia house, Marcia! It's too dangerous.'

'Well, I can't take him to mine,' she snapped. The fact that her mother was becoming confused these days ought to allow greater privacy. But Marina would wander in at the most inconvenient moments. Then, worse, she would suppose they were still back when she, the one-time fabulous beauty, had kept herself in funds by attracting men. Reluctant to be preyed on by a now-dud elderly good-time girl, Marcia's fellows fled. 'I am not having it happen with Corellius.'

'Fair enough.'

The night was still young when my cousin went off to her tryst. Tiberius insisted she be put in a hired carrying chair, which we paid for. I saw the doorway spies taking an interest, though they did not tail her.

If they had, they would have been tired out. Marcia must have made it to the house, urging the bearers to go fast. She gained admittance at the discreet back entrance, giving a special knock for Corellius. Their night of passion never happened. He sent her straight back to us with a message: 'Crisis! Bruzenus has been kidnapped. Nobody can imagine how. The whole house is in uproar, but he is definitely missing. A baker's boy was paid by a stranger to bring in a message to Dolazebol. If he wants his man back, he has to make an exchange for Squilla.'

'Juno! There's no mistake?'

'The messenger brought that ghastly torque as proof. It must have been difficult to wrench off his neck – it's bent and there was blood on it.'

'Nice touch! That would emphasise his danger.'

'Corellius is furious,' Marcia told me. 'He called it point-less and amateur. He said to tell you this is not official. It's the crazy agent, pushing for a fast recovery of his girlfriend. The swap is tomorrow, at sunrise, in the Porticus of the Danaids.'

I said that was good. There would be fifty statues of murderous brides, fifty more of their luckless bridegrooms, plus Apollo and the stone oxen carved by Myron, all for people to hide behind.

The satire was too fine for Marcia, who frowned. 'Each of the people being exchanged must have only one person bring them. Those are the conditions. Otherwise the whole deal is off.'

Tiberius was looking apprehensive, but I laughed.

51

It should have happened on a bridge. That is the classic location for parleys between enemies when they reach the final compromise. For an exchange of hostages, it is ideal. Everyone can see what is happening. They have an excellent view of the planned handover spot, even in longueurs when nothing is happening. No gangs of men can burst out of hiding. If you choose the right river, even a clandestine boat will be swept away.

Ritellius seemed to have forgotten this part of spies' training.

It was a calm, bright morning at the end of the hour after cockcrow. The rectangular top of the Palatine Hill lay silent, bathed in thin sunlight. In the city below, daily activities had started. Children were being roused and dressed; the sick who had finally dozed off were shaken awake again by cruel nurses; obsessive athletes entered gymnasia; every third pigeon opened one eye. After the festival night preceding, both inanimate and human detritus was being shovelled off the streets. Business began again. Nobody noticed that the imperial area was in the grip of an exercise.

Nothing new there, anyway. The Praetorian Guards were always annoying us with special checks and shakedowns.

Up here, the south-western corner was dominated by

Domitian's palace, with its enormous marble halls and private garden stadium; the whole lay strangely still. Iron entrance gates, which, ironically, had been installed after Nero's reign, were locked. Guards stood there as well. Gates at the foot of the hill, gates in monumental arches, gates giving access to the ramp and the Cryptoporticus were also closed to the public. Nobody had thought to close off the pinch-point at the top of the Steps of Cacus, so I climbed from the Circus Maximus corner and gained access.

The narrow steps, named after a fire-breathing, cattle-herding cannibal monster, brought me up between the Temple of the Victory and the House of Augustus. This was ideal for the precincts of Apollo on their massive platform above. Less ideal was that I ran into a cluster of men conferring: Philippus, with his assistants Rubrius and Fuscus, and the Princeps Peregrinorum. Titus had left his eight *phalerae* at home, no doubt hoping for a roughhouse, which might damage his treasured medals. When the others scurried off to hide in the cella of Apollo's Temple, Titus crooked his finger. 'Come with me, little Albia, if you want a good time!'

I went with him because I thought he had the most sense. With the exchange due in the Porticus, people up in the temple might be out of sight but they would never hear anything, and would be unable to take useful action without running down a long steep flight of steps. Rubrius and Fuscus might take those six at a time but if Philippus, who was not athletic, tumbled on the slippery marble, he risked a broken pelvis.

Titus and I ensconced ourselves in shade behind a corner Danaid. Naturally he patted her shapely posterior. Our dryad had been supplied with a jug and a big pot, from which water leaked, to symbolise the punishment the guilty sisters had imposed on them in Tartarus, endlessly attempting to fill up a holed pithos after killing their fifty husbands. Well, forty-nine husbands. Hypermnestra spared hers as his reward for respecting her virginity. I would have had mixed feelings about that, except that they went on to found a dynasty.

'Admiring my spear?' asked Titus.

I had no such intention but I feared we were in for a long wait there. Delay in a hostage exchange is traditional. Indeed, not turning up at all has precedents. To fill time, I dutifully expressed an interest in my companion's beautifully maintained military equipment.

We chatted. It became lengthy. Unsurprisingly, Titus was a weapons hobbyist; a friend of his, now dead, had made special adaptations to the very spear he was carrying now. Titus explained various technical points, how a lead weight could be added to the head to improve penetration, though that slowed the flight, or how your spear could be fletched with leather strips or feathers to help rotation, which kept flight straight and hits accurate. 'You can bind your handhold for extra grip, but must position only two fingers actually on the binding because you want the shaft to slip through your hand as you throw.'

'Neat!' All I knew was that Roman spears had iron heads that were intended to bend when they stuck in an opponent's shield. 'They can't pull it out, so throw their shield away and are at your mercy. Next stop, theta-ed.' 'Theta' was military slang, the Greek initial for *thanatos* or death. Thanatos, son of Night and Darkness, twin brother of Sleep. Theta was the mark put on a dead soldier's record.

'Good girl!' Titus was full of mock-approval for this basic knowledge.

'I was married to a soldier once. An accident waiting to happen; if there was a broken board, he stepped right on it. I was glad we lived here. In the north, keeping him off ice on ponds would have been hell. But a dear boy.'

'Well, bear up, they can't all be crack men. Have to expect a few duds.'

'Don't call him a dud, Titus. I loved him.'

'Still, you've got a nice new one now.'

'Smoke-blackened and hair on end.'

'All right if you can get it. I bet he's hot stuff!'

'True.'

He had been. I hoped he would be again.

He was waiting for me back at home. He had declared that if I failed to return in time, today he was off to the Circus on his own. I knew people would warn me this was not a good start to a marriage.

In truth, though he tried not to show it, Tiberius was desperately worried about me attending this hostage exchange.

Titus and I talked about spears again. It was better than having to talk about chariot races. Thinking of Rutilius Gallicus, I said having an interest in weapons was at least better in an old soldier than writing awful epic poetry. The Princeps, ever open to dangerous new ideas, looked interested. Now *he* was thinking of composing some twelve-book nightmare, and it would be my fault.

One thing we reminisced about was how, in the terrible defeat at Carrhae, the Parthians won because they shot barrages of arrows further than the Romans could hurl their javelins. The enemy stayed out of reach while the legions were massacred. Afterwards Rome developed spears that could travel longer distances, out-firing the Parthians.

355

'So even the army's classic weapons are redeveloped occasionally?' I wanted Titus to say what was so special about his friend's adaptations.

'Nothing was. He thought he made some mystery improvement, but bugger me if I can tell any difference. He liked to tinker. No harm in that – though it got him into big trouble. I've just brought this one today because we always spent a lot of time talking about the need for better fire-power than Parthia. So, in my old pal's memory, I hope to loose off a Lucullan today.'

Lucullan! I jumped.

'Princeps, you knew Sallustius Lucullus, lately governor of Britain?' He gave me a laconic nod. 'You presumably know what Domitian did to him. Any comments?'

'None,' said the Princeps, in his well-turned voice of finality. 'We had a shared interest in weapons. We tinkered with spears in a workshop. Mates. We never talked about politics.'

'Who mentioned politics?'

'You were going to.'

A slave in palace livery entered the Porticus. He strolled towards the temple.

Our three colleagues slithered out between the over-ornate Corinthian Composite columns. The boy shouted. They came down the steps openly. Rubrius called across to us: 'The exchange is cancelled.'

52

Philippus said Ritellius had sent a message to their office
in the palace. It had taken time to arrive because of
the locked gates. There was no explanation for his change
of plan. But hitches, often deliberate, were customary in
intelligence.

None of the others was sure what to do next. Ritellius,
a crazy man, was controlling events. Nobody knew how to
contact him.

To me, delay was good. While the Princeps had been
gossiping about spears, half my mind was forming a suspicion. Sometimes information you barely noticed consciously
comes back to you of its own accord. I suddenly had a new
idea about the groomed False Nero.

I volunteered to slip down the Cryptoporticus, the straight
covered way to the Forum, which ended nearby. I said I
would call at the Parthia house, to ask Corellius what he
knew of this delay; Ritellius must have sent new instructions
to Dolazebol. They fell for it. The rest of them were going
back to the palace.

By the time we all left the Porticus of the Danaids the
gates had been opened; people were everywhere.
Nevertheless, a lone woman could slip through if she made
herself look innocuous. The few Praetorians in the

Cryptoporticus were inspecting visitors coming in, not me going out.

I wondered if someone was following me. Well, let them.

My rapping at the Parthians' back door summoned Corellius. 'No action at the Porticus. What's occurring here?'

Corellius told me yesterday's uproar over the Bruzenus kidnap had simmered down. Dolazebol had stayed in today. 'He's putting on a show of concern, though the two of them are always squabbling. Bruzenus has ambitions. Dolazebol never wanted to bring him to Rome, but strings were pulled, so he had to be included. It's typical of Parthia. Dolazebol believes Bruzenus is plotting behind his back, but now he has to make a show of rescuing him from Ritellius.'

I made Corellius let me in. We dived into his room; if Marcia had been last night, she had left no evidence. However, the agent confessed she was there – and Dolazebol had learned of it. He had had her taken to the women's room; Corellius could not stop it, and was despairing of how to rescue her.

'If Dolazebol has taken against Squilla, in his mind there will be a vacancy . . .'

'Never mind that.' I was brisk. 'Marcia won't be moved by him. I want to follow up what you said about Bruzenus. To me, it sounds as if it could be *him* who is plotting with the palace traitor. Dolazebol either doesn't know, or could be playing a shrewd game. If Bruzenus' plot fails, Dolazebol plays the innocent; if it succeeds, he welcomes the result and joins in. Either way, if Dolazebol has been excluded from the plotting so far and is angry about it, he may not actually want to retrieve Bruzenus from Ritellius.'

'Oh, he has to,' Corellius assured me. 'Even though they

loathe one another, he must save face. He cannot let a Roman capture a fellow Parthian.'

'Well, we'll see. Something else intrigues me . . .' I fired off questions: 'Do you keep a list of visitors and was one of them yesterday the Fabulous Stertinius?'

The agent looked startled. 'Yes.'

'How often does he come?'

'Every two days.'

'Not for concerts?'

'He gives music lessons.'

'Who to?'

'Bruzenus' nephew. I keep away. The repertoire they are practising is horrible.'

'I bet! Nephew, name of?'

Corellius, apprehensive, saw I had a reason behind my questions. 'My complement list for the Parthians is sketchy. Half are just called "family members" – their names are so hard to pronounce, we never quibbled. "Nephew".'

'Describe.'

Corellius shrugged feebly. 'I never see him really.'

'Is he kept apart?'

'Choice, I think. He seems unhappy to be here. He stays in his room like a moody lad. He's older, though. Thirties?'

Oh, rats. 'This is not moody puberty. He is hidden, hidden in plain sight – right under your nose, Corellius! Show me your money.'

'*What?*'

'Get a purse – hurry!'

I knew from searching his room that he kept a purse under his mattress. As soon as he dived under and produced it, I grabbed the bag, tore open the top strings, slewed out coins across the bed. I picked out what I wanted: a silver sestertius, *Nero on the reverse, bare-headed and togate, seated on a curule chair to distribute coins to a citizen.* I flipped it. Obverse: *Nero, youngish, straight nose, forward chin, curly hair on a bull neck, chubby cheeks, smiling.* 'That "nephew" bear any resemblance?'

Corellius grasped the point.

I told him to take me to the women. It might have worked: the bored Parthian ladies might have introduced me to Bruzenus' nephew. In the room with them was Marcia. I sent her a swift glare, as she knelt on the floor pretending to play with the grey and white kittens. By her standards, she was looking anxious.

Then a figure arose from a low divan and I was greeted by a maliciously smooth voice: 'Ah, Flavia Albia, come in. We have been expecting you!'

Dolazebol.

I had space to jump back to the doorway, away from him. Corellius was there. I assumed he would let me go past him, making my escape.

Wrong. Instead, he opened his arms, grasping the door frames to block me. He gave me a shrug of apology. I groaned.

My lovely cousin had fallen for a double agent.

53

With no escape, I might as well try to learn something. I had a bad feeling I would never manage to pass it on, but instead of allowing Dolazebol to run this scene, I took charge. I strode forwards, announcing to the Parthian ladies that I was looking for Bruzenus' nephew. He was wanted by the Roman authorities for impersonating Nero. To have any chance of saving him from justice, they must surrender him to me.

This caused a flare-up. Dolazebol clearly tried to dismiss my claim as nonsense. He looked almost beseeching as he attempted to calm his womenfolk, which went badly wrong on him. 'Ladies, ladies, don't blame me. It was Bruzenus, always Bruzenus and his special friend. He talks to Rome in secret. The scheme was never going to work; it was crazy.'

Even his questionable diplomatic charm was failing. Women conferred together in shock. They arose from their cushioned couches, like gorgeously coloured butterflies. One in particular, Asxen, Bruzenus' wife, rounded on Dolazebol, loudly attacking him in Greek so we could follow her outburst.

The young man was *her* nephew. She loved him. Others had used him. *He* was innocent. None of the women had been told before why he was brought to Rome; now they knew, so they saw how he had hated what was being done to him, and they were furious.

Stirring the mix, I said, 'This is so dangerous. You must be terrified. False Neros are killed cruelly. If the Romans catch him, your poor young man will die like all the others.'

Dolazebol let out a shout, calling for his men. Marcia and I might be about to disappear for ever – yet surely he was too clever to risk the consequences. Besides, he could still blame Bruzenus for everything, and with the women in uproar against the plot, I felt braver.

Asxen continued in her deliberate Greek: 'So that is why he was kept out of sight! He is a lovely musician but they made him practise terrible old tunes. Well, he went out for a good time and has not come home. He climbed through a window and escaped, Dolazebol – in spite of you and Bruzenus.'

That confirmed what Stertinius had said yesterday about his pupil bunking off. It was oddly reminiscent of Nero, who famously prowled the streets at night with violent cronies, beating people up for their own amusement. If the young Parthian's doting aunt was right, his idea of adventure was harmless, but if he had failed to come home, where was he now? Hopefully, he had not fallen foul of the vigiles.

Asxen turned to me. She was weeping. 'Please help him. His name is Haxamanis.'

'I will help, but I need to leave here.'

The distraught aunt grasped both my hands, unthinkingly impeding movement. Marcia jumped to her feet and came to me. Kittens tumbled in all directions over the floor, while the white cat Vindobona suddenly clambered up a carpet that was hung on a wall. He clung to the knotted wool with sharp claws, running right up to the ceiling.

Furious that no male attendants had appeared, Dolazebol yelled out again. He began to move towards the door, striding in his curl-toed Persian boots. If the guards arrived, we were done for. But it never came to that.

Vindobona launched himself downwards. He landed on the envoy's neck, digging in needle claws; he was a big creature, with some weight. Dolazebol shrieked.

As the cat attached himself, the Parthian forgot us while he tried to grasp him. I shook off Asxen. I dragged an arm around Marcia to pull her with me.

Corellius still blocked the exit.

'*Bastard!*' My cousin Marcia, the boxing queen, bounced on her toes, making fists. She caught her two-timing lover completely by surprise. It was classic – four moves: jab; cross; hook; uppercut. Her jab was relaxed, the rest were power punches. The girl really meant it. Corellius went down without a murmur.

Holding hands, we stepped over him.

We ran to the front doors, where a man dressed as a gardener saw us coming, so he quickly opened them; we ran out headlong. I had the impression Trebianus' spy would close the doors after us, then impassively go back to watering a large plant in an urn.

Just as those doors were meeting together, the white cat shot through the closing gap. Vindobona must have dashed between the gardener's legs. On his heels raced two beautiful, extremely fast, silky-haired sighthounds. Ecstatic in the chase, they sped down the Forum, full of grace and eagerness, as if coursing in some desert of their remote homeland.

Vindobona disappeared, fleeing for his life up the Via Sacra, a long-haired, desperate streak of white.

54

I sent Marcia home. Her street, that of Honour and Virtue, was only a step away. I knew she had really liked Corellius. Wounds of the heart needed attention.

I had other plans. Steadying my breath, I walked straight to the ivory workshop around the corner from the Arch of Titus. Outside in an open space, they were working on a batch of furniture, attaching finely carved panels to various cupboards and couches, using giant pots of fish glue. This pungent gel was even being spread on the doors of a carrying chair where it would dry in the sun to give a crackled finish. I knew they brushed on glue, left the surface to go tacky, then powder-painted the item, which would set in crinkles. My father had told me. It is a trick for creating new 'antiques'.

The workers must have been taking advantage of the still-early morning period. Anyone who was out and about had things of their own to do; fewer members of the public would start complaining at the fish-scale smell. Covering my nose, I asked for Ilia. Nobody took much notice so I went to where I had found her last time. When she saw me marching in, she put aside her work protectively.

'Stop messing about, Ilia!' I had no time for finesse. 'I am on to you, woman. You have been leading the spies a fine dance, but the game's up. You deal with me now – and I know exactly what you have been playing at.'

The woman looked truculent, but under my verbal assault I could see her weakening.

Fired up by our narrow escape from Dolazebol, I blazed away: 'It's your choice, Ilia. Either you tell me the truth or soldiers will come and take you in chains to prison. Listen: I *know* Ritellius has not been at your father's house. I dare say your honest old father would cudgel him for how he has behaved to you and your poor dead daughter. But you, you still support that bastard. Agents watched your home for him, while all the time your cheating husband was holed up elsewhere – and you knew it.'

Her face set in an unpleasant mask. I needed something stronger or she would confess nothing. Ritellius had completely trapped her in his lifetime of schemes.

'You lied about everything, Ilia. I know when the freedmen informed you Ritellius had done a bunk that it wasn't even soup you threw at the messenger, was it? You worked here all along. The palace man saw you here. It was a glue pot you heaved at him.'

This guess of mine, pure bluff, began to work. My certainty about that incident made Ilia think I knew much more.

I kept up the pressure. 'Ritellius is engaged in a dangerous caper. You know his bolthole. I'm sure you trot along to him, bringing food, even money. He has taken a hostage who must be there right now; perhaps you have seen the man. It's not for your benefit. He intends to swap his hostage for Squilla. Squilla, his eternal darling. Squilla, the subtle goddess with the lush blonde hair, who will supplant you, Ilia. If Ritellius survives, then whatever nonsense he has promised you, he and Squilla will be together. Not you. He uses you, but he wants her.'

She knew I was right. She had known all along.

'The Lupercal.' Ilia finally turned on her husband. 'The dirty double-dealer is hiding in the cave of the Lupercal.'

55

I was beginning to know the circuit around the base of the Palatine Hill much too well. It can be a long, hot pavement hike.

As I set off, I gained company. Fuscus, the silent man who worked for Philippus, must have followed me down the Cryptoporticus. It was little consolation that if Dolazebol had harmed Marcia and me, this man would have been outside the house. Eventually, he would have reported to someone that I was most likely killed. I doubted he would have broken in and saved us.

He had a runner with him, whom he sent up the hill to tell Philippus where we were going. I never actually heard him say, 'Send reinforcements,' but with Fuscus little was voiced aloud.

The Cave of the Lupercal, a centuries-old venerated spot, is supposed to be where the shepherd Faustulus discovered chubby little Romulus and Remus being nursed by a she-wolf. As an adopted child myself, I took a passing interest in this myth, though I considered old Faustulus had caused much trouble in the world.

The craggy hole lies deep in the Palatine bedrocks, beneath the House of Livia. Augustus, in his lordly way, had assumed ownership, built villas for himself on top, and reconfigured the natural cavern with expensive artistic decorations. No wolf would venture into it now.

Outside, observing from a discreet distance, we found Rubrius and the Princeps. Rubrius was lying on the ground, to minimise the target he presented. Titus, with a sardonic expression, stood at attention alongside, braving any missile that might be shot from the cave. When we arrived, he decided to check inside. He told us to wait. He laid a hand on his sword pommel; he had decreed that on an exercise like this in Rome, a Princeps Peregrinorum was entitled to bear arms. However, he did not bother to draw the sword.

He went in. There was a pause. He reappeared and told us nobody was there.

We followed him in. Titus, inevitably well-prepared, had a flint about his person, which he struck on the scrumptious Augustan tiles. Shielding the flame with a big careful hand, he lit a small lamp that stood there, waiting for his gentle attentions.

We were in the modern version of a wolf's cave. It had been turned into a fancy cavern, finely decorated everywhere with glistering coloured mosaics and marble pieces, plus patterns created with numerous shells to suggest this was still a natural feature. A fancy white eagle surveyed us from the central roundel of the ceiling. For a hillside cave, the Lupercal was surprisingly dry, though pongy.

We found evidence of human habitation. Someone had been there, possibly as recently as last night. Maybe more than one. It was impossible to be sure because the place was used by courting couples. They left behind food rubbish, then pooed and peed in dark corners. Romans know how to treat a venerated shrine, at least when the guards go off duty. Ritellius must have been confident he could scare them away.

Rubrius and Fuscus decided to return to the palace for further orders. Titus and I chose to wait.

'Where are your men, Titus?' My voice sounded echoey in the cave.

'What men?'

'Princeps, I do not believe you came out today without full military support.'

He smiled. Though he gave me no answer I knew he would have troops when he needed them.

Eventually we heard scuffling sounds. I nudged Titus, suggesting he should blow out the lamp, but he kept it alight so we saw who entered.

It was a big, shaven-headed man of Germanic build, wide-shouldered. He had faded blue eyes and the white-skinned, freckle-peppered colouring of a one-time red-head. He wore a patched brown tunic and heavy-duty combat boots, meticulously strapped. I glimpsed weapons fastened to him under a cloak that he had trussed close to his body. He also had a hat. This would have concealed his face, but he took it off as he entered the cave.

When he saw us, he bellowed, 'This place is requisitioned, so get lost. If you're here for a shag, go and fuck somewhere else.'

His voice was cultured and arrogant. His language was easy and crude, a man who had been expensively educated in rhetoric but who affected to despise it. I did not take to him.

'Gaius Ritellius!' the Princeps replied, in a smouldering tone of welcome. He must have owned the spies' handbook,

369

because he used the same script as Dolazebol. 'Come in, man. We have been expecting you!'

He had pulled out his sword. It slid from its underarm scabbard with a telling whoosh. The blade was in good fettle. With his spare arm, he pushed me flat against the grotto wall, a safety measure. 'Do not make me use this.'

Only a fool would have done so, but we were dealing with one of life's ludicrous risk-takers. From his look, Ritellius intended to jump the Princeps. It never happened. Instead, Fuscus silently reappeared right behind Ritellius. He fixed him in an arm lock, applying a bright dagger to his throat. It was the grip, not the blade, that was making him gasp.

Rubrius joined us too, tough-talking: 'Where is Bruzenus?'

Half choked, Ritellius spluttered, 'Let go, Fuscus. Stop enjoying it!' Old comrades, I thought. Same training course.

Rubrius nodded to Fuscus, who loosened his grip marginally.

The big maverick then admitted he had stalked Bruzenus yesterday night, when the Parthians were out on the town after the Games. They had gone in a noisy group to visit their own exotic animals, their camels and elephant, out at the Imperial Menagerie. Ritellius tailed them until a message was brought to Bruzenus; without saying anything to his companions, the henchman split off from the others, taking only a few guards. Ritellius went after him. Bruzenus then seemed to be searching city entertainment places.

'Trying to find his nephew,' I explained. Rubrius quirked up an eyebrow. 'Potential Nero. Being trained in statecraft and harping, but he's run away from home.'

If we wondered how such a mountain of flesh as Bruzenus could be overcome and carried off, Ritellius had borrowed

370

– stolen – a delivery cart. It was night as the Parthians were coming home from the menagerie. Once Bruzenus left the main party, in the dark he became more vulnerable. Emerging from the festival crowds, Ritellius had jumped the hard man, the way Fuscus had just grabbed him, with a knife at the man's neck. Threatening to slit the Parthian's throat if he called to his guards, Ritellius had dragged Bruzenus away down a dark side-street, trussed him, gagged him, put him on the cart and drove off like Pluto emerging from Hades.

'You had better hope Dolazebol really wants to get him back,' I scoffed, from against my wall. Dry or not, it was clammy to the touch and the mosaic tesserae scratched my bare arms. 'Do you know about the plot with Bruzenus' nephew?'

There were four men here with me; clearly none of them had worked it out. I rounded on Ritellius. 'You have no idea how many layers of intrigue your stupid stunt has interfered with! His name is Haxamanis. He was at the Parthia house, being trained for public duties. Squilla presumably knows. For that alone, she will be lucky if Dolazebol ever lets her go. But the only possible reason for Rome to take an interest is if your louche girlfriend also knows who Bruxenus has been plotting with here. Who is his "special friend" in Rome? If she is genuinely on our side, we need her to say so. What exactly have you told Dolazebol about swapping her?'

Ritellius grumpily told us his plan. He had the captive Parthian, still tied up and hidden in that other pastiche of ancient times, the Hut of Romulus. He had found a notice saying 'Men at Work', which of course meant the men had vanished for a month. The structure was closed for

371

renovation; it so often required new reeds and wattle, nobody would think anything of it. Bruzenus could be well-hidden there.

The supposed meeting at the Porticus of the Danaids had been a feint. To unsettle the Parthians (he claimed), Ritellius had sent Dolazebol a new message at cockcrow, telling him a changed plan.

Instead, he would transport Bruzenus from the hut on the cart, which he had originally found there laden with tools. 'He's in the cart ready now. All I have to do is jump aboard and drive it.'

In the new plan, they would travel along the hilltop to the palace's banquet hall. Dolazebol was to bring Squilla. There was a monumental fountain, a complex nymphaeum; they would arrive on either side of it, then each send a hostage around to the opposite side of this water feature.

After the exchange, Ritellius would whisk his girlfriend away on other transport. To cover their escape, he asked Rubrius that the authorities should arrest the Parthians.

Rubrius and the Princeps quickly conferred. They decided they might as well let this caper go ahead. Most of us thought it was lousy, but it was so vague, no one offered to pick real holes in it. We had run out of time. Ritellius told us everything was due to happen in the next hour.

Rubrius let Ritellius go to fetch Bruxenus. Rubrius himself rushed off with Fuscus to organise official forces.

One fault with the changed plan, as Titus told me while he and I hurried from the Lupercal and up the Steps of Cacus, was that when such arrangements are altered for strategic reasons, you are supposed to bring the critical event forward;

the point of changing is to interfere with any counter-measure your opponent has.

Ritellius had put his plan back. It gave more scope for the adventure to go wrong, which Titus prophesied would happen.

'So why has he changed it?'

'Because he's an idiot.'

'He thinks he is clever.'

'That,' opined the Princeps, 'makes him an idiot of the worst kind.'

I saw another flaw. Ritellius wanted to free Squilla, so he could run away with her. But if she knew the name of the palace traitor, other people would try to stop that. She was in most danger from the Parthians. Yet Philippus wanted to grab her; Abascantus, or whoever it was, wanted to prevent him.

In the doom-laden words of Simon the scribe, I now foresaw implacable wrath and ruination.

56

Titus went off, claiming he had to answer a call of nature. 'Just popping to the three-seater at the nymphaeum.' I walked around for a while until things started happening, when I scuttled to the pre-arranged meeting point.

The Parthians arrived first. They brought their large colourful palanquin, forging through the crowds. The palanquin seemed to have come up from the Vicus Tuscus near Anacrites' house, using one of the old roads, then in front of the palace it had to slow and negotiate bystanders; soldiers were attempting to ease out the public, but once the iron gates reopened, people came swanning everywhere. It was impossible to shift them by citing national security; they just stood watching curiously.

Not everyone was a gormless tourist. In one of a series of forecourts, a large formal space backing onto the audience chamber, I had seen Perella, with her satchels hung on her. An extremely old musician was playing a hammered zither. She had her arms raised as she began to dance sensuously for a fascinated audience; they looked suspiciously like plain-clothes troops. Even though it was a ploy, she danced with such dignified intensity, they were hypnotised.

The Parthians would have passed Perella before turning

374

around into the less busy area that Ritellius had chosen for the exchange. By the time the palanquin made its stately entrance, I was there alone, positioned by one of the columns outside the magnificent double-height dining area. I watched the conveyance being carried slowly into the fountain court. This noble piece by the architect Rabirius occupied a large open space in front of the ceremonial hall, one of the features those dining inside could view. Surrounded by columns, its oval bowl had a central island covered with brilliant marbles, where splashing and sliding water added movement and sound. Exquisite statues were dappled with shifting flakes of light, cast up by the fountains. All around there were marble features in grey, yellow, purple, white and green. Highly polished, and with rare patterned borders, they made an incongruous setting for what was about to be played out.

The red-swathed palanquin drew to a halt on one side. Bearers lowered the weight. The men stood motionless. None of the rich curtains moved. Swinging tassels gradually stilled.

Almost at once, Ritellius arrived in his cart. The low Hut of Romulus, from which he had come, huddled behind Augustus' monuments. Clearing the Temple of Apollo, which was right in front of the banqueting hall, the cart lurched forwards awkwardly, grumbling under the weight of obviously heavy contents. It was probably Ritellius who had turned an open vehicle into a covered wagon, using hoops and dustcloths. That hid whoever was inside.

He pulled up and parked on the far side of the fountain, away from the palanquin. He jumped down; for some reason, he unhitched the mule. Almost hidden by a huge horse blanket, the mule pricked up long ears, looking around with eager intelligence. Ritellius stood by it, arms folded, also waiting.

Stand-off.

Nobody moved. I noticed, with a chill, how the crowd who had milled about before had suddenly drained from the hilltop. The precincts lay deserted.

A light breeze whiffled sporadically. The sun, grown in strength with the day's passing, warmed stone pavements, curved walls and the high roofs, tiled in marble that made Domitian's palace resemble a temple. Bruzenus must be melting. A grossly overweight man lying inside a closed wagon, roped up so it was impossible to change position, he would be sweltering in much distress. Yet I was close enough to hear he never groaned.

Silence.

In that silence, I became aware that the ground trembled. Imperceptible reverberations grew in strength until it was clear that something tremendous was coming this way from the Cryptoporticus nearby. Then from behind the Temple of Apollo appeared a full-sized adult Parthian war elephant.

A mahout guided her progress, though his control seemed precarious. In the back section of a stylish howdah were three people: Dolazebol, Squilla and a male servant. Midway between palanquin and cart, the elephant halted beside the imperial fountain, which it eyed with wily interest.

Unhurried, Ritellius unfolded his arms. He showed no surprise that the red palanquin was a diversion. He called up to the envoy calmly, 'Send Squilla to me. Set her down! I shall then release Bruzenus.' He sounded fully in command. He might be clapped-out and paunchy but today he was sober. The sight of his lover seemed to fire him with even more confidence.

Dolazebol's servant slipped past the mahout in his lower seat, planed over the elephant's head in a spread-eagled face-down position, slid the length of its trunk, landed securely. Without a word, Dolazebol gestured to the mahout. The man spoke to the elephant, which raised its trunk, curled it around Squilla, lifted her and brought her down to ground level.

She thanked the beast with a caress of its trunk. I could see she was wearing only a straight white tunic, no jewels. She was barefoot, looking less than clean, though her long hair swung like pale gold leaf, as sensuous as ever. She seemed unfazed by the situation.

The servant, who had a small curved dagger in his waist sash, seized her arm, controlling her.

Ritellius strode to his wagon. He ripped cords away, letting the coverings fall.

I heard him curse.

In the cart, instead of the trussed-up corpulent Bruzenus, were only workmen's tools, reed bundles and building materials. Ritellius must have thrown all that stuff aside when he had first taken the cart; someone had since put everything back. It was this jumble that had given the cart weight as Ritellius drove there. Now he helplessly shook a rope end, which told its story: Bruzenus had escaped.

Oddly, it was Dolazebol who exploded. He let out a cry of betrayal, just as his elephant moved forward, raised herself, placed two enormous feet on the edge of the imperial fountain, filled her trunk with water and delightedly began bathing.

At Dolazebol's anger, curtains were flung open on the

Parthian palanquin. Out spilled retainers, all armed with bows and arrows. They ran straight towards Dolazebol. He must have expected Bruzenus to arrange something like this. He yelled for the mahout to move the elephant, but one of the archers shot the mahout. The great beast, full of fun and mischief, refilled her trunk and began to spray water at the running archers.

Ritellius recovered enough to throw himself on the servant who was holding Squilla. I ran out and dragged her away from the action. Ignoring what was happening all around us, I shook her. '*Who is the traitor? Who, Squilla?*'

Blank expression. Big, innocent kitten eyes. She would not say. The slut-heeled goddess was keeping her saleable goods safe.

Someone burst past, knocking Squilla from me. Perella! She pushed the golden beauty on her back, over the hard edge of the fountain. Amid those twinkling mosaics, strong dancer's arms held Squilla, strong hands dipped her head back into the water, so white-gold hair swirled in the bowl, then clung to her as she was yanked out into the air again.

'Name him!' Perella ordered. Without waiting for Squilla to refuse, she dunked the younger woman backwards once again. Now I helped. This time we kept her under water longer.

We dragged Squilla half upright, again ordering her to name the traitor. This time, she murmured something. 'Bruzenus.'

'Try again!' snapped Perella, coldly.

'Abascantus.'

Letting her sit up, Perella and I leaned for a moment on the fountain edge, full of relief. Then Ritellius, much larger and more solid, barged between us, gathering up his girlfriend.

For once that mysterious look of half-amusement vanished. With a truly sweet smile, Squilla fell on his neck.

Perella pulled a knife from her satchel. She lunged at Ritellius. He smashed her away. I turned to help her up, as she cursed. He was wounded, blood pouring from his neck, but age or bad planning had diminished her old skill so Perella failed to finish him.

Heedless of his hurt, Ritellius had swept up Squilla; they ran to where his mule was standing. He wrenched off its horse blanket. It was saddled for riding. He flung himself on. Squilla scrambled behind him, clinging with her arms around his waist. He turned the mule's head and galloped towards the front of the palace, intending to make a dramatic escape down Domitian's covered ramp.

It was a good mule. It was the best mule I had ever seen, probably Sabine. Sparks flew under its hoofs as it raced off. For this escape, he must have blown all the cash he could lay hands on. Ritellius was making his exit on the fastest mule in the west.

57

He reckoned without Bruzenus. Left alone, he must have broken his ropes. He had replaced the tools in the cart, covering it carefully. We worked out later that he had then struggled down the Steps of Cacus. Somewhere at the bottom by the Circus Maximus, he had encountered a two-horse racing chariot. Knocking the surprised driver from his perch, Bruzenus had jumped on, sped around the Palatine and brought the vehicle to the top of the hill via the Cryptoporticus. It was a straight run, driveable and out of view. All he needed was to crash past a few startled Praetorians. Those boys probably admired his nerve.

Now, torqueless and with bloodstains on his ripped silken tunic, he burst upon our scene. It seemed incredible that such a large man could perch securely in the fragile basket, but his feet were dainty. Racing horses are powerful so these could pull his weight, and he turned out to be an expert driver. As Ritellius and his sweetheart started what they thought was their ride to freedom, Bruzenus in the chariot rushed after them.

After him ran Perella and I, zigzagging between the Parthian archers. Behind us, we heard loud trumpeting: Dolazebol had managed to reach the mahout's position and was trying to bring his war elephant under control. His headdress had fallen off, so he tossed back long braids of hair from his eyes, as the elephant began moving. Her tough skin had repelled the Parthians' arrows, which she shook off angrily, but she was still at the fountain, with Dolazebol in the driving seat, shouting at her.

The Parthian archers came under attack. Mounted men had appeared – those who had been watching Perella's dance, directed by Titus, who was riding with them. I suspect he had hidden their horses in one of the inner courtyards. The mounts were small, sturdy and fast. Their versatile riders were army-trained for scouting. A chance to round up Parthians in Rome was their big treat.

Perella and I left all that behind as we followed the mule and chariot. In the ramp chase, the mule was fastest. It easily took the hairpin turns in the tall dark corridors. Behind, Bruzenus' chariot was delayed when one of its wheels bounced off the flat onto the upper-level steps. At that point we nearly caught him up as we entered the top of the ramp. Somehow he managed to force the skewed vehicle back onto the roadway ahead, we saw, then he went careering on downhill. The chariot's suspension must have suffered from hideous bumping, but the axle held as he teased it on around the double-backs. Though not so nippy as a Sabine mule in such confined spaces, the racers were trained for circling at the spina ends in a circus. Perella and I could see the chariot ahead of us sometimes, as the horses slowed for corners. Descending the steep slopes behind them, we two were forced to lean back, feeling the hard pull on our legs. We hurried, but we could not run.

No members of the public were on the ramp sections, though a couple of Praetorians jumped for safety into refuges.

The ramp becomes slightly narrower as it goes down. That was a problem. The horses went slower. Bruzenus punished them with a long whip. Wheels skidded and screeched. Wheel bosses crashed against the tall walls. Near the bottom is the lavatory niche. The ramp floor has a step there, before a turn. The step looks original; it may be a deliberate obstruction.

A large Praetorian Guard emerged from using the hygiene bucket. The horses shied. The chariot bounced on the step. It crashed, stuck fast. Bruzenus fell out.

Perella and I rounded the corner above. We then jumped aside into a viewing balcony that overlooked the House of the Vestals, to avoid suddenly being crushed as Dolazebol's huge elephant came powering through. Stepping at a run, she passed us, swaying from side to side, crashing her howdah on the walls while Dolazebol clung on in the driver's seat. She was spooked by the narrow, half-dark corridors full of shrieking people.

The fear-mad beast reached the chariot wreckage. Bruzenus was trapped underneath, helpless because of his bulk. The elephant laid into the chariot, tugging pieces with her trunk as if clearing a pathway through some dense jungle. The Praetorian had a knife out, cutting free the frantic horses. They, too, were distressing the elephant.

With terrifying noises, she trampled Bruzenus, this way and that. She was using her tusks too. Dolazebol was white-faced and screaming but unable to stop her. Afterwards, she forced a way over the wreckage and went trumpeting on to the Forum.

This was one of the darker spaces, not lit sufficiently by the high windows for us to see blood and burst intestines. I climbed over everything. Perella stayed, with her knife

out, helping Bruzenus into Hades. It was no act of kindness.

I kept running. Once through the monumental arch and
on the flat, it was easier. But I slowed. Nowhere could I
see the mule with Ritellius and Squilla. The elephant had
stopped on the Via Nova, upending stalls like matchwood.
People yelled and fled. A couple of the mounted scouts
must have come down by another route; they cautiously
rode around the elephant, though keeping at a distance.

There used to be a very ancient lavatory, a place so
sordid that women in my family had been barred from
using it. Hearing the commotion, out of it strolled the
Princeps Peregrinorum. He must have a weak bladder.
Normally when a man emerges looking nonchalant, adjusting
his spear, you think, *That must have been a big relief.* Titus,
of course, had a real spear.

He surveyed the scene, appraising this new emergency,
with the Parthian envoy aloft on his elephant. I stood still
and braced myself. Titus drew back his arm and launched
the Lucullan spear at Dolazebol.

58

He missed.

'Fallen short! Oh, bad shot, Titus.'

The Princeps turned to me. 'Just because a man names a weapon after himself doesn't mean it's any good! The Lucullan was rubbish. He knew it. Never mind being executed. This spear was the biggest disappointment of his life.'

59

Catching wild animals is a duty of the aediles. Where is an aedile when he is needed?

The elephant had found a sweetmeat stall, one I knew since it was a favourite haunt of Dromo's. There, a young serving-girl fearlessly approached the huge beast. She seemed to know what to do. One at a time, she offered cakes and pastries. The elephant stood taking them, responding to her gently; it plainly intended to stay there until she stopped giving more. Dolazebol could not make it shift.

A commotion in the other direction caught our attention. Now I guessed where Ritellius would have gone. 'The ivory workshop!'

The Princeps and I raced there.

Anticipating trouble, some of the ivory workers were hurrying to carry their expensive pieces into a lock-up; it looked like a practised procedure for occasions of social unrest.

Inside the workshop we found Ritellius. He was bleeding badly, too badly to have ridden far. Ilia, in tears, was kneeling by her husband, trying to staunch blood from the wound Perella had inflicted. Squilla was standing on the sidelines, white-faced, not helping. All as expected.

We arrived at a critical moment. We heard wheels, amid

hoofs clattering. It was a raeda, a four-wheeled mule-drawn formal carriage. Plank seats, cloth top, not comfortable but swanky. Only six people were allowed a wheeled carriage in Rome by day: those holy daughters of Rome, the Vestal Virgins. Seven if you count the Empress. (Not holy.)

The raeda was driven by Fuscus. Rubrius jumped out. Fuscus began turning the vehicle. Rubrius grabbed Squilla, marched her out to the carriage, bundled her inside, closed the curtains.

'Where are you taking her?' screamed Ritellius after them.

'The Vestals' House. Shut up. No one will touch her there.'

But a new menace was arriving to threaten the escape. 'Parthians! He'll never get through!' muttered the Princeps, rushing back out to the street.

'Watch!' replied Rubrius, also assessing the danger: a newly arrived group of Parthian foot-soldiers, who all carried bows and full quivers of arrows. How had they got here? The envoy must have guessed where Ritellius would bring Squilla.

The Princeps stamped and threw up his arms at them, as if shooing cows. They moved back slightly, then started jeering. The workshop men waved axes and staves.

A moment later the Parthians also brought up a spectacular battle drum, so large it was carried on a donkey. When it was struck, the deep sound from that membraned monster could be heard for miles. They began drumming it. It truly was the most frightening sound most of us had ever heard – and now it was desecrating the sacred Roman Forum.

Mounted men came with it. These heavy, exotic figures were covered with chain mail and even their horses were fully swathed in scale armour. Their leader was carrying, two-handed, a lance as heavy as an oar, plated with metal and nearly five yards long.

'Cataphracts!' groaned the Princeps. 'It's Carrhae all over again!'

There were four. I remembered Trebianus complaining that cataphracts accompanied Dolazebol on his carnival parade coming to Rome. Even I could see these were the real thing. They looked terrifying and I knew that at Carrhae armed warriors like this had wreaked appalling damage.

Despite our horror, a response was immediate. Alerted by the war drum, the Roman scouts last seen up on the Palatine reappeared in force, trotting towards us on their small tough ponies. Their Princeps shouted. Signalling the presence of enemy troops, he raised his arms, holding the corners of his cloak. The scouts sped up and fell to, fighting the Parthians. Parthian foot-soldiers tried replying, though to shoot arrows in a Roman street and hit targets is not the same as firing off across an open plain. But they had brought a fire pot and were now using bitumen. Anything could be set alight.

Fuscus chivvied the mules to set off with the raeda. After only a few paces they were forced to a stop, their way blocked by the armoured cataphracts.

We heard Squilla's shrieks of terror from inside. Back in the workshop, Ritellius broke from Ilia. He hauled himself upright: jaw clenched, knuckles white, a man of action, a true spy. Somehow he made it back outside to his own bright-eyed Sabine mule, threw himself into the saddle, pulled at toggles, cast aside his cloak and revealed himself armed with various weapons, including a bow and arrows.

Meanwhile the Princeps, on foot, headed straight for the

cataphract who was holding the huge lance. Fearless, he carried out a trick that Roman mercenaries had used in Parthia: he ducked right beneath the horse, then with his sword slashed upwards at its unprotected belly, disembowelling the poor creature. The horse collapsed. The cataphract fell heavily, then lay helpless in the street because of the weight of his armour, while members of the public set about him. The mounted scouts yelled in triumph and began closing around the other three armoured men, ready for the kill. Fuscus was able to move the raeda. He drove off unnoticed.

Ritellius rode up, leaned down from his mule and captured the fallen cataphract's war lance. Infuriated by this outrage, Parthian foot-soldiers began chasing him. Ritellius was riding around in wild circles, taunting his opponents with the captured lance. Soaked in blood, wild-eyed and whooping, he was unforgettable.

He pulled up when he saw Dolazebol. Now on a stolen mule, the envoy rode straight at Ritellius. Ritellius turned away from him, kicked up his own faster mule and seemed intent on escape. Dolazebol pursued him.

Abruptly, Ritellius turned in the saddle. Holding on with knees and thighs, he fetched out his bow. He raised both arms, nocked, aimed, released and fired off an arrow backwards. A Parthian shot. Exquisite.

Dolazebol, with no protection, took the arrow in the chest. It had pierced some vital organ. He fell from his mount, dead even before he landed.

The crazy Ritellius let out more whoops of triumph, more insults to the opposition. He set off in the direction the raeda had taken Squilla. Fiery arrows pursued him. He rode only a short distance. His adrenalin failed and he fell, now fatally wounded.

His watching wife reached him a moment before she lost him. I ran after her.

He was dying in front of us. Ilia sobbed, devastated. She dropped to her knees beside Ritellius.

'You were the one, darling . . .' His voice failed. His life gave out. But he left this final courtesy to his wife of forty years. She would always think those words meant something, and undoubtedly live comforted.

But I had seen the look in his eyes as he saw off Squilla into what he hoped was safety. Ilia had been fooled again. Gaius Ritellius died lying.

I turned away. Rubrius crouched beside the corpse, checking that the rogue agent really had been killed. They would want to be sure, when Eutrapelus theta-ed his personnel record.

'Squilla?' I asked. 'Is she safe now with the Vestals?'

'The Vestals won't touch her,' said Rubrius, rising. 'She will be given to us.'

I took it at face value. Since she had named the traitor, she should be allowed to exist in some very small town in an obscure province. If that never happened, her fate was not my business.

Here in the street by the ivory workshop, the Parthian war drum at last fell silent. It was looted, and never seen again. Chaos ended. Marching feet in large numbers. Brisk orders. Trumpets. A batch of extremely haughty lictors arrived, men bearing rods and axes, escorting a most prestigious personage: Rutilius Gallicus, the City Prefect. He was in command of the Urban Cohorts. Their task is to quell riots. This they achieved with skill and efficiency, as usual. Locals, who knew what the Urbans are like, dived into their premises, out of the way. Foreigners were rounded up, not gently.

Rutilius inspected the mopping up. Now that the trouble was all safely contained, other officials ventured down from the Palatine to look.

Flavius Abascantus, the Secretary of Petitions, was heard to say to a colleague, Claudius Philippus, that this Parthian upset was deeply unfortunate. In my hearing the man blatantly claimed that his own relationship with Dolazebol and Bruzenus had been like going into enemy territory to make maps; a scientific experiment. The exploration had needed stealth – but it had had to be done. We all knew he was lying, but he brazened it out, still believing he was in control, still thinking himself untouchable.

One last fiery arrow landed by the ivory workshop. A stray. No one knows who shot it. Fizzing, this alien firework stuck head down in a large cauldron full of fish glue that was standing in the open air.

I saw Rubrius and the Princeps gape in horror. I covered my ears with both hands, eyes closed. There was no time to run. We all braced ourselves for what must happen next: an enormous explosion.

60

Nothing happened.

Fish glue is an extremely stable commodity. Inert, it carries no risks when used in normal work situations. It is not a fire hazard.

61

It took a few moments more before we experienced the event that would supersede everything else when the *Daily Gazette* wrote up today's events.

After they had rounded up the Parthians, tidy-minded members of the Urban Cohorts collected all the arrows they could find, lest these be used as weapons in some other mêlée. Under Rutilius Gallicus, the Urbans were as keen on riot-prevention as they were on riot-quelling.

One assiduous Urban found the burning bitumen pot, which he thought required safe disposal. He carried out no risk assessment and did not consult his superiors. Intending to pour the stuff away, he took the pot into the ancient public convenience, where it came into contact with a bubble of gas that was emerging from the drains. Sewer gas is a flammable medium.

The lavatory was badly damaged. Many people suffered injury, some never recovered from the shock. Those with hairy posteriors experienced serious singeing, as the *Gazette* solemnly reported.

When I could, I left the scene. I still had one more thing to do.

62

Marius lived in a single room, high up in a grim building. In this my young cousin was like most people in Rome. Until I married Manlius Faustus, I had done the same.

His was a tenement full of metal workers and bale-laders, huge men who made much noise when they were around, though they went out early and worked long hours, which gave respite to late-sleepers. He lived there because he had refused the Eagle Building, saying my father charged too high a rent. Falco is a soft touch, so that tells you much about his finances. I never went there without seeing mice. The creaking stairs, with half their treads missing, housed the thickest spiders' webs in Rome. The smells could be tolerated only by a young man.

Nobody heard me enter the room, which was always unlocked. Burglars had given up on the place. Marius and his new friend were lying on the narrow bed, top to toe like brothers in a poor household.

I opened the cranky shutters, one half missing. This let in light and let out the inevitable odours from a room where two young men had lain comatose for many hours after going on an all-night bender. Luckily neither had been sick.

As I expected, the new friend of my cousin looked right. The plotters had chosen him well. He was thick-set. Older than Marius, he had overlong light-coloured hair, which curled on his muscular neck. His nose was straight, his chin jutted. As far as I could see through his half-closed lids as he lay snoring, he had blue eyes. He looked fairly clean, with his fingers well-manicured; his expression had pleasant potential.

Against a wall stood his instrument, the finest ivory-inlaid cithara I had ever seen.

I shouted curses until they both woke.

'Now we're in trouble!' groaned Marius, kicking at his crony.

I sat on the stool Marius used when practising his flute, a seat hand-whittled by his father Petro, who considered himself a dab hand as a carpenter. If you braced your legs, you could almost prevent it wobbling.

Once they stopped comparing their hideous hangovers and were alert enough to listen, I told the pair that I knew about their night in the bar. So who had provided them with cash for it?

'Corellius,' said Marius. 'He gave me a big purse yesterday and asked me to keep Nemo safely out of trouble while a crunch was going off.' Corellius? Maybe Marcia's double agent was a triple one.

'*Nemo?*' The new friend looked confused, although it must have been one of those mornings when many things felt confusing. I dismissed the pretension: 'A letter's wrong there, surely.'

'Like Odysseus fooling the Cyclops,' Marius said hastily, sounding proud of this half-baked allusion to Homer. 'As in "*I am nobody*".'

'Very literate!' I was sour. 'Get real. He is somebody all right. This person's name is Haxamanis, and knowing him is bloody dangerous. Being him is worse. Worst of all would be if he ever acted as the person he has been trained to impersonate. But that stunt ends here,' I told Haxamanis, who looked relieved.

'He just wants to be free to play his music!' Marius complained, with fellow-feeling.

'*His* music can be played all he likes,' I replied crisply. 'The dross he was learning, Nero's compositions, he must never pluck or sing again. Is that clear, Haxamanis? Now, Marius, listen. This is the deal, which applies to you both.'

'Will we like it?' Give him credit, even with his head cracking and his tongue furry, Marius was valiant.

'You will love it. I have screwed this from persons of influence.' I had been to the palace. I had issued threats of non-cooperation, then promised compliance. I had made them see sense. Their offer was generous.

'Does he have to go home to Parthia?'

'No, he has to stay in Italy. He is never to go east again.'

'Is he under arrest?'

'Do I look like a death squad? First, take your new friend to the barber in Fountain Court, old Appius, and have his hair dyed very dark. Next, you and he will be provided with a ramshackle cart, plus enough money to live on for the next few months, depending how many bars you waste it in. Once the cash is gone, you must earn your living. Starting as soon as you have sobered up today, you are to drive away and lose yourselves. Down south, Bay of Neapolis or wherever you like. You can bum around busking. It's your dream, I know it.'

'Who will tell my mother?' Marius had his priorities.

'Leave Rome, then I will. And, Haxamanis, I shall tell your auntie.'

The young Parthian looked thrilled, then wary. He could not quite believe it. They had taught him Latin, which he spoke well: 'This is true for me? No more Nero?'

'No, my dear,' I comforted him gently. 'All that is over. Trust me. You need never be Nero again.'

63

The plot was foiled. Philippus would survive, Trebianus also. The Princeps Peregrinorum would be awarded his ninth *phalera*, citation never stated, all details of his noble activity suppressed. Perella would go back into retirement, still brooding on the injustice done to her.

Domitian would live to tyrannise another day. So far, Flavius Abascantus was still flaunting himself as secure in the Emperor's trust, but unknown to him, Eutrapelus, the old record-keeper, had now looked out the personnel scroll of one Gnaeus Octavius Titinius Capito, an equestrian. Quiet hands would place that scroll in front of our Master and God after he came home. Quiet men would tell him why.

Titinius Capito would take over from Flavius Abascantus, an appointment that the palace would achieve slickly and discreetly. Abascantus would disappear from the public record. Historians will no more understand the reasons for these changes than they can account for why, during the reign of Domitian, two serving provincial governors were executed. Capito would go on to serve as Petitions Secretary in the cabinets of four emperors.

I would work with Titus Capito. I'd work against him too. In addition, another name from this investigation would resurface – mainly to my detriment: Karus. Julius Karus would become all too familiar.

An aedile who had been struck by lightning would receive an award from our ever-benevolent emperor. The aedile would give the money to his wife, since they lived by plebeian principles and shared everything. Anyway, he conceded, she had earned it.

After I had seen the boys off to the barber, I went to find my husband. He had been at the Circus Maximus but had returned to our quiet house for lunch. The two sinister observers had been removed from outside. Fortunately, I had brought food with me, or there would have been none.

'Come home,' ordered Tiberius. 'I never see you. I am sick of this. We need to find a steward and staff. Come home to choose frescos, keep Dromo in hand, and look after your husband. Stay at home right now,' he said, 'and go to bed with me.'

This is the life of a bread-winner. You work long hours, you crawl home, craving the long sleep of the exhausted only to find that your soulmate has spent all morning at the Circus; he is bright-eyed and wants love-making.

My husband was himself again. So I had no complaints.

GET ALL
THE LATEST
LINDSEY DAVIS
NEWS

Go to www.hodder.co.uk/lindseydavis to subscribe
to the Lindsey Davis email newsletter

Visit Lindsey's website at www.lindseydavis.co.uk

Or head over to the official Facebook page
/lindseydavisauthor

H
HODDER &
STOUGHTON